Letters
to
Love

ALSO BY SORAYA LANE

Letters
to
Love

soraya lane

Montlake
Romance

Published by Montlake Romance Publishing, Seattle

www.apub.com

Amazon, the Amazon logo, and Montlake Romance Publishing are trademarks of Amazon.com, Inc., or its affiliates.

ISBN-13: 978-1503947863
ISBN-10: 1503947866

Cover design by Lisa Horton

Printed in the United States of America

*For Sophie Wilson, my editor. You pushed me so hard on this book,
and I'm incredibly proud of the final story. Thank you!*

CHAPTER ONE

February 2008

Bella,

I have something to tell you. I'm pregnant. I promised Gray we'd keep this a secret, that we wouldn't say anything until we were both back, but keeping this from you is killing me. I'm only eight weeks, so it's early days, but you have to promise me that you'll take care of my baby if anything ever happens to me. You're the only person I would trust with my child, except for Mom and Dad, of course, but it's you I'd want to raise my baby if something happened to me or Gray. I know you hate me putting myself in danger so often, but serving my country means a lot to me, and I think we just have to agree to disagree on what I've chosen to do for a job. I love this baby so much already, our little "button." See you soon, and don't tell Mom yet!

Love, Lila xoxo

~

August 2015

Bella Anderson turned up the music, smiling as the wind blew back some strands of hair that had escaped her ponytail. She had the window down, preferring the natural breeze to her SUV's air conditioning, hand dangling out and strumming a beat on her door. It was her favorite part of the day—she was about to stop for a coffee at her local café, chat to the cute barista as he made her latte, and then make notes before meeting clients for the day. Only today she might have to order an extra shot after the night she'd had trying to get her two nephews to sleep in their own beds.

The song ended and she turned down the radio before pulling into a parking space. Bella reached for her bag, slinging it half over her shoulder as she went to pull her keys from the ignition.

"... *a serious crash in Napa Valley has closed one of the main* ..."

Napa Valley? Her ears pricked, pulse ignited. She dropped her bag and turned the volume back up.

"*Police say fire crews are at the site, using the jaws of life to rescue the two occupants of the car. They are not releasing any details at this stage; however, they are believed to be a man and a woman. The SUV was hit by a truck traveling in the opposite direction in a head-on collision.*"

Bella gripped the steering wheel, heart beating fast. Napa Valley was a big place. There were hundreds of people traveling on the road. And plenty of them would have two occupants in the vehicle. *But something didn't feel right.* She let out a big breath and reached for her keys, then her bag, slowly getting out and walking numbly toward the café. It was still quiet out, the lull before the morning rush, just the time of day she liked best, only now it seemed too quiet.

The firm, no-nonsense voice of the radio announcer kept running through her head. *Napa Valley. Head-on collision.* She gripped her bag tighter. No more thinking about the stupid news report.

"Ma'am?"

She looked up and blinked when she realized she was being spoken to, forcing a smile. "Sorry—I was a million miles away. Latte to go, one sugar."

"Anything to eat today?"

Bella always ordered a croissant or bagel, but her stomach was churning so hard right now that just the thought of her coffee was enough to make her want to be sick. But she had to eat. *And stop getting all paranoid.*

"Ah, maybe a bagel. Cream cheese and jam, thanks." She paid and took her receipt.

"We'll bring it over."

"Thanks," Bella said.

"Hey."

Bella looked up, smiling at the gravelly voice that always made her grin. There was something about flirting with this particular guy that always kick-started her mood. "Hey yourself."

He wiped down part of the coffee machine with a white cloth, somehow managing to make the simple action look sexy, especially when he winked as he did it.

"You heading out this weekend?"

Bella bit down on her lip to slow her smile. "Are you asking me out?"

"If you ever said yes to me, I might keep asking."

She leaned against the wall across from him. If only he knew that if he *actually* asked her out instead of just teasing, she'd probably be the one saying yes. "I'm actually already taken this weekend. Threesome would you believe."

He raised an eyebrow. "Don't tease me like that."

"Two boys."

"You just ruined the mental picture I had going on."

Bella took the takeout cup from him when he held it out, laughing at the bemused look on his face.

"They're six and four, my nephews," she told him. "Their parents are away on a romantic break. So we'll be ordering in pizza, snuggling up, and watching DVDs, followed by three of us crashing in bed all together."

He rested his elbows on the counter and leaned forward. "Sounds like a good date."

"Two lattes and a long black!"

Cute guy whose name she didn't know pulled a face and straightened. "And so the day begins."

Bella waved and crossed back over to collect her food. She stopped to take a quick look at the newspaper, then glanced back over her shoulder before heading for the door and walking out. She was tempted to check the news app on her phone for an update about the crash but thought better of it, deciding to call her sister instead.

The phone rang, and she smiled, imagining what her sister would say when she answered. Lila would laugh and tell her to stop worrying so much. That she'd survived war zones and dodged bullets, that Gray was an amazing driver and would never crash, blah blah blah.

"Hey, you've reached Lila. Leave a message."

Bella hung up and redialed. They were probably still in bed, cursing the phone for ringing and ruining their fun morning sex. And when Lila called her back, she'd tell her sister that she was stupidly paranoid and to stop freaking out.

Nothing.

She put the phone in her bag again and took a quick sip of her coffee, burning the tip of her tongue. *Damn it!* She hurried down the road and jumped back in her SUV, sliding the coffee into her cupholder. Bella checked the clock and decided to make the quick drive over to her parents place for peace of mind. She didn't want to worry them but . . . She didn't have her first client for an hour, which meant she had time to shoot past their house before heading to her appointment.

Bella started up the engine and indicated before pulling back out onto the road, accelerating hard and reaching for her coffee once she could take a hand off the wheel. She laughed at how uptight she was, knuckles almost white they were gripping the wheel so hard. A few minutes ago she'd been flirting shamelessly with her coffee guy, and now she was a bundle of nerves again, pulse hammering away like she'd just run a marathon.

This is ridiculous. My sister is fine. Gray is fine. I'm being paranoid.

She drove fast to her folks' place, foot hard on the accelerator, until she saw their street sign and slowed. They'd lived on Blossom Avenue all her life, and just seeing the familiar big house on the corner, the trees lining the street as she pulled in, lifted her spirits.

"In breaking news, we've just had confirmation that the two motorists involved in the head-on collision in Napa Valley have died at the scene. Further details will be . . ."

Bella gulped and quickly turned the volume down, not needing to hear anymore. And then she saw them. No lights flashing or sirens blaring, just two cop cars pulled up directly outside her parents' place, disturbing the otherwise perfect, nothing-out-of-place neighborhood.

Bella pulled into the driveway, drained her coffee now that it was more warm than hot, and pressed her forehead to the steering wheel for one long moment. Then she took a deep, shuddering breath, jumped out of the car, and folded her arms tight across her body as she walked up the front path to the door. She guessed no one would answer if she knocked, so she just turned the knob and let herself in.

It was silent. Eerily silent. No laughter, no talking, no TV blaring, or clatter from the kitchen. Just deathly silence. Followed by a wail that cut straight through Bella, made her double over in pain when she realized the animal-like noise had come from her mother.

And then she ran, heels clacking loud on the wooden floor as she shot straight past two police officers in uniform and straight into her mom's arms.

~

"I need to go and collect the boys," Bella said, her voice straining.

Pain shot through her, bursts of emotion like knives stabbing every inch of her body. She bit down hard on the inside of her mouth, refusing to cry. Not yet. She was still holding her mom in her arms, keeping an eye on her dad sitting in his chair by the window. He hadn't said a word, silent tears running down his cheeks now that the police had left. Bella had so many questions, so many things running through her head, but she was also thinking of everything she had to do. Things she had to set in motion. Everyone she had to look after. She was in coping mode now—she had to be.

"Will you bring them here?" Her mom's quiet voice surprised her.

Bella dropped a kiss into her hair. "No. I'm going to make some calls, contact Lila and Gray's lawyer, then take the boys home early. I want to keep things as normal as possible for them." *As normal as things can be when both your parents have just died.*

Her mom nodded. She gave her a final big hug, arms wrapped tight around her, then crossed the room to place a hand on her dad's shoulder. It was the first time in her life she'd seen him cry. Her big, tough-as-nails, amazing military dad; a man who never cried, never complained, never asked anyone for anything. And now he was sitting as still as a statue, body shuddering with emotion as she touched him.

"I love you, Dad," she whispered.

He squeezed her hand back and nodded.

Bella squared her shoulders, not looking at her mom again. If she did, there was no way she could leave the house. But her mom and dad had each other, and she needed to be there for the boys.

Her hands shook as she reached the car and leaned in for her phone. She had four clients scheduled for the day, and she needed to call the first two at least and explain that she couldn't make it. Her assistant could deal with the rest, not to mention the next week.

"Hi Rachel, it's Bella." Her voice was on autopilot, the words spilling from her mouth even though her brain felt like mud, trying to process what had happened. "I've had a family emergency, and I'm not going to make it this morning. But if you head into the showroom, you can still look over all the lovely taffeta fabric and let me know if there's anything you like. We can pair the drapes with the final wall colors another day."

She made small talk, sucked back a deep breath as she had a similar conversation with her next client about her house, and then slumped back against the car. Suddenly, interior design seemed trivial, stupid. *Lila is dead.* She balled her hands into tight fists, nails digging in hard to her palms. *Gray is dead.* She stuffed her fist to her mouth, biting down on her knuckles as burning hot tears filled her eyes. *They're gone.*

She shook her head, refusing to believe it.

The sound of her phone ringing pierced her thoughts, jolting her back to reality. The number was showing as private, and she answered, thinking it could be the police or someone else she needed to hear from. Something else she needed to force herself to be strong for.

"This is Bella," she answered, voice shaking as she tried to compose herself.

"Bella, it's Noah."

The deep, raspy voice on the other end only brought everything back. Lila and Gray's wedding, Noah's speech, arguing with him when she'd found him kissing the other bridesmaid, seeing him goofing around with Gray outside the delivery room the day Cooper had been born, him dressing up as a clown at Will's fourth birthday party.

"You've heard, haven't you?" she whispered, hardly able to trust her own voice.

"Yes, I've heard," he replied. There was a pause. "Are you looking after the boys?" he asked.

Bella nodded, then realized he couldn't see her. "Yeah. I'm going to get them now. I've been staying at their place. Are you here or away?"

Noah was a Navy SEAL, had worked with Gray for years and known him for even longer. They'd been best friends since school days, until Gray's family had become foster parents so they could take him in, and since then they'd been as good as brothers. But he was nothing like Gray, and despite all the teasing over the years, she'd never wanted to become one of his conquests. *Unlike another one of Lila's bridesmaids.*

Normally, Noah wound her up—he was a larger-than-life guy who always seemed to put the cat among the pigeons. And he often went too far. But suddenly hearing his voice today seemed to soothe her, made her feel closer to Lila and Gray somehow.

"I'm heading back to the US now," Noah said, voice crackling as the line faded in and out. "I'll be back in Cali within forty-eight hours."

She didn't ask how he knew about what had happened, because she didn't care. Maybe he'd been listed as Gray's next of kin.

"I'll—" Bella took a deep, shaky breath, trying to stop herself from sobbing. She bit hard on her lower lip for a long beat. "I'll let you know the arrangements."

The crackle of the line was the only sound until Noah's voice echoed back at her. "Stay strong. I'll see you soon."

And then all went quiet.

Bella pulled the phone from her ear, shuddering as she pushed it into her pocket, the wind suddenly freezing as she wrapped her arms around herself. Her body shook as she fought the emotion, the burning hot terror within her that she'd been desperately trying to ignore. Her legs gave out beneath her, made it impossible to stand, and she collapsed onto the grass outside her parents' home, praying they couldn't see her as the tears started to spill from her, the gasps of pain stealing her breath away.

She'd always thought she'd lose her sister to a war zone, waited anxiously every time Lila was away, and instead, she'd died in a car with her husband just miles away from home. The tears were more violent, running down her cheeks and into her mouth, her head hanging as she fought to breathe.

Gray had wanted to do something for their anniversary, and Bella had planned it with him to help surprise her sister, had offered to look after the boys so they could have an entire week of spending time together, just the two of them.

And now they were gone, and there was nothing she could do about it. Not a goddamn thing.

CHAPTER TWO

Bella sat straight backed, one arm around each of the boys as she nodded and smiled and pretended she was happy to see all the well-wishers who came past to pay their respects. The service had been long, filled with words of hope and talk of better places, but Bella hadn't been able to take her eyes off the massive photo of her sister on an easel beside her coffin. It was still propped there, Lila in full dress uniform, with the photo of Gray positioned to face her from the other side.

She looked down at the boys, hating how quiet they were, listening to their sniffles instead of their usual laughter. She also looked around and saw that it was finally her chance to get up and leave, to get in her parents' car for the private burial. They had to deal with the guests and refreshments afterward, but it was a relief to be leaving it all behind, at least for a short time. The church was packed full of friends, family, and military, and Bella was feeling suffocated.

"Come on," she urged in a voice she hoped sounded happy and not fake. "Let's go meet Grandma and Granddad outside."

The boys stood, and she kept hold of their hands as they walked out. Bella kept her head down until they were out in the afternoon sunshine.

"Hey, boys!"

Bella bristled at Noah's loud voice assaulting them the second they walked out. He ran up and swung first Cooper and then Will up into the air, one on each hip, his big arms supporting them. She noticed his hat on the step, the only thing missing from his otherwise immaculate Navy uniform. The gold buttons were shining as brightly as the smile he was giving the boys, and even though she should have been happy to see their faces alight, she still bristled. Trust Noah to sweep in and manage to make even their parents' funeral fun.

"Are you traveling with us?" she asked, doing her best to keep her tone light.

Noah made the boys squeal when he pretended to drop them, irritating her even more.

"Noah! Don't be disrespectful," she muttered.

He gave her a puzzled look, and the boys looked startled. Bella glanced away and wished she'd held her tongue.

"Sorry—just trying to give these little guys something to be happy about," Noah said, setting them on their feet and reaching for his hat.

Bella wished the ground would open up and swallow her, but still—this was a day of mourning, and Noah should be more sensitive to that. "It's just—"

"I get it," Noah interrupted, ruffling Cooper's hair and getting another grin out of him. "Let's go. I'll drive; Bella can ride shot gun."

"We're going with my folks," Bella said, not moving.

"I told them I'd take you."

"Please can we go with Noah?" Will begged.

Bella forced a smile. "Of course." It was the least she could do, given what they were going through. She had to remind herself that anything that made the day easier for the two boys was to be welcomed. "Let's go."

She waved at her parents when she saw them and pointed at Noah, briskly following his long stride. He paused to hug and back-slap another guy in uniform, laughing before grabbing the boys' hands and swinging them along beside him. Bella had always hated the way he made a joke out of everything, and today it annoyed her even more. It was her sister's damn funeral, not to mention his best friend's; could he take nothing seriously?

Soon they were in her car, the boys in the back and Noah driving. She listened to their banter and kept her forehead pressed to the glass. The last thing she needed was to hear Noah talk crap, not when she was about to lower her sister into the ground.

"You okay?" Noah asked, his voice breaking her thoughts.

She realized the car had gone quiet. "No."

He didn't say anything for a long while, not until she looked over at him, changing her position in her seat.

"I'm just trying to make them smile, Bella. Surely even you can understand that."

Even her? What was that supposed to mean? Just because she wasn't giggling her way through the worst day of her life. She rolled her shoulders back and grit her teeth. She wasn't even going to answer that. He'd been back in the country less than two days, and already he was getting under her skin.

"Let's just get this over and done with," she muttered.

"And then we need to talk," Noah said, his voice lower than usual, making it sound husky.

Bella glanced at him, hated how damn handsome he looked in uniform. He was clean-shaven, his hair shorter than she was used to. The last time she'd seen him, he'd had shaggy hair and a straggly beard, no doubt trying to fit in to wherever he was being posted. Maybe that's why she was so taken by his all-American appearance. His jaw was strong, matched the rest of his body, like he was carved from marble. He might manage to irritate her almost every time she saw him, but even she couldn't deny how handsome he was.

Bella had no idea what he wanted to talk about, but she'd planned on doing her best to avoid the man, not have a private conversation with him. She wanted at least some time to mourn her sister and brother-in-law in peace today.

"We're here."

They'd followed the two hearses, their car leading the others, and they pulled into a graveyard flanked by a long stretch of grass on each side. A shudder trawled Bella's spine as Noah parked the car, and she slowly got out, forcing her feet to cooperate. She got Cooper out on her side and held his hand tight as they made their way around to Noah. He'd already gotten Will out, and she cringed as he lifted the boy up onto his shoulders. She wanted to tell him to put him straight down, but the look on Will's face stopped her. He was close to tears again, and the last thing the little guy needed was her barking orders.

"You okay?" she asked Cooper, her voice barely above a whisper.

He glanced up and nodded, but she knew neither of them were any kinds of okay.

"I don't want them to put Mom and Dad in the ground," he confessed, gripping her hand tight. "I don't want to throw the dirt on them."

She bent down and wrapped her arms around him. "We can each throw a flower, then walk away. We don't have to watch."

Cooper nodded and threw his arms around her for a quick hug. She held him, focused on her breathing as she tucked his little body against hers until he was ready to step back.

"Ready?" she asked.

He nodded and they set about following Noah again. It was only minutes later that they were all gathered around the two deep holes in the ground, where Lila and Gray would be lowered side by side, but for Bella it felt like an eternity as she stood there and waited. Her mom was on one side, shoulder pressed to hers, and her father on the other side. Gray's parents stood to her right, with Noah the only person separating them. When she glanced at him, he smiled down at her, but she couldn't bring herself to smile back. The sooner he left, the better, as far as she was concerned. He might have been Gray's best friend, but he'd already disrupted the little bubble she had around the boys, and she wanted to get everything back to normal. Or as normal as life was ever going to be for them from now on.

Bella tuned out as a prayer was spoken, watched as the first handful of dirt was thrown on the coffin. Cooper jammed his body to hers immediately, his hold on her hand almost painful, and she shook her head at her mom and pulled him away, walking away from the gathered crowd. When she stopped to take him into her arms, his eyes were wide, heart beating so hard she could feel it against her hand.

"I don't wanna throw the flower," Cooper whispered, only just audible.

"Look up," Bella said, pointing to the sky, not about to make him do anything he didn't want to do.

Cooper did as she asked. "Why?"

"Because remember how I told you Mommy was up there, in heaven?" Bella asked. "She's up there looking down on us, making sure you're okay. That's just her body in that coffin. No one's throwing dirt on Mommy because she's already up there in heaven."

Bella wasn't convinced she believed the words coming from her own mouth, but she said them anyway, prepared to do anything to comfort Cooper.

"Your dad's up there, too."

Bella turned at Noah's deep, raspy tone. She watched as he carefully put Will down beside his brother.

"You're sure?" asked Cooper.

"Positive," Noah replied, bending so he was down at their level. "Your mom and dad are up there, along with some of my buddies I lost a while back. Everyone we love goes up there."

The boys exchanged glances before Will pointed to some trees. "Can we go climb them until it's time to go?"

"No," Bella said.

"Sure," Noah said at the exact same time.

She spun to stare at him, open mouthed as he ignored her and crouched low again to be on the boys' level.

"Go have fun," he said. "Climb until it's all over, and I'll come get you."

They ran off without a backward glance, and Bella planted her hands on her hips.

"You completely disrespected me," she fumed. "Not to mention the fact that all those people over there expect us to be showing our respects."

He shrugged. Bella narrowed her gaze, suddenly certain he was amused by her anger.

"I don't actually give a damn what anyone else thinks," he said, mimicking her pose, arms folded and making his jacket look like it was about to burst at the seams as his muscles bunched beneath. "Those boys have just lost their parents, and if they want to deal with it by climbing trees, then who cares? They shouldn't be expected to do anything."

"Me. I care!" she hissed, wishing she'd just checked her anger and bitten her tongue.

"I'm not here to argue with you," Noah said, reaching for her and dropping his hand when she stepped back.

"I've just lost my sister, Noah," Bella choked out. "I just want to stand there and throw some damn dirt and bury her."

His smile was kind, but it still managed to irritate her. "Then go. I'll watch the boys."

"They're my responsibility," she muttered. "The one thing she asked me to do."

Noah moved closer and she let him, not stepping back this time.

"Bella, did Gray ever talk to you about who he wanted to look after the boys if something happened?"

She dug her nails into her palm as she made fists with both hands. "Me. It was always going to be me. Lila made that beyond clear."

Noah's sigh chilled her, the piercing look in his blue eyes telling her he was about to tell her something she didn't want to hear.

"I don't want to argue, Bella, not now, but Gray always told me he wanted it to be me. That's why I got back so fast. Why I managed to get leave at all."

Bella's heart started to beat hard, her legs turning to jelly. Bile rose from deep in her stomach, burning her throat, but she swallowed it down, refused to be sick, wanted desperately to stay strong.

"The boys are mine, Noah. Don't you dare try to take them away from me," she choked out.

She was greeted with silence. Painful, long silence that stretched on too long. But his eyes never left hers, and she knew in that moment that he wasn't going to back down.

"Noah, please!" she begged, her voice barely a whisper.

"I would never take them away from you or your family," he said in a measured, low voice. "I'm just telling you what Gray's wishes were."

"Yeah, well my sister made her wishes pretty damn clear, too," Bella snapped, finding strength in her anger.

"I plan on honoring his wishes, Bella. If that means we look after them together, then so be it, but I'm not letting him down." he said, his tone firm. "I'm sure it will all be recorded in the will."

"Fine," she muttered, holding her ground.

"And Bella?"

She wished she were sitting with her head between her legs, to fight the nausea, to let the blood rush to her skull.

"Yes?" she managed.

"I'm sorry. I'm just so damn sorry. They meant a lot to me, too." His voice cracked as his eyes left hers, and he stared at his feet. Hearing the emotion in his tone made her tears start again, hot as burning embers as they started to stream down her cheeks. *I'm sorry.*

"Me, too," she choked out, stumbling back a few steps.

"I'm here for another day before I have to head back to my team," Noah said, composing himself as he stood with his feet shoulder-width apart, back straight as he met her gaze. "I'll be there for the will to be read, and I'll be back on home soil within a month, maybe two."

Bella forced a smile. "Just remember that blood's thicker than water, Noah. No matter what claim you think you have, they're my nephews, and I'm not going anywhere."

She swore his eyes flashed with something, a hint of *something* she just couldn't put her finger on. But then he turned and headed toward the boys, and she waited a long beat before collapsing to the ground. Sobs wracked her body like they had every few hours since she'd first received the news. She put her fist to her mouth, silently grieving her sister. Her brother-in-law. She understood why the boys didn't want to go back to the burial, because she didn't either, and if she didn't have to stand there being brave for their sake, she wasn't going to.

Bella fought to catch her breath. Noah wasn't going to take the boys from her, wasn't just going to walk in and think he had rights to them. Or at least she wasn't planning on letting that happen—not on her watch.

$\sim$

Noah took his first sip of whiskey and grimaced as it bit his throat on the way down.

"To Gray," he said, holding his glass in the air.

A handful of their military and Navy friends stood around him, glasses raised. "To Gray," they echoed.

Noah could feel eyes on him. He turned and saw Bella watching, her mouth drawn in a tight line as she stared daggers at him. He took another sip and stepped away, motioning for her to come join them. She shook her head and turned away, so Noah went back to toasting his buddy. He didn't have the best track record with Gray's sister-in-law, but he'd been close to Lila, and she'd always sworn that her sister was a lot of fun. The only time he'd ever seen so much as a glimpse of that had been at the christening of one of the boys, when she'd accused him of being a manwhore, and he'd laughed and crushed her body to his and kissed the hell out of her. She'd been willing at first, then slapped him hard across the cheek and hardly spoken a word to him since.

"You remember when we were hazing him?" One of the guys was just about bent over double with laughter.

Noah grinned. "Way he told it, you guys served it to him big time."

"More like he was a pussy and just about crapped himself!"

Noah chuckled, about to take another sip as a warm hand closed over his forearm. He'd long since discarded his jacket, shirt-sleeves pushed up to his elbows now that he was having a drink.

"Care to join us?" Noah asked, knowing it would be Bella. He looked down and was rewarded with brown eyes the deep shade of chocolate, only they weren't anywhere near as warm as her skin.

"No," she said, "and I need you guys to keep it down."

He took her by the arm and walked them a few paces away, out of earshot. "They're remembering Gray," he told her. "Everyone in the kind of job we're in loses a lot of buddies, and having a drink and a laugh is the only way to deal with it sometimes."

Noah knew she was hurting, but the problem was that they'd never seen eye to eye.

"I'm just doing my best to deal with this," she said, eyes swimming with tears that made him uncomfortable, reminded him of why he was back in the US, standing in Lila's parents' house.

"We all are," he replied. "Which is why you need to let these guys grieve in their own way."

He watched as she bit hard on her lower lip. "Noah, about what you said . . ."

Noah took a few steps back, grabbed her a drink and set it in her hand. She looked perplexed, maybe annoyed that he'd moved away when she'd started to speak, but she did raise it and take a hesitant sip. The face she pulled afterward made him chuckle.

"That's awful!"

"Burns like a motherfu . . ." he let his voice trail off. "You get my drift. But after the burn it starts to numb, and that's a good thing."

She sighed. "We're always at loggerheads, but whatever Gray and Lila wanted, I'll do it. And if that means you and I have to get along so the boys can spend time with you, then I'm just going to have to deal with it. Because if that's what Gray said to you, then I'll bet on him having put it in writing."

Noah took another sip, and she followed his lead. "That's all we can do, Bella. I didn't want this any more than you did."

She nodded. "I know."

He held up his glass. "To Lila and Gray."

"To Lila and Gray," she repeated, clinking her glass softly to his.

Noah chuckled and jumped when one of the guys grabbed him and held him in a bear hug until he held his glass to his lips and drank down the rest of the whiskey. He saw the disapproval in Bella's eyes, but he didn't stop. Everyone had their own way to grieve, and this was his, with the guys, dealing with it the only damn way they knew how.

~

Bella toyed with the stem of her wine glass as she sat alone at the dining table—the same table she'd often sat around with her sister and brother-in-law, eating home-cooked meals and ending up in heated debates about everything under the sun. She smiled as she reached for a letter, taking one she'd read at least a dozen times already since they'd passed.

She touched the dog-eared edges of the paper and unfolded it, sucking back a familiar shudder of emotion as she read her sister's handwriting. When she'd collected them at the time, saved every single one her sister had sent her over the years when she'd been posted overseas or away from home training, she'd never expected to reread them, missing her like crazy and trying to pretend like she was still here, still alive. And yet here she was, pouring over them every night once the kids were in bed, a lifeline to the past that she was sure she'd cherish forever.

March 2011

Dear Bella,

It's breaking my heart being away from Will. Remind me how I thought I'd be able to do this? Thank you so much for staying with Gray while I'm away. I honestly don't think he'd cope on his own. He's fine with all the practical stuff, but Will needs to be able to crawl into your lap for a cuddle. I'm not saying Gray isn't good at cuddles, just that sometimes nothing beats a mom to snuggle up to with long hair and squishy breasts. Of course, you haven't breastfed, so I'm sure yours are all pert and firm! Haha, seriously

20

though, I think it'll be good for you to hang out with Gray. You've known him for so long, but please, can you just take note of the way he treats you? That's what you deserve, and I know you get all grumpy with me if I bring it up, but Serena agrees with me. Brody just isn't . . . I don't know. There's something about him. I don't like the way he speaks to you. He's all sugar in front of Mom and Dad, but when we've been out and I've seen you two together, it makes me uncomfortable. I'm glad you guys aren't living together, because I honestly think he'd try to keep you away from us if you were.

Maybe I'm just worried and paranoid because I'm stuck over here, and you're at home, but still, just be careful. Make sure Will sees my photo every day, and play him my video clips. I don't want him forgetting his mom.

Love, Lila xoxo

Bella wiped the tears from her eyes and carefully put the letter back in the box, putting the lid on and pushing it away. In time, she'd read some of the letters to the boys to help them remember their mom, but it had been a long day, and thinking about the past was only making what had already been a bad day even worse.

CHAPTER THREE

Two months later

October 2014

Dear Bella,

I know I've already said it a million times over, but try to be nice to Noah, okay? He's a really nice guy—you just have to give him a chance. He'd do anything for the boys, and that makes him a friend, not the enemy. Gray keeps saying that if you'd only say yes and go out on a date with him . . .Haha, don't worry, I long since gave up hope of us all going out on a double date. But just be nice to him. He might come stay for a few nights when he's back, and Cooper and Will love their Uncle Noah. It's so hard for them having both of us away at the same time, not to mention my worst nightmare come true. But let's not go into all that. I'm just pleased you're there with them! You do realize that I fully expect you to get a sitter if you get asked out on any hot dates, though, right? Serena told me that she's seriously on the lookout for you. Haha, wish I could see the look on your face right now.

I'll see you soon. Kiss the boys for me, and make sure you read to them every night for me. And don't kick Noah out of the house if he turns up to stay!

Love, Lila xxoo

Bella sat at the counter and stared at the fridge. The paint-splattered pictures and randomly placed photos made her smile every time she looked at them, and today was no different. Except that today wasn't a normal day. Today was the day that Noah moved in, and there was no way she was ready for him to arrive. It was early; the boys were still asleep, curled up in her bed together and leaving barely an inch of room for her, but they all seemed to sleep better when they snuggled. Half the time she woke with one body on top of her and one smooshed to her side, but she was getting used to it. Nothing about the past two months had been easy, but she'd made it, and that was all they had to do. She'd fake it until they actually made it out on the other side, and then she'd be able to look back on how tough everything had been with a smile. Or at least that's what she was hoping.

A knock sounded out, and Bella took a deep breath before rising. Maybe she shouldn't have read the letter about him from Lila this morning, but she'd wanted to remind herself that her sister and Gray had loved Noah and had entrusted him with their boys for a reason.

Noah unsettled her; he always had, but then she was also kind of looking forward to having someone else in the house to help her out. Dealing with the boys was . . . she smiled to herself, thinking of Will and Cooper's little faces. They were angels a lot of the time, but when they were bad, she wondered how she'd even last another day. And the fact that she was almost looking forward to having some adult time with Noah, of all people, told her that maybe they were driving her just a little mad. There were only so many times she could soothe their anxiousness and explain why bad things happened to good people without wishing for help. Her parents had been amazing, but she was the one in the trenches day in and day out, and it was tough going at the best of times.

But then having Noah here wasn't going to be any kinds of easy. She'd settled into a routine of holding it together during the day, watching the clock until bath and bedtime, knowing she'd be able to collapse and lose it once the boys were in bed. Sitting at the kitchen table rereading Lila's letters had become her own little ritual, a way for her to grieve without anyone seeing, and now she was going to have to keep her game face on 24/7.

There was another loud knock and Bella swung open the door. Noah was standing on the porch, two bags at his feet. "Hey," he said, looking awkward but smiling anyway.

She smiled back, wondering if maybe she would have been better off struggling on her own than inviting the big bad wolf at the door in. Then again, it wasn't like she'd exactly had a choice in the matter. They'd both been sitting there when the will was read, and Lila and Gray's wishes had been as clear as the co-parenting agreement she'd had to sign with Noah. "Hey."

"Hey." Noah raised an eyebrow as she leaned against the door. "Can I come in?"

Her gaze swept over his broad shoulders, T-shirt stretched tight beneath his leather jacket, faded jeans, and scuffed boots. He was the kind of guy who always looked at ease, so damn comfortable that she'd always wanted to do something, *anything*, to wipe the smug look off his face. And all she'd ever managed to do was rile herself up in the process.

"The boys are still sleeping," she said as she stepped back, waving him in. "They're getting better, but the crying every night is tough."

"They sleeping in bed with you still?" he asked, eyebrows raised.

She bristled. "They've just lost their parents. I'm not about to march them back to their own beds at 2:00 a.m."

Noah held his hands up. "Just asking," he said. "Gray always said they both crept in during the early hours. One of the things he loved about being home."

Bella wished she hadn't snapped. But Noah just always seemed to push her buttons. Always had, probably always would. If she was like this when he'd just arrived, she hated to think what it was going to be like in a few days, a week, a month .... Hell, she hadn't really thought this through at all. If the funeral and burial were anything to go by, they really weren't to be trusted together at all.

"Getting them into anything resembling a routine has been almost impossible, but at least now they're not wetting their beds because I don't try to get them to stay in their room," she continued, not caring that he hadn't meant to offend her. No matter how sympathetic he might be right now, he had no damn idea how tough caring for the boys had been.

"You don't have to explain yourself to me."

"Well, I'm just—"

"Bella, I'm not trying to tell you how to be a parent. It was just a question," Noah said, giving her a look that made her wonder if he was ready to run for the hills already.

She took a deep breath and held up her chin. She wasn't great at apologies, and although she knew she'd snapped, she wasn't about to buckle and give him one yet anyway. "So you just got back, huh?" she asked, changing the subject.

Noah nodded. "Yeah."

She knew better than to ask him where he'd been. "Want a coffee while we can sit in peace?"

He nodded and left his bags in the hall, following her into the kitchen. "I can make it."

"No, it's fine. You can pay me back by dealing with the breakfast rush when they wake up." Truth was, she liked to stay herself busy to keep her mind off everything. The more her hands were working, the less her mind had time to wander off into dangerous thoughts that threatened to ruin the careful, meticulous fence she'd managed to build around herself and the boys these past few weeks.

Not to mention her serene smile that masked the storm clouds that were brewing inside of her, the face she'd perfected to use whenever anyone asked her how she was or how badly she missed her sister. Her cracks only appeared at night, in the dark, when the house was quiet and the boys were long in bed. She gulped, not wanting to dwell on that again.

"How do you take it?" she asked, composing herself.

"Black. Three sugars."

Bella pulled a face. "Gross." She was about to lecture Noah on the perils of sugar but changed her mind. Her sister had been sugar-free and organic for years, and in the end it hadn't helped her one bit.

"So how are the boys? Happy to be back at school and pre-K?"

Noah had settled at the counter, leaning forward as he watched her. It was unsettling being alone with him—after all the years she'd known him, they'd never actually been *alone*. Well, apart from one time, but Bella conveniently blocked the ill-advised kiss they'd once shared from her mind, not letting it surface. She'd been around plenty of military and Navy guys her entire life, with her dad and his friends, and then with her sister and Gray, and the only one she'd ever dated she'd sworn would be her last. She was the first to be thankful when it came to honorable, brave men and women serving their country, but date one? *No, thanks.* Marry one? *No freaking way.* First, there had been Brody. She grimaced just thinking of his name. Then there was the fact that she'd spent way too many nights, weeks, and months worrying about her dad not coming home to go through the same with a boyfriend or husband, and she sure as hell wouldn't want her own kids to go through what she had. Only now she was a mom, *technically*, and her kids had Noah as their new dad, which meant despite her best efforts, she was in the exact position she'd never wanted to be in.

"So I'm guessing you've confirmed everything at your end with the lawyer?" Bella slid Noah's coffee across to him and took a sip of her own tea. She was drinking herbal, trying to get herself used to green tea and failing miserably. But using her sister's fancy pink and yellow teacup at least made her smile.

"I'm still kind of in shock, but I've already sold my place. Put mostly everything in storage, except the odd thing like my desk." She shrugged. "This is home now."

Noah grunted. "It's a lot to process. Especially the fact that they left everything jointly to . . ." His voice trailed off.

"*Us?*" She laughed. "Yeah, that was the bit that shocked me the most, too." Learning that all their assets had been left jointly to Bella and Noah had been unsettling, but they had to raise the boys, which meant they needed access to everything until the kids were old enough to inherit. They'd been entrusted with everything, and the weight of the responsibility was heavy on Bella's shoulders at the best of times. Not to mention the fact that she'd sold her condo. She'd been so proud of owning her own place, of her business taking off enough to mean she no longer had to rent, and now it was gone like she'd never had it in the first place.

"That shocked you more than them giving us joint custody?"

She took a sip of tea, grimaced, and tipped it down the drain. "I'm still in shock over that, too. But I've had a couple of hands-on months to get used to the idea, I guess."

"Not liking your tea?" he asked, changing the subject.

She frowned. "It's disgusting. I'm trying to be healthy, but all I want is coffee."

Noah stood and moved around into the kitchen, flicking the kettle back on and taking the cup from her. She watched as he rinsed it out and dried it before making her a coffee, adding a spoon of sugar, and passing it to her.

"This is what you should be drinking."

"If I wanted to be a diabetic," she quipped, even though her mouth was salivating at the thought of sweet, sugary coffee.

"If you want to survive looking after two boys and still keep smiling, take my advice."

Bella bristled. "Oh, because you've got so much experience?" Her face flushed from anger, wanting to get up and give him a big shove for walking in like he knew exactly what it was like to parent two kids.

"I can imagine," he said. "Do you want it or not?"

Bella pushed it away just to make a point. "No, thanks."

He just shrugged like he couldn't give a damn, and it made her wish she'd just taken the coffee instead of making a big deal out of it. But still, who the hell did he think he was?

"How do your parents feel about this whole situation?" He settled back down next to her and wrapped one hand around the coffee mug. "Sorry—bad choice of words. I meant about the will. Us looking after the boys."

Bella took a deep breath. Her parents loved Noah. Always had, probably always would. It seemed she was in the minority getting all riled up by him, because he seemed to make most woman swoon, including her mom. And then there were Gray's parents who lived an hour or so drive away but kept telling her how wonderful it would be when Noah was around to help take care of the boys as if it were the best thing in the world that she not only had to learn how to parent but to co-parent, too. She doubted she'd ever agree with that rationale.

"They just want what's best for the boys."

"So they don't want to try to take over or anything?" he asked.

Now it was her turn to raise her eyebrows. "Lila was always pretty clear with them that if anything happened, I was to be the one."

"Same here. With Gray," Noah affirmed, the look on his face telling her he was used to getting what he wanted. "Every time before we shipped out or had to do anything that could risk his life, we'd have a beer, watch a game of football, and he'd make me promise to take care of his family."

Bella balled her fists. Maybe she was just really bad at sharing, but she hated that Noah had been left as much in charge as she had. The guy was a serial dater who'd never had a long-term girlfriend and spent more time offshore than he did on US soil. How the hell was he supposed to be ideal dad material?

"You're pissed, aren't you?" he asked.

"No." She got up and poured a glass of juice for something to do, wishing they hadn't been sitting so close. Just because she liked to think she was immune to his charm didn't mean she wanted to be so near to him that she could smell his citrusy cologne. The way he looked at her—hell, the way he looked at *all* women . . . it was like his dark eyes could see straight through her, like he was giving her every inch of his attention, as if she were the most important person in the world, and it unsettled the heck out of her.

"So I thought I'd take the boys tree climbing again," he said, draining his coffee and taking the cup around to load it into the dishwasher—and sending her back to her seat just to keep some distance between them.

"Because it was such a great idea last time?" She tucked her long hair behind her ear for something to do, trying to stay calm.

"They seemed to enjoy it." Nothing seemed to faze Noah, and he sure as hell didn't seem to be picking up on her signals. Or maybe he just didn't care.

"Noah, we have to talk about how we're going to make this work. I mean," she sighed, "you need to respect my boundaries and what I've put in place with the boys' routine, and we need to talk about all the other stuff. All of Lila and Gray's stuff."

"You mean like what we're going to do with the house and the cars?" he asked.

"I'm not selling the house if that's what you're getting at." She made a fist and found it impossible to unclench. "Their wishes were set out very clearly."

"For God's sake, Bella, what the hell is wrong with you?" He was glowering at her now, dark brows pulled together, his gaze almost black as he stared at her. "I wasn't angling to sell the damn house!"

"What's wrong with *me*? I've just lost my sister, Noah, that's what's wrong," she hissed.

"Yeah? Well in case you've forgotten, I've just lost my best friend. The one person in the world who actually gave a damn about me. So how about we cut the crap and you just tell me what the hell I've done in this lifetime to piss you off so bad."

Noah wasn't easily riled. He was used to being in stressful situations and dealing with a lot of crap, but Bella annoyed the hell out of him. One minute she was sweet as pie, sugar, and all things nice, and the next she just about snapped his head off.

"Let's get a few things straight before the boys come down," he said, trying to channel his inner negotiator. He was not going to lose it over her attitude, not when he was trained to deal with high-octane situations for a living. And he wasn't going to admit to her that he didn't have a clue what to do in this situation, because he wasn't used to going in to a job blind, but this was exactly what he was doing here.

He watched as she reached for her glass, even though there was hardly anything left in it. Her hands were visibly shaking, and she looked close to tears, but they needed to establish some ground rules. He was hurting, too, and he wasn't going to be treated like crap for stepping up to follow his friend's wishes, just because he was out of his depths.

"What's that?" she finally said, voice low. Her eyes met his— dark pools of emotion, swirling with pain and disbelief as she blinked, the gold flecks more visible than ever. But there was also a softness there, a beauty in the way she looked at him that made him wish they weren't always at odds.

"Number one: I'm not going anywhere. If you think you can be a bitch and push me away, then you've marked me as the wrong guy."

"Oh yeah?" she snapped. "If you think that's me being a bitch, then you really have no idea."

Noah raised an eyebrow. "You're kidding? If that wasn't you being a bitch, then maybe I *should* run for the hills."

Bella bit down on her bottom lip, eyes downcast, before bursting into laughter. He smiled back, watching as laughter quickly turned to emotion, and tears started to run down her cheeks. Noah went to move forward, knowing he should comfort her, but not comfortable with crying. Was he supposed to give her an awkward pat on the back, or would she bite his head off for touching her?

"I'd lend you a handkerchief, but I don't seem to have one on me," he joked, patting all his pockets.

"Don't," she whispered. "No jokes."

"Am I that bad for trying to keep things positive?" he asked, putting some space between them again as he stepped back. "I'm just trying to do the right thing." What he needed was for her to give him a damn break, tears or not.

"No," she murmured, clearing her throat. "I just don't like crying in front of you, and you joking just makes me feel even more stupid."

"We all cry. Don't beat yourself up about it."

Now it was her raising an eyebrow. "You're telling me that Mr. Tough Navy SEAL can shed a tear?"

"You think I'm that much of a bastard that I wouldn't cry over losing my best friend?" Whatever he'd done to make her dislike him so much, he'd sure been convincing. "Christ, Bella, I'm not made of

31

stone." He wasn't about to let her see him get all emotional, but she was giving him some serious shit right now.

"I just didn't think you'd cry," she clarified. "Not that you wouldn't be upset. Sorry."

"Uncle Noah!"

Saved by the kid. Cooper screamed his name and came hurtling toward him, barefoot and running fast across the wooden floor. He'd never been more pleased for a conversation to be over.

"Hey, buddy!" Noah said, jumping off his chair and dropping to the ground, arms open. Cooper never slowed—just launched into his arms. Noah tipped backward, pretending he'd been so fast that he'd knocked him clean over.

"Geez, when did you get so strong, huh?"

Cooper leaned back and showed off his teeny muscles, hands bunched, dropping his soft toy to the ground.

"Wow, you've definitely been working out," Noah said, squeezing each bicep before reaching for the fallen bunny. "And who's this guy?"

"No one," Cooper muttered.

"Doesn't look like just no one," he said, examining the worn rabbit. "Looks pretty loved to me."

"That's Flopsy," Bella said, suddenly standing behind him and reaching down for the toy. She cradled it in her arms and dropped a kiss to the toy's head. "And he's very special. You don't have to act all tough guy to impress Noah."

Noah glanced up at her, recognized the frown, and cleared his throat, scooping Cooper up with him as he stood. "No way. I had a . . . uh, dog toy when I was a kid. Took him everywhere with me."

"You did?" Cooper looked surprised, one arm looped around Noah's neck as he stared into his eyes.

"Yep, I sure did. Hell, I'd take this guy everywhere with me if I were you. I need to get *me* one of these Flopsy guys."

Cooper glanced at Bella and reached out a hand, taking the rabbit and tucking him under his other arm. "Yeah. Okay."

Bella shot Noah a grateful look, and he smiled back at her. He was going to have to learn to read her if they were going to make this co-parenting thing work, although he was guessing that could be easier said than done. Lucky he'd done some serious time with the boys whenever he'd been on home soil, because it was paying off now.

"So where's your brother?" Noah asked, walking Cooper with him back into the kitchen and opening a cupboard door.

"Asleep."

"Coco Pops or Fruit Loops?" he asked.

Cooper made a face and pointed to the bread instead. "Just toast."

Noah set him down and put a couple of slices in the toaster. "How about you go get him, and then we can all have breakfast together."

Cooper ran off, Flopsy being dragged by the ear as he shot through the kitchen and ran up the stairs.

"Was that true?" Bella asked.

"Was what true?" He turned and flicked the kettle back on before leveling his gaze on Bella.

"What you said about your toy dog?"

He chuckled, even though there was nothing funny about what he was about to tell her. "Bella, I was a foster care kid. I was lucky to have the clothes on my back, and until I found Gray's family, I hardly ever went to school with food in my belly." He shrugged. "It was a long time ago, so don't go feeling sorry for me, but no, I never had a dog. Or any toy for that matter. Just me."

"But you said it anyway," she murmured.

"I love those boys like they're my own, Bella. Always have, always will. That means anything they need, whatever they need me to say, I'll do it." He paused, staring at her. "I might not be a natural with them, but I've had to work damn hard for everything in my life. That means I ain't no quitter, no matter how tough the going gets."

Footsteps echoed out above, thundering feet as the boys ran down the hall and continued down the stairs.

"Sorry for being a prize bitch," she said, arms folded over her chest as she watched him.

"Apology accepted," he said straight back, happy to move forward.

Bella smiled. "Good."

They both laughed as the boys skidded on the floor and bumped into him, the lighter feeling between them a relief to Noah. He glanced up at Bella, saw the way she looked at the boys. She might not like him, but he was sure as hell going to find a way to make this work. Because like it or not, they had both been booked for this parenting gig, and the only way to move was forward.

"Noah!" Will yelled, arms wrapped around his legs so tight he couldn't move even if he'd wanted to.

"Hey, buddy. How's my little soldier?"

He dropped when Will finally eased up his commando hold, and pulled them both into his arms. Will was two years older than Cooper, but he was tall and lean, where his brother was built like a little tank.

"You guys been good for Bella?"

"Yup," Will said, eyes shining with what Noah guessed was excitement.

"Did you just get back?" Cooper asked, quieter now that his brother was up.

"Yeah, I arrived back in last night and took the first flight I could to get home to you guys." He was seriously jet-lagged from all the flying. He had been in the Middle East for the better part of the last couple of months, but it had been worth all the hours now that he was with the boys. He was just lucky this had been a short deployment and not like his last six-month one.

"You shoot anyone?"

"Cooper!" Bella exclaimed.

"What?" he asked, shrugging like it was the most normal question in the world. "I asked Dad that all the time."

Noah glanced at Bella, then at Cooper. "And what did your dad say all those times?"

"Only the bad guys," Will answered before his little brother had a chance. "He always smiled and said he only shot the bad guys so we could all sleep easy."

Noah's smile faltered, but he quickly auto-corrected it. It was some kind of messed-up shit that left him, and not Gray, here with the boys. "He was a pretty awesome dad." It was the truth and also all he could think of to say. Tears welled in his eyes, emotion like a fist to his gut as he swallowed it back and took a deep breath, refusing to let it surface in front of the boys. Or in front of Bella.

"Yeah," Cooper said.

"You sure he's not just over there killing bad guys?" Will asked, head cocked to the side as he looked up at Noah. "Like, hiding in the hills going *pow-pow-pow*," he asked, holding his fingers up to make a pretend gun, "and waiting for when he can come home?"

"Yeah, buddy, I'm sure," Noah said softly, on his knees now with an arm around each of the boys. "But I sure as hell wish I was wrong."

Noah looked up at Bella, smiled sadly as tears streamed silently down her cheeks. There was nothing he wouldn't have done to bring Gray back. Hell, Lila, too. She'd been like his sister, and Gray his brother in every way except blood. He'd have died for either of them, sacrificed himself a hundred times over to keep their family together, to give the boys the fairy-tale upbringing he'd always wished for as a kid. To make sure Gray had his wife, and the kids had their mom.

Because he knew what it was like to be the boy without a mom or dad. To be the kid looking at all the dads at a ball game and wishing he had his own sitting on the bleachers cheering him on. To have a mom to snuggle up to and wrap his arms around tight and never let go. These were things he'd never had, but it had never stopped him from imagining what could have been.

He was going to be a dad to these boys no matter what it took, and no one, not even Bella, would ever be able to stand in his way. He didn't care if he was the crappiest dad around, so long as he was there and he was trying.

"Come on, guys, no tears this morning," he announced, winking at Bella. "We're going out for pancakes."

"Pancakes?" Bella asked at the same time the boys screamed, *"Pancakes!"*

"Yeah, pancakes. Waffles. Whatever you guys want, so long as it's drowning in real maple syrup. What do you say?"

"Yay!" squealed Will.

Cooper held up his hand for a high five.

"It's a school morning," Bella whispered, her tone firm. "I don't want to be the bad guy here, but—"

"Screw school," Noah muttered, watching the boys, loving the way they smiled and shoved each other, reminding him of the way he'd always been with Gray. "It's just one morning. I say we need to have some fun."

He stared at her, looked into eyes that reminded him of milk chocolate, not breaking the stare even as her gaze threatened to turn him to stone.

"Noah," she said, lowering her voice and turning her back slightly so the boys couldn't see her face, "I've spent the past two months doing everything in my power to keep things normal for the boys, to keep them in a routine. They're going to school today, and they're having breakfast here."

He smiled but shook his head. "I appreciate that, Bella, but sometimes in life you've just got to live in the moment. And in this moment, we're going out for pancakes. I'm starving, and the boys deserve to enjoy themselves."

"Noah . . ." she cautioned, her look fierce as he turned away from her.

"No school today, boys," Noah announced, not about to let Bella ruin a morning off for the boys when what they needed was some fun after everything they'd been through. "We're going to stuff ourselves with syrup, run all that sugar off at the park, and then we'll come home and you can show me how good you are at shooting hoops. What do you say?"

The boys whooped and yelled and ran back upstairs, and Noah grinned as he watched them, not fazed by Bella staring daggers at him.

"Don't give me that look, Bella. I'm not your husband, and besides, it doesn't suit you." Her face flushed a deep red, and he shrugged. "If you don't want to join us, head in to work or go to the gym or something. Hell, get your nails done."

"Don't act like I want to get as far away from the boys as I can," she seethed, hands on hips. "I don't want to drop them at school to get rid of them; I want to keep them in a routine, to keep some normalcy in their lives."

"I never said you didn't," Noah said, softening his tone, not wanting to piss her off to the point of no return. "I'm just saying that if you want some time to yourself, take it. Otherwise, put a smile on that dial and come join us."

Bella stared at him for a long moment before disappearing upstairs, the rage just about steaming off her. He was trained not to underestimate anybody in combat, yet the first mistake he'd made where Bella was concerned was to do exactly that. She might be cute and tiny with a ponytail that bounced when she walked, but she was only sugarcoated on the outside. He was pretty sure he'd bargained for a lot more than he'd realized when he signed the co-parenting agreement, and that was before he got to thinking about the kids themselves.

CHAPTER FOUR

Bella was so tired it was like her eyeballs were only hanging on by a thread and could fall out at any minute. She gratefully sipped her coffee when it arrived, happy to sit back and let Noah take the lead with the boys. She should have just done what he said and gone to the gym, let him have them for the morning, since it was his fault they weren't in school. But after two months of making all their decisions and being with them all the time, it just wasn't that easy to walk away. She'd no idea whether Noah was capable of looking after them. And it was all very well that he was super fun and full of enthusiasm now; she only hoped that he'd actually stick around when the going got tough. Like bath time, bedtime, tantrum time, crying-for-mom-and-dad time . . . She blew out a breath and looked out the window, redirecting her thoughts. She couldn't let her anger show in front of the boys. She and Noah needed to present a united front to them.

"You okay?"

She looked back and straight into Noah's eyes. His gaze was locked on her, and she was powerless to pull away from his intense stare. Bella reached for her coffee again to break the spell.

"Not really," she admitted, not seeing the point in lying.

His smile was kind, but she wasn't ready to pretend that everything was fine after the way he'd undermined her that morning.

"Uncle Noah, are you going to marry Bella?"

She almost dropped her coffee cup. "Cooper, no one's getting married."

"Maybe we should," Noah quipped back, eyebrow arched and laughter in his gaze.

"Yeah, that'd be cool," Cooper said, grinning and nudging his brother with his elbow.

"Um, except for the fact that it won't be happening," Bella said, not about to let the boys get all carried away just because Noah enjoyed teasing.

"Bella's got cooties—that's why I can't marry her."

"What're cooties?" Cooper asked, looking confused.

"Girl germs," Noah whispered, head bent low to the boys as if it would stop her from hearing.

They squealed with laughter, and Bella reached over and thumped Noah on the arm, smiling when he howled with pain and cradled his arm. She had to admit, the boys were in great spirits with him around, and taking the morning off from school had meant no tears about leaving her or crying that she might not come back, either. They were terrified of losing her now, didn't really understand how their parents had gone away for a holiday and never came home. Not that she was ever going to admit to Noah that it hadn't been the worst idea in the world.

The boys went back to eating their pancakes, and Bella leaned into the seat, coffee in hand. She didn't have a big appetite at the moment—not after everything. Unlike Noah, who was devouring a plate of eggs, bacon, and hash browns like he'd never eaten in his life.

"Noah, we need to talk about keeping the boys in a routine," she said, only bringing it up because the boys were now content, eating and playing with their superhero toys. "I make sure we're up at the same time each day and that we follow the same routine to the letter before heading off to school, to avoid any tantrums or excuses. I've had to learn to be strict, but kind."

"Sounds good," he said, laughing at something that Will said and pretending to shoot Spiderman, which made the boys giggle.

"Noah! You need to take this seriously," Bella told him, holding her coffee with a shaky hand.

He looked up and gave her a quick salute. "I got it: routine, no tantrums, strict."

She wished he got it, that he didn't have to try to turn everything into a joke or a good time. "I need your support, Noah. We have to be a team, and I'm just trying to get you up to speed."

Bella reached for her fork again and started to push a piece of pancake around on her plate.

"You're too thin," he said out of the blue.

She stared at him, gripping her fork to keep from dropping it. "Excuse me?"

"I'm just sayin'. You look better with a little meat on your bones, and you need to eat to keep your strength up."

She bit down on the inside of her mouth, not wanting to snap at him in front of the boys. "My weight is none of your business," she said in a low voice, "and I'm not exactly finding it easy to keep food down right now." She also didn't like the idea that he'd noticed that she used to have more "meat on her bones." She wondered which part he was talking about because she'd lost it everywhere— including her butt and her boobs—the parts of her she didn't really want to lose. "You know, I have no idea why Lila liked you so much."

"Oh yeah?" he muttered, smarting from her words.

"Yeah," she shot straight back.

Noah took another mouthful of bacon, put his fork down, then leaned back into the booth seat. The casual way he moved, the way he didn't seem to give a crap what anyone thought, it made her wild, made her blood boil to the point where she wondered if he just did it because he knew it annoyed her.

"Your sister was my closest female friend," he finally said, hands behind his head, making her want to stare at his arm muscles even though she was trying so hard not to. "We were pretty tight, and I would have taken a bullet—hell, a *hundred* bullets—to save her."

"Oh." Bella didn't know what to say, but she'd walked straight into that one.

"Gray was my best mate, and she meant the world to him. I cared for her like she was my own sister, and before you ask, I'd have definitely told her if she was starting to look all skinny, too."

Bella forced a smile. "I bet you wouldn't have."

"Yeah, I would have," he said with a grin, eyes shining with emotion after talking about Lila. "And she would have told me to stop checking out her ass, and then Gray would have given me a bloody nose. But I still would have said it."

They both laughed. "You really liked her that much?" Bella asked, all jokes aside.

"I did," he confessed, drumming his fingers across the tabletop now. "She was a great girl, a great wife to Gray, and a damn fine mom."

Bella was touched by Noah's tribute to her sister. It was heartfelt and genuine. She swallowed a lump in her throat.

"They had a lot of fun as a family," Bella said. "I want to do everything I can to replicate that, but we also need to be careful that the boys keep learning. That they keep up their little friendships at school to maintain that normalcy. And for the record, I take back what I said about doubting why Lila liked you so much."

Noah nodded an acknowledgment of her sort-of apology and considered Bella. He got what she was trying to say, and it wasn't that he didn't appreciate what she'd done. Hell, she'd been the sole parent to two grieving kids, and by all accounts she'd done a damn fine job of it. But they were different people, and he'd put money on it that Gray would have wanted the boys having fun and not taking anything too seriously, especially given what they'd been through.

"There is everything to lose here, Noah," Bella continued. "This isn't just you needing to be the fun uncle—this is real life."

"Is that a challenge?" he asked, raising an eyebrow and failing to make her smile.

"This isn't some mission, Noah—I'll say it again; it's real life. This is the lives of two little boys who depend on us for everything," she hissed in a low voice.

"You're saying that what I do for a job isn't real life?"

"You guys exist in a bubble, forgetting about everything else and focusing on one thing only. You're used to living on adrenaline. It's about the excitement of the chase, living in the moment, until you're debriefed and on to the next task."

He chuckled even though she was seriously starting to piss him off, not wanting her to see that she could rattle him. "Glad to know you're such an expert on the life of a Navy SEAL." He slung an arm over each of the boy's shoulders. "You guys ready to go blow off some steam?" he asked, smiling at Bella and knowing he'd just pissed her off by taking charge.

The boys nodded, and Noah waved the waitress over, wanting the bill. She was pretty, brown hair pulled back into a ponytail, and he tipped her and gave her a wink when she put the bill in front of him. "Thanks darlin'," he said.

Bella was clearly annoyed; the look she shot him when he spoke to the waitress was pure hatred, but he ignored her. He'd only done it to aggravate her, and it had worked—childish, but amusing none-theless.

"Let's go."

They all rose, heading for the car. Once the boys were buckled in, he jumped behind the wheel, still weirded out that he was driving Gray's SUV. If he was going to be hanging around, he had to get rid of his own pickup and buy a family wagon just so he didn't have to use Gray's. Although the kids might not like the change, especially since their mom's SUV had been wrecked in the crash.

He glanced up and hoped Gray could see them, that he was looking down and watching how hard Noah was trying to keep everything together. Because if there was one thing Gray knew about him, it was that he'd always vowed never to have his own family, never to have children. *And look at me now.*

He stopped at a light and could finally focus on Bella, see the confused look on her face. "You know, I think we need to call a truce here," he said, not wanting to strain things between them to the point that they were at war. "We're both different, and we just need to find some common ground."

"Meaning I need to step back when I've been the one doing it alone?" she asked, shaking her head.

"Let's just agree to disagree sometimes. And maybe you could cut me some slack, given I've just arrived back."

She shrugged. "Sure. When you've been in the trenches here for a couple of months, I'm sure you'll be begging me for help."

Noah chose to ignore that. "I think the whole point of this is that we both balance the kids in different ways. It's why we're both here together."

Bella was great with the kids. He'd seen her enough times with them over the years to know that, and she had always helped to look after them in the past. But he wasn't just going to be bossed around like he was a husband under the thumb. He had things he could bring to the boys' lives, too.

He looked over at her in the seat beside him and stifled a chuckle. She'd be raging if she knew that he thought she looked incredibly cute right now. But even if he'd wanted to go there with Bella, he wouldn't. He wasn't looking for long term—never had been. All he wanted was a good time, great company, fun sex. He didn't break hearts because he never let things go too far—always made it clear that he wasn't looking for more. And Bella was the kind of girl to take home to your mom, the woman who was looking for a husband, 2.5 kids, and a white picket fence. Only Noah didn't have a mom to take any girl home to, he sure as hell wasn't going to get married, and . . . well, he'd just inherited the fence and the kids. Which meant he had a lot of stuff to wrap his head around.

"We definitely need to work out some ground rules," she said, looking out the window. "We need to figure out how we're going to make this work and how we can both keep smiling and not have to pretend like we're okay." She paused. "We *need* to have that conversation instead of you just joking around and acting like it's okay to wing it."

Noah hoped he hadn't hurt her feelings, but all he'd said was the truth. "Okay," he agreed, deciding to agree for the meantime, to avoid bickering.

She opened her door when he pulled up to the curb, getting out and then leaning back in, eyes locked on his. "I know I've been snappy with you," she said, "but it's hard to have you come sweeping back into our lives when I've worked my butt off and given everything up to make things feel normal."

He nodded, opened his mouth to say something. He shouldn't have just taken charge, but it was what he was used to doing. And he did think that having fun was more important than being serious with the kids right now.

"I'm busting!" Cooper suddenly announced. "It's coming now!"

Noah leaped from the car and yanked the back door open, grabbing Cooper and positioning him against the wheel of the SUV, helping him pull his jeans down.

"Not on the—" Bella protested.

"Hey, look, it's like a fountain!" Cooper exclaimed. "I'm like a dog piddling on the tire!"

Noah took one look at Bella and burst out laughing, tears streaming down his cheeks. One thing about the boys—they sure were a reality check when he needed one. Although Bella didn't look at all impressed by his impromptu decision to let the kid go against the vehicle.

~

Bella walked down the stairs, exhausted. Her eyes were bleary from having to cuddle the boys in bed for so long, to get them to sleep; her jeans were still damp from the splashed water during bath time; and she was ready to drop. They'd been so excited about having Noah back, and the fact that he'd zoomed around the house chasing them after their bath hadn't exactly helped.

She paused, listening to the clink of glasses and wondering what Noah was doing. It was kind of nice to have someone else in the house, instead of having to leave the TV going just to have some noise. She hated putting the boys to bed upstairs and walking down to silence, listening out for every bump and bang. But as nice as it was not to be alone after dark, she wasn't convinced about that someone else being Noah. Not after butting heads with him all day. And not when she was ready for her customary glass of wine and letter-reading session.

She wiped at her eyes and walked down the rest of the stairs, wishing she didn't think about her sister so often. Lila kept popping into her head the second she wasn't doing something, which was why she'd kept herself so busy the past few months that now she was on the brink of exhaustion. There was so much she still needed to do, so much she'd ignored, like her business, but the boys had been all consuming. And so had dealing with a whole heap of loose ends.

What she wanted was to pick up the phone and call Lila. Moan to her sister about how tired she was, which would invariably lead to a lecture about how people without children had no idea what tired actually was. Bella smiled. She couldn't pull that one on her now, because she knew *exactly* how exhausting it was running around after two boys and never managing to get more than four hours' sleep in a row. At least she had her best friend, Serena. Serena might not have children, but she was good at pouring herself a cocktail and listening to Bella when she needed a good moan. Bella grinned. For about ten minutes, anyway, before she told Bella to grit her teeth and get on with things, which was why Bella loved her so much.

Bella pulled out her phone and wrote her a quick text.

Noah is killing me. Why would she do this to me?

She went to put the phone back in her pocket, but it buzzed. Bella smiled when she saw Serena had texted her straight back.

Just admire his muscles. He must at least have that going for him?

Bella chewed on the inside of her mouth to stop from laughing. *He's ruining everything. I haven't spent the last two months trying to replicate Lila's routine, for him to come here & cause chaos.*

Serena's reply came straight back again. *There's nothing wrong with a little chaos. Chill & enjoy the fact you're not in that big old house alone. xo*

You're right. He's driving me a little crazy, that's all.

Bella smiled at Serena's response: *Then use his babysitting skills & get out of the house! We could finally get a drink.*

You always have the best ideas, S. No wonder I love you so much.

Serena replied again instantly: *Hey, if I were you, I'd just be enjoying the eye candy.*

Bella chuckled. *Yeah, I know you would!*

She thought more about the point Serena had made about Noah babysitting. She hadn't really thought about that—the fact that having him around could actually free her up a little. And part of her liked the idea of throwing Noah in the deep end, leaving him alone with the kids to fend for himself.

Bella left her phone on the hall stand as she passed and walked into the kitchen, a smile still playing across her lips at Serena's words. She found Noah wiping down the counter. There wasn't a dish in sight, and the light on the dishwasher told her it was already going. For the first time since she'd known him, he'd managed to pleasantly surprise her.

"Someone's sure trained you well," she joked, crossing the kitchen and reaching up for a glass. She filled it with water and leaned back, wishing she had more energy, and then she might have taken Serena up on her suggestion of a drink out. "Or else this is a ruse to make me let my guard down before you surprise me with something hideous." She should have text Serena earlier in the day—her friend was always good at putting her in a better mood and making her chill more.

"They're full on," Noah said, completely ignoring her and putting the cloth he was using down. He turned to face her. "Playing with them for an afternoon is one thing, but . . ."

Bella laughed, finishing his sentence for him. "Playing *mom and dad* ain't easy. Which is exactly why I wanted them staying in routine and going to school instead of playing rookie with you."

"You can say that again." Noah chuckled. "The not-easy part, I mean."

He blew out a breath and reached past her, his arm skimming hers. Bella stayed silent, didn't move. She hated the way her body reacted to him, the way she looked at his muscled arms, was drawn to the size of his shoulders and the height of his frame, the chiseled lines of his face. There was no denying that he was a gorgeous man, but she didn't need gorgeous, and she didn't need a SEAL. They were the two things at the very top of her "not-for-me" list.

"Can I tell you something," she asked, deciding then and there that she had to trust him—where the kids were concerned, anyway.

"'Course you can," Noah replied.

"Some days I don't think I can do it. This whole being-a-mom thing, taking care of the kids and making sure they're fine and running their lives, organizing everything . . ."

"Bella," Noah said, putting down his glass and shaking his head, "looking after the boys is overwhelming. It would be for anyone, and it sure as hell probably was for Lila at times." He smiled, his head dipping down ever so slightly so he was looking directly at her face and into her eyes. "You want to scream or yell, just do it. Take a swig of whiskey, drown your sorrows in a bottle of wine. Whatever you need to do? Hell, I say just do it."

"It's not that easy," she muttered, sipping her water and wishing a few drinks were enough to help her.

"Look, it doesn't matter if they don't make it to school or pre-K some days. It doesn't matter if we all just hang out and shoot hoops or watch a DVD. We just need to get through each day as best we can and make sure the boys are happy."

She shook her head. "No, you're wrong. That's okay for the first few weeks, but they have to go to school; it's important. They can't miss out and—"

"They're four and six years old. School isn't that important yet," he disagreed, filling his glass and then turning back to stare at her. "I hate all this bullshit and pressure put on little kids. I mean, what the hell? Playing at home, climbing trees—that's what's important at this age. Not bullshit homework and all that crap."

"Noah, this isn't the fifties," she said angrily, wishing she hadn't even brought up the whole topic of not coping. "And you can't just talk over me in front of them and change the rules or go against my wishes."

His laugh annoyed her, made her want to storm out of the room like an angry toddler.

"No, this is the real world, and we don't always get our own way," he said, leaning back against the counter and folding his arms across his chest. She doubted he ever changed his mind when he fixed on something; there was a glint in his eye that gave her the impression he never backed down. "This is a world where people we love get taken away from us too soon, where crazy kids take guns to school, and children all around the world are starving. All I'm saying is that it's okay to put the boys' happiness first and make our own set of rules for a while."

She stared out the window into the darkness, didn't want to look at him for fear of bursting into tears. This wasn't her. She wasn't the one who cried when things didn't go her way or had to bite her lip in romantic comedies to stop from weeping. But ever since the accident, she'd been an emotional wreck, and the worst thing about Noah was that as much as she wanted to hate him, he was right.

"I just want what's best for them," she said, keeping her voice low so he wouldn't hear the crack in her tone. "I want to do everything for them that Lila would have."

"So do I. Why is it you keep treating me like the enemy when I'm the one person in the world right now who knows what you're going through? I miss Lila and Gray like crazy, like you do. And I know I haven't been doing it as long, but I'm parenting the boys now, too. We're on the same team, you and I, whether we want to be or not."

"So why is it so hard?" she asked. "Why does it seem so impossible to be teammates?"

He laughed. "Because for the better part of eight years we've done everything we could to avoid each other."

"Because you've always been a douchebag," she murmured.

"And you've always been such a goddamn princess," he fired straight back.

"Princess?" Bella laughed. "Now that's just mean."

Noah smiled, enjoying the lighter mood and the banter with her. "Oh hey, I forgot to say that I found a box when you were upstairs," he added. "I thought it was something belonging to the boys; then I saw a letter from Lila on top."

Bella's blood ran cold. She'd only had them out because she'd wanted to read one to the boys before bed. She hadn't expected Noah to go snooping.

"Noah, they're private!" she said, rushing over to the box and taking off the lid to see which one was on top. Her heart dropped when she saw that the letter about Noah wasn't there.

"Don't stress. Gotta say I had a chuckle," Noah said.

Trust him to find the only one that made mention of my sister's stupid idea about us dating.

"So she thought we should have dated?" Noah continued, holding up a piece of paper and smiling as he reread something.

Bella stormed over and snatched it from him. "It's not funny. They're all I have left from her. You shouldn't have been snooping around like that."

Noah's smile faltered. "I was just trying to have some fun. I didn't mean to upset you. I saw my name—that's the only reason I looked."

Bella bit hard on her lip to stop from crying, placed the letter on top of the pile, and shut the lid.

"I bet Lila would be having a laugh up there right now. At us," Noah said tentatively.

Bella took a deep breath. She could tell that he was genuinely sorry that he'd upset her. And she thought about it—Lila *would* have found the situation damn funny. Did she need to stop being morose, give herself a break, and lighten up every once in a while? Yes, Noah's judgment had been a little off but . . . suddenly it didn't feel as bad as before. She went and poured herself a half glass of wine and settled down on the sofa.

"So would you have ever gone out with me?" she asked, wishing the second she'd said the words that they hadn't just come out of her mouth, even though she'd only said them trying to be funny. Only they hadn't come out funny.

"Honestly?"

She grimaced. "Maybe not."

He sipped his wine, sat back, and grinned. "I thought you were super hot when I first met you. I mean, come on, what guy wouldn't? But then I realized you were way too uptight for me."

"So you're saying you would have shagged me, but you wouldn't have dated me?"

"Something like that," he said with a laugh.

"I should be offended, but strangely I'm not. Maybe it's the wine." She shrugged, channeling Serena and deciding to just chill and not get all worked up over what he was saying about her. He was probably half-right—she'd give him that. "So do you want to know if I would have dated *you*?" She would never admit it to him, but perhaps a hefty glass of Chardonnay was all she'd needed to feel a smidge better.

He pulled a face. "No."

"Well, I wouldn't have," she told him anyway.

"But you would have . . ."

"No!" she said, before he could say anything further. "I don't do one-night stands."

"How very upstanding of you."

His grin annoyed her. "There's nothing wrong with having morals."

"Oh, I have morals," he said. "I'm just selective about when I flaunt them."

"Yeah, like in front of my parents when you act like such an upstanding citizen that they can't stop raving about you."

"What's not to love?"

"Ugh!" she threw one of the cushions at him, narrowly missing his head. "You are so infuriating, you know that?"

"Says the pot to the kettle."

"The answer is no," she said, refusing to look at him and staring into the dark red pool of her wine instead. "I don't date military guys. I had way too many nights worrying about my dad, and then about Lila, to ever go there."

"Technically, I'm not military, but I get your drift. But what's your problem with it, exactly?"

She sighed. "Don't get me wrong, I respect any man or woman who serves our country. I'm one hell of a patriot; I just don't like my family being in the line of fire."

Humor shone from Noah's gaze, and she knew he was about to make fun of her, try to embarrass her, only this time she was prepared.

"So if I quit the Navy you'd date me—is that what you're saying?"

She felt the flush rise from her neck up into her cheeks, and no amount of fighting it helped. Bella held her chin up, refused to let him see how easily he could affect her with his choice of words. She could tell he was enjoying teasing her.

"Did I not mention the whole douchebag thing?" She was proud of her words, liked that she'd actually come back with something instead of hiding behind her wine.

"Douchebag . . . that's interesting," he replied, eyes fixed on hers. "And reminds me—did I forget to mention that I wasn't drunk enough to forget our kiss? You didn't seem to think I was a douchebag then."

She shuddered, being deliberately dramatic. "Don't go there, Noah. Just don't."

His laugh sent shivers down her spine and made her belly swirl. She hated the way he could make her feel.

"All I'm saying is that you didn't seem to mind me so much that night."

She took a big breath and raised her chin, refused to surrender. "We all make mistakes, Noah. I'm just lucky I realized mine within seconds."

Noah finished his drink and set the glass down, then rose to retrieve the bottle. He wasn't big on wine, but it was going down just fine, and he was liking getting Bella all riled up.

"You know, you should be like this more often," he called out, seeing the baby monitor on the table and grabbing it on his way past, once he had the bottle in hand.

"Like what?"

She suddenly jumped up as he leaned forward with the wine, bumping straight into his shoulder.

"Oh my God, the monitor!" she went to rush past him, and he held it up.

"It's fine—I've got it."

"They could have been crying, calling out, and I'd—"

"Have heard them," he assured her. "We would have heard the monitor from here, don't worry."

She stared at him for a long minute and then sat back down, holding out her glass. "Fill me up. And talk about that damn kiss one more time, and I'll give you a serious black eye." Bella's smile was slow. "And a bloody nose."

"I think we get along better when we're drinking," he joked, not bothering to acknowledge her threat. He knew when to push, and he also knew he'd almost pushed her too far.

Bella laughed, snuggling back into the sofa again. "You reckon? Because I'm pretty sure we've both been drinking whenever I've ended up thinking you're a jerk. I doubt tonight's going to be an exception."

"Ouch." Usually hearing anyone talk bad about him was water off a duck's back, but suddenly he actually gave a damn what Bella thought of him. He had no idea why, but Gray had loved her, and he kind of wanted to impress her. Although all the thoughts he'd once had about wanting to take her to bed had to go—hadn't he already given himself that pep talk? Noah glanced over at her again, at the way her tank top had slid low to show off a lacy bra, at her jean-clad legs tucked underneath her and the cute pink toenails peeking out. *Damn.* She might be uptight and seriously not his type, but he doubted any heterosexual man could be staring at her right now and not think wicked thoughts.

"So how are we going to make this work?" she asked, killing the flirt and pulling them back to reality. "What's the plan?"

"We live here together, we share looking after the kids, and we just make it work as best we can. We need to agree to disagree on some things and just figure it out along the way." He knew she'd hate that, that she was big on planning.

She gave him a look he couldn't decipher. "So you're planning on staying?" she asked. "I mean, permanently?"

"It's what Gray wanted, and from what it said in the will, Lila, too. Besides, I've signed the paperwork."

Her tone was as hesitant as her expression when she finally replied. "I just wasn't sure if you'd want to do it—long term, I mean. Whether you *could* do it. It's going to be . . . tough."

He nodded, annoyed that she thought so little of him that she expected him to bail when the going got tough. "Sorry to say, but you're stuck with me. I'm hanging around for the long haul."

"I'm just worried about the kids losing you, too. About how I explain to them when you have to go away."

"You explain it to them like Gray and Lila always did. They got it." He shrugged. "Kids are resilient. They understand things so long as they're explained."

"I just wonder if they'd be better off without—"

"Without what? Me?" he scoffed. "Seriously, if you think they're better off without me because there's a chance I might not come back from an assignment, then you're crazier than I thought. Hell, I could get hit by a car tomorrow and be gone."

"Nice," she muttered, putting her glass down with a bang on the coffee table.

"Bella, I didn't mean it like that. Bad choice of words," he tried to apologize.

"You know what? Don't bother," she said, standing. "I need to get some sleep. I'm in the master; the spare is all made up. Make yourself at home."

He should have told her to go to hell, that he wasn't the villain here. That the kids were better off with him in their lives. Only he wasn't sure he was right. There was no way he was going to walk away from the boys, not when he'd promised Gray a thousand times over that he'd look after them if anything ever happened to him. But what the hell did he know about being a dad? He hadn't had one of his own when he was a kid, had been taken in by Gray's family when he was fourteen, long after he'd bounced from one crappy foster home to another.

Instead of snapping at her, being an asshole, he rose and stopped her, hand on her arm.

"Just let me go, Noah," she said, not looking at him.

"Bella, I'm not going anywhere," he murmured.

"You've already said that."

"Just give me a chance," he said. "Give me a chance to help look after these kids instead of expecting me to be a fuck-up."

She still didn't look at him, but her body softened, her arm no longer rigid as he held her.

"Can you just give me that?" Noah asked.

Bella finally lifted her gaze, brown eyes hard to read. "Yeah, I can give you that."

He wished he hadn't touched her or stood so close to her in the first place. She smelled like shampoo and perfume, nothing overpowering—just a light aroma that stayed with him even as she walked away. Noah listened to her head up the stairs, the just-audible creak of the floorboards as she disappeared for the night. Then with one hand, he retrieved both their glasses by the stems and with the other, picked up the bottle.

Life had a way of changing course when he least expected it, just like it had so many years ago for him. He walked into the kitchen, left her glass in the sink, and poured a little more into his, sitting alone at the table. He needed a moment to think, to gather his thoughts. Because he wasn't good at dealing with this shit, with the memories that plagued him, even though he'd told Bella otherwise, made out like he could compartmentalize and not blame himself for things.

When he'd thought no one loved him, when life couldn't get any worse, along came Gray's parents. They figured out he was alone, found out that he was skipping out on foster families and bouncing around the system, and they made it their mission to take him in. It had taken them a while to get the paperwork sorted; they'd paid a lawyer even though he knew for a fact they hadn't had a lot of spare cash at the time, and they'd been the first people in his life to do what they'd promised. Teachers had felt sorry for him and offered to help, given him lunch and done their best, but no one had ever really stepped up and followed through, actually helped him out when they said they would, even though he'd come to school with countless black eyes and bruises. But Gray's family had been different, and so had Gray.

Tears pooled in his eyes as he sipped his wine, the room dark except for the light in the kitchen and the lamps Bella had left on.

He missed Gray like crazy, and he doubted he'd ever get over losing his best mate. He didn't let the first sob escape until the house was dead silent, until he knew for sure that Bella was behind a closed door, and even then he suffered in silence, let his body heave but forced the noise down.

"I'll do it even if it kills me," he muttered once he'd composed himself, hoping that Gray could hear him, looking skyward. "Those boys are gonna be loved. If it's the one thing I do in this lifetime, it'll be making sure those boys are loved and looked after every damn day of their lives."

He finished the wine, swallowing his guilt and pain along with it, before putting his glass in the sink and flicking out all the lights. He trudged up the stairs in the dark and headed for his room, almost pausing for a second outside Bella's and then cursing himself for being so stupid. She'd made her feelings for him brutally clear more than once, and if she wanted him in her bedroom, she wouldn't have walked off in a huff for bed. But no matter how much she tried to push him away, something about Bella made him curious, especially now he'd seen her let her guard down a little. He'd always known Bella the perfectionist, Bella the interior designer, and now he'd seen Bella at home, Bella with the boys. And it was this second version of Bella that intrigued him.

Noah pushed open the door to his room, stripped, and slipped beneath the covers. He'd hardly slept in days, which meant he was well overdue for some shut-eye.

CHAPTER FIVE

August 2014

Dear Bella,

I'm worried about you. Seriously, you need to go on a second date with one of these guys! Give one of them a chance. They can't all be as bad as you think, and don't keep comparing them to Brody. He was a first-class jerk, and I know all it's done is make you hate military guys even more than you already did, but geez, do you want to end up alone? The crazy cat lady? I know you don't actually have any cats yet, but you're already worrying me. It's okay to say yes and have fun and let your hair down. I don't want you being so careful that you end up at fifty alone and wishing you'd opened yourself up a little more. I saw you hurt, and I saw you fight back, and I believe in that strong woman. I believe in you, and I want you to be happy.

I love you, Sis, but you need your own Gray, not just me in your corner. Someone who has your back, someone to love you, someone to have gorgeous little Bella babies with. See you next week, and if you haven't been on a second date with one of those guys by the time I get back, then I'm going to take your love life into my hands, okay?

It's tough over here. The things I'm seeing, the things I hear. It's scary to be a woman in this position, knowing what I know. But if we don't have strong women in the world, prepared to fight for a cause, it'd be a pretty sad world. I know we have to disagree sometimes, but I honestly do feel like this is my calling, that I'm doing the right thing by being here. Even if I miss home so bad that it's almost crippling some days, the pain I feel at being away from my boys.

Lila xxoo

Noah woke with a start, bolt upright at the noise. His heart was racing, pulse igniting as he threw the covers off and leaped from the bed, pulling on his boxers as he ran out the door.

"What's happened?" he muttered as he watched Bella disappear into the boys' room. The scream was piercing, would have damn near woken the dead it was so loud.

He rushed in after her, saw her bent over the bed, arms engulfing one of the boys in a cocoon. Then the other woke and when he realized it was Will, he took the initiative and dropped to the boy's bed, pulling him up to hold him.

Noah stared at Bella, still bleary-eyed and trying to figure out what the hell was going on. "This happen every night?" he asked, hoping he was wrong.

She nodded. He could see her clearly with the two nightlights in the room sending out a soft wash of light. "It's getting worse, not better," she murmured, soothing him as she cuddled, one hand stroking Cooper's hair, the other holding him tight as she held him to her body. "It's why I sometimes just put them in bed with me from the start, so we all get a decent sleep."

"Am I doing the right thing?" Noah asked, nervous as hell all of a sudden, even though he was used to doing so much with the boys. He wasn't used to doing the hard stuff, though—he'd always been the fun uncle who could pump them full of sugar, send them crazy playing in the yard, and then flee the scene. And he sure as hell wasn't used to dealing with their emotional needs.

"You're fine." Her smile was soft, her face serene, even though Cooper was still crying, his little body shuddering every so often as he tried to catch his breath, traumatized from whatever had woken him. He was clutching his toy bunny as hard as he was holding on to Bella, the toy squished to his face.

Noah got it, and he knew Gray would have, too. If Cooper was having night terrors, then it was something Noah could deal with, something he could work on with him. The terrors were the worst part of his job, the flashbacks, waking up cold and sweaty, sheets tangled and damp from memories that wouldn't go away and that hit when you were least expecting them. He blinked, taking a deep breath and pushing them away like he always did, not letting them get to him. Just because he knew the theory about how to help didn't mean it had worked on him.

"What do we do now?" he whispered, thinking Will had fallen asleep, but too scared to put him down in case he woke. He was feeling hot, on the verge of breaking out in a sweat, having to hold the little guy.

"I think I'll take Cooper into bed with me," she said, struggling to stand with the big four-year-old in her arms. Noah wanted to reach out to steady her, but Will had suddenly tightened his already vice-like grip on him.

"Not without me," Will cried out, suddenly wide-awake. "I want Bella, too."

Bella sighed and nodded at him, walking from the room. "Bring him in. Can you just lie him down on the other side of me?"

Noah followed, glancing away when he noticed how short Bella's nightie was. It had ridden up high, was showing off almost all her thigh and her butt, and when they passed the nightlight, he was pretty sure she wasn't wearing underwear. When she dropped to put Cooper down, he crossed to the other side and laid Will down, except Will wasn't letting go of him, arms looped firmly around his neck.

"What do I do here?" he asked, suspended over the bed.

Bella turned, Cooper still in her arms. "Won't he let go?"

Noah shook his head. "No." It was harder to see in Bella's room, although a small light from the hall was on so he could just make out her face, hair tangled around her from the way Cooper had been looping it through his fingers.

"You might have to hop in with us all," she said. "Sorry."

Noah put Will down gently and lay down beside him, his body tight to his, length to length now they were on the bed. His body temperature rose instantly, not used to being jammed so tight to a little person who seemed to be trying to attach to him like glue. He also wasn't used to sharing a bed with . . . anyone. He liked his own space, especially because he knew that he was usually woken in the night by his own terrors.

"'Night," Noah said, voice low and quiet, refusing to give in when the boys were so settled finally.

"Thanks, Noah," Bella whispered back.

He didn't know what it was, but something about Bella's tone softened something inside him, told him that he needed to give her a break even when she blew at him as icy as the Antarctic. Neither of them had banked on this happening, on having to step up and figure out how to make the best out of the worst situation, but here they were.

He wriggled one arm free of Will, the other still wrapped around him. Gray would be having a chuckle at him now. He had Bella in his bed, something they'd always joked about happening only when hell froze over, and Gray's two boys were making sure he wasn't going to get close to her.

～

Bella stretched and had to thrust her arm out to stop from falling out of bed. Light was filtering in, the sun already starting to shine, and she moved away from Cooper. He was like a tangle of limbs to sleep with, and her neck was sore from having him half on top of her all night.

"Morning."

"Noah!" She glanced down, quickly adjusted her nightie to make sure she wasn't showing any nipple. Her breasts were straining to escape, the fabric all twisted around her. "I forgot we were all sharing the bed."

"You get much sleep?" he asked, rubbing at his eyes.

"A little. You?"

He shook his head, pulling up into a sitting position, doing the same kind of extraction she just had. Noah's chest was bare, his shoulders against the fabric headboard, fabric she'd chosen for Lila when she was designing her interior. Her sister hadn't been worried about everything looking perfect—the complete opposite of Bella—her only concern being not wanting anything to look too girly. Gray liked masculine, and so Bella had worked hard to find just the right look for them. Now, seeing Noah pushed back against it, she realized the room was perfect. His hard muscles looked at home against the dove-gray color, the white waffle duvet covering his lower half, making even the linen look sexy.

She averted her eyes, looked at his face. There was something about his big broad chest, muscled arms, and the sprinkling of dark hair arrowing down his belly that was making her want to curl her toes into the sheets.

"You sleep like this every night?" he asked, voice low.

"Yeah, except I'm usually the meat in the sandwich, with both of them attached to me."

"I think we need to take turns, get a decent sleep every other night."

She nodded. "Maybe." In reality she doubted Cooper would let her out of his sight, but it was worth a try. He'd started to twirl her long hair between his fingers when he was anxious, like she was his life-sized comfort blanket. "Noah, how long do we have you here for?"

"Awhile."

Bella didn't like how vague his answer was. "You're not telling me because you don't want to tell me, or do you actually not know? Because as much as I appreciate your help, like last night, I want to know if you're just going to break my carefully bandaged together life I've created with the boys and then just leave us to pick up the pieces."

He shrugged, but he wasn't looking at her now, the connection broken. His gaze was firmly on the boy snuggled asleep next to him. "I'll let you know as soon as I know. That's the best I can offer because my job isn't exactly nine to five. But for now you can get back to work, do your thing, and leave me with the boys."

She bristled, hating the frosty tone she'd used on him, but finding it impossible to talk to him any other way. "I don't need you telling me when I can go and how to get on with my life," she replied sharply.

Noah shrugged. "Suit yourself."

Bella gripped the covers and told herself not to be so damn pigheaded. She could make up her own mind, and the truth was she did need to get back into the office.

"So you're happy to take over everything with the boys so I can go off to work for the entire day?" All this time she'd struggled, kept putting her clients off and leaving her assistant to keep everything ticking over, but all of a sudden she needed to get out of the house, needed some time to herself, even just for a few hours. She wasn't actually convinced she could leave them for that long without making sure everything was okay, seeing them eat their milk and cookies after school and watching them as they played and did some homework. But throwing Noah into the deep end with no lifeline did sound appealing.

"You got it," Noah said, like it was the easiest task in the world. "I'll drop the boys off at school if they wanna go, and try to get a few jobs done around the place. Hell, I might even try to make us dinner."

"We love our fine dining here," she said sarcastically, knowing full well the child care alone should send him to breaking point.

"Never know—I might surprise you."

"About the dinner part or the actually taking them to school part? Because if you don't promise to get them to school, I'm not leaving them with you."

Noah slipped from bed then, careful not to disturb Will as he moved. She wanted to look away but couldn't, watched him, the release and pull of his muscles rippling down his back as he stretched, the only clothing he wore, his boxer shorts. Bella swallowed hard. Every inch of him was firm, honed, taut, and she'd be lying to herself if she didn't admit to wanting to explore his body to see exactly what those muscles felt like. Especially when he was so annoying!

"I'll get them to school. Stop getting your panties in such a knot."

She grimaced. It was one thing knowing she deserved a normal life, to continue parts of her old life, but ever since Lila had died, she'd gone into fierce mama bear mode, and letting go wasn't so easy. And even more so when Noah tried to waltz on in and upset the apple cart that she'd finally braced from tipping over. Although she did have to admit that the boys had smiled a lot already in the short time he'd been back, and that wasn't something she wanted to put an end to.

～

Noah stood under the water and cursed the thoughts he was having about Bella. He turned the faucet to cold, forced himself to stand there, to suffer in the freezing water as punishment. But he just groaned and *still* thought about her; the edge of nipple that had escaped when he'd first glanced over, her hair all messy and tangled from sleep, full lips taunting him. He seriously needed a distraction.

"Uncle Noah!"

He turned the water off and stepped out, grabbing his towel and pulling the door open. "What . . . ?"

He quickly tightened the towel around his waist, Bella's startled expression making it hard for him not to laugh. Her mouth had formed a perfect O, her eyes roving down his body, then up, before her cheeks turned a deep shade of pink as she blushed.

"Sorry," she muttered, spinning around and grabbing Cooper's hand as he went to dart away.

"I heard one of the boys call for me," he said, running his fingers through his wet hair.

"He was being silly, wanted you to talk me into staying and not going to work."

Bella was all dressed up, black slim-leg trousers, high stilettos, silk blouse. He would have liked to unbutton it a little more, but . . . *cold shower.* If he kept thinking like this, he'd need another cold blast of water.

"Boys, Bella needs to go to work." He shrugged. "You have me to play with. What's the big deal?"

Cooper hung his head, eyes downcast. "She might never come back."

His words were low, muttered so Noah could only just make them out. "You guys haven't been that bad for her, have you?"

"Noah," Bella cautioned, shaking her head and giving him a hard stare that he didn't understand.

He checked that his towel was tucked in tight before bending down, looking at Cooper on his level. When Cooper wouldn't look up, he glanced at Will, who had just appeared in the hall. He was staring at his toes, too, watching as he wiggled them into the thick carpet. It was hard not to laugh given he was dressed in full Spiderman costume, but Noah fought it and kept a straight face.

"What's going on, guys?" he asked.

"Cooper reckons she won't come back, 'cause last time Mommy and Daddy left, they never came home, even though they promised."

Noah had never been overly emotional, but his throat choked up when Will raised his eyes and looked at him. There was nothing but honesty in the boy's face—and sadness. He hoped that Bella would step in, because he had no idea what to say, was only capable of holding it together by gritting his teeth and steeling his jaw.

"What happened to your mom and dad was an accident," Bella said, eyes meeting his like she knew he needed saving. "No amount of promising could have changed what happened, and if there was anyway your parents could have walked away from that crash alive, could have changed what happened, they'd have done it in a heart beat." He swallowed. "There's nothing they wouldn't do or have done to be here with you boys. *Nothing.*"

"But Dad promised," Cooper whispered. "He told us that when he made a promise, he always kept it. Always."

Noah stood, looked at Bella, and wished she had some magical answer that could make everything better, would make the boys understand. "This was one promise your dad couldn't keep, buddy. It wasn't his fault."

Cooper started to cry, and Bella folded him in her arms, bent low. She was watching Noah over Cooper's head, her chin nestled into his hair. Noah, taking his cue, went to Will and scooped him up. Bella's smile was kind, her eyes brimming with tears. Noah doubted this whole thing was going to get any easier any time soon, but damn it, he hoped so.

"Want to come watch me shave?" he asked Will. "You can use the back of a toothbrush, and I'll cover your cheeks in shaving foam."

"Cool," Will said, wriggling to get down. "But I'm not sure if Spiderman needs to shave."

Noah laughed. "Oh, he does. Definitely."

"Wanna come, Coop?" Noah asked, beckoning for him to join them. "Bet you can show your brother what to do."

Noah watched as he reluctantly let go of Bella and headed into the bathroom with him. It was all he could think of at a moment's notice—he hadn't expected them to be so upset about her leaving for a few hours.

"Just go," he mouthed as Bella stood and stared.

She didn't say anything, then finally nodded.

Bella felt like her feet were rooted to the spot. She wanted to go, was desperate to visit a couple of clients that she'd been seriously neglecting, and make her way into her office to deal with, no doubt, a desk full of mail and samples, but she couldn't. Now she knew what her sister had meant when she'd said that leaving her children for even an hour sometimes hurt like hell. How she'd ever left them to go on tour, Bella would never know.

Through the open door she could see Noah standing, his golden-brown back bare except for a tattoo that she wished she could get a better look at, a white towel still just slung around his waist like it was about to drop. She averted her eyes and looked into the mirror instead, seeing the two little boys staring at their faces, now covered in white foam. Will was giggling and Cooper was smiling, but it still didn't make it any easier for her to head out for the day and not feel like she was abandoning them.

Then her eyes found Noah's. She realized he'd been staring at her in the mirror the whole time, or maybe only for a second, and she hadn't noticed. She hated the way he made her feel, the way he unsettled her and made her stomach flip into somersaults every time he leveled those icy-blue eyes on her. *Ugh.* She seriously needed to get out of the house and away from him.

Bella turned, grabbed her bag, and hurried down the stairs. She collected her keys on her way and marched to the door, locking it behind her and jumping in her SUV. With the boys, she'd been driving Gray's vehicle because they'd wanted her to, but she needed to collect fabric samples and drive to her client's house after the office, and it was nice to be in her familiar vehicle, to pretend for a sec that nothing had actually changed in her life. Besides, it wasn't littered with wrappers and half-eaten potato chips.

She dialed Serena before she drove off, smiling when her super bubbly, glass-half-full girlfriend answered.

"Hey. Don't tell me you've actually left the house. Alone?"

Bella laughed. She'd promised Serena she'd call her the first time she was alone and actually available to grab a coffee.

"I'm alone, and I'm out of the house, but I don't have time for coffee," she told her. "I'm heading into work."

"I'll meet you there. Give me fifteen, and I'll bring the coffee."

Bella was going to say no, but she needed some downtime. To just chat for a bit about nothing and everything, to have some adult time before she started work. It wasn't like she'd had no adult time since she'd taken over looking after the boys—she saw plenty of her parents, countless people had called in, and now there was Noah—but Serena was different. She was fun and she wouldn't mention what had happened, or if she did, there would be no treading on tiptoes so she didn't offend Bella.

"I've got news by the way."

"Oooh, cute bartender you liked asked you out?" Bella asked, finding herself smiling just for the hell of it for the first time in weeks. "Or was it the new associate you have your eye on?"

Serena laughed. "Even better. I'll tell you soon."

Bella hung up, still smiling as she drove the rest of the way and pulled into a parking space. She grabbed her bag and headed up, walking up the stairs instead of taking the elevator. She shared space with a few other people, had one corner of a large open-plan office. Her assistant hadn't been in the last few weeks—Bella had given her time off—but today Bella arrived to find her assistant standing talking to one of the other guys on her floor.

"Bella! Oh my God, how are you? I wasn't expecting—"

"Hi, Kate. Just coming in to clear a few messages, make some appointments," Bella said with a smile, ignoring the looks of pity she was receiving. This was why she'd avoided everyone—because she didn't need those looks and stares, not when she'd finally made it out the door and stopped thinking about her sister for longer than a minute.

"But are you sure—"

"Go grab a coffee, Kate. Take your break now," Bella told her, smiling curtly. They were usually pretty close, friends even, but today she just needed to get to her desk and have coffee with Serena. She pulled a ten-dollar bill from her wallet. "It's on me—and thanks for all your work holding the fort down for me."

Kate touched her arm and smiled before taking the money. "I'll see you in half an hour. You want anything?"

Bella shook her head. She crossed the room and made it to her desk, sighing as she slumped down in her chair, not able to see even an inch of the glass top. As she'd expected, there were so many things to address, she had no idea where to start.

"Hey, gorgeous!"

Bella grinned when Serena called out, silencing everyone in the office as she walked in, coffee tray in hand. She was blonde and tall, her legs endlessly long in a knee-length skirt and pumps. Bella bet the male attorneys in her office found it impossible to work with her around.

"I so needed this," she said, holding her arms out for a hug when Serena reached her desk.

Serena wrapped an arm around her, squeezing tight. "You look fab."

"No, I look like a train wreck compared to you." She gratefully took her coffee and slowly took a sip. "I need an IV line pumping caffeine into me these days."

"You're a mom of two boys now, Bells. Stop being so hard on yourself."

"So tell me your big news?" she asked, dying for some of Serena's gossip.

"It's kind of *your* big news," she said, looking like she was about to start laughing. "Oh, the coffee's double strength by the way, in case you're bouncing off the walls later."

Bella knew better than to let Serena distract her. "What do you mean *my* big news? You're not making sense." All Serena was doing was making Bella suspicious.

"So, you know how I signed you up with that new Internet dating site a while back?"

Bella groaned. "Please tell me you didn't."

"I did actually. Because we all know that you need a date. Or two. Or ten." Serena laughed. "I actually told your sister all about my idea, and she wholeheartedly agreed, so I'm just honoring her wishes."

Damn Lila. Her sister would have been the first one to sign her up if she'd had half a chance, or the time to actually sit down and make her a profile. She'd been hassling her for the better part of a year. Bella imagined her laughing and applauding Serena's work.

"You make it sound like I'm desperate and dateless."

Serena frowned. "Um, you are. When was the last time you went on a date?"

Bella pulled a face straight back at her. "I've been on dates."

71

"Excluding coffee dates. I mean getting-dressed-up, looking-smoking-hot, hitting-the-town kind of dates."

"Never. You know I hate that sort of thing."

"No, you hate that you used to do that sort of thing with Brody. That doesn't count." Serena sipped her coffee. "Most guys don't get that drunk all the time—or that annoying."

"So what's your point?"

"You have a date Friday night," Serena said. "I'm going to baby-sit the boys, unless you want your mom to know that you're going out, and then you could get her to do it. It's just casual—nothing to get all worked up over."

"Serena!" Bella groaned again, slipping forward and resting her head on a large pile of fabric. "Why do you do these things to me?"

"Because I'm your best friend and I want you to meet the man of your dreams."

"Says the so-called best friend who's just found a guy online for me who could be a rapist or a serial killer."

"So you want me to babysit? You can't cancel on him. And he wasn't from the Internet—he's real. Could've saved myself the time writing your profile."

"I don't need a babysitter; Noah can look after them. You gave me the idea in the first place, remember?"

"How's that going? Because if you need me to get rid of him, I don't think it would take a lot to make a case and give you sole custody of the boys. You're their aunty by blood, and it'd be better for them to have one stable parent rather than being shared between you."

Serena was so confident, made it all sound so simple. "Gray wanted Noah in their lives," Bella said simply. "It might not be easy, but I need to at least try to follow their wishes."

"Fair enough. Pity you've always hated him so much; other-wise, it could have been cute, the two of you looking after the kids together, falling in love—"

"Stop!" Bella didn't know whether to cry or laugh. "And I haven't always hated him. 'Hate' is too strong a word. I just—I don't know—he's not my type. Besides, that's the last thing we'd need to complicate things anymore than they already are."

"Oh, I forgot that you don't like sexy-as-hell, muscled bad boys," Serena said with a wry smile.

"He's Navy."

"Oooh, even worse!"

"Did you not hear the part about me not wanting to complicate things?"

They both laughed and sipped their coffees. The idea of a date was killing her, but a blast of Serena was exactly what she'd needed. And she was right—Lila had been encouraging her to date, to give some guys a chance rather than write them off if one little thing about them didn't seem perfect. Her trouble was that after Brody she'd been happy to be on her own for a while. He'd been the perfect guy on paper—ex-SEAL turned cop, handsome, charming. But when he drank, which wasn't all the time but often enough, he changed, like he was a different person. Once every few weeks, or sometimes every couple of months, they went out for a big night, to have fun, and she'd end up in tears and on her way home in a cab alone. She couldn't recognize the person he'd turned into but knew that by the next evening he'd be back to Mr. Charming again.

"We kind of slept in the same bed last night, but nothing happened; we had the boys in with us," she told Serena, wondering why the words were even coming from her mouth. "Then this morning he ran out of the bathroom with a towel around his waist, and I swear to God, my jaw hit the floor."

Serena arched an eyebrow. "He's super hot, right?"

"Yeah. He is."

"So . . . you *do* want to go there?"

Bella shook her head, as much to convince herself as Serena. "No way. He's firmly out of bounds, and besides we've never really gotten along. I bet he's slept with way too many women to count, and he's so damn cocky. Seriously, the man thinks he's God's gift to women. I've seen the way he flirts. Besides, haven't you listened to all the times I've moaned about him?"

"So go on this date on Friday. Give him a chance."

"You're not going to let me say no, are you? Who is he?"

Serena rose. "I have to get back to work. But you're going on this date, Bella. He's going to pick you up."

"You gave him my address!" Bella shrieked, silencing the entire office. She blushed and took her last, long gulp of coffee.

"Yeah, I did," Serena said with a smirk. "And by the way, he's your cute barista, the one you always flirt with. I was chatting to him the other day, mentioned you, and he said he's been wanting to ask you out for ages. I just played Cupid, and it's only a drink. I know you're going to say that it's too soon, but I think you should do it."

If her day could have gotten any worse, it just had. "Please tell me you're kidding," she gasped.

"No. Sorry." She shrugged. "Worst-case scenario, you have to find a new coffee shop."

"But he makes great coffee!" Bella groaned.

"So let him make you great coffee after you have great sex with him," Serena whispered. "Just give yourself permission to have fun every now and again. Not every man is going to break your heart, okay? And you need a break from the boys sometimes; otherwise, you'll go crazy."

Serena was starting to sound like Noah. "Fine, I'll do it. But seriously, you can't do this to me again."

"Scouts honor," Serena said, holding her fingers up in some sort of weird sign. Bella sighed.

She shrugged. "Just do it. Go out with him, flirt, have fun, and then tell me how wonderful I was for setting you up in the first place. Okay? Otherwise, I'll give your phone number to all the other hotties I have lined up for you from the website."

"Fine," Bella grumbled, "but give my number out to any of those guys, and I'll kill you."

Serena waved, and Bella was left with a sinking feeling in the pit of her stomach and still with a pile of things that had to be opened and dealt with. She had samples waiting to take to clients, bills to pay, new fabrics to consider and give her recommendation on—and all she wanted was to curl up in a ball and sleep. Or read a book, go for a pedicure. Anything except deal with the real world and the fact that she was going to be collected in a few nights' time for a date with the cute barista that she'd thought she'd been harmlessly flirting with all these months.

And Noah. She was going to have to look Noah in the eye and tell him she was going on a date. She'd expected she'd be the one having to deal with him going out and bringing women home, not the other way around—not for a second. So why was she so worried about telling a man she had no romantic feelings for that she was going on a date?

Bella ripped open the first parcel just as Kate walked back into the office. She needed to stop thinking about the man she now shared a house with and focus on work. Just because he'd looked insanely good without a shirt on did not mean she needed to change the way she felt about him. He was still the one who'd disrupted everything the moment he'd arrived.

He was still Noah who'd slept with one of her sister's bridesmaid. Noah who was way too much fun when it was time to be serious. Noah who always teased her for being too uptight.

"Need any help?"

Bella stood up, needing to get out of the office. "Could you open all these, send any unsolicited samples back, put the bills in a pile for me to pay, and sort everything else out for me? I'm going to call in on a few clients, make sure I haven't lost them since I've been out of touch for so long."

Kate nodded. "There are lots of cards personally addressed to you, too."

Bella didn't need to deal with anything else relating to her sister's death, had opened enough sympathy cards to last her a lifetime. "Thanks. Would you mind opening them for me? Write a quick note back to each one, thanking them for their thoughts, so I don't have to? Then jot down a list of everyone who's been in touch so I can thank them personally when I'm ready."

Kate's smile was sweet, and Bella hoped she hadn't been too dismissive before, when she'd first arrived. "No problem."

Bella hurried back to the car, needing the fresh air. She had to keep herself busy and stop thinking about Noah, the cute barista guy, and the fact that she was so behind on work that she was in danger of losing the clients she'd spent years accumulating.

~

Noah was exhausted. Six hours of being a solo parent, and he was in awe of anyone who had to deal with kids day in, day out. He dodged past Cooper to grab the phone, pressing it to his ear and spinning around to make sure the boys weren't about to kill each other. They'd been good, but he was pretty sure they were starting to get tired, and he was seriously regretting his decision of not making them go to school when they'd begged to stay home. *Maybe it's time to admit that Bella might be right about her whole routine gig.*

"Hello."

"Gosh, you sound like Gray."

He stopped, smiling as he listened. "Hi, Christina." He recognized Bella's mom's voice immediately.

"How are you getting on? The boys okay?"

Noah glanced at them and grinned. "Yeah, when they're not shoving each other and arguing. And driving me around the bend." He hadn't expected child care to be so . . . draining. Exhausting. Overwhelming.

"They didn't go to school today?"

"Unfortunately not."

"Bella made that same mistake early on. Think she learned her lesson real fast."

So she'd been talking from experience when she'd told him not to give in and let them stay home. Maybe he should've listened.

"How are the two of you getting on? It must be hard on you being back and thrown straight into suburbia. And I know Bella's worked so hard to get the boys into a routine that works for them, to help them feel a sense of normalcy despite everything."

"Yeah, you can say that again, about being home." He cleared his throat. "That came out all wrong—sorry."

"My husband was the same. Always desperate to get home to us, but found it impossible to settle in straightaway. I could always see his struggle."

Noah grunted. He wasn't sure what to say. On the one hand, he'd always craved stability, the idea of a home life, but it also terrified him, especially when the guys he trusted with his life every day had become his family. Not to mention the fact that he was feeling like a jerk for throwing his weight around when it was dawning on him big time how hard it must have been for Bella jumping straight into parenting when he'd gone back to work and left her to go it alone for the toughest couple of months.

"Well, it's nice not to dive for cover every time I hear a bang, but I'm not gonna lie and say being back is any kind of easy," he joked.

"Is my daughter there? I wanted to give you two some space, but I'm dying to see those kids. I miss them like crazy."

"I'll bet you do," Noah replied. "Bella's actually at work still. Went into the office first thing, and I haven't seen her again yet."

"Oh, well that's good. She needs to get back into a routine, balance the boys with work—otherwise, she'll go stir-crazy. We've all been thinking it but not sure how to say it. She's been so tired and overwhelmed that it seemed best just to let her figure things out and ask for help when she needed it."

Noah jumped to grab a wayward ball, his arm shooting out to grasp it, and shook his head at the boys. Bella's mom had given him a serving without even knowing it, just letting him in on that little bit on how her daughter had been coping, or trying to cope.

"I'll get her to call you. I'm about to start on dinner—you know, trying to impress her."

"Good luck," Christina said. "Goodness knows you'll need it with that one."

"I know what you mean," he said with a laugh. It wasn't a secret that the two of them had never exactly gotten on, so he was sure there would be a whole lot of people laughing about the fact that they'd been lumped together.

"Just be patient with her. She's actually a lot of fun, more like Lila than you probably realize."

He smiled. He hadn't seen it yet, but something told him not to doubt her mom's words.

"If she's anything like Lila, then your husband might have to get out his shotgun, Christina. Gray always swore that he had the best girl in the world, so I'd have to take my chance on her sister," he teased.

"She was a great girl, my Lila," Christina said with a big sigh.

"Lila was one *hell* of a girl, no doubt about it."

The ball he'd only just retrieved and thrown back made a loud smash as it went straight through the window. *Shit.*

"And that's my cue to hang up," he said.

Christina said good-bye, and he put the phone down, folding his arms across his chest as he stared down at the boys. They were silent, hadn't made so much as a peep since the smash. There was glass all over the carpet, but the puppy-dog expressions facing him made it impossible to be angry. Lucky for them he still remembered what it was like to be a kid.

"Does Bella ever let you play ball inside?" he asked.

Cooper and Will both shook their heads. "Nope," Will said.

"She gonna kill us?" Noah asked.

"Yep," Will said, still dressed in his Transformer's suit, but with the sleeves and legs pushed up. He'd gotten hot earlier but refused to take it off, so Noah had done his best to turn it into a summer version.

"Then how about I take the blame. No need for you guys to get in trouble. But next time, no throwing like you're pitching at a Giant's game, okay?"

Noah headed for the laundry, getting everything he needed to clean the glass up. He was feeling like a Stepford wife, only there was no way he could keep it up very long.

"Did you ever help your mom cook?" he asked as he scooped up the mess.

"Nah," Will said. "Just baking, like biscuits and cakes."

"Want to help me make dinner anyway?" He had no idea how he was going to keep an eye on them and cook, but if they helped him it seemed like a win–win.

"Cool. What're we making?" Will's eyes were bright, his expression so much lighter than it had been earlier. When the excitement of his arrival had worn off, Noah had seen glimpses of the boy's pain, even in the way he played with his brother and stared off into the distance. "I love making all sorts of stuff," Will continued.

"You used to make stuff with your dad, right?" Noah asked.

Will nodded. "Yeah, but mostly with Granddad. We do model planes and stuff. I kinda help, and he does the hard bits."

"Sounds cool," Noah said, hoping Will wouldn't ask him to help build a model. He could teach the boy to shoot a gun or hoops—even throw a ball—but he was crap at making things.

"I'll show you one day," Will said.

"Sure thing. Now give me five, then I'll check out what we have." Bella had always been organized, so he was betting the fridge would be full.

He finished cleaning up, made a mental note to vacuum later once the kids were in bed, and headed into the kitchen, with the boys following a step behind him. He opened the fridge and looked in the pantry, checking off a few ingredients. Cooking wasn't exactly something he was amazing at, but he knew how to throw a meal together when he had to.

Bingo. Pizza bases. "You guys like pizza?"

"Yeah!" they both agreed enthusiastically.

"Pizza it is, then. Will, grab that stool and stand on it," he said. "Little man, you can sit on the counter next to me."

He got the boys set up, pulled out all the ingredients he needed, and turned on the oven. The kids might be hard work, but they were also one hell of a lot of fun.

"Bella's gonna freak," Cooper said. "She doesn't like mess."

Noah laughed. "You let me deal with Bella. She doesn't scare me."

Both boys laughed—until a soft voice made them all stop dead.

"Who's not scared of me?"

Cooper and Will burst out laughing as Noah dropped the knife he'd been holding and held his hands up in the air. "Guilty as charged."

She dropped her bag and walked over, coming around to drop a kiss into Cooper's hair and leaning to press one to Will's cheek. Noah smiled when her long hair brushed his arm, the gentle scent of her perfume wafting up to him.

"Why didn't you kiss Noah?" Will asked innocently and with his cute little lisp.

"Because I've been naughty," Noah said, winking at Bella as she shot him a grateful look. "I'll be expecting one next time if I'm good."

"Looks like you guys are making dinner?" she said, completely ignoring him.

Noah watched as she stepped back around and sat down at one of the stools. She looked beat. He swatted Cooper's hand away from the cheese when he tried to steal it, halfheartedly attempting to stop him.

"You okay?"

"Just tired."

He checked that Will wasn't too close to the edge and turned around to get a couple of beers from the fridge. Noah popped the tops and slid one over to her.

"Oh, thanks." She smiled, hesitantly, but he was pleased her lips turned up instead of down or into that awful straight line she set them in when she was mad. He'd seen that way too many times yesterday.

"I don't usually drink beer."

"It's cold, and you deserve one." Noah took a long pull of his. "Tell me all about your day."

She looked embarrassed, a strange look passing over her face as she stared at the bottle he'd passed her. "Work was crazy, but my clients all seem to understand my absence. Well, all but one." Bella took a sip, sighing when she put the bottle back down. "That one I told to go to hell."

"I'm impressed." He dragged his eyes from her, not wanting to look at her any longer. For a woman he'd vowed never to touch with a forty-foot pole, she was sure stirring up his admiration a lot. Although it was hard not to admire her; she had long hair that curled just on the ends and eyes so warm when she fixed them on the children, the look transferring to him sometimes and making him feel like everything was actually going to work out. And her lips . . . damn, he definitely needed to stop staring at those soft, pillowy, full lips of hers. Hell, her entire mouth was sexy as sin. "What did you say to her?"

She shook her head. "I don't even want to go there. But I had coffee with a friend and . . ."

Her voice trailed off, and he watched as she took another sip of beer.

"What?" he asked, waiting for her to finish her sentence.

"Please tell me the boys went to school," she said, her tone sharper.

He watched as she looked around, like it was dawning on her that there were no school lunch boxes waiting to be washed on the counter, and then there was the mess in the living room, the general chaos.

Noah decided to just 'fess up. "No. They wanted to stay home. Will wouldn't get out of his costume, and Cooper begged me to watch a DVD and—"

"Noah!" she hissed, slamming her beer bottle down and glaring at him. "You can't do this. How can you think this is okay?"

He had a mind to tell her that he'd do whatever the hell he wanted, only he knew that she was right. "I get it," he said. "I won't do it again unless there's a good reason."

"I've worked so hard to—" She suddenly stopped talking, and he cringed when she looked past him. "What happened to the window?"

"Entirely my fault," he said, not about to land the boys in trouble. "In hindsight, playing ball inside probably wasn't the best idea."

"You think?"

Bella looked like she was about to explode. "The glazier is coming in the morning—it's fine. The boys had a nap on the sofa, and I got rid of all the glass and—"

"You let them have a nap!" Bella threw her hands up in the air, and Noah found himself cringing again. "They'll never go to sleep tonight."

He decided not to admit to anything else and just to keep his mouth shut about what they'd been doing.

"Noah, I left you here today thinking it'd make you realize—"

"I learned my lesson. I get it. Enough said."

Bella looked exasperated, but she didn't say anything, just folded her arms over her chest.

Noah held up a hand before she could explode again. "You don't need to explain yourself, but Bella, you've had months to figure this all out. I've gone from being the fun uncle to having to figure out how to be that as *well* as set some ground rules. Give me some time."

"Are you going to stop being Mr. Cool and work with me as a team?" she asked.

Noah conceded, "Yes."

He watched as her mouth opened, then shut. Eventually, she just nodded. "Okay. Truce. But don't go overriding me again. Or telling me what to do. Or not listening."

"Deal," he said, holding out his hand.

Bella hesitated, then reached for it, her palm fitting snug against his. "Deal."

Noah shook her hand and then let go to retrieve the pizzas. "Dinner's ready! Who's hungry?"

Spiderman ran into the kitchen, and Noah laughed when he realized that in the meantime Cooper had pulled on a Batman costume with a muscle chest on it. There was something about those kids that put a smile on his face, no matter how hard he tried to resist.

CHAPTER SIX

Bella flopped down onto the sofa, kicking off her ballet flats and shutting her eyes. She had no idea how she managed to get through every day, even with Noah helping. Between work and school and pre-K and dinners and bath time . . . . She sighed just thinking about the past week. She could hardly believe Noah had been with them since Monday.

"Wine?" Noah called out.

Bella groaned, wishing she could say yes. "I can't."

Noah appeared. The living room and kitchen were open plan, with a separate lounge that served as a TV room off to the side. She was stretched out on the sofa in the living area, enjoying the silence.

"You're not pregnant, are you?" he asked, grinning like he thought it was the funniest joke in the world.

"No. I'm going out."

He frowned. "You have plans?"

"I didn't realize I had to ask your permission." She liked the idea of him realizing how exhausting it was to be on sole parent duty all day *and night*.

"I was hoping to head out for a beer, but I can stay home. It's not a biggie." He shrugged. "I only just figured out what day of the week it was when one of the guys sent me a text earlier to say it was beer Friday."

Bella smirked to herself. "Beer Friday? Not with these little ones around." Then she relented a bit. Noah had given up his night out pretty quickly. "I have no idea how parents manage to have a life outside of kids," she added.

"I think that's half the problem," Noah said, disappearing again. If she bothered to crane her neck, she would have been able to keep watching him, but she was too tired and too lazy.

She shut her eyes again, knowing she needed to head upstairs and get ready, but not wanting to just yet. But she also had to tell Noah where she was going, in case something happened and he needed to get in touch with her.

"Here," he said, interrupting her thoughts. She looked up to find him standing over her, a half glass of wine in hand. "It'll help you unwind."

She took it, grateful that she could sit for a little. "Thanks." Although she was starting to worry; she was relying on her nightly glass of wine a little too much these days!

"I thought my job was full on, but those kids? *Damn*," he swore.

Bella grinned. "Yup. I miss so much about my old life."

"Like what?"

"Don't even get me started," she said. "I mean, aside from the obvious with Lila and Gray, I miss reading until 2:00 a.m. without worrying that if I don't have a few hours of sleep by that time, I might miss out on any at all."

"Not having to worry about eating right because it's only you," Noah interjected.

"Or having to get home by a certain time."

They both laughed.

"And then I look at Will and the obsessive way he plays Spiderman, or the thoughtful way Cooper constructs things from blocks, or the pictures they paint me that I get to stick on the fridge, and I know that no matter what I miss, they're the most important people in my world and probably always will be."

They sat in silence. Bella sipped her wine, waiting the tears out, knowing that if she just sat quietly and stopped thinking about the past, they'd eventually pass.

"You have a tat?" Noah suddenly asked. "I didn't pick you as the type to get ink." She glanced down, saw that with the arms of her blouse pushed up, tonight it had been in plain view. It surprised her he hadn't glimpsed it before now.

"Just two letters," she said, holding the inside of her wrist out for him to look at. "I got it just after the service."

"You've changed since they passed," he said. "More than just what you've lost—it's changed your outlook or something."

The L and G were just tiny, barely there bits of ink, but she liked it. True, she'd never wanted a tattoo before, but at the time it had felt right, and it still did.

"Maybe that's why I said yes to going on a date tonight," she muttered.

Noah almost dropped his beer on the tile floor. "You did what?"

She shrugged. "It's just a drink. I'll be a couple of hours max, so if you want to head out after, we can just tag in."

The boys came running in then. They'd been happily playing in Cooper's bedroom but had obviously tired of whatever it was they'd been doing.

If Noah had been a dog, she bet the hairs on his back would have been raised, bristled like he was about to have a standoff, teeth bared. The way he was looking at her was . . . primitive somehow. Like he had a claim on her.

"Someone you've been seeing?" he asked, and she watched as he got up and went back into the kitchen. He was making the kids pizza again because they'd loved it the first time, and she got up to join him, settling on the other side of the counter to give him some space.

"Long story, but my friend organized it. I don't actually know the guy that well, but he's picking me up at eight."

Noah set the knife down and stared at Bella. She reached over to steal a piece of cheese. "Hold up. You don't know him, but he's coming to the house?"

She shrugged. "I know where he works. He's not a complete stranger."

Noah was frowning. "You don't strike me as the blind-date type."

"Serena will kill me if I pull out, so I'm going along with it. She's on some crusade to honor Lila's wish and find me love."

His laugh was low, husky. "I wonder what she would have thought if she'd known about our kiss?" Noah raised an eyebrow, staring at her until she dropped her gaze and looked down at her beer. She glanced at the boys. They'd been way too quiet since they'd come downstairs, no doubt ears flapping as they listened to the conversation he was having with Bella.

Bella glared at Noah. They'd sworn never to speak about what had happened between them; she'd practically begged him not to tell her sister, and now he'd just gone and said it out loud. And it wasn't the first time he'd brought it up since arriving back, which was twice too many times for her liking.

"You're lucky I didn't slap you when you tried it on," she said, not wanting him to know how much he'd rattled her. "And I think we can both agree that nothing like that will ever be happening again."

"Slap me? Sweetheart, you were practically begging for it."

Her jaw hit the floor. "Noah!" she hissed, glancing at the boys. "I was *not*."

"I'm guessing that's why you don't usually have more than two glasses of wine," he said with a grin, sliding the pizzas into the oven once he'd finished the toppings. They were pretty simple—just cheese, pineapple, and ham for the boys, with extra vegetables on theirs. "Don't trust yourself to behave?"

If she could have thumped him, then she would have—or worse—but when the boys looked at her, she just smiled sweetly, like Noah teasing her and talking about something he knew infuriated her was perfectly normal.

"Why did Noah kiss you?" Will asked.

Bella dropped her forehead to the counter, realizing the boys had heard everything. "No more questions," she muttered. "Seriously, Noah, I'm going to kill you for this."

"Didn't you like it?" Cooper asked. "I wouldn't like a girl kissing me. Except for Mommy. Or you."

She slowly raised her head. Just like that, the boys had pulled her from her own thoughts, made her smile and forget about being annoyed with Noah—just like that.

"Hey, do we have any pie?" she asked Cooper.

"I dunno. Why?"

She laughed. "Because if we do, I reckon we should throw it at Noah. Get him all smooshy with it all over his face."

Noah's lips kicked up at the sides again, his smile infectious. "If you stay home, I'll let you."

His smile might have been mischievous, but she knew something about her going on a date had rattled him, and after what he'd just put her through, she was more determined to go than she'd been all day.

"Sorry, no can do."

He bent over, whispering something to the boys.

"I missed that," she said, leaning in closer.

"Noah said you had cooties anyway," Will whispered.

"Oh, did he now?" she muttered, flicking a piece of cheese at Noah and receiving a slow smile for her efforts.

"Do that again, and I'll—"

"What?" she asked innocently. "You'll do what, Noah?" Bella felt alive for the first time since the accident, actually enjoying herself without having to try so hard. She flicked another piece of cheese.

"Uh-oh," Cooper said, laughing when Noah grabbed them both down from the bench before firing a piece of capsicum at her.

"And it's war," Noah said.

The boys ran at her, and Bella bolted, jumping off her chair and running for the stairs.

"Get any food in my hair, and I'll—"

"What?" Noah called out, leaping at her and grabbing her by the arm so the boys could tackle her and topple her down on the first few steps of the stairs.

He was looking down at her, grinning as the boys pinned her. Noah was holding a piece of tomato in his hand, but he didn't throw it, just watched as they pretended to get her, play punching as she tickled.

"I'll unleash these little monsters on you," he finally finished, gaze never leaving hers.

Bella kept tickling the boys, but she never took her eyes from Noah, watching the way he was looking at her. She had to admit that he wasn't as much of a douchebag as she'd once thought. It was nice to laugh, to smile just for the hell of it. There was something upbeat about him that was impossible not to feed off.

"How about we let Bella go get ready for her hot date," he told the boys.

They groaned and held on to her tight, and she cuddled them right back. "How about we find a DVD to watch, eat those pizzas the second they come out of the oven, and then have a bath before bed? I'm not going out until later."

She didn't want them to be anxious that she was leaving, and after being away from them all day, she was kind of looking forward to hanging out with them for a bit.

"A few hours away from us, and you can't get enough, huh?" Noah asked, holding out his hand.

"A day away from these little rascals, and I'm feeling all soppy about leaving the house again at all," she confessed, leaving them to rough and tumble as she pulled up.

Bella looked up at Noah, wished she hadn't put her palm in his. There was something about him that had always made her want to run a mile in the opposite direction, and tonight was no different. His stare, the blue gaze that seemed so piercing yet so magnetic, the memory of exactly what his lips had felt like on hers—too hot, too intense, too damn intoxicating. She liked to stay in control, to know exactly what she was doing and when, and Noah tipped her way too far in the opposite direction.

"You know, I thought it would be *you* all pissed off with *me* when it came to the opposite sex," he said, releasing her hand but still holding her gaze.

"Let's not get carried away," she muttered. "I'm just going out for a drink. You're not going to wake up and find a half-naked stranger making himself coffee in the kitchen."

He laughed. "You sound fairly sure about that."

"That's because I am. I don't do one-night stands—never have. I'm a relationship kind of girl."

"Nothing wrong with having fun," he joked. Or at least she thought he was joking. "And I don't recall you worrying about whether or not we were in a relationship when you kissed me in your parents' kitchen."

"Enough with the kiss story!" she hissed, balling her fist and connecting with his bicep. "Mention that again, and I'll knock you out." She actually had no idea how she'd do that unless she had a hunk of wood or metal in her hand, but still.

Noah caught her hand, laughing when she winced. "If you didn't get so worked up every time I mentioned it, it'd be no fun, and I'd stop."

She hated that he had hold of her, the way she felt when she was so close to him. Noah was nothing like her type, never had been, never would be. But still. He unsettled her, and she didn't like it one bit.

The boys tackled her around the legs again, almost dropping her, and Noah let her go.

"Pizza," she mumbled. "Let's go check the pizza."

"Do you always just change the subject instead of dealing with stuff?" he asked. She could tell he was loving this, his smile never wavering, even as he walked backward into the kitchen, still watching her.

"When it comes to you? Yeah," she told him. "Now stop talking and just deal with the pizza. *Please.*"

Noah shrugged. "Come on, boys—you heard her."

CHAPTER SEVEN

Dear Bella,

Something happened between you and Noah, didn't it? I quizzed him before we left, but he wouldn't say a word. Come on, tell me! Your letters are the only thing that keeps me going over here. I read them over and over every night, and I need some gossip. I keep telling you how great he is, but man, you guys always seem to rub each other the wrong way. You're gorgeous, he's gorgeous, you're both fab—I just don't get why you always end up pissed at each other. No, scrap that: you *get pissed off with him, and he always finds the whole thing insanely amusing. At least give him a chance to just be your friend—it would be great if we could actually hang out with both of you at the same time. If you knew what he'd been through, what he's come from, I think you'd feel differently about him. But that's his story to tell, and he doesn't seem to share a lot with anyone but Gray. And me sometimes. Anyway, just have a few drinks with him one night, and let him open up a little. Personally, I reckon you guys were getting it on in Mom and Dad's kitchen after Will's christening, but Gray just keeps telling me I should be an author since I'm so good at coming up with stories.*

See you next week, love you. Hugs for the boys.
Lila xxoo

Bella put her lip gloss down and listened out for the boys. She almost wanted an excuse not to go, wished one of them would wake and call out for her so she could cancel, but so far they hadn't made a peep. She sighed and walked out of the bathroom, spritzing herself with a little perfume and grabbing her purse. She checked she had her phone and credit card, glanced one last time in the mirror, and then quickly looked away. She was wearing jeans and heels, a black silk blouse unbuttoned a little lower than she usually would, her diamond "B" necklace hanging on the fine platinum chain around her neck. She wasn't big on jewelry, but it was the one thing she always felt bare without.

She quickly put away the letter she'd been reading, skimming over the words because she almost knew it by heart. There was something about the way her sister had always tried to push her toward Noah that was unsettling her, especially when it was impossible not to check him out when he walked downstairs half-naked in the mornings, wearing just his boxer shorts. Not to mention the fact that she was struggling to peg him as the complete idiot she'd always seen him as. Or maybe it was just the fact she was going on a date that was unsettling her.

"It's just a drink," she muttered to herself as she walked down the stairs. Then the doorbell rang, and she just about bolted straight back upstairs to dive into bed and hide.

"Don't wait up," she called out to Noah, thinking he was still watching TV. Instead, he appeared in the doorway, folding his arms as he leaned against the jamb.

"I won't." He glanced at the door. "You going to get that, or do you want me to?"

She shook her head. "Definitely not. See you later."

Bella paused before opening it, took a deep breath, and glanced back at Noah. He was still watching, unnerving her. She quickly opened it, relaxing a little when she saw her date standing there.

It was stupid to be nervous; they'd flirted for months since she'd started getting coffee there, and the only difference about tonight was the fact that he wasn't working.

"Wow, you look beautiful."

Bella smiled as he stepped closer and kissed her cheek.

"*And* you smell incredible."

"Thanks. Shall we go?" Bella groaned as a noise behind her alerted her to the fact that Noah had come closer. Her own personal guard dog. He was almost as bad as her dad had been when she'd first started dating.

"Where are you heading? Just in case the kids need you, sweetheart."

Bella could have killed him, wished the ground would just open up and swallow her.

"You have kids?" Her date looked visibly shocked.

"No," she muttered. "I mean kind of—it's a long story."

"Noah," he said, moving past her and holding his hand out. "I'm Bella's—"

"Housemate," she quickly interjected before he could say anything else.

"Corey. Nice to meet you."

"See you later, Noah," she said, pushing past him without making eye contact. She straightened her shoulders and hoped that her butt looked good in her jeans as she walked off. She could kill Noah later.

"You've never mentioned your children," Corey said as he walked around to his side of the vehicle.

Bella sighed, wondering why she even expected a guy to open her car door for her these days. Just because her dad still did it for her mom didn't mean modern guys would for her. She wondered if Noah would have opened her door and then wished her brain would just shut the hell up and stop thinking about him.

She got in and smiled at Cute Barista Guy. She needed to stop calling him that, but it was hard when she'd called him that for the better part of the last six months.

"It's a long story. My sister passed away, and they are her children."

He nodded and started the car. "Ah, I get it. So you live there and help out their dad?"

Bella wasn't sure what to say. She really needed to figure out an easy, straight-to-the-point way of telling this story that didn't involve her getting emotional or making it sound all weird—preferably that avoided both.

"He's the other guardian. Not their dad. Their father, my brother-in-law—he died in the accident, too."

Corey took a moment before answering, like he was trying to process the whole situation. "That's intense. I'm sorry. But you guys live together?"

She took a deep breath and wondered if she should just ask him to turn the car around. This was not the best start to what was meant to be a fun evening. "Yeah. I know it sounds weird, but we're just trying to do what's best for the kids."

He laughed. "I'm guessing he doesn't have a girlfriend, then."

Bella shifted in her seat, not sure what was so funny. "Why?"

"Because no woman would let you live with her man." Corey chuckled again. "Sorry, but it's true. You're way too beautiful."

Bella wasn't sure what to say, although the flattery was nice. "Noah and I are just . . ."—she paused, wondering what they actually were—"friends, I guess. Acquaintances who'd probably never see each other if the kids weren't in the mix."

"So long as I have nothing to worry about," he said with a wink, touching her hand, his palm covering hers as he took a hand off the wheel.

Bella smiled back, but suddenly that spark of chemistry she'd felt every time she went in for coffee seemed to have sizzled out.

Or maybe it was the fact that when Noah winked at her, it made her stomach drop and just about hit the floor.

"So where are we going?" she asked.

"Thought we'd just head somewhere quiet for a drink. Get to know each other."

She wished she could snap out of her funk and just enjoy being out with a cute guy, but all she really wanted was to stay home. Bella took a deep breath and told herself not to be so stupid. He was funny, gorgeous, and sweet; there was no reason this wasn't going to be a great night. She just had to get Noah out of her head.

"Do you meet all your dates making coffee for them?"

He shrugged. "Not all. Sometimes I meet them making hot chocolate."

Bella laughed. "Well, you are a barista king, so it's no wonder."

Corey smiled over at her, and she grinned back. The truth was, all she wanted was for the drink to be over, so she could curl up in bed with the boys or run into Noah shirtless in the hall. But she owed it to Corey, not to mention Serena, to have fun, and that was exactly what she was going to do, even if it killed her.

~

"So how did it go?"

"Shit!" Bella cursed, dropping her keys and leaning against the wall, heart racing.

"Sorry—didn't mean to scare you."

Her eyes adjusted to the dim light in the hall, and she glared at Noah. "You thought you wouldn't scare me by appearing in the dark and jumping out?"

Noah thrust his hands into his jeans pockets. "Something like that."

"What are you doing waiting up for me, anyway?" she asked, moving past him and kicking her shoes off in the kitchen, flicking the kettle on to boil.

"Just wanted to make sure you got home okay."

"He wasn't an ax murderer, and he didn't pull any moves on me."

Noah's chuckle was soft. "Good."

She spun around, wanting to be angry with him, but not having any idea why. "Did you really have to do that tonight? Act all Mr. Tough Guy and make out like we had children together or something?"

"For starters, I did not make out like we had children together. I just wanted the chump to know what he was in for if he wanted to date you. And second,"—he laughed—"if you thought that was me being all tough guy, then you're definitely mistaken."

"Ugh!" she muttered, putting both hands on his chest and shoving him back. "Just stop it!"

"What?" He looked more amused now than he had before, but when she went to shove him again, to vent her frustration that she was usually so good at keeping a lid on, he grabbed her wrists. Tight.

"Whatever your problem is, it's not my fault."

"Maybe *you're* my problem," she argued. *"Let go."* Bella struggled, but his hold was vice-like.

"No."

They stood staring at each other in the half light, Noah's face too near to hers, his body dangerously close. Her breath was coming in soft pants, her heart racing as he pulled her hands down to her sides, still gripping her, still not letting go. They stood like that for what felt like forever, the noise of the kitchen clock ticking so loudly, every second taking an age.

And then he stepped forward, into her space, way too close for comfort. Noah's eyes dropped, his gaze on her lips. Bella wanted to get away, to think about the sweet guy she'd just been on a date with, the guy she should be giving a second chance. Not Noah. Not the one man she wanted to steer clear from.

"Mommy!"

Noah froze and Bella groaned. He bent lower after hesitating, and just as she shut her eyes, almost let it happen, he took a step back, the light falling across his face.

"We can't do this," he whispered.

She gulped, hands shaking as she balled them. He was right—of course he was right! But he'd been about to kiss her, his mouth had been so close. What had she been thinking?

"Anything happening between us is every kind of wrong," he muttered, stepping even further away. "Right?"

She nodded, forcing her head to comply. She knew that, so why did she feel oddly disappointed? "Yes, of course." It hurt being rebuffed, but she knew he was right. "I've had a few glasses of wine . . ."

"We just got carried away in the moment," he added when her sentence trailed off.

"Mommy!!"

"I have to go," she whispered when one of the boys called out again, waking from slumber and forgetting that mommy was no longer there.

"Come back down when they're settled," he said, voice low, the only noise in the kitchen the crackle of the baby monitor and the clock ticking. "I went out to collect the mail after you left, and there was something for us."

She hesitated, wanted to ask him more, then remembered the heartbreaking cry. "From the look on your face, I'm starting to think you waited up to show me the letter, not to make sure my chastity was still intact."

Noah nodded. "Something like that. But you'll want to see it before you call it a night."

She went to walk off, then turned back around. "Any idea who it's from?"

His smile was sad—genuine, but full of sadness. "Your sister," he told her. "It's from Lila."

Bella's body went cold, her skin becoming clammy as she gasped for air, forgetting all about their near kiss. She ran for the stairs, needing one of the boys in her arms, not wanting to hear Noah's words echoing through her head. There was no way the letter could be from her sister. Which meant someone was either pulling a nasty prank on her, or Noah . . . . She took the stairs two at a time, even though her body just wanted to shut down and not move. The look on his face, the way he'd held her before—he might like to goof around, but this wasn't the type of thing he'd joke about.

"I want Mommy." Cooper's sob sent her racing through the door, dropping to the bed and finding Flopsy for him, tucking it into his arm as she bent to cuddle him.

Life was cruel. Life was mean and unfair. But the idea of one last letter from her sister? Maybe something she'd sent that had been lost when she'd been away serving? That was something to live for, something to smile about.

CHAPTER EIGHT

November 2014

Dear Bella & Noah,

If you're receiving this letter, then life hasn't exactly gone according to plan for us. I knew when I was going on this tour, the one that I'm certain will be my last, that I had to write this, even though it's the toughest thing I've ever done.

We knew when we had a family that there was a chance, however tiny, that we could leave our kids without parents. Serving my country is something I'm so proud of, and Gray is so passionate about what he does too, but working in conflict zones comes with risks. Whatever happened to us, know that we would have done anything in our power to stay with our kids, to be there for them and see them graduate, to watch them learn to navigate the world and become adults. The burden we've put on you is enormous, and I know you guys haven't always been the best of friends, but we decided to put you both down as co-guardians so you could bring the boys up together, share the load. Bella, you're the most amazing sister, and you always have been since we were little kids and you'd stick up for me on the playground at school. You're also an incredible aunty, and I know the boys will think of you as their own mom once the memory of me starts to fade, as much as it kills me to even write that.

Noah, Gray loves you like a brother, and so do I. You might butt heads with Bella a million times, but she's also super sensible and careful, and that means the boys need you, too. They need you to teach them how to surf and catch them when they fall out of trees, to say yes when they need some freedom, to do all the things Gray would have done with them. And I need you to give Bella a break sometimes. Please.

But most of all, I want you two to like one another. And to be honest, if you're both single right now, I have a feeling that . . . Gray's shaking his head at me, so I'm not going to say anything else. Except for this: Go look in the top drawer to the left of the dishwasher. You'll find a blue piece of paper with the names of a couple of babysitters we've used and trusted before. Don't ask Mom or Dad to come over; I want you to just phone a sitter and tell them you need a couple of hours to go out. Tuck the boys up first if you want to, then go.

Noah, if Bella says no, make her do it. Every Thursday you're going to receive a letter, and it means a lot to me that you guys take time away from our crazy kids to have a date night. Bella, don't roll your eyes. Yeah, it's called date night, and yeah, it's with Noah. Wish I could see your face right now, and the way Noah's looking at you! Anyway, tomorrow night you're going to the beach, and every Friday night you need to make time for something I have planned. I want you to head to the place where the cool Mexican food truck is, order whatever looks great, then chill on the beach for an hour. Just talk, relax, enjoy. Because if you don't take some time out from the boys, they'll drive you mad, no matter how much you love them.

Bella, I love you so much. I know you're going to be struggling, and Mom and Dad will be heartbroken, but please just get over yourself and enjoy Noah. He's a great guy. And Noah, give her a chance, okay?

Until next week, Lila xoxo

Noah stiffened, watching as Bella gulped like she was a fish out of water. She balled her fist and pushed the letter away, tears running down her cheeks as she turned to him. Less than an hour ago, she'd almost been in his arms because of lust, and now he was trying to decide whether he should be offering her comfort in his arms from grief.

"I thought when you told me it was from her that it was some kind of mistake," Bella said, voice shaky as she brushed the tears from her cheeks. "Have you read it?"

He nodded. "Yeah, I did. If I'd realized it was from her before I opened it, I would have waited, but it was addressed to both of us."

Her smile was sad, tears still brimming against her lashes, threatening to fall. He wanted to step closer and wipe them away for her, to cradle her in his arms so she could just cry her eyes out if she wanted to. But he didn't. Bella had this strong exterior, this look about her that she'd perfected, but something told him that it was all an act to compose herself. He wanted to see the real her, for her to just trust him enough to let her guard down, even though he got it. The only person who'd ever seen him with his guard down, without his game face on, was Gray.

"Do you think there are more? Do you believe her?"

Noah chuckled. "Yeah, I believe her. She wouldn't have had this sent to us if she wasn't going to follow through."

Bella brushed more tears away, a look of fierce determination passing over her face. She nodded, like she was trying to reassure herself about something, pep-talking herself. "The lawyer must have sent it, right? I'm going down there first thing to ask for the rest of the letters."

Noah touched her shoulder as he passed, before sitting down at the kitchen table. He was having to step it up, trying to be in touch with how she was feeling. "Or you could just let this play out like your sister wanted."

He may as well have told her that the sky was green, the look she gave him was so surprised. "You're kidding, right? Are you actually suggesting we do what she says?"

Noah shrugged. "Bella, what almost happened before, we can't let that happen again. But going out as friends one night a week? I don't care what she wants to call it, but it doesn't sound half bad."

"But . . ." Her voice trailed off as she continued to stare at him. "You're sure?"

"Yeah," his voice was husky now, deeper than before, and he cleared his throat. "Just so long as we're both clear . . ."

"Oh, we're clear," she said quickly. "So, friends getting to know each other better?"

"I think we need to be better friends for this whole"—he paused, searching for the word—"*arrangement* to work. So, yeah."

"It's been tough—having you here, I mean. Having someone else around." She blew out a sigh. "I just keep worrying that it's all going to get too much for you, and you'll bail, and I'll end up at square one again, starting from the very beginning with the boys."

Noah frowned. "That's not going to happen. I know it was probably disruptive when I first arrived, but I'm trying, Bella. I am."

He watched as Bella pushed off from the table where she'd been leaning and reached for a glass, hands shaking as she filled it with water. "Trust my sister to still be calling the shots even when she's gone and damn well left me." Her voice cracked, barely audible.

Noah hesitated, not sure what to do, whether he should follow his instincts or just leave her the hell alone. But she was hurting, hurting so damn bad that he could see her pain, and he hated just standing by. He leaned forward, thought about it and decided: *To hell with it.* He walked closer and slowly, carefully, placed a hand on each of her shoulders, squeezing, wanting her to know he actually cared about how she felt. It had been stupid to try to kiss her, but giving a damn was something else entirely.

"It's okay to cry," he murmured. "You don't have to be strong for me."

She tensed under his touch, went stiff as a board before sighing and relaxing a little, water glass still in hand. "I feel like all I've done these past couple of months is cry."

"Not true," he said. "You've also kept your chin up and gotten on with caring for two crazy-busy, grieving little boys. Not to mention trying to keep your business afloat and being strong for your parents."

She set the glass down and groaned as he pressed his thumbs into her shoulders, gently starting to massage her bunched muscles. "I'm failing epically at the keeping-my-business afloat part."

They both knew that it wasn't just about money. Both Lila and Gray had excellent life insurance policies, and the kids were taken care of, the house and cars paid off. Her sister and Gray might have been on average wages, but they'd been careful with their money, and both sets of parents had helped them out financially when they'd started their family. But Bella was proud, and she was independent, and Noah knew she wouldn't want to just step away from the business she'd started from scratch.

"All I'm saying is that you don't have to be strong for me. You can let your guard down," he told her, hands falling away as she turned. He was okay with dealing with other people's pain; he just wasn't good at letting anyone see his.

They stared at one another a long while, tears still shining in Bella's eyes. "Says the guy who always has his guard up," she murmured, eyes studying every inch of his face.

He didn't like the scrutiny, wasn't used to someone so openly searching him like that, as if he were a hard-to-read book. "You've got me all wrong," he lied, not wanting to go there, for her to see through him.

She gently shook her head, the barest of movements. "No, I don't. And that's why I always thought you were an asshole, because I never took the time to actually figure you out."

He cleared his throat, wanted to step back and get the hell out of Dodge, but at the same time didn't want her to know how right she was. "So what have you figured, smarty-pants?" he joked.

"You're not fooling me, Noah. Not for a second." She surprised him by reaching for his hand, her fingers searching his out for barely a few seconds before letting go. "You might pretend like nothing fazes you, the tough Navy guy who's all about fun when he's off duty, but I don't buy it. Not anymore."

Noah wanted to change the subject real fast. "So are we going tomorrow night or not? I mean, tomorrow's Saturday, but I guess we can break the rules this one time," he said, putting her on the spot, wanting the focus off him.

"Yeah, let's do it," she said, chin held high, shoulders straightened, like her sister bossing her around from the grave was the kick in the pants she'd needed. "Just don't go trying it on, okay? Friends hanging out—just like you said."

He grinned. "So we're friends now? Lila would have kittens to think we'd progressed that far."

She laughed, the pain gone from her face, eyes full of happiness for a short burst at least. "Yeah, I reckon we're friends now. After everything we've been through, we deserve it."

He held up a hand and backed up a few steps. "See you in the morning then, friend."

She smiled. "I'll phone the babysitter first thing."

Noah turned to go, before spinning back around. "All that and I forgot to grill you about your date. Did he sweep you off your feet?"

"He was a nice guy." She shrugged like it was no big deal. "We had a good time."

He winked at her, wanting to keep the smile alive on her lips, needing to joke around with her. "Well, lucky it didn't go too well; otherwise, you might not have been free tomorrow night for our friendship date."

She bit down on her lower lip, a gesture he found sexy as hell and made him wish he'd just gone to bed and not engaged at all. "Goodnight, Noah," she murmured.

He forced his feet in the other direction. If only she knew what he was thinking about her right then, there was no way she'd want to be alone with him. Not for a second. Lucky for both of them he was good at keeping his word, at doing the right thing when he had to. Or at least he always had been in the past.

~

Bella thought she'd been a bundle of nerves the night before, but compared to the way she was feeling right now, it'd been nothing. At least with Corey she'd felt okay about getting all dolled up, whereas with Noah she didn't know how to feel. Whether it was okay to look like she was going on a date versus not wanting to look like she was making a big deal out of it. She had to co-parent with this guy until the boys were eighteen, for God's sake, and they'd almost kissed in the kitchen!

The fact that she was so conflicted over him made her even more tense. He was so annoying and difficult, and then other times . . . she sighed. He could be positively charming when he wanted to be. And besides, she had to give him a chance. If they couldn't become real friends, then what chance did they have of making their situation work?

"Seriously, Lila. Did you have to do this to me?" she muttered, standing in front of the closet with her hands on her hips. Then she glanced at her sister's clothes, pushed to the side to make room for her own, and a fresh wave of tears hit her when she was least expecting it. "Just come back," she whispered. "Just come back and tell me it was all a mistake, that you didn't meant to leave me."

She stepped closer, reached for a hot-pink blouse that her sister had loved, and leaned in to inhale the flowery scent of Lila's perfume, faint but still there. Bella breathed deep and shut her eyes tight, fighting the pain. "Not tonight," she said. "I am not doing this tonight."

The doorbell sounded out, and she jumped back, pushing the memories away along with her pain. She reached for a pair of jeans, faded and skinny, pulled them on, and then considered the tops she had hanging, eventually taking down a scoop-neck T-shirt embellished with tiny jewels over the front. Casual, but cute. She slipped into a pair of flats at the same time that Noah called out the sitter had arrived. Bella quickly spritzed her hair with perfume, checked her lip gloss, and pushed some gold hoops through her ears. Satisfied with how she looked, she grabbed her purse and ran down the stairs, almost crashing into Will as he came careering up.

"Whoa," she said, holding out a hand to steady him. "Slow down, Tiger."

"Wow, you look real pretty," he said, smiling up at her as she bent to give him a quick hug.

"You sure you're alright without us for a couple of hours?"

"He's sure."

Noah's deep voice made her look up, the commanding way he spoke telling her exactly how powerful he'd been in work mode when lives were at stake. He was wearing dark jeans, boots that looked well loved and a charcoal-gray T-shirt that fitted him like a glove, just tight enough to show off his biceps, make it hard for her not to stare at his shoulders, at the muscles she knew were hiding beneath the fabric. Noah might have annoyed the hell out of her for years, but he was damn fine to look at, and she'd be lying if she didn't admit it, at least to herself.

"You look beautiful," he said, eyes not leaving hers for even a beat.

Will had gone silent, but he was still standing there, looking between them, watching the exchange. She touched his shoulder. "What were you looking for?" she asked, ignoring Noah and the heat flaming inside of her.

"My Lego car. I wanted to show Lauren."

"Go grab it. I'm just going to say bye to Cooper before we go."

Will ran past her, and she turned to watch him go, delaying the moment she had to look back at Noah, because right now he scared the hell out of her. Will seemed so big beside Cooper sometimes, but on his own, running away, it struck her how small he still was. How vulnerable.

"Should I not have said that?" Noah asked, hands thrust into his pockets when she finally faced him.

Bella blushed, which only served to infuriate her. "I'm not good with compliments."

He laughed. "Then just say 'Thank you,' and forget it. Friends say that kind of stuff, right?"

If only it were that simple. "Ready to go?"

"Yep, ready whenever you are."

Bella moved quickly past him, introduced herself to the sitter, and chatted a few minutes before finally saying good-bye to the boys. She recognized Lauren from the service, and both Will and Cooper were climbing all over her, so any worries she'd had faded almost immediately.

"Want to drive?" Noah asked when she finally stopped ignoring him. He was holding up the keys.

"No, you go for it," she said, following him out and almost running smack bang into him when he went to the same side of the car as she did, opening her door.

She must have sighed without realizing, because his gaze was uncertain when she finally looked up at him.

"Was that not okay either?" he asked.

"No," she said, "it's perfect. Thank you."

"I don't want to offend you," Noah said, showing a rare hint of vulnerability. "I learned all the manners I know from Gray's dad, but I'm well aware that half the women in the world might want to slam me in the head with a phone book for opening doors for them."

Bella couldn't help but laugh at him. "Yeah, sad but true. I never really get why men behaving well could be interpreted so wrong. I mean, you clearly know I'm strong enough to open a door on my own, right? It's not like you're assaulting my rights as a feminist."

He held up his hands, backing off. "Damn, you should have told me you were a feminist."

"What, with a sticker on my forehead or something?" Bella jumped in and held out her hand so he couldn't close the door for her, teasing him. "I just believe that women can do anything, that we're a million times more capable than men. No offense."

"None taken," he said when he got into the driver's seat beside her. "You're probably right, anyway."

"But it doesn't mean I don't like doors being opened for me and seeing seats given to pregnant women on public transport."

His grin was infectious, the strain between them long gone, as if it had never existed in the first place. "Well, I'm glad we got all that straightened out. And for the record, a woman doesn't have to be pregnant to get my seat. Just sayin'."

"It's stupid, but I was really stressing about this whole . . ."—she hesitated—"un-*date*. For want of a better word, anyway. It seems weird going out on a predetermined outing."

"More than your hot outing last night?" he teased, glancing at her as they pulled out.

"Yeah, way worse than last night," she admitted. "I don't know, this just seems . . . ." This time she didn't finish her sentence because she actually didn't know what she was trying to say. She was tongue-tied in her own mind without even trying to express herself to Noah.

"Me too," he said, thrumming his fingers across the steering wheel. "I don't usually date, so this being all set in stone—like what you said, I get it. We should have just planned an impromptu coffee or something because this is downright weird. I know that sounds terrible, but it's kinda true."

She gave him what she hoped was a fierce stare. "So how does it usually work? If you were going on a real date, I mean, not just an outing with a friend? You'd just catch some gorgeous woman's eye in a bar and a few hours later she'd be in your bed?" Heat rose in her cheeks; she wished it didn't annoy her so much to think of him being such a manwhore. She was trying to keep the conversation light, and in the end she'd done the exact opposite.

"Something like that. Except it's probably closer to an hour, not a few."

His tone was so sure, his face straight, until she thumped him hard on the arm, and he howled more with laughter than pain.

"Noah! That's disgusting."

He winced and rubbed his arm. "And so not true. I'm only teasing you." He cradled his arm like he was injured. "I used to talk a lot of smack with Gray, but he didn't hit me as often as you do. I think he was way better at being a friend."

"You're lying," Bella accused.

"Yeah, he actually didn't hit me at all. It was more like me jumping in and trying to hit someone else and him making quick work of parting us."

She rolled her eyes. "I was talking about the women."

"I was only partly lying about that. I do meet women in bars and hook up sometimes—I'd be lying if I said I didn't. And you know what? That never makes me nervous, but for some stupid reason I felt weird about coming out tonight. It feels a little contrived."

Something in Bella died and fluttered back to life again. It might have been a line, but she couldn't help the small groan that passed through her lips. "You're telling me you had to work up the nerve to come, right?" she asked, biting her lip to stop from laughing. "On our stupid friendship date, if there's even such a thing."

"Oh yeah. Gray was the smooth talker—super confident and never gave a damn about being turned down. Me, I'm a bundle of nerves even being alone with a beautiful woman like you."

"Stop bullshitting me!" She had to admit that he was kind of funny. He'd made her stop being nervous and laugh, and it had been a long while since she'd just let herself do that.

"I'm kidding about tonight—of course I am. I'm just trying to have fun." His smile was kind. She guessed he'd been the class clown, always making someone laugh, to make friends and be the center of attention. "But Gray was so confident with everything, from work to girls. He'd been brought up to believe that he was awesome, and I mean that in a good way. His parents were always there for him, telling him to go get whatever he set his mind to. He was confident, and nothing fazed him."

"And you never had that," she thought, realizing too late that she'd actually said it out loud.

"Yeah, something like that. So I kind of just watched him, took it all in, slowly started to realize that I wasn't butt ugly and stupid."

She burst out laughing. "It took you all that time to realize you weren't butt ugly? You honestly didn't notice all the girls drooling when you walked by?"

Noah grimaced. "Now who's laying on the compliments?"

"So tell me honestly," she asked, tucking one leg under her and wriggling to face Noah so she could watch his expression. "Were you surprised, when he met Lila, that he settled down?" She liked that they'd branched into neutral territory, that they were able to talk about Gray and Lila, and she was able to find out more about her sister's husband, about his past.

"Gray? No way," he said. "I mean, yeah, it was crazy to see him fall head over heels for one woman, but he was different with Lila. He didn't give a damn about anything but her once they met, and they were so cool together. She never seemed to want to hold him back. Loved that he was so serious about his work, never wanted him to stop hanging out with his friends."

Noah smiled, eyes on the road, but she could see the softness in his expression. "Even so, she ended up tagging along on every guys' night we had. We all loved her, the way she'd crawl into Gray's lap one minute, curled up on him and driving him wild, and then the next she'd be doing shots and shooting pool with the rest of us and driving him even more crazy."

Bella smiled, thinking about her sister for the first time without being overcome with emotion. "She was pretty cool like that. The complete opposite of me."

The car slowed and Bella glanced out, realizing that they were already at the beach, and Noah was pulling into a space. He didn't say anything until he cut the engine, turning to her after he'd pulled the keys from the ignition.

"I reckon you're a whole lot more like Lila than you realize," Noah said, voice low, eyes locked on hers.

Bella shook her head. "You're wrong," she murmured, not trusting her voice, gulping as his eyes moved, knowing he was studying her face.

"Or maybe I'm right, and you just don't want to admit it."

Bella breathed out, gasped once he got out of the car. What the hell was wrong with her? This wasn't a real date. This was just Noah and her hanging out and grabbing some dinner away from the kids. So why was her heart hammering like crazy, her hands shaking at the thought of being alone with him? This was Noah, the guy who'd always driven her mad, annoyed the hell out of her. The guy she'd growled about every time she'd had to be around him.

Noah, she repeated in her mind. The one guy her sister had always vowed was perfect for her, laughing every single time Bella had ranted and raved about what a jerk he was. *Noah.* The guy who was strictly off limits, no matter what. The guy she was *supposed* to be just hanging out with, like the friends they were, *like the co-parents they were.*

He came around to her side, and she quickly pushed her door open, needing the fresh air, the scent of the ocean hitting her immediately.

"You want me to go grab some dinner while you find a nice spot to sit?'

Bella nodded, smiling over at him. It was like he'd just read her mind, knew she needed a little space. "Sounds good. I'll have whatever you're having."

He hesitated, pushing the keys into his pocket. "You okay?"

"Fine. Just hungry."

It was a lie. Her stomach was churning for an entirely different reason, but she wasn't about to tell him that.

"Okay, I'll catch up with you in a few."

Bella watched him go, studied his frame as he slowly disappeared. He was so male, so masculine and strong. The things that had once annoyed her about him were starting to fade, making way for feelings she wished she could stamp out and never think about again. But Noah was a link to her past that she didn't want to extinguish, a reminder of what had been. And he was also the one person capable of protecting her, of helping her to hold everything together when their very existence felt so fragile. Only she had to balance that with not letting anything more develop between them. They couldn't hurt the boys, and if they ended up romantically involved . . . it could end in an epic disaster.

~

Noah managed to navigate his way back to Bella, juggling three plates of food. He was going to make another trip back for drinks, rather than embarrass himself by dropping the lot. As a teen he'd done a stint as a waiter, and although the tips had been not bad, his waiting skills had never improved, especially when it came to carrying one too many plates.

"Over here!"

He spotted Bella straightaway, her hands in the air as she waved to him. Something about her had snuck up on him without his even realizing it, and for a guy who'd made a career of never being caught unaware, it surprised him. It scared him, even. Her T-shirt rode a smidge too high with her arms raised, and he caught a glimpse of her stomach, flat and toned. He bet she worked out, went to the gym as part of what he was sure would be a meticulously planned weekly schedule. Until the boys had come along and demanded every part of her, including part of herself she probably hadn't even known she could give. And the only reason he knew that was because it was exactly the way he was feeling, like he'd been emotionally wrung out at the same time that he had to pretend like he was holding together just fine. When he wasn't. Not even close to it. And he also had the added issue of feeling crappy about not realizing when he needed to back her up instead of trying to show the boys how much fun he was.

His phone rang then, vibrating in his back pocket.

"Need to get that?" Bella asked when he neared.

She took two of the plates from him, and he pulled it out, checking the caller ID. He had to answer.

"Hey, Mom," he said, grinning as he said it. What had started as a joke between Gray and him had quickly transformed into a habit, sticking for life.

"Is this a good time?"

He mouthed "Sorry" to Bella and set down the plate he was holding, beside her on the sand, walking a few steps in the other direction as he talked. "It's fine. I'm just out grabbing some dinner. With Bella."

"I wanted to make sure you're okay. We miss the boys so much." *And Gray.* He grimaced, knowing that the name was hanging there, unsaid. "We're thinking of driving up next week, if that's okay."

"Any time you want to see them, just jump in the car and start driving," he said honestly. "I miss you, too."

"Is Bella doing okay this week?"

He nodded, smiling over in her direction. "Bella's doing good, considering. She's a whole lot stronger than I ever gave her credit for."

"Well, we miss you. Promise you'll still be there when we arrive?"

"Yeah, I'm not going anywhere. Not for a while anyway." The truth was, Noah wasn't sure he'd ever be going anywhere again—not like he used to. So much had happened, so much had changed. He was feeling conflicted over his career right now, but he pushed the thoughts away.

"See you soon," he said.

"All our love to Bella and the boys," she said. "And to you."

When he finally ended the call, he turned to see Bella watching him, her expression curious.

"Gray's mom?" she asked.

"Yeah. She's hurting pretty bad, wants to drive up next week."

"Fine by me." She touched the spot beside her, held up the plate of food he'd put down. "Dinner looks great."

"I got a bit of everything in the end—thought we could share," he said. "Mexican's my favorite. It was way too hard to choose just one thing."

Her smile was warm, touched her entire face. "I couldn't help but overhear that you called her 'mom.'"

"She's the only mom I've ever known," Noah admitted, looking out at the ocean, his gaze fixed in the distance, taking in the bright blue waves. He wasn't used to talking about his feelings, had never been comfortable talking about the past.

"They took you in, right?" Bella asked softly.

"Yep. Only family I've ever had."

"It's amazing they only had one son. I mean, that she only had one biological child."

"Gray was the only child after five miscarriages before him. And she tried for another unsuccessfully for years after. I doubt she tried again after I arrived though." He grinned, surprised that he actually wanted to talk to her about it. "Gray and I were brothers in every sense of the word."

Bella stayed silent, picking up one of the plastic forks and starting to eat.

"You miss him?

"Like crazy." He sighed. It was like he'd had his own limb ripped off, he missed Gray so damn bad, the pain so intense sometimes it was all he could do to pick himself up and keep going. Not to mention having to put on a brave face all the time for the boys.

"I don't know about you, but I'm starting to wonder why I ever disliked you quite as much as I did," Bella blurted.

He laughed, finishing a mouthful before answering, pleased they'd moved to another subject. "I never disliked you. Well, not really."

"And by 'not really' you actually mean . . ."

Her smile was infectious. "Look, I thought you were so far from being similar to Lila that I wondered if you were even related. You were so uptight and annoying and . . ."

"Oh, don't stop," she said, rolling her eyes when he paused, "I can take it." She plucked at the skin on her arm and made him laugh. "It's pretty thick."

He shrugged. "Then I saw that you were a whole lot more like Lila than I'd realized. You're strong, determined, fierce, beautiful—just like her."

Noah knew his voice had dropped an octave, could hear the huskiness of his tone. Bella was looking at her plate, her gaze lowered, no longer focused on him.

"When we were younger, we were like twins," she said, holding a taco between her fingers and slowly eating it, her eyes finally, haltingly, meeting his.

"That changed as you got older?" Noah used a napkin to wipe the sauce from his fingers. Mexican was great, but it was always messy.

She sucked in her bottom lip, just for a second, her eyebrows drawn together ever so slightly. "As we got older, we grew apart for a while. I was so angry with her for choosing to go into the Army, and there were a few years there where we barely spoke."

"What changed?" Her words had taken him by surprise. He'd known she had a hang-up about military guys, but ruining her relationship with her sister over her career choice? Not what he'd expected to hear.

"When we were growing up, Dad did his fair share of stints away from us, leaving Mom with two little girls terrified they weren't going to see him again. Then, as we got older, his going away got even harder because we understood what could happen."

Bella stared out at the ocean, putting her food down, wiping her fingers, and then leaning back, hands out behind her. Noah didn't say anything, didn't need to, because she was going back down memory lane and the last thing he wanted to do was to interrupt her or try to fill the silence when she so obviously needed time to process.

"You know, I haven't talked about all this stuff in"—she glanced at him—"ever, actually. Except for when I was yelling at Lila about leaving."

Noah nodded. "Whatever you tell me, it's just between us. I'm not the kiss-and-tell type."

She smiled fleetingly, her face softening at his joke. He liked it, and it made him want to work harder to keep her looking at him like that.

"Why do I get the feeling that we're not talking about just secrets anymore?"

He grinned. "It was a figure of speech—nothing more. But I don't share bedroom secrets either, for the record."

They both laughed, the mood between them more relaxed than it had ever been, despite the subject matter. The only other person she could just talk with was Serena, and she hated off-loading on her friend all the time. Her mom and dad were great, but there was only so much she wanted to share or talk about with her mom. The last thing Bella wanted was to add to her mom's already full worry load.

"When Lila was due to ship out the first time, when the reality of her deployment hit home to me, everything changed between us. It was like the two years of shit between us had never happened, and all I wanted was to have those years again, just to enjoy my sister."

"And now you'll be wishing for them even more," Noah said softly.

"Yeah," Bella murmured. "From that day on, I focused on positives. I was so immensely proud of her, just like I'd been of our dad, but I was so scared of losing her. I didn't want my sister being part of that world."

"Would you have felt the same if she'd been a brother?"

"Maybe not—or maybe it would have been exactly the same. I don't know," she said honestly. "Lila and I were only eighteen months apart in age. We played Barbie's together; rode make-believe ponies and galloped around the yard; shared the same room, even though there were two spare in the house and Mom had never intended us to. So to know she was in a combat zone and might not make it home? It terrified me."

Noah spread his hands out, food long since consumed. "And that's why you never wanted to date military guys?" he asked.

She shook her head. "No. I mean, yeah, I didn't want to have another person to worry about, especially once Gray joined the family, but military guys—I don't know. I've been there, done that, I guess. I know the type, and it does nothing for me anymore. Sorry."

"That's fine. I wouldn't date a brunette, so I get it. We all have our types."

He stifled a laugh when she reached instinctively for a strand of hair. It was bullshit; he loved all women, but it was good to see the surprised look on her face. Besides, she was technically a brunette with a ton of blonde streaks, so she didn't really fit either category.

"You know, from what I recall, the bridesmaid of Lila's I found you in the restroom with was a brunette." Bella made a face. "Not to mention married."

"The hair thing was a joke," Noah said. "And I had no idea she was married. You can call me all sorts of names, but marriage wrecker ain't one of them."

Bella stared at him, and he chuckled and sat back. He decided he'd pushed her hard enough, and steered the conversation back to less contentious topics.

"So tell me what happened to you. What did you decide to do when Lila joined the Army?" he said.

"Me?" Bella shrugged, looking more relaxed again. "Not much to tell. I was older, I went off to study design, worked with an interior design firm for the first few years before deciding to branch out on my own."

Noah played with the sand, letting it trickle through his fingers, again and again. "So you ended up going solo, doing your own thing, and your sister became the ultimate team player." He thought about it for a minute, chuckling. "Kind of makes sense, given your personalities."

"You're saying I'm not a team player?" she asked dryly.

"I'm just saying it makes sense. So how do you get on with your soldier dad, then? I mean, you've always seemed close."

Bella's smile was sweet. "I adore my dad. If there was ever a daddy's girl, it was me. Still is."

"I know you didn't want them in harm's way, but the way you feel about the military, about men, sorry *people*, serving their country . . ." He wasn't sure exactly what he was trying to ask her, or maybe he was and just didn't want to hear the answer.

Her eyes met his, unwavering. "I admire every single man and woman who's brave enough to serve our country, Noah. But I'm selfish." She shrugged. "There's no way to sugarcoat it, because believe me if there was, I'd do it. I want my family safe, and I want them close to home. I wanted stability once my dad retired, pure and simple."

Noah got it, he did—in theory anyway. "Sometimes we don't get to choose."

"And sometimes your sister and brother-in-law can somehow survive the shittiest times abroad, serving when so many others didn't, and then end up getting killed when a truck driver slumps against the wheel."

"Shit happens," he said, saying exactly what ran through his head and then wishing he'd stopped to filter it. "Life ain't fair, and it sure as hell ain't just."

"I guess I couldn't understand why Lila had to do it. I mean, she was so smart and she could have done anything, could have just had a normal life and gone to college and not had to risk her neck all the time."

Noah shook his head. "No, she couldn't, because she thrived on the adrenaline. What else could she have done that would have given her that, except maybe law enforcement? Hell, she and Gray used to go to the shooting range for fun!"

Bella suddenly flopped back into the sand, head back, looking straight up at the sky. Her long hair fanned out around her, hands at her sides, fingers pushing back and forth through the sand.

"One day, I hope I can find a way to show you why Lila's job meant so much to her," Noah continued.

Bella nodded. "I'd like that. I want to understand, but . . ." She shook her head. "I hate that it's like this missing jigsaw piece, that I still can't figure out how she felt, what made her . . ." Her voice cut off. "It was different for you. I can understand why you did it."

He leaned back and lowered himself down beside her. It would have been so easy to shut his eyes, to rest beside Bella, where he felt safe, breathing in the fresh, salty air. He was so, so tired, every inch of his body, every muscle, tired to the bone.

"Is it because I'm so clearly a fuck-up?" he asked.

Bella pushed up on one arm, looking down at him. The sun was low, almost gone, which meant he could look straight up at her without having to squint. Her eyes were so brown, so warm, he realized he could look into them all day without tiring. They were the kind of eyes that made him feel alive but safe, all at the same time, a feeling of peace—something he'd rarely felt in his life—when he was the subject of her gaze

"You're not a fuck-up, Noah," she murmured. "You might have annoyed me in the past, but I never thought that of you. Never."

"But I am," he muttered, shutting his eyes to block her out, not wanting to see that honesty, to read her face. "I'm great at what I do, when I'm at work. I'm a damn good SEAL—I'd never leave a man behind, and I'd sacrifice myself for another without thinking."

"Yet you think so little of yourself?" Her tone was incredulous.

Noah kept his mouth shut. He didn't want to talk about himself. He stared into the distance.

"Give me something, Noah! I've tried to open up to you properly—I'd love it if you could do the same, just a little." She pushed at him, shoved his arm lightly. "Tell me what makes your job so damn important to you?"

"No," he said.

Bella went to stand, pushed herself up, but he made himself grab her and stop her from moving away. He forced himself out of his comfort zone.

"Look, in the Navy, I have a family of guys, a home. I know that I fit in and people rely on me; it gives me purpose. But when I'm not working?" He opened his eyes, saw that Bella was still looking down at him. She blinked, flushed when he caught her studying his face, slowly lowering herself again so she was looking up at the sky once more. "I'm a loose cannon when I'm not at work. It's no wonder you always thought I was an asshole."

Bella's fingers brushed his then. He almost wondered if he'd imagined it until he moved his own, the only part of his body that moved, fingertips searching, then staying still. Deadly still.

"I think we both need to give ourselves a break," Bella finally said.

"Maybe," he replied. Although he wasn't convinced she was right, not about him, anyway.

Bella's fingers left his, made him wish he'd done something to keep them there, but if he had, it might have pushed things one step too far.

"Tonight's been nice," she said, voice low as she brushed sand off her jeans and stood.

Noah did the same, collecting their paper plates and napkins. "You sound surprised."

Bella burst out laughing. "I am!"

Noah watched her, moved closer, then decided he was being stupid. What he wanted to do was kiss her cheek, brush his lips over hers, make it something more. But he didn't. Because everything he loved, everything he wanted, always somehow turned to shit. And he couldn't go there with Bella. They had two little boys to care for as their own children for the rest of their lives. There was too much at stake to screw anything up where Bella was concerned.

CHAPTER NINE

Bella took a deep breath and placed her palms down flat on the counter, needing a minute to gather her thoughts. She loved having her family around, thrived on being surrounded by people she cared for, but everything was starting to get the best of her. So much for being told as a teen that girls could do anything. It was the worst lie she'd ever believed. She slipped her phone back into her pocket, ignoring another text from Corey, not sure what to say in reply. He was keen to see her again, and even though she knew she should say yes, something was holding her back.

"You okay?"

The deep timbre of Noah's voice caught her off-guard. Ever since the "date" last Saturday, she'd tried her best to avoid him, kept busy, made use of his being there and not having to be anywhere else, so she could get on top of work. Things should have been easier, because he was making an effort to stick to her routine, not even laughing at her when she'd pinned a weekly schedule to the fridge. But the way she was feeling about him . . . it was stupid. She'd been on a real date with a super nice guy, and instead of thinking about him, she was imagining things being different with Noah, what it would be like to be in his arms for just a moment, to give in to the part of her that was insanely attracted to him. And then she reminded herself of all the reasons why she couldn't go there.

Now it was the end of the week again, and she'd taken the day off, and ever since Noah had arrived home with the kids, it had been chaos. Gray's mom had arrived, her own parents had turned up, and then ten minutes ago her kooky Aunt Iris had arrived uninvited. Not that she had to be invited, but still. Bella was ready to collapse, and she hadn't even made them all coffee yet.

Bella slowly turned, came face-to-face with Noah. "Not really."

"Anything I can do to help?" His offer was genuine, concern etched on his face.

"I just want . . ." She blew out a breath, reaching for the counter again, needing to hold onto something. "Is it so bad to wish for an hour of my old life? To run a bath, read a book, just be *me* with no one needing me?"

The look he gave her broke her apart, made her want to pool on the floor and then pull herself together and stop being so broken.

"You're doing fine. It's just overwhelming having so many people in the house." He smiled. "And being reminded over and over again of what happened."

"Oh my God!" She lurched forward, pushed past Noah as she raced for the back door. "The letter was due yesterday!" How had she forgotten something she'd been looking forward to all week? The days were running into each other, the week passing in such a blur that she could hardly remember whether it was the end of the week or the beginning.

She heard Noah behind her, but she was determined to get there first, jogging barefoot out to the mailbox. There were a few letters, mostly bills, but there, grouped in with everything else, was a cream envelope with Lila's familiar, flowing writing on the front. If they hadn't written each other every single time Lila was away, she might not have recognized it so readily, but there was no denying it was her sister's hand.

Bella passed Noah the stack of miscellaneous mail without looking, her eyes locked on the envelope in her hands. She slid her nail under the seal, pulling out the paper and scanning the words so fast that she made herself stop and reread them slowly, savoring every word.

She couldn't decide if it made losing Lila harder or easier, but however much it hurt to be reminded of her sister, the letters brought her back, which was something Bella wouldn't give up for anything in the world.

November 2014

Dear Bella & Noah,

I'm trying not to laugh as I write this. Actually, I'm alternating laughter and tears because I also keep thinking about the boys and what it would be like for them growing up without us. But that only brings me back to why I'm doing this, to give you guys time to get to know each other away from the kids. They've got you, so I know they'll be fine, but it still tears me up.

This idea for date night is a bit more traditional than the other one, but it still involves food. I want you to head to Tony's. Nothing too fancy, just fun and happy. Order pizza and red wine, watch the world go by, and tell each other something you've never told anyone else before. Don't roll your eyes, Bella—just go with it. Live a little, okay?

Can you both do me a favor, too? I want you to check on Dad, make sure he's okay. I know Mom will be getting plenty of hugs and lots of love, but Dad will be hurting more than you realize. Be there for him, give him a big kiss, and tell him that I loved him more than a daughter could ever love a dad. He was the best, and I want him to know it.

I love you both, too. Snuggle those boys for me, and please don't ever leave them to cry in the night. I know it's a big ask, but they're only little for such a short time.
Lila xoxo

Noah came closer, his hand on her shoulder as he peered over, reading from behind her. Bella shut her eyes for a second, let herself enjoy the moment of Noah's touch, how safe she somehow felt with him so near, even though half the time she was terrified of how he made her feel.

"Another date?" he asked softly.

"Yeah," she croaked before clearing her throat. "Want to go now, so we can escape the others?"

Noah's laugh was deep, his fingers tightening over her shoulder before letting go. "Honestly? Yes. But we can't."

"We were supposed to have the sitter booked for tonight, so we could go," Bella said, annoyed that she'd been so busy with everything else that she'd forgotten something that had been so important to her sister, important enough for her to pre-plan in case something happened to her.

"So let's ask Gray's mom to stay tomorrow night and take care of the boys."

Bella gulped. "And tell her about the letters?"

Noah seemed unconcerned as he motioned for them to go back in the house. "Only if you want to, if you're ready to go there. Otherwise, we just tell her that we're going out for pizza. She won't even blink an eye."

Bella followed him. "You mean she won't think it's a date, is that what you're saying?"

He winked. "Sweetheart, there's no chance anyone in that house right now would think we were going on a date, or anything even close. They're all probably exchanging looks, wondering how the hell we're managing to live in the same house without killing each other. And we've got nothing to hide; we're just going out as friends, so what's the big deal?"

Bella folded the letter and slipped it into the pocket of her jeans. "You're right." She doubted even her sister would have believed how well they'd be getting on. Or maybe it was just that they'd been too busy to get on each other's nerves for a few days.

"Come on, let's brave the crowd," Noah said, holding out his hand.

Bella had no idea why, but she took it, palm to his as they walked back in the door.

"How is this man still single?"

Bella fought the urge to roll her eyes. She was far too old to be so childish, but seriously? Her Aunt Iris had always had a soft spot for Gray, and she seemed to have transferred that love straight over to Noah.

"Try living with him—then you'll know," Bella said dryly, chewing on the inside of her mouth when Noah shot her a filthy look.

Her mom stared at her, and her aunt made a strange clucking sound. She got it: Noah charmed the pants off most women, *literally*. She shuddered at the thought, remembering exactly why he'd managed to annoy her so many times in the past.

"I'm kidding. He's great. Stand-up guy and incredible with the kids."

"So you *are* sharing a room?" Aunt Iris asked, her eyebrows raised.

Bella's jaw dropped, no words coming out, as she glared at her mom, willing her to say something, anything, to get her crazy aunt to stop.

"Anyone for more coffee?" Noah asked, grinning as he rose. "I'm gonna head out and shoot some hoops with the boys."

"I'll make more coffee," Bella said, wishing she'd just shot her aunt down straightaway. Sleeping together? The thought made her shudder. She'd been grieving for her sister and trying to figure out how to parent two little children. She hadn't exactly had time to jump into bed with Noah. *Even if she had thought about it.*

Noah followed her out, and she groaned as soon as they were out of earshot. "Seriously, what have I done to deserve all this?"

His low, deep laugh made her stand straighter, pulling up from her slump. "Sweetheart, they're . . ."

She stared at him, unblinking.

"Shit, did I just call you 'sweetheart' again?"

Bella bit down on her lower lip, and then they both burst into laughter. Within seconds Bella had tears running down her cheeks, and she had no idea whether they were from laughing so damn hard or because she actually felt like she was on the brink of exhaustion. Or maybe an emotional meltdown. Either way, she was ready to keel over.

"What are you two finding so funny?"

At the sound of her dad's commanding voice, Bella wiped the tears from her cheeks and turned, sidling over to the man who sounded so fierce but had always been soft as a teddy bear with his girls.

"Nothing, Daddy," she said, slinging an arm around his shoulders and giving him a quick hug.

"You haven't called me 'daddy' since you were a girl," he grumbled, putting an arm around her waist. "I know when you're about to pull the wool over my eyes. Noah?"

"Sorry, sir. If she's pulling the wool over your eyes, then she's doing the same to me."

"Noah!" Bella scolded. "I'm not doing anything to anyone. Is there something wrong with wanting to hang out with my dad?" She gave her father a big hug, not sure what to say, but wanting to show how much she loved him, Lila's words echoing in her mind.

She watched as Noah exchanged glances with her father, and she pushed away from him, pretending to be offended.

"How are you enjoying your leave?" her dad asked Noah as Bella began rummaging in the cupboards for some cookies to put out for the boys.

"Busier than usual with the kids, but for once I'm not desperate to get back out there,"—Noah cleared his throat—"sir."

Her dad smiled. "I appreciate your respect, Noah, but it's fine to call me James. I'm sure I've told you that before."

Noah nodded. "Just habit."

"It's me who should be calling you 'sir.'" Her dad blew out a half-breathing, half-whistling sound. "I spent my entire career with the military, but the things you've done with the Navy? I have more respect for your SEAL team than you could imagine."

"It's just what I do," Noah said nonchalantly, as if it were no big deal. "They're my brothers, and wherever we get sent, we just do whatever we have to do to get the mission done and get us all home safe."

"Do you talk about what you've done, what you do, with anyone, son?"

Bella looked up, considered her dad's face. He was a man with two daughters, had only ever called Gray 'son,' and he'd just said it to Noah like he was his son-in-law. Maybe it was because they were in Gray's kitchen, or maybe her dad just felt a connection with Noah. Either way, it unsettled her.

"No, sir—I mean, James," Noah said, hands at his sides, fists clenching a little, telling her that he was uncomfortable. She doubted it was her dad's doing—more the subject matter. "I don't need to brag about what I do for a job. We get in, get out, and everyone on that team knows what we've done. I don't want a pat on the back; I just want to get out without my head being blown off."

"And what if next time it does?" Bella asked, her voice shaky as she spoke up, interrupting their conversation and making both men turn to her. "Get blown off, I mean. What if the next time you go away, you don't come back?"

"Bella, that's enough," her father scolded.

"No," she said, holding up her hand to silence him, stronger now. "It's a fair question, Dad. Noah and I are parenting Cooper and Will together, and I need to know what I'm up against. What I'm going to tell those little boys if their second dad doesn't come home."

The kitchen was suddenly silent. All Bella could hear was her heart thumping in her chest, pulse starting to race, knowing she'd overstepped but not able to stop herself as raw panic set in.

"They've already lost Gray. Is it fair for them to worry about losing you, too?" she asked.

Noah folded his arms across his chest and watched her for a long moment. "I'm going out to shoot some hoops."

She squeezed back tears that threatened to fall. "You might be one of the bravest men in the world, Noah, and the Navy's damn lucky to have you, but you're not just a SEAL anymore. *You're a dad.*"

He walked from the room, leaving her standing there, ready to scream from the frustration of everything. From the pain of losing her sister, from the despair she felt at losing Gray, her feelings for Noah. *Everything.*

"That was unfair, Bella," her dad said, his angry stare making her feel like an in-trouble teenager all over again. "That man is one of the most elite—"

"I know exactly what he is, Dad," she interrupted, not letting him tell her off. "Noah is incredible at what he does—I know that. But all I care about right now is holding this family together. And if he can't be a stable parent in the boys' lives, then maybe he shouldn't be here at all." It was harsh, she knew, but how could she open the boys up to more heartache? To even more loss?

"Don't you make that man choose, Bella. That's not fair to him, and it's not fair to our country." His voice was low but commanding, demanding respect. "You go out there and apologize to him."

"James!" Her mom exclaimed, walking in on them and seeing part of their heated exchange. "What on earth is going on?"

"Nothing, Mom," Bella said, chin held high, refusing to back down. "Dad's trying to give me a lesson in respect, which, for the record, I don't need." She shook her head. "I'm so proud of you, Dad, for what you did for our country. I'm proud of every man and woman who serves, and I respect Noah's work more than you could imagine. But I can't help the way I feel, and right now I'm terrified of losing him when I've just started to trust him, just started to count on him. *To need him.*"

Her mom cleared her throat, glancing sideways, and Bella realized she was trying to tell her something. She turned, saw that Noah had come back in without her realizing, his face flushed from whatever he'd been doing, hands on his hips as he caught his breath.

"Now you've all heard it, can we just get on with whatever the hell it is we're doing?" Bella said, cheeks blazing.

Noah was staring at her, her mom was giving her a tight smile, and her dad looked more bewildered than anything else.

Bella left them all in the kitchen, needing some fresh air and some time to herself. Sometimes the weight of what she'd lost was too much to bear, just like the weight of what she still had to lose made moving on with her life seem impossible.

~

"You ready?"

Bella looked up at Noah's call. She was snuggling Cooper on the sofa, reluctant to get up and leave him, or maybe she just didn't want to face Noah and go out on the date Lila had created for them. What she'd said the day before was still burned into her brain, refusing to let up. And she was upset with herself for not just showing her parents the letters. She didn't know why, but she just wanted to keep them to herself a little longer before having to share them, because right now she was living in a bubble where her sister was still with her, like she was just away serving and writing like she always had.

"You okay if I leave, little buddy?" she asked, giving Cooper a squeeze and dropping a kiss into his hair.

"Bella, they're fine," Gray's mom said, smiling over at her. "It'll be nice for the two of you to have a night off, and there's plenty of room over here. Come on, Coop."

Bella watched as he rocketed off the sofa and onto the other side of his grandma, Will already in position, snuggled up to her. They had a DVD on, had already eaten dinner, and didn't seem concerned in the least.

She glanced back at Noah and rose. He had a tense look on his face, an expression she didn't recognize, but it made her get moving. Bella slipped her heels back on and touched his arm.

"You okay?" she murmured.

"Fine," he said quickly. "Let's just go."

She grabbed her purse and keys, and they both walked out, but she hurried around to the driver's side. He either didn't notice or didn't care.

"You sure you're okay?"

He shut his eyes, head back. She watched the heavy rise and fall of his chest.

"No," he eventually muttered.

"What's wrong?" she asked, leaving the keys in the ignition, but not turning the car on. "Has something happened?" Her heart sank. "Are you being deployed?"

When he finally opened his eyes, he stared straight ahead, not making a sound, but she noticed the hard balling of his fists, the vein bulging at his neck.

"I've just had word that . . ." He slammed his hand into the dash. "Fuck! I can't be telling you this."

Bella slowly reached for him, took his hand, linked their fingers tight, even though he resisted. "You can trust me, Noah. If you need to talk, I'm here."

She considered him as he exhaled, studied the strong lines of his face, his jaw carved from stone, cheeks soft from just being razored, when they usually had stubble. In the past, she'd seen him mostly with a beard, no doubt trying to blend in when he was serving in the Middle East, but the way he was right now was how she liked him best.

"I can't be talking about work. It's not something we're allowed to do."

"If you're not telling me about a mission, any details about a deployment, won't I hear about whatever it is on the news anyway?"

She held her breath, watched him, waited.

"A Chinook—sorry, a helicopter—was just taken down by an RPG—I mean a rocket-propelled grenade. They'd just dropped down a team—part of a team—before they were hit. We've lost some guys." He shook his head. "We're like brothers, Bella, all of us."

She nodded and gripped his hand even tighter, relaxing when he finally did the same back. It wasn't like him to open up so easily, but she was grateful that he was talking to her now, getting it all off his chest.

"You want to stay home?" she asked quietly, feeling guilty for ignoring him so much after the conversation in the kitchen the day before.

"No. I can head out on my own for a bit if you—"

She released his hand and fired up the engine. "I'm not leaving you alone. We can eat pizza, and you can have a drink."

He smiled, eyes still trained straight ahead. "Thanks."

She drove them quickly to the restaurant, knowing where it was because she'd been there before with Lila when they'd had a night out, just the two of them. Noah never said a word, and when she parked, she got out, met him around the other side, and they walked in silence into the restaurant. She was starting to wonder if they'd done the right thing in coming, and then Noah silently reached for her hand.

Bella asked for a table, and they walked hand in hand, following a waitress who was so happy and bubbly that she made Bella cringe.

"Two beers please," Bella ordered. "Make them Buds."

Noah dropped into a chair, his fingers falling away from hers. She sat down, too, leaning across to him.

"I'm sorry," she said. "For what it's worth, I'm sorry about the guys you've just lost, and I'm sorry about the shit I said yesterday."

Noah's eyes were glassy when he looked up. "I have these dreams," he said, elbows resting on the table as he reached for the saltshaker and twirled it between his fingers. "I wake up and look down, and my hands are covered in blood. I think it's my own, then I look across and Gray's slumped down, he's been hit, and I slam my hands into his stomach and try to stop the bleeding, try to save him."

Bella shuddered, the mental picture hard to push away. "Is that what wakes you?" she asked, surprised he'd suddenly opened up to her like that. "I hear you get up sometimes."

"Yeah." He ran a hand through his hair, hair that was starting to grow out from the shorter look he'd been sporting. "It's so vivid, and at the time it seems so real."

"You know I have huge respect for what you do, for what you put yourself through, right?" Bella asked, nodding her thanks when the waitress dropped two beers to the table. He took a long pull of his, and she sipped hers. She wasn't big on beer, but given what he'd told her earlier, she wanted to have one with him, had felt like she needed it, too. "You kind of walked in on half the conversation yesterday."

He shrugged. "How about we talk about something else. I need to get my head out of what I can't control."

Bella sat back, took another sip. "Well, okay. How about Lila's challenge—tell me something no one knows about you." She'd meant to lighten the mood, but it merely intensified.

Noah's lips moved, the corners of his mouth tilting upward as he gave her an impossibly sexy look, eyes barely connecting with hers. "That sounds dangerous."

"Come on—there must be something. And don't go confessing to how many women you've slept with. That would just be gross."

He clasped both hands around his beer bottle, eyes leaving hers as he stared out the window toward the street. It wasn't dark yet, but the light was fading fast, and there was something nice about the streetlights slowly firing into life. He wasn't going to back down from Bella's challenge, but what could he tell her?

CHAPTER TEN

Noah sipped his beer for something to do. He didn't want to lie, but he didn't want to make himself more vulnerable than he already had by talking about his fallen comrades. His brain was scrambling, still trying to process what he'd heard, what had happened to the team. He didn't know the guys personally, but the loss still hit him hard, reminded him how easily it could have been him. It hadn't bothered him before, had always been something he was prepared to sacrifice, his life secondary to protecting his brothers and completing his mission. And then he knew what he was going to tell Bella.

"I've never valued my own life," he said, the words falling from his mouth before he could stop them.

She held his gaze, her expression impossible to read. She looked like she was holding her breath, her stare unbreakable. "And now?"

"Now, I don't have to be told that my life's important, because I look at those little boys, at the way they look up at me and trust me so completely, and I know."

The air was silent between them, the noise of the restaurant disappearing, less audible than the crackling radio silence from Bella. Before she could respond, say anything and make him feel like shit for being honest, he grinned. He wasn't ready to talk more about his job, about what the future held for his career, preferring to joke around and push the thoughts away. His confession to her had scared him, truth be told. He wasn't used to losing control over what he said like that.

"And I'm scared of cats."

Bella's smile was low, but it was there. "You're lying."

"I'm not."

The waitress arrived back at the their table. "Are you ready to order?"

Noah smiled apologetically and reached for his menu. "Sorry—we haven't even gotten that far yet. Can you give us a few minutes?"

"Sure thing."

She lingered too long, batting her eyelashes, and Noah felt uncomfortable for Bella.

"Sorry," he muttered once the waitress left.

Bella raised an eyebrow. "Not your fault women want to fall at your feet."

"Yeah, every single one but you."

The second he'd said it, he regretted it, but Bella recovered quickly, ignoring it. He might be able to get himself in and out of some of the toughest situations his job threw at him, but put him at a table with Bella, and he was useless.

"So, about the cats . . ." she muttered.

Noah breathed a sigh of relief. "It's the claws that get me. I mean, they're just way too smart for their own good, so freaking intelligent, and then to arm them with razor-sharp claws, for Pete's sake?"

Bella looked relaxed. She'd leaned back into her seat, beer in hand as she studied him. "I'm allergic, so there's no chance I'll be getting one for the boys. You'll be able to sleep easy."

He chuckled.

"Sorry. I didn't mean—"

He held up his hands. "Hey, we're both saying stupid things tonight. Let's just give each other a break, huh?"

"Good idea." She tipped back her beer and finished it as he downed the rest of his.

"Pizza or pasta?" he asked.

"Lila said pizza, so pizza it is."

"Hey, she can't exactly tell us off if we don't obey her," he teased.

Bella laughed. "Don't apologize for that," she said as he groaned again, "but we're having pizza. She'll probably blast me with lightning from up there if we don't do what she says, just to show me she's still boss."

They settled on pepperoni, and Noah made sure to let Bella order so he didn't have to deal with the overly friendly waitress. He always flirted with pretty women, but for the first time since he could remember, the one he was sitting across from was enough to hold his attention. Bella's smile was easy, even though he knew that every time they talked about her sister, it would be like gnashing on a raw nerve ending. He knew it because it was how he felt every single day.

He slid her second beer across to her and picked his own up. "So you haven't told me your secret."

"Does it count as a secret if it's something I told Lila, but no one else?" she asked, face serious.

Noah nodded. "Yeah. I'd say it does."

"My ex," she started, ripping at the label on the bottle.

"The one I met at Gray and Lila's wedding?" he asked. He recalled a tall guy, remembered him standing at the bar when he'd gone up to get shots.

"Yeah, him. He was a former SEAL, and he beat me up so bad one night that I ended up in the hospital."

Noah froze. He angled his head, was about to look away; only the honesty in her gaze told him she was telling him the pure truth.

Anger thumped through him, threatened to knock him out of equilibrium when he was so used to being able to hold it together, no matter what the situation. So this was the truth behind why she hated military guys so much.

"I don't know what to say." It was the truth—what the hell could he say in response to that? He reached for her hand, squeezing it and looking straight into her eyes, needing to say the right thing. "No woman should ever have to be scared of a man. I'm sorry it happened to you."

She looked down at his hands. "I never thought it would happen to me, but I guess that's what just about every victim of domestic violence says."

"And Lila was the only person you told?" he asked, just to make sure he understood the situation.

"Yep. I swore her to secrecy, wouldn't let her breathe a word to Gray because I knew what he'd do, and I didn't want him taking matters into his own hands."

"Did you file a police report?" he asked before forcing himself to stop asking any more questions. He needed to be more gentle with her, understand what she'd been through.

She nodded. "Yes. But he lied, made up such a bullshit story about what had actually happened, and I dropped the whole thing. I'm not proud of myself; I should have done more, but it is what it is."

He gripped his beer bottle in his other hand, afraid it was going to smash in his hands because he was holding it so tight. Anger thumped through him, as he thought about someone, *anyone*, laying a hand on Bella. "And your parents?"

"My dad would have killed him." She grimaced. "I'm not kidding, he would have."

Noah didn't doubt it. "So what did you tell them?"

"Lila told them I'd gone away on vacation, I called a day later to tell them that I'd been so stressed with work that I'd treated myself to a trip, and I spent a week in the hospital and then a week on vacation in Mexico. When I came back, I explained my bruises as a bad experience going paddleboarding. Which, for the record, I never tried, even though I watched couples learning on the beach every day."

Noah breathed deeply, relieved when the pizza arrived. He let go of Bella's hand slowly and took a slice, burning his mouth by trying to eat it too quickly.

"The second part to that secret is that I haven't really dated much since then."

"And you think all military-type guys are assholes," he added.

She shrugged. "Pretty much. I hate that whole macho thing, but I know that's only a certain type of guy. My dad and Gray weren't like that."

He ducked his head, then forced himself to look back up again. *I'm not like that either.* They were the words he wanted to say, should have said, but for some reason they just weren't forming when he needed them to.

"I know you're not like that, Noah," Bella said softly as she held a large slice of pizza, twirling some cheese off with her fingers. "You don't need to prove yourself."

He finished his mouthful. "How do you feel now? About what you went through? I mean, it must be hard to trust again."

She put the slice back down. "I know you're not going to go around hitting women or getting into fights, and neither are most trained military guys, but you're still the type. Big, tough, strong. Women drop like flies around you. You're all work and then way too much play on the short bursts of time you get away from the Navy." She grimaced. "I can't help what I think, and yeah, it affects the way I feel about men."

She was right. He was all of those things. But the fact that he was a SEAL didn't define the way he was in his personal life. There was a whole lot more to his fucked-up ethos of not wanting anyone to get close to him than just his career.

"I might know this guy if he was actually a SEAL."

She shrugged. "He said he left because he got into a fight with one of the instructors who was giving him shit."

"Bullshit. He was never a SEAL. Guys who say that kind of crap are just embarrassed about being in the ninety percent who never make it through training. If anyone so much as threw a punch at an instructor?" He whistled. "They'd receive a hiding. And besides, I know plenty of SEALs who love a fistfight, but not one who'd hit a woman. And none who go around bragging about their jobs."

Bella pursed her lips. "I just believed him, never thought to question him."

Noah smiled, deciding not to engage any further. The only way to prove Bella wrong about SEALs was to show her, and he couldn't do that over pizza. "I'll prove it to you, Bella, that I'm not like that. Just to show you that men, especially military guys, don't need to be physical to be real men."

She smiled, but he could see she was uncomfortable. He was trying his best, wanted to make everything okay for her, but nothing had prepared him for this kind of situation. "Can we just change the subject now?" Bella said.

Noah didn't need to be asked twice. It wasn't exactly comfortable conversation, and he had no intention of pushing her for more information if she didn't want to talk about it.

"So, uhhh, do you ever think the kids need a pet?" he said, clutching for any safe topic to bring up.

She looked puzzled. "A pet? I thought we'd just decided against a cat."

"I was thinking a dog. Maybe a Golden Retriever."

Bella groaned. "Seriously? I'm only just getting used to picking up after the boys. I don't need a freaking puppy to contend with, too."

"It was just a thought. If I were around more . . ." And he realized he'd said too much, just when he'd been trying to get their chat back on lighter ground.

"*Are* you going to be around more?" Bella asked.

He wanted to reach for her, needed to connect with her, but instead he just stared. "Maybe."

They went back to eating their pizza, slice by slice, in between sips of beer. Noah was happy to stay quiet, lost in his thoughts, and Bella seemed content for the meal to pass in almost silence, too. He didn't know when it had happened, but being with Bella and not saying a word didn't feel awkward at all. And that wasn't something he'd encountered often in his life—outside of work, anyway.

They drove home mostly without saying much and said a quiet "Good night" once they were home. Bella disappeared up the stairs first, and Noah hung back and filled a glass of water before heading to bed.

∼

"Noah!" Bella urged, hand on his shoulder. "Noah!"

Noah jumped and grabbed at the person touching him, going for the throat. He needed to protect himself, didn't know where he was, why it was dark.

"Noah!"

The strangled, choked cry hit through the wall in his head, brought everything crumbling down, made him enter reality. The room was dark, a little light filtering in from the hall, but the second he let her go, she reached for the lamp and flicked it on.

Noah stared down at his hands, expecting to see blood. Expecting them to be stained red and dripping, but there was nothing. He looked up, saw the wide-eyed look on Bella's face, the way her fingers were pressed to her neck.

Fuck! "Bella, I'm so sorry," he whispered, pushing the tangled sheets away and fighting to get out of bed.

She backed up, making him feel like the biggest jerk in the world.

"I thought you were someone else. It took me a second to come back to reality," he admitted, the dream still fresh in his mind—the blood, the smell of gunpowder, the burning heat of the sun as they hid against the rocks, searching for cover.

"I didn't want you to wake the boys," she whispered. "I've just gotten Will back to sleep."

Noah reached for her, stepped into her space when she went to back up again. Her hair was messy, falling over her shoulders. Her nightie was made of satin and fit her tight from her breasts down to just above her knee; it was hot pink, with a lacy edge around the bottom that he wished was a few inches higher so he could get a better look at her thighs.

"I would never hurt you," he said honestly, keeping his voice low so they didn't wake the kids. "Not in a million years."

She moved again, and he took her hand. He wasn't holding tight—she could have broken free if she wanted to—but she stayed still.

"You just did," she whispered.

"I know." He couldn't deny it, but he could show her just how gentle he could be, that he believed in touching a woman with all the gentleness in the world.

Noah watched her, took in the soft rise and fall of her chest, the wide-eyed expression, the way her mouth parted when she knew he was staring at it. He'd been wanting to kiss her for a long while, to feel her mouth against his and taste her lips, but until now he hadn't had the opportunity.

He paused, gave her the chance to get the hell out of Dodge, but she didn't move an inch. Noah lowered his mouth, softening his hold on her wrist as he stepped into her space. She lifted her chin as he bent to her height, touched her mouth to his so tentatively he wasn't even sure he'd kissed her, but he wanted her to know she held the power, that she wasn't being forced into anything. He knew he should pull away again, like he had the other night, but he just didn't have the strength to say no this time.

When a soft moan escaped her as he tried to pull back, Noah let go of her wrist entirely and circled his arms around her body, drawing her closer, fighting a groan as the soft satin of her nightie brushed his bare stomach. He deepened the kiss, pressed his lips harder to hers, crushing her mouth, waiting for what felt like forever before touching his tongue to hers, exploring.

They stood for a long beat, mouths fused, bodies tight. Bella's hands were slipped low around his waist on one side, the other to the back of his head like she was trying to stop him from ever moving away. But kissing wasn't enough for him, was only making him want her more, to explore every curve of her body, to feel every inch of her soft skin.

"You have no idea how long I've been wanting to do this," Noah muttered when he finally pulled his mouth from hers, transferring to her neck, kissing along her collarbone, loving every little soft moan that came from her lips.

"We should stop," she murmured, but he could barely hear her and decided to ignore her completely. The way she was pressing into him, her fingers digging into his skin, told him she wanted it to stop about as much as he did.

"Why?" he asked, not really caring what her reasoning was so long as she kept grinding against him, head tilted back as he made his way across the top of her breast.

"Because it's a bad idea," she whispered, gasping as he flicked his tongue down lower, teasing her. Bella grabbed hold of his hair and yanked him up. "A very bad idea."

He laughed and went back to pleasuring her mouth, his hands low and skimming over her bottom.

"*Bella!*"

The soft call from the room down the hall made them both freeze, even though it was virtually impossible for him to stand still and not do anything with Bella's warm, sexy body rammed hard up against his.

She sighed and dropped her head to his chest, forehead first, her lips connecting with his skin. "That's my cue to go."

Noah laughed. "I would, but . . ." He gestured down low, his erection visible against his boxer shorts.

"Yeah, I think I'll go," she teased.

"*Bella!*" It was Cooper, and he was more insistent this time.

"Go," he whispered, cupping a hand under her chin and stealing one last kiss.

Bella kissed him back before turning, glancing over her shoulder before disappearing out the door. He had no idea what had just happened, but it was damn good, and he wished it didn't have to end.

CHAPTER ELEVEN

Upstairs it was mayhem. Bella could hear squealing and laughter, not to mention way too much water splashing out of the bath. But the fact that Noah was up there with the boys meant she could get the dishes done and run around like a crazy woman, tidying up, before sprinting upstairs and getting the boys' beds ready for them. She wasn't too proud to admit that it was like the movie *Groundhog Day*, with every day repeating over and over again, but she was starting to get the rhythm of things. When she'd been the one looking after them, taking turns with her parents on the rare occasions that Gray and Lila had been deployed at the same time, it hadn't bothered her to bend the rules and not be so strict. But now that she was here full time, getting them to bed before seven-thirty meant she had a few hours to herself. *With Noah.* She pushed the thought away as she let the soapy water run out of the sink; she was still finding it hard not to think about the kiss they'd shared two nights ago.

"I'll be there in a sec," she called out as she went into the boys' room and pulled the drapes, fingers gliding slowly over the dark blue taffeta. She could still remember planning the room for Will, the dark blue paired with a much softer shade on the walls.

"Don't come in!" Noah called out amid a burst of giggles and even more splashing.

"Why?" she called back, thinking it was a game the boys were playing and sneaking closer, avoiding the squeaky floorboards.

"Noah!" Cooper squealed, followed by hysterical laughter from Will—or at least that's what it sounded like.

Bella waited, both hands on the door, before pushing it open and bursting into the bathroom.

"Whoa!" she exclaimed, clamping her hands over her eyes. Noah was naked, *in the bath with the boys*, the few bubbles that were left doing *nothing* to hide his bare skin.

"Shit—sorry," he swore.

"Money for the swear jar!" Will happily announced, holding up his hand for a high five from his brother.

Bella peeked between her fingers, seeing Noah with a hand over his crotch. It didn't matter that she'd instantly blocked her gaze—the image of him lying back in the big bath, completely stark naked, was burned into her memory. Even now, with his shoulders so broad, slick with water, one big arm resting on the edge of the bath, his legs hardly fit in the confined space. Then she laughed. All that view, and she hadn't noticed the bubbles on his head.

"Hey, I like the hairdo," she said, dropping to sit on the closed lid of the toilet.

"Thanks," he muttered. "I was coerced into this, in case you were wondering."

"Oh, I'm sure it was really hard for the boys to convince you," she teased straight back. Something had changed between them, an easiness that hadn't been there before. Even though she was seriously twisted in knots over the kiss they'd shared, the kiss that was as ingrained in her memory banks as the view of him naked, she still felt more comfortable around him than she ever had. They hadn't talked about what had happened. She wondered if maybe it had only happened because they'd both been so emotionally charged from what they'd talked about, and she was happy to just sit on the memory.

"Hey, have you booked the sitter for Friday night?" Noah asked.

Bella nodded. "I have."

The boys were playing with little boats, making circles in the water and climbing all over Noah in the process. She loved the fact that they were so comfortable around him, and their little naked bodies, so skinny and all sharp elbows and knobby knees, always made her smile.

"I meant to tell you earlier, but I have to head back to base. Tomorrow, if I can."

Bella froze. She clenched her fingers together, the little bubble of happiness she'd felt at listening to the boys giggle and talk disappearing like it had never existed in the first place.

"You're being deployed?" she asked.

Noah's face softened, his smile kind. "No Bella, I'm not. If I was deployed, you'd know about it, because one minute I'd be here and the next I'd be gone. Fast. That's usually how it works for my team."

She gulped. "So you're just . . ."

"I need to get back, see some of the guys. It's hit everyone pretty hard." He looked sad. "There will be memorial services to attend, too."

Of course: the helicopter going down. She hadn't spoken about it to anyone after he'd told her, but it was all over the news now, so it was no longer a secret.

"Does the whole thing mean you could be deployed sooner, though, because of the men they lost?"

Noah shook his head. "No. They're part of a different SEAL team."

She hadn't asked him questions about how he was able to take so much leave or whether he was just between deployments. She didn't know or understand how the whole thing worked. All she knew was that she liked having him around, and she was nowhere near ready to face the prospect of losing him. Not yet.

"So you'll be gone a few days?"

"I'll be home Thursday night. Maybe you could call me as soon as the mail comes?"

Bella rose, taking the towels down from the heated rails and placing them close to the bath so Noah could reach them. "Sounds good. I'll let you get out."

She was numb walking across the hall into the boys' room, and she dropped to the bed and waited for them to come running in, wrapped in their fluffy white towels, with wet hair and little bodies wrinkled from being in the water too long.

⁓

Noah pulled up outside the house, turned off the engine, and leaned back in his seat. He was knackered. Seeing the guys had been great—he'd missed them like hell—but it had also drained him. Losing Gray had been hard enough, especially on top of everything else he'd had going on, but attending the services for the men who'd been on the Chinook? *Damn.* The graves were marked by white headstones now, part of a row of men killed in combat. The only saving grace was that their bodies had been recovered so quickly, or at least the three guys they'd buried the day before had been. There were still more to come. Which meant there were more men to say good-bye to and more services to attend in their honor, as well as reliving so much of what he'd seen in person.

Noah was craving sleep, more because he wanted to escape his thoughts than from genuine tiredness. He was trained to go without, although all the training in the world wouldn't make him voluntarily give up his eight hours a night.

A tap on the window made his eyes open, the noise putting his body on high alert.

"Sorry!"

If it had been anyone else, Noah would have glared, but it was hard for him to be angry with Bella. She had a wide mouth, her smile making him forget everything when he was cast in her web, and her brown eyes showed her emotions. Right now they were dancing, vivid, but at other times, when he knew she was thinking about her sister, they were damp and swimming in sadness. Even then she looked beautiful, but nothing beat her infectious smile right now. But he'd had the time to do some thinking while he'd been away from her. What was happening between them was so confusing. He owed it to her to be more honest about himself, about what she was getting herself into. But then part of him just wanted to enjoy the happiness they had and not worry about the future.

He pushed open his door. "It was too nice sitting here in the sun. Thought I'd get some shut-eye." It was a half lie, because he'd been sitting thinking about her, not sleeping, because he hadn't expected anyone to be home.

"I'm just about to go collect the boys," she said, reaching into her bag and plucking out a letter. "This came."

"Oh yeah?" Noah had all but forgotten about it. "What are we up to tonight?"

Maybe that's why she was so happy. "Ugh, the shooting range. You'll probably love it, but I'm just happy I got to sit in the sun, drink my coffee, and read something from my sister."

Noah matched her smile, but he wasn't so convinced her happiness was a good thing. The letters from Lila were sweet, and he was grateful that they'd brought Bella and him together, but he was smart enough to know that they weren't going to go on forever. Maybe this was the last one, or the one after could be. Whenever they stopped, he knew it was going to hit Bella hard.

"You okay to go get the boys without me?" he asked, taking the letter from her.

She smiled at him, the sun shining down on her face. It made her look younger than she was, as if she didn't have a care in the world as she held up her hand to shield her eyes.

"No problem. Mind if I take your wheels? My car's in the garage, and you're blocking me."

Noah nodded and passed her the keys, but his hand brushed hers and connected for a moment. Bella took hold of the keys but didn't remove them from his palm, stepping closer and standing on tiptoe to press a soft, warm kiss to his cheek.

"It's good to see you," she whispered.

"You, too," he managed, voice gruff. He refused to give in to his instincts and wrap his arms around her right there in the driveway. If something happened between them . . . *no*. He placed his own kiss against her skin, to her forehead. Whatever the hell was going on with Bella and him had to stop, no matter how badly he wanted it to be otherwise.

Noah backed up. "See you soon," he said, heading for the house.

Bella looked confused for the split second he watched her before walking away, but he chose to ignore it. He'd lost enough in his lifetime already, and he didn't need to let anyone else close. Even if it hurt like hell to admit it. And besides, once she knew the truth, knew everything about him and what he'd done, maybe she'd want him the hell out of Dodge anyway. He pulled out the letter and leaned against the hood to read it.

November 2014

Dear Bella & Noah,

I know there's every chance that the two of you are so sick of each other, being in the house all the time and trying to get on with everything, that the last thing you want to do is spend even more time together. But part of me hopes that I'm completely wrong and you're loving hanging out. Maybe that's the part of my brain that needs to believe everything's okay even though I'm gone. All I can do is hope, right?

Bella, you're gonna hate the sound of this, but I want you guys to go to a shooting range. Let's not start a political debate here (for the record, Noah, Bells is a die-hard Democrat, and she's not so convinced that the current gun legislation is tough enough). Anyway, just give it a go. Noah, show her what you're made of, make her see what a thrill it is to feel the weight of a gun in her hands, waiting to squeeze the trigger to take out the target. I reckon she'll love it.

And maybe it's about time you started to show her the real you. I'm just sayin'. ☺

Lila xoxo

Bella wasn't sure if she'd done something to upset Noah or if he was just struggling with what he'd been through back at base. Either way, she was determined to enjoy herself, more to prove her sister wrong than anything else. But so far there was nothing about the shooting range that she liked, except for the man walking beside her. Noah had stopped to talk to the manager, discussing things she had no idea about, and finally they were ready to start.

"Do I need a bulletproof vest or anything?" she asked.

Noah's mouth kicked up into a smile as he glanced down at her. "No vest. I have no plans for trying to shoot you."

She tucked her arm into his, surprising herself by how comfortable she felt around him. The four days with him gone had passed slowly, and although she didn't mind taking care of the kids solo, it was better with Noah around.

He pulled away, and she was about to protest when she realized he'd stopped for a reason.

"This is the rifle range," Noah said as casually as if he were telling her the temperature. "I thought we'd do this rather than handguns, given your pro-liberal stance."

"Ha-ha," she muttered, staring at the large guns waiting to be used, "I don't have a big problem with guns—not when they're used correctly, but I've just never wanted to shoot anything before."

Noah held up his hands. "Hey, I don't particularly want to shoot anything live either. I'm not into gunning down animals for sport, and I don't like when I have to take someone's life out in the field, but I do it to save my own ass and my brothers' asses."

She shuddered, a vibration trailing the entire length of her spine, tingling its way through her body. She didn't even want to think about the situations he'd been in with a gun. "So you're gonna show me what to do?" Bella asked.

Noah nodded. "It's about time you knew how to use one. I bet you'll love it."

"I seriously doubt that." The truth was, she was kind of excited, even if she didn't want to admit it.

He ran through some safety tips with her before lifting the gun and passing it to her, positioning it in her hands. Noah moved behind her, his big arms circling her body. Bella breathed out and relaxed into his hold, loosening up and refusing to be daunted by the gun or scared by the man. The latter was troubling her more than the guns, which were at least taking her mind off what they were about to do.

"I want you to put the butt of the gun just here," he said, guiding the rifle up so it was sitting where he wanted it. He pushed her right elbow out, made her hold it high. "When you look through the lense, focus on the target and place your trigger finger gently, ready to squeeze it."

Bella was focused, or as focused as she could be with the warmth of Noah behind her, his chest to her back, his mouth so close to her ear as he guided her. He was a great teacher, she'd give him that, although she was pretty certain this wasn't the way he'd learned to shoot. His arms encircled around her made her feel safe, as if there was no possible way she could come to harm with him in charge.

"When you have the target lined up, I want you to take a deep breath and then slowly exhale," he murmured to her. "When your body is relaxed and your breath is halfway out, that's when you squeeze the trigger."

She did as he instructed, breathed out, and pulled the trigger. The slight kickback of the gun took her by surprise, and she lifted her head.

"Sorry—I should have warned you about that," he apologized. "But good going for a first shot. You're a natural!"

Bella blinked and squinted into the distance, seeing that she'd managed to hit the target, just not square in the middle.

"Huh," she murmured with a grin. "Not bad."

Noah looked proud when she turned to face him. "Must be the incredible teacher you had."

She laughed. "Can we go again?"

"Go for it. We're the only ones here right now, so we might as well make the most of it."

Bella picked up the rifle again—she'd slung it down after her first shot—but hesitated. She liked the idea of trying another shot, but she much preferred the idea of being in the circle of Noah's arms again.

"Would you mind showing me again?" she asked, smiling as sweetly as she knew how.

Noah didn't hide his surprise, eyebrows shooting up at her question. He took her hands in his and slowly lifted the gun higher, positioning her again from behind. This time, when she was ready to squeeze the trigger, he stayed in place, not moving away. His body was hot, and hers was getting hotter by the second, flames shooting through every part of her. She shot again, hitting her target almost perfectly, but she never lowered her gun, not until he made her, his hands guiding it down as carefully as he'd aided her in raising it.

"You did good," Noah whispered in her ear.

Bella let him make the rifle safe, waiting, hoping that something was going to happen. They stared, eyes locked, watching one another for what felt like forever. She reached for him, touched her palm to his cheek, thumb rubbing gently across stubble that she guessed had been there for a couple of days already.

"I missed you," she confessed.

Noah opened his mouth, looked like he was about to say something, then turned away. "My turn," he eventually said.

Bella felt rebuffed, but she didn't want to make a big deal out of it. Instead, she stood back to watch him. He collected a different rifle, loaded it, and settled in, raising the gun so fast as he effortlessly hit his target, over and over. When he finally stepped back, gun discharged, the look he gave her left her cold.

His eyes, usually blue and bright, seemed dull, his mouth braced in a tight line.

"What is it, Noah?" she asked.

"You did great tonight," he replied. "I reckon you get the thrill now, huh?"

She nodded, but she wasn't fooled by his turning the conversation around on her. "You want to talk?"

He grimaced. "There's so much you don't know about me, Bella. I had time to think while I was away, and I need to be honest with you. I just . . ." He didn't want it to come out wrong. "I'm just not cut out for a relationship, and I think you need to hear why before you decide if you even like me."

She pursed her lips. "Seriously? You actually think I could dislike you more than I used to?"

His frown told her he was serious. "Yeah."

"I think we need to get a beer then," she said. "Or a strong coffee."

Noah pointed back the way they'd come. "There's a bar in there. Nothing fancy, but it'll do."

"Sure thing." She let him do what needed to be done with the rifles, and then they walked toward the bar. There was less than a yard between them, but Noah was being careful not to touch her, so it might as well have been an ocean separating them.

He'd decided on whiskey. Noah had never been a big drinker, but since he'd started opening himself up little by little to Bella, it was exactly what he needed right now. Besides, he knew he was more than likely going to be called up again soon, knew he wasn't going to be extended much more leave before he was back in training or deployed. His final decision about the promotion he'd been offered was hanging over him, strangling him with its constant presence. There was one job offer firmly on the table, an instructor position that on paper looked great, but it wasn't active and he loved action. But the other job on the cards was making him think. It was higher up and more strategic, with more responsibility. It would mean him making a difference still, working from base but assisting and advising in high-octane situations. Only that offer hadn't been made yet, although he knew he was one of only two candidates being considered.

He was so close to walking away from the job he loved, the job that had always meant more to him than anything else, and the worst thing about it was that he couldn't talk to anyone about his plans. Only his superior knew about them, as he'd put feelers out for different positions for him within the Navy. It was the thought of no longer being beside his brothers out in the field that was so hard. Tougher than hard—it was as good as paralyzing.

"What's troubling you?" Bella asked, the softness of her voice enough to make him smile.

Noah stared into eyes that reminded him of milk chocolate. "I'm trying to make some decisions that affect us all," he admitted.

"Decisions you can't talk to me about?"

Noah nodded. "Yeah."

They sat in silence a while longer, both spending more time looking at their glasses than each other. Noah knew he needed to open up to Bella more, tell her why he kept pulling away, but talking about his feelings hadn't ever come naturally to him, and he doubted it ever would.

"Are your night terrors still happening?"

Bella's question surprised him. "Yup. I doubt I'll ever be able to sleep like a civilian again. They're not something new—more of an ongoing thing." What he didn't tell her was that one of the only nights he'd slept easy was the one with her and the boys in bed, and other mornings for a few hours solid when one of the kids, usually Will, crawled in with him.

She touched his hand, reaching across the bar, fingers curling over his. "So it's not just this particular one that troubles you?"

Noah frowned. "Sadly, no. But you know I don't, uh, talk to anyone else about all that stuff, right? The whole night terror thing is just between us."

"Oh yeah, and all the other girls' whose beds you wake up in all tangled in the sheets."

He chuckled. "First of all, I haven't woken up in your bed yet. And secondly, that's why I keep things casual, don't have many . . ."—he grinned at her—"*sleepovers*."

Bella groaned and shoved at him, her hand leaving his to push at his shoulder. "Gross. And you have actually woken up in my bed, that very first night when the boys were all needy."

Noah cleared his throat twice, wanting to open up to Bella, but not sure how to find the words. And then she looked at him, her face so open and her eyes so kind and bright, that he knew he had to.

"After you told me about your ex and why it made you have this idea about military guys, I've been wanting to be honest with you. I've wanted to tell you about my past, and I think it'll help you understand why I can't get into something with you. Because when I was growing up, bouncing around different homes, I had it pretty rough," he told her.

Bella moved so she was facing him, beer bottle cupped in her hands as she gave him her full attention.

"I didn't have a lot, but I did have a girlfriend. She was a runaway, living on the streets, and we looked out for each other. She taught me the ropes, how to stay safe and all that kind of stuff, and I . . ." His voice trailed off, the memories still hard to process almost two decades later. "Let's just say I was a pretty mature fourteen. I was fifteen before Gray's family took me in, but even with everything going on, I kept going to school, lied about where I was living, showered in the gym, managed to keep my head above water and avoid drugs."

Her eyes were wide. "I didn't know you actually lived rough," she said. "I just thought you had it tough in foster care." Noah nodded in reply.

"Her name was Bree, and she was older than me," he continued, not wanting to stop now that he'd started. "I loved her like I'd never loved anyone in my lifetime before, and I would have done anything for her, but every little bit of money she got together went straight into her arm."

Bella gasped, eyes never leaving his even as her brows pulled together at what he'd just said. "Heroin?"

Noah breathed deep, saw Bree the way he'd found her. "I tried so hard to get her to stop, to look after her, but I was only a kid. One day I came home from school, and she wasn't there. She was gone. I searched and searched, and when I finally found her, she had a cord wrapped around her arm, needle on the ground beside her. Her eyes were rolled back into her head, her lips purple." Noah downed the rest of his beer. "She was gone."

Bella had tears in her eyes as she pulled her bar stool closer, hand dropping to his thigh. "I'm sorry."

He sat up straighter and motioned for another drink, glancing at Bella's and seeing it was still over half full. "It was a long time ago, but losing her has made it tough for me to let anyone too close, to care too much about another woman like that."

"Is that when Gray's family took you in?"

"Yup." He pulled some notes from his wallet and put them on the counter when the bartender slung him another whiskey. "I didn't turn up for school that next day, just stayed with Bree's body. Gray was the only friend I had and the only person I'd been honest with about my living conditions. He came searching for me the next night, he and his folks, and they weren't taking no for an answer. His dad gave me an ultimatum, told me that this might be my one and only chance to make a better life for myself, a lifeline when I needed it most." Noah paused, remembering the way Gray's father had held out his hand to him and never budged until he'd finally grasped it back. "It took me about five minutes to process what they were offering me, and I was smart enough to know I had to say yes. They took me in that night, fought tooth and nail to keep me, and I give them full credit for the man I am today. For who I was able to become."

Her smile, as usual, was kind. Although maybe he just kept on thinking of it as being so kind because he'd never seen this side of her before, until he'd moved into the house. Previously, he'd been more often tasked with her frown, her eyes cast skyward whenever she'd realized he was joining them.

"It's a pretty awesome success story, rising from the streets to being one of the country's most elite fighters."

Noah shrugged. He'd never needed or sought out praise, but at the same time he was sensible enough to know that she was right. The media was filled with negativity, particularly about kids who'd grown up rough and just ended up rougher and tougher as adults. And it was one of the reasons he wanted to help other young people. But it wasn't the reason why he'd just opened up to Bella.

"I guess what I'm trying to say is that I'm not good at relationships. Letting anyone too close, opening myself up to experiencing loss like that again. I loved Bree, even though I was only fifteen when I lost her." He paused, considering his words before saying them. "I'd lived so much by then, had experienced so much, and the way I felt for her wasn't just some teenage crush. I haven't let another woman get that close to me again."

Noah was glad they were the only people in the bar, the music low. It was easy to talk, and he didn't have to worry about anyone overhearing them.

When Bella spoke, he found himself leaning forward to hear her, to connect with her. Her words were considered, careful when she was usually so much more organic with him, seeming to say whatever was on her mind.

"You want me to know this because you think I don't see the real you. Is that it?"

He went to speak, then shut his mouth, took another burning sip of whiskey. "Or maybe I just want to you to know that if I'm giving you mixed signals, it's because I don't know what the hell I'm doing."

"For the record, I think we're both pretty mixed up about . . ."—she hesitated, then motioned between them—"this. *Us.* Whatever the heck's going on between us is all kinds of confusing. But I've already realized that every thought and assumption I'd made about you was off the beaten track. I owe you an apology."

He shrugged. "No, you don't. I was a jerk to you because it was fun playing on you being uptight and wanting everything to go perfectly whenever we were all together. It's not unusual for the sister of the bride to want the bachelorette party and pre-wedding day dinner to go off without a hitch when she's spent months organizing them. Or the boys' christenings or birthdays. I deserved it all, every time I received the wrath of Bella."

"How about we just call it even and start fresh. Put all that behind us and just"—she smiled—"move on."

"And this?" he said, not sure how to express himself. "We just let this be what it ends up being?"

"I like you, Noah," Bella said, her voice lower than usual, eyes darting to the side, tongue flicking out to moisten her lips. "I never thought I'd say it, but I do. I'm starting to realize why Lila cared for you like she did."

"This was the side of me your sister got to see. The real me, not the me I try to be for the rest of the world."

She stood and leaned forward, pressing a warm kiss to his cheek. She lingered, her breath soft as she murmured. "I'm the one person you don't have to pretend with—not anymore."

Noah stayed still, rooted to the spot, until Bella stepped back and nudged her glass further over, clearly not wanting to finish it. He took her cue, drained his, then grabbed his wallet and keys and headed for the door. He held it open for her, waiting for her to pass through, admiring the curve of her butt in the tight jeans she was wearing as she walked a few feet ahead of him. They got into the car silently, neither of them saying a word as they drove home. He kept glancing at Bella, but her eyes were trained straight ahead, her expression hard to read. Until she reached for his hand, her touch light, and she didn't let go until he pulled into the driveway. Then she was silent as she looked at him, eyes wide, before slowly getting out of the car and heading for the front door.

Noah couldn't take his eyes off her, wished to hell he wasn't so screwed up about relationships. Because if ever he'd wished he could rewrite his past and start afresh, it was now, but even if he could, there was still something he hadn't told Bella, something she might hate him for keeping from her. She was so beautiful, so perfect in so many ways. Only Noah didn't need perfect. He didn't deserve *perfect*. Not for a second did he believe he deserved anything in life, and he sure as hell knew he wasn't good enough for a woman like Bella. Never in a million years.

The house was deathly quiet. The interior was dark except for the soft low lights in the hall and the one out front that illuminated the porch and reflected back inside; otherwise, it was just her, standing alone, breathing softly and trying to get to grips with her thoughts. *Noah.* She should have run a mile when he'd told her about his past, should have withdrawn emotionally anyway, but instead, it had only made her want him all the more. Because all the manwhore comments she'd once thrown his way, the anger she'd felt at the way he was so casual about his relationships with women—suddenly it all made sense.

Bella listened to his footfalls in the silence as he made his way up the three steps to the porch. Any minute now he'd be walking through the front door, which meant she had about thirty seconds to decide what to do.

"Bella?"

She sucked in a big breath and checked her nerves the moment she heard his deep, sexy voice. Everything about him was so . . .

unnerving. But instead of being scared of him, it only made her want him all the more.

Bella turned as she heard the door shut behind him. She moved toward him, crossing the couple of yards that were separating them and recognizing the surprised look on his face as he first watched her, then in the split second as surprise turned to . . .

She didn't let him say anything. Didn't hesitate. Didn't give him the opportunity to question her or tell her no.

Bella stormed the final few steps and reached for his face, one hand to his cheek, the other clutching the hair at the back of his neck as her lips parted and she kissed him, mouth frantically covering his, desperate to explore every inch of him. To taste him and savor him, to lose herself to the desire pooling in her belly, her want for him numbing everything else.

"Bella . . ." he muttered, but she ignored him, pressing hard to him and forcing him against the wall.

If he wanted to stop her, he could have easily, could have pushed her back or gripped her arms and forced her away, but Noah showed no sign of wanting to put an end to what she was doing to him. Bella's kisses were hungry, but Noah's were hungrier, his mouth catching up to hers and taking charge, the keys falling to the wooden floor with a jangle as he cupped her bottom and pulled her up into his arms. She locked her legs around his waist, groaned when he spun around so she was the one with her back to the wall. For so many years she'd played it safe, hadn't been with any man, let alone allowed him to take charge, but she trusted Noah. His arms were strong, his touch firm and his intentions clear, but nothing about him physically scared her.

His mouth pulled away from hers, his breathing heavy and hot as he stared down at her, their lips only just parted. "I think we should take this upstairs," he muttered, kissing her again, plucking at her lips.

Bella moaned as his tongue found hers again, so gentle this time, driving her wild, making her tingle all over like she hadn't in . . . forever. She'd never felt desire like this, was desperate to explore every inch of Noah's skin. It was forbidden, it shouldn't be happening, but there was nothing she was going to do to stop it.

"Let's go," she managed when he let up long enough for her to catch her breath.

His arms were locked around her as tight as her thighs were against him. "You sure about this?" he whispered.

She nodded, kissing his jawline. "Yes."

"I can't offer you more," he said solemnly. "I wish I could, but I can't. *We can't.*"

Bella looped her arms around his neck. "I know."

He hesitated, waiting as he stared at her like he was expecting her to change her mind. But she had no intention of stopping what they'd started.

"This is enough," she said, even though she'd never had casual sex before and had no idea why she was telling him she didn't need more when she sure as hell wanted more from him than one night in bed. "We're still just friends."

He kissed her so tenderly she would have slipped straight off him if he hadn't been holding her. And then he carried her up the stairs like she was a featherweight, bracketed in his arms, with her head against this chest, listening to the steady beat of his heart as he stealthily took her to his bedroom.

CHAPTER TWELVE

August 2007

Dear Bella,
I think I'm in love. I can't stop thinking about him. About his
kisses, his hands . . . OMG, he has the most beautiful hands.
So strong, but so gentle. Ugh. I know I sound like a lovesick
teenager. Please go around for dinner to Mom and Dad's on
Sunday night, because he's going and I want you to meet him.
He might be taking a friend, a guy that's like his brother. He
sounds nice—maybe you should meet him? It would be so cute if
we could double-date.

Nothing's happening here, just boring training at base. I wish
I were home so we could go out for a drink and talk. I miss you,
wish we hadn't wasted so much time being at loggerheads. See you
soon, Sis.
Lila

Bella lay in Noah's arms, their bodies slick with sweat, sheets tangled beneath them. She kissed his chest, absently ran her fingers across his skin, tracing every inch of him, wishing they were alone in the house instead of having to be as quiet as mice so they didn't wake the boys up or, even worse, Gray's mom, who was in the guest room at the other end of the hall.

Noah was silent, the only noise his breathing as his chest rose and then fell. She propped herself up on one elbow and looked down at him, pushing her hair back as it fell over her shoulder and down onto Noah.

"Leave it," he murmured, eyes half-closed. "It feels nice."

She grinned and tossed it back so the long strands were against his bare skin again. "You work out way too much," she muttered.

Noah made a noise that she guessed was a laugh, his chest jumping. "Why's that?"

"Because no man's body should ever look this good." She bent to kiss him again, kissing a path all the way to his nipple. She pulled up to look at his tattoo, the edge of it visible from where she was, on his upper arm.

"You don't strike me as the kind of girl who likes guys with tats," he said as she scrutinized him.

She raised a brow. "I'm not, unless they mean something. I'm guessing yours are SEAL related?"

He nodded, sitting up and pulling her with him, leaning back into the pillows. They hadn't had time to rid the bed of all the dress pillows and cushions, although most had scattered to the floor.

"I got the trident-and-eagle one on my arm when I made the SEALs," he told her, arm twisted around so she could study it. Bella traced the outline with her fingertips, admiring the black ink. "The year I made it, the dropout rate was over ninety-five percent. It's usually a little better in the odds department than that. I went with the other guys, and we all got tats."

"What—the rate's actually more like ninety usually, right?" she joked.

His face was serious. "Yeah, something like that."

Bella bit her lip. She'd known it was tough, but she'd thought it was a rumor that it was actually *that* competitive. "And the one on your back?"

She hadn't seen the back one properly—only a glimpse of it when she'd seen him without his shirt in the bathroom. Tonight she'd been a whole lot more interested in his front than his back. Bella smiled as she thought about what they'd just done, how she'd behaved. She was always the one who waited to be asked out when it came to guys, so taking the initiative and making it dead clear to Noah what she wanted from him wasn't exactly something she had a whole heap of practice at.

He sat forward, leaning low so she could see his shoulder from behind. "The grim reaper seemed a good idea at the time, when I was nineteen and excited about the idea of blowing bad guys apart."

She studied it, surprised by how dark and sinister it appeared, so unlike how she thought of Noah. "You wish you didn't have it?"

He sat back up. "No, it's part of my history, a period of time I went through, so I don't regret it. I just wish my younger self hadn't had quite the same outlook as he had back then."

Noah settled back, and she lay against his chest again, listened to the steady, calming beat of his heart. She had no idea where they went from here, but so long as she was in his arms right now, she didn't want to think about what came next. As if reading her mind, Noah's left arm encircled her, held her to his body as he dropped a kiss into her hair. They were naked and relaxed, some-how coming together just when she'd worried things were going to fall apart.

"Just when I close my eyes, the boys are going to wake up," she whispered, lids heavy as she snuggled back further into Noah, using him as her pillow.

"And then Judy's going to poke her head out the door and see you making a naked dash across the hall," Noah said with a chuckle, his big chest rumbling against her ear.

Bella gave in, let her eyes flutter, so tired and so relaxed that it was impossible not to submit to slumber.

"Bells?" he asked, his other arm coming around her as he said her name. "Sweetheart, slide into one of my T-shirts, and we can go jump into your bed. That way you're ready for when they wake."

She shook her head, murmuring no as she held on to him tighter, not wanting to give up the position that felt so damn comfy. His muscles bunched as he pulled her forward.

"Come on," he insisted, swinging his feet down and rummaging for a T-shirt for her.

Bella grumbled when he passed it to her, but she couldn't complain once she had it on. His scent surrounded her, the faint aroma of his cologne clinging to her senses as she wrapped her arms around herself and enjoyed the soft, worn fabric against her skin. Noah pulled on a pair of boxers, and she admired his torso and arms again, his thick thighs. The only difference this time was that she didn't give a damn that he knew she was checking his body out, not after what they'd just done.

"Let's go," he whispered, holding out his hand.

Bella quickly scooped her clothes up to take with her and padded silently out into the upstairs hall and across to her room. She dumped her clothes on the ground and pulled back the covers, slipping into bed at the same time as Noah. She turned and backed into him once he'd flicked off her bedside lamp, wriggled back so she was hard against him as he spooned her. She could feel his arousal, knew that she was teasing him by wiggling so hard against him, and as much as she wanted him to pleasure her again, to do wicked things to her again and again, somehow she slipped into slumber without even realizing it.

~

When Noah woke, he reached for Bella. Usually he woke exhausted from a less than peaceful sleep, but for the first time since he'd been in her bed last, he'd woken thinking of the night before . . . and without being tired. Without even stirring. Only his hand didn't connect with Bella like he'd expected. It connected with something that burst into giggles.

His eyes popped open, and he looked straight into Will's, bright blue and full of laughter.

"We've been watching you," Will announced.

Noah pushed up to see Bella with her eyes still shut, Cooper lying half over her and playing with a strand of her hair.

"I haven't been," she mumbled without moving. "It's all on them."

"What time did you guys come through?" Noah asked, running a hand through his hair.

That made Bella sit up, suddenly awake. "Remember, you carried Will through and decided to stay in bed with us all?" she asked, giving him a look that reminded him of the fact that it was not normal for him to be waking in her bed.

He flopped back down. "Oh yeah. I just didn't, ah, glance at the clock when I brought him in." Noah winked at Bella and enjoyed the blush he received in return.

"Can we play?" Will asked.

Cooper wriggled over Bella and made her groan, no doubt painfully elbowing or kneeing her in a tender place on his way over.

"Transformers. I'll be Commander Starscream," Will announced.

"I'm Bumblebee!" squealed Cooper.

"And I'll be Arcee," Bella said, laughing at him. "She's the only girl one, so I don't get much choice. You, on the other hand, are probably allowed your pick."

Noah found it hard to take his eyes off her, searching her face, wondering whether he'd just fucked up the only good thing he had. Because he was finding it hard to convince himself that Bella honestly believed that them having sex hadn't complicated things and that they were still just friends.

"Hey, Noah?" Cooper suddenly asked, his expression thoughtful as he clambered over Will and curled up beside him. "Do you ever think about Dad?"

Noah choked up, his throat instantly filled with emotion at the way Cooper was looking up at him, so trusting and open. "Yeah, buddy. All the time." He looped an arm around him and kissed the top of his head, leaning over to do the same to Will. "All the time, no exaggeration."

"Me, too," Cooper said. "I wish he was still here. And Mom. I miss her so much."

"So do I, buddy, so do I." Noah kept his arm around him, met Bella's tear-filled gaze, and realized that no matter how easy one individual moment might feel, nothing about what they were doing was easy or okay.

"I know you stayed all night in Bella's bed," Cooper added, changing subject like they'd just been having a conversation about something as nondescript as the weather instead of his father's passing. "It's okay to want to cuddle her. She tells us that all the time. Her cuddles are nice and warm and soft."

Noah laughed then, his sides heaving, close to splitting as he laughed harder than he ever had in his life. Bella joined him, tears spilling down her cheeks as she laughed and laughed, the boys looking on like they were both crazy. If only all he wanted from Bella was a cuddle, life would be so much easier.

∾

Noah stared at his hands. During the day, he could clearly see that there was no blood on them. He wasn't crazy. But at night . . . he shuddered. Nothing in his training could have helped him to deal with the night terrors he'd experienced since the deployment he'd been on when everything had turned to shit. When he'd held one of his men in his arms, blood all over himself, covering every part of him and drenching his clothes as he hauled the guy to safety. Only to lose him before their backup arrived, before he could get him into the Chinook. And then there were the brothers who'd been gunned down alongside him.

He leaned down on the counter, wishing he could block the memories and just force them away forever. When he was deployed, he was focused—nothing clouded his judgment or hindered his thoughts. But that was because he'd never formed relationships that meant he couldn't give his all, never given that part of him away to anyone. All that had changed now, and it terrified him.

"I'm just heading out again," Bella called out.

Noah hauled himself up, didn't want her to see him like that. There was so much he still needed to tell her, about why he'd stepped up for the boys, what he was thinking of doing. He just had no idea how to blurt it all out.

"You need me to collect the boys this afternoon?" he asked.

She leaned in the doorframe, dressed for work in a pencil skirt, pretty blouse, and heels. She looked gorgeous, and what he wanted was to storm the distance between them and forget about everything with her in his arms, her body jammed against his, pillowy lips surrendered to him.

"Noah?"

He blinked. "Sorry?"

"You look like you're a million miles away," she said. "I asked what you thought of going to my folks' place for dinner. Mom's been asking, and she just left me another voicemail. I don't think I can keep avoiding her."

He grinned. "I love your folks. Phone and say yes, and I'll meet you there tonight, so you can work all day."

Bella hesitated, folded her arms across her chest, and then gave him a shy smile before coming closer. "About last night," she started.

Noah reached for her, stroked his fingers down her shoulder. "We don't need to talk about it. It just . . ."—he smiled—"happened."

She looked embarrassed. "I don't want things to be awkward between us."

"Hey, you'd already seen me naked in the bath. This was just me getting one back."

Bella leaned into him, and he put his arms around her. "Last night was great, but we're still just friends, right?" he murmured.

She nodded against his chest, probably thinking the same thing he was: that they didn't have a choice. "A friend that needs a hug every now and then to combat the severe sleep deprivation I'm experiencing these days. I think natural moms have different hormone levels—you know, after childbirth and all that. Must help them."

He chuckled, moving a step back, hands on her shoulders now. "I dare you to say that to a group of moms and come away without war wounds," he joked, liking how easy things felt between them.

She laughed. "I'll see you tonight. I think Dad's been looking forward to seeing you again."

He nodded and watched her go. He knew he made it look easy, the way he was with the boys most of the time, but in reality it was anything *but*. Opening up to the boys was natural in a way, but he had to force himself to be so relaxed with them, to shut down the side of him that was always on the defensive and used to keeping everyone at arm's length. And Bella? She'd done something to him. For years he'd tried to get under her skin, had wanted to irritate her enough to get her attention, desperate to kiss her again after the fleeting fumble they'd had when she'd been tipsy. Trouble was, now that it had happened for real, he had no idea what his next move was. He couldn't let her down gently and move on; they lived in the same house, for God's sake, and besides, he didn't want it to be just a one-night exchange—he still needed more. But how could they sleep together again without things starting to look a lot like a relationship?

Noah stared out the window, watched her SUV reverse out the drive. He wanted her in his bed, body warm to him, stopping the nightmares. He wanted her naked skin skimming his, wanted to kiss her over and over until her lips were plump and pink.

He grimaced and continued to stare out the window at nothing in particular. It was time he was strong and put an end to what was going on. He just had no idea how the hell he was going to do that without ruining everything.

Gray's dad has always taught him that honesty was the best policy, but right now he wasn't so sure.

~

Bella walked into the café, trying to keep her shoulders back and her head held high, even though it was almost impossible. She was long overdue coming in, but she hadn't exactly been looking forward to it or had a lot of spare time on her hands. She gripped her purse tight, remembering the last time she'd walked through the doors, the day when she'd been so worried about Lila, even though a voice in the back of her head had been telling her that everything was fine, that she was being silly. If only she'd flicked back a few texts to Corey rather than complete radio silence.

"Hey, stranger."

She gulped and forced herself to keep moving. "Hey, Corey."

"I was starting to think I'd never hear from you again."

Bella smiled. "Guilty as charged. I'm sorry."

"You've got a lot going on—I get it."

She knew he was still expectant, though, that he wasn't going to be prepared for what she was about to say. In her experience, good-looking guys were very rarely used to being the one let down, and she had no idea where to start, except by being honest.

"I'm really sorry that I haven't called you back. It's why I wanted to come down in person and see you."

He raised an eyebrow. "I'll make you a coffee, and we can grab a table and chat. It's still quiet."

Bella hesitated, wishing she were better at this sort of thing. "Corey, I had a really good time the other night . . ." she started, clearing her throat.

His smile faded but didn't disappear entirely as he looked up, no longer focused on the coffee he was making her. "Why do I feel like there's a 'but' coming?"

She was the one forcing the smile now. "I've been through so much these past few months, and if I'm perfectly honest, there's someone else."

He pushed the cup that was supposed to be hers to the side. "It's that guy, isn't it? The one you're living with?"

Bella balled her fists, not sure what to say. Her nails were digging into her palms, her discomfort rising. "I really don't want to go into details . . ."

"Look, I get it. Maybe we would have had a chance before, but after everything you've gone through and the situation you're in?" He shrugged. "I guessed as much, to be honest, after the way he looked at you. That buzz we've had between us kind of fizzled the moment we went out together, right?"

Bella took a deep breath, grateful that he was being so understanding. "So I can still come in for coffee? Because you make *really* great coffee."

Corey laughed and stepped around the counter, opening his arms and giving her a friendly hug. "No hard feelings. Just keep me in mind if you have any cute single friends."

They both laughed as she hugged him back. "I sure will. You're a great guy."

Bella waited for him to make her a takeout coffee and then left, waving at him over her shoulder as she did so and feeling relieved. They'd only gone out once, but letting him down had seemed impossible. She needed to learn to back herself more often.

She jumped in her car, put her coffee into the holder, and dialed her assistant. She ran through some tasks she needed her to do and let her know where she was going to be, then called Serena as she drove.

"I was just thinking about you," Serena said with a laugh when she answered.

"Oh, really? Were you seeing me let down the sweetest guy in the world?"

She could almost see Serena frowning. "Eek, no. Sorry. I take it you told Corey he wasn't the one?"

"Yeah." Bella groaned. "He was so cute, but it just wasn't meant to be."

Serena stayed silent except for a long sigh.

"I haven't seen you in so long, and there's no way I'm going to have any free time this week." Bella missed her friend. With Lila gone and not enough hours in the day to even chat to Serena, she was feeling like a ship all alone at sea. Noah was great, but he was different, their relationship still awkward in so many ways, even though they were spending so much time together. "I miss you."

"How's Noah?" Serena asked. "And I miss you, too. Just in case that's not implied."

"Want to meet him? Noah, I mean."

"What? Are you kidding me! *Yes.* All I remember is that he was handsome and cute. I'm a little hazy on the details from whenever it was I last saw him."

Now Bella was the one laughing. "Just promise me first that you never fooled around with him? At Lila's wedding or anything? I couldn't stand it."

"You like him, don't you? I mean"—Serena exhaled—"you *seriously* like him."

"Maybe." *Yes.* "I don't know. But I need to tell you something else—we've been getting these letters . . ."

"Letters? From who?"

Bella's breath was shaky as she let it go. Just telling someone else even a little bit was a huge step, instead of holding on to it as her little secret, something that only Noah knew about.

"From Lila. She wrote them before she died, and I've been getting them every week for a little while."

Serena was silent. "From Lila?" she asked, her voice unusually soft.

"We're going around to Mom and Dad's tonight for dinner. I know they'd love to see you, so why don't you come, too? I'll tell you all about it then, but it's just between you and me."

"Okay. I can't wait to hear more."

Bella laughed. "I've stunned you so much, you haven't even asked the one thing you always ask me."

Serena laughed back. "What's she cooking?"

Bella burst out laughing. "Seriously, is that what you're making your decision on?" She was pleased she'd called her friend. They always had the same silly conversation whenever her mom asked Serena over; it was a long-standing joke that Serena only said yes when she heard the menu, because Bella's mom always cooked whatever Serena requested. "Fried frogs legs. What do you say?"

"You should have started with that. I'd have said yes straightaway."

They both laughed. "For the record, I still haven't forgiven you for the whole date thing, but I'm prepared to let it go. And second, she's doing her famous sweet-and-sour chicken over rice. I put in the request."

Serena made a noise that sounded like her smacking her lips together, and Bella gave her the time and said good-bye. Then she left a voicemail for her mom, telling her she had another guest, knowing she'd love to see Serena. They'd been best friends through school, with Serena spending as much time at their place as she could, since she was a friend of both Bella and Lila. They'd had a lot of fun over the years, and she was part of the family, the kind of family friend who could just pop around for a coffee uninvited or let herself in with the key hidden under a stone near the front door. Which was something Serena had done a lot when her parents were going through a divorce.

Bella turned up the radio, determined to enjoy the rest of her drive time. Between the boys and work, she hardly had any time to herself, with no one talking to her or touching her or wanting her. Or all three at once. She needed to make the most of every moment on her own. And keep her brain off Noah, which was easier said than done. Especially when all she could think about every time she wasn't busy was the slow, gentle curve of his smile, eyes the color of the ocean on a perfect summer day, and that body of his, carved from pure muscle. She turned the music up even louder.

~

Noah marched the boys from the car, trying to be stern. He wasn't good at being the tough parent, but this was one of those times that he didn't have much choice.

"You know I'm still very angry, right?" he muttered as he kept a hand on each shoulder, walking them up to the house.

They were both quiet until Cooper let out a giggle and slapped his hand over his mouth.

"If you're so angry, why do you keep cracking up?"

Noah made a grumbling sound that came out as more of a growl, but it didn't seem to worry, let alone frighten, them. "I'm not cracking up."

"Yeah, you kind of were," Will said.

"Bella is going to kill me. I mean, who do you think is going to clean all that up?" Noah asked, shaking his head and wishing he'd had time to clean up before driving over. But they were expected at six, and he hated being late more than he hated leaving a mess behind.

"Hey boys!" Christina, Bella's mom, came rushing out the front door, arms open wide and bending low as the boys ran toward her.

"Grandma!" they both shouted.

"Oh, wow," she exclaimed, looking at Noah over the top of their heads. "And wow again."

"They got into the face paint while I was trying to tidy up the house."

Christina cracked up as she glanced from face to face.

"See! Grandma thinks it's funny, too!" Cooper said excitedly.

Noah groaned. "Do you see what I'm dealing with on a daily basis? They're killing me. And Bella's gonna kill me."

They all had a laugh, and Christina ushered them into the house as he followed. "Don't worry—I'll get them cleaned up."

They'd left a trail of paint through the living room at home, not to mention the state of the bathroom after they'd tried to wash it off their arms and hands. Now it was just their faces covered, completely smeared in green, yellow, and red paint.

"Hey, Noah," Bella's dad called out as he walked through the kitchen. "Come take a load off."

Noah smiled gratefully and joined James on the sofa. "Seriously, the respect I have right now for stay-at-home parents is insane."

James chuckled. "I hear you, son. Whenever I was home from deployment, I'd take the girls to give Christina a break, and I swear it was tougher than anything I went through when I was serving."

They both chuckled, and Noah felt strangely comfortable. No matter what either of them said, child care was nothing on some of the things they'd seen. Tougher in many ways and requiring huge mental strength, but the mundane details of being a parent . . . it wasn't comparable to seeing children left burning and still alive alongside their blown-to-pieces parents in a war zone, friends dead alongside you when just a moment ago they'd been talking shit about life back home. Those were the unsaid things hanging between them and why he liked spending time with Bella's dad.

"So how's my girl?" James asked.

Noah looked up, smiling as the boys ran through, arms out in the air as they pretended to be planes and received a raised-eyebrow look from their granddad when he caught sight of their faces.

"She's good. Coping well." Noah watched as James rose, crossed into the kitchen to take a couple of beers from the fridge, passing him one on his way back. "I think she's stronger than anyone probably ever realized."

They were silent a few minutes, clinking beer bottles and both sitting back to take a sip.

"She always was strong. Lila was the one who showed everyone how strong she could be, but Bella was always the strong silent one. Determined, but without anyone having to know about it."

Noah met her dad's gaze. "Sounds a lot like me."

He laughed. "Yeah, which is why I always wondered why you managed to rub her up the wrong way so bad."

Now it was Noah laughing. "You noticed that, too?"

"The whole world noticed it," James said, still chuckling. "But things seem a little less heated lately. I hope she's giving you a break."

"She hates what I do," Noah said bluntly.

"Yep, no way to sugarcoat that. But it ain't so much that she hates what you do, as it is how scared she is of losing you. It puts kids through a lot having a parent serve, so give her time."

Noah considered his words. He shouldn't be talking about work with a civilian, but then James was a retired lieutenant general who had served most of his lifetime and dedicated everything to the Army. He needed to talk to someone, and right now that someone being James felt right.

"What would you think of me if I said I was thinking of retiring?" he finally asked.

James studied him, leaning forward and watching him. "I'd ask if you had rocks in your head," he said bluntly. "You can't give up being a SEAL to be a—a *stay-at-home dad*."

Noah sipped his beer. Maybe the old man hadn't been the best person to talk to after all. "I don't want to be a stay-at-home dad, but even if I did, I know now that it'd be worth it. Those boys are freaking amazing, even if they do almost kill me every day."

"Gray was still serving, and so was Lila. They'll cope with it."

Noah shook his head. "But it's me who doesn't want to do it anymore. Not when I have the boys to consider after everything they've lost." He hung his head, staring at the bottle slung between his hands. "I'm the best at what I do because I've never had anything to lose. Things have changed. *I've changed.*"

James was still staring at him when he looked up. "You need to do what's right for you. But don't let anyone talk you out of doing what you love, what you're passionate about, because you'll only end up bitter and resentful."

"Bella doesn't know about all this, and even if I wanted to tell her, I can't," he said softly, wishing he could have spoken to her about it. He didn't know what it meant, what was going to happen, what he even wanted.

"What will you do?" James asked, sitting deeper in his chair now, no longer looking so alarmed.

"I've been offered a position. I'd be training the recruits, still traveling a bit to places like Alaska for cold weather training, but essentially I'd be based here in California. And then there's another position, higher up, something I can't talk about yet."

"And it's what you want to do?"

Noah's hands started to shake. The decision was huge, almost impossible to process. "I don't know. I honestly don't know." He was so conflicted, the choice running through his head day and night. "I don't know if I'll ever know, but I have to make the decision soon."

"There's a time limit?"

Noah nodded. "Yeah. I'll have one more deployment, sounds like something's heating up, and I'll be out of here sooner rather than later, but that's strictly between the two of us. I shouldn't be talking to you about any of this."

"You have to do what you have to do, son," James said. "Just make sure you're doing it for the right reasons."

Noah agreed. The problem was that he no longer knew why he was doing it. Before taking over custody of the boys, he'd have sworn that the only way he'd have ever retired was when he was forced, but things had changed. He'd changed. Life had changed.

"What are you guys talking about? What does Noah have to do for the right reasons?"

Noah clamped his mouth shut and wished to hell he'd just stayed silent rather than chewing it over with her dad.

"Ah, nothing much," he said.

Her dad rose and opened his arms. "We're just shooting the breeze. Come give your old dad a hug."

Bella shot him a look that said she wasn't convinced.

"Hi, everyone!"

Noah looked up, not knowing they were expecting anyone else.

"Hi," he replied, studying the woman's face, trying to place her at the same time as Bella spun around and hugged the blonde. "I know we've met before, but . . ."

"Serena," she said, holding out her hand as he stood, her other hand on Bella's shoulder. She slid her palm against his, her smile hard to read as she blatantly checked him out. "We've met a few times in the past."

Noah tried not to feel too guilty. Given how beautiful she was, he was pretty damn certain that he would have been more than friendly to her at whatever events they'd been to together. He had a habit of liking all of Lila's cute friends.

"Hi, second daddy," Serena said when she let go of his hand, giving Bella's dad a big hug.

"Hi to you, too," James said, holding her in his arms and hugging her back as if she were one of his daughters.

Noah remembered Bella talking about Serena and suddenly recalled that she was the friend who'd set her up on the date. He grinned. "So you're the one to blame for Bella's hot date the other night, huh?"

She spun around and held up her hands. "Guilty."

"Bella went on a date?" her dad spluttered. "Get out of here!"

"Bella what?" Suddenly her mom was in on the conversation, head poking around the corner from the kitchen. "Who did she date?"

"Oh my God, Noah!" Bella exclaimed.

Noah exchanged glances with Serena, who dived straight in and turned the attention off him.

"The cute coffee guy. I set them up."

"How did it go?" her mom asked.

Serena smiled sweetly at him, raising an eyebrow and answering before Bella could. "He was nice, but I think her heart's already taken."

"What?" Her mom sounded all breathless, like she'd missed out on the most important piece of news.

"We're not discussing my love life! No more questions," Bella said, looking embarrassed as she followed her mom back into the kitchen.

Noah stared back at Serena, hearing what she'd said but refusing to let her bait him. He was staying out of this, and besides, there was no way she was seriously talking about him. He still held her gaze, not wanting to be the first to back down. *She absolutely isn't being serious, or she's talking about someone else.*

Bella walked back in with a glass of water. "We're going to pretend like that entire conversation didn't happen and start over, okay?"

They all laughed, but Noah shut up when she gave him a sharp stare. Serena didn't look the least bit worried.

"I'm going to go find the boys, play with them awhile," she said.

Bella flopped down onto the sofa beside him the moment Serena disappeared, kicking off her heels before tucking her feet up.

"How was your day?" Noah asked, steering into neutral territory.

"Exhausting. I'm just so tired."

"You can always ask us to help out more," James said. "You two don't have to go this alone. We love having the boys."

"We should take them up on that," Noah said, "before they realize what little gremlins the boys really are and rescind their offer."

Bella laughed and reached for his beer, taking a big sip before passing it back to him. "I needed that."

He raised it for her again, but she shook her head. "No, thanks." Bella glanced between her dad and Noah before continuing to speak. "You guys seem a little suspicious. Like you were talking about something secret before I barged in."

Noah traded glances with her dad again, pretending like he had no idea what she was getting at.

"You know, the one time Lila got all upset about Gray talking to Dad, he was asking for her hand in marriage."

Noah laughed and her father chuckled. "I can assure you I haven't asked for your hand, sweet maiden."

Thankfully for Noah, Christine called out that dinner was almost ready, and Bella disappeared off to the kitchen, flashing them a wide smile as she got up. He finally turned to her dad.

"I haven't seen Bella smile like that in a long time," James told him.

Noah gulped, sipping his beer for something to do. Because despite the fact that he'd lost his best friend only a few months ago, he didn't recall a time when he was so settled and prepared to smile either.

~

Bella twirled her wine glass between her fingers and sat back, staring out into the street. Serena was getting ready to leave, Noah was doing the dishes with her dad, and her mom was snuggled up on the sofa, watching a DVD with the boys. It had been a nice night, but it had also been one of those nights that made her miss her sister terribly. Because they'd always had family dinner nights and had enjoyed playing with the boys and arguing over what dish they wanted their mom to make. And now here she was, an only child.

She also couldn't stop thinking about what she'd overheard her dad and Noah talking about. It kept playing through her mind, something about a decision, making sure it was for the right reason. Was it about deployment? Would he have spoken to her father about it before her? She shuddered. How could she be contemplating a future with someone who didn't include her in his decision making? Noah wasn't just disruptive; he'd turned her life upside down when it was already in a state of turmoil.

"You okay?"

She smiled up at Serena as her friend sat down beside her on the porch step. "I'm fine. Just reminiscing."

Serena slung an arm around her. "Are you thinking about how much you used to despise Noah? You know, compared to how much you *lurve* the man now."

Bella scowled. "Honestly, S. I could strangle you sometimes."

"So you wouldn't mind if I asked him out? He's pretty darn cute."

She knew she was being baited, but she couldn't bite her tongue and not say anything. "You so much as—"

Serena just laughed and clinked their glasses together. "Just kidding. And you can just take things slowly with him, see what happens."

Bella took a big sip of wine, then another. "It's not that simple."

"Mmm," said Serena, sensing Bella's reluctance to talk and seeking another way to get her to open up. "Can I ask about the letters? Tell me about them."

"Lila wrote letters in case anything ever happened when she was away serving. They've been mailed to us every week for a month now." She stared out into the dark. "I'm not sure if they're a curse or a godsend."

Serena's smile lit up her face. "That's incredible. Have you told your parents? Let them read them?"

"No." Bella sighed. "It's complicated. I mean, they're personal, for Noah and me, to bring us closer together or something. Each letter has a message for us, sometimes for me, and tells us what date to go on. It's cute."

"So you've been going on them, these dates?" Serena asked. "You fox!"

"They're not real dates, more just friendship outings or something. It's kind of how I stopped being so—I don't know—resentful of him, and started—"

"Falling for him?" Serena's voice was softer now, all hint of teasing gone.

"He's gotten under my skin, but I want so bad to be able to push him away."

"I don't think you mean that. I mean, he's made you happy, made you and the boys smile. Is he so bad?"

"He's caused nothing but chaos from the moment he arrived back, and now I think he's being deployed and I don't . . ." She stopped talking, about to cry and not wanting to.

Serena looked sympathetic. "Honey, of course he's caused chaos. He's a bachelor trying to be a dad, not to mention the fact that he's used to a crazy kind of job and not perfect domesticity."

"Believe me, we're far from perfect domesticity," Bella grumbled.

"He's made you feel things you haven't felt in a long while, that's all. And what makes you think he's being deployed?"

"Nothing. Just fragments of something I overheard."

"Didn't your mom tell you about eavesdropping when you were a kid?" Serena asked, nudging her in the side with her elbow. "It's dangerous. If you're worried about something, just ask him."

They didn't say anything for a while, just sat side by side.

"Speaking of your mom," Serena suddenly said, picking up their conversation right where they'd left off, "you know that you have to show the letters to her, right? They'll mean a lot to her."

Bella knew she was right, but keeping them just for her had been easier to deal with, or maybe it had just been easier to pretend they were real, as if they were actually arriving from her sister. Not sent by a lawyer who'd had them in a drawer in case they ever had to be sent. "I'll tell her. Tonight."

Serena reached for her hand, holding it loosely, but the fact they were connected helped.

"You know I love you, right?"

Bella leaned sideways so her head could rest on Serena's shoulder. "I know. I love you, too."

A noise alerted Bella to the fact they were no longer alone. She pulled up and looked back, gaze landing on Noah. He was standing in the doorway, leaning his shoulder into the timber, hands thrust into his pockets as he watched them. The casual, relaxed way he watched her always unsettled her—she doubted that would ever change. Only now it didn't frustrate the hell out of her as much as make her pulse quicken and make her wish he was touching her at the same time as his eyes roved over her body. She still had to fight the urge to snap at him, push him away, but she knew it was because she was scared of how he made her feel, and for a self-confessed control freak, being organic and open with her feelings didn't come naturally to her.

She chastised herself. Why was she trying to make excuses for the way he made her feel? He *had* caused chaos and disrupted her life, frustrated her more than any other human being ever had!

"Am I interrupting?" Noah asked, the warmth of his blue eyes in complete harmony with the upturn of his mouth and his softly spoken words.

"Not at all."

"Yes!" Bella shot back at the same time.

Serena rose and touched a hand to Bella's shoulder, leaning down to whisper in her ear. "Don't be so scared of the past that you close yourself off to the future. Playing it safe isn't always the right decision."

Heat rose through Bella's body, making her cheeks burn, and she hoped that Noah hadn't heard Serena's low words. She doubted he had, but the idea of him knowing they'd been talking about him embarrassed her.

Bella took a breath, watched Serena go, waited until she'd disappeared into the house. Then she forced herself to stand, left her wine glass on the step as she turned to Noah. He pushed off from where he'd been leaning, stopping only when she put her hands on her hips.

"Yes, you're interrupting, Noah," she said, her tone low. She'd finally started to give part of herself to another human being, to a man, and he was driving her crazy, making her second-guess her every thought.

He looked amused, folded his arms across his chest. "Oh, I am, am I?"

"You're interrupting my life," she told him, walking faster now, slamming her hands to his chest, shoving him back. Her emotions were spiraling. She wanted him, she wanted to be rid of him, but she was suddenly angry and scared, too. "You've interrupted everything. You've made me—" She hit out, harder this time, wanting to force him back, to take back some control.

"What?" he asked, catching her hands before she had the chance to shove him again, holding tight around her wrists. "What else have I done?"

His smile disappeared, replaced by a harder stare, his jaw carved from stone.

"Everything," she managed, fighting for her arms. "I don't want you to go," she whispered.

"I'm not going anywhere. What made you think that?"

Noah's stare never wavered, eyes locked on hers.

"You talking to my dad. When I walked in, I—"

"Bella, I'm not going anywhere."

190

She shook her head. "But if not now, then someday." Her words were barely audible.

"And if and when that day actually comes, for certain you'll be the first to know."

And then she gave in. Bella fought one last time to slam her palms into him, to hurt him, and when that didn't work, she slammed her lips into his instead.

Noah didn't react at first, still had hold of her, was still restraining her. But when she stood on tiptoe and kissed him like her life depended on it, he wrapped his arm tight around her, not letting her go, hardly even letting her breathe.

"Noah," she whispered when she pulled back for a second to gasp, to fill her lungs with enough oxygen to do the same thing all over again. She slid her fingers tight into his hair, gripping at him, not wanting to let him get away now that she'd finally given in.

"Your dad better not have a shotgun handy," Noah muttered, spinning them around so it was her back to the side of the house, walking her until she was hard against it.

Bella groaned, arching back, head to the wall as he kissed down her neck, mouth hot. She yanked him back up by his hair, loving what he was doing, but impatient and wanting his lips back on hers, needing him like she'd never needed anything in her life before.

He kissed her relentlessly, over and over again, until Bella finally pushed him back, gasping for air.

"Noah," she whispered, palms flat to his chest.

Noah pressed his forehead to hers, body low so he could match her height, his intense blue eyes piercing into hers.

"I'm sorry," he murmured.

"For what?"

He stepped back, taking her hands in his. "For causing you pain, for worrying you. For everything."

Bella squeezed his hands back, still watching him, staring into eyes that made her feel like she was so out of control that it terrified her. She breathed in and out, trying to calm down, trying to think of something else to say.

"I think I'm going to tell Mom, if it's okay with you. About the letters," she said.

Noah smiled, the soft porch light playing across his features, his strong jaw and full lips mesmerizing in the half light. "They're yours to share, Bella."

The moment was over, felt like it was long gone, and Bella wrapped her arms around herself, moving back into the light.

"I'm going to head back in," Noah said, shoving his hands in his jean pockets, looking as confused as her.

"I think I'll just take a minute out here," Bella said. She wanted to pull him back, just forget about everything and be in his arms for a few more minutes; only their problems weren't as simple as a quick kiss and make up. They'd hadn't slept together since that first time, although the air around them felt constantly charged.

Heat flooded her body again as she watched him walk away, a tremor of something she couldn't identify sending ripples through her. Noah was safe but dangerous, irresistible and so not her type, all at the same time, all rolled into one. She couldn't rely on him, couldn't get close to him, couldn't . . . she tried to push him from her mind and couldn't. *Because part of him is so damn right it's killing me.*

Bella righted herself, took a few breaths until the boys were gone, then forced herself to walk inside and head to the downstairs restroom to check her makeup. Her lip gloss was long gone, and she ran the pads of her fingers around her mouth to check for smudges, not wanting her mom to know she'd been making out with Noah on their porch. Then she stared at herself in the mirror, blinked back at the woman staring at her. It had been a long time since she'd felt like this, since she'd had a flutter in her belly that she couldn't shake. Serena had been right: she was falling for Noah. And no amount of pretending was going to change that. Just like no amount of wishing was going to change his job and the fact that with the click of someone else's fingers, she could lose him.

The one thing she could do was head inside and confess to her mom about the letters. It was about the only thing within her power to control right now.

CHAPTER THIRTEEN

M om, do you have a few minutes?" Bella walked in to the living room where her mom was tidying up. The boys were still upstairs playing hide-and-seek in pairs with Noah and her dad, and she couldn't avoid telling her mom any longer, wanted to tell her before the night was over. She was used to sharing everything with her mom and sister, and lately it felt like she was bottling everything up, ready to burst from the frustration of it all.

"One minute or a hundred, darling. I've got all the time in the world," her mom said, putting down the coffee mugs she'd been carrying and giving Bella her full attention. "What's on your mind?"

Bella squirmed, fidgeting from one foot to the other. "Can we sit down?"

"Is it that serious?" Her mom laughed, but when Bella didn't laugh back, the look on her face became less humorous.

"I'm just tired. I want to curl up and talk."

"Go sit down. I'll make us a coffee. See if you can manage to rest a little before the boys come back down."

"You gave them way too much sugar," Bella groaned as she flopped down into a sofa.

"Isn't that what grandmas are supposed to do? Feed 'em up, then send 'em home?"

Bella smiled, realizing how idyllic this would all look to an outsider, to someone who didn't know what they'd all been through. Two little boys, a mom and dad, and doting grandparents.

She stared blankly at the TV as she waited, wishing she had a few hours to herself to watch *Grey's Anatomy*, then thinking how selfish that sounded when the boys she was looking after had lost their mom and dad. Her life seemed like a series of guilt trips lately.

"Does it make me an awful person to wish for some time to myself?" Bella asked when her mom returned and placed two steaming mugs on the coffee table.

"No, sweetheart, it doesn't. The boys are full on." Her mom sighed. "Find me a mom who doesn't wish for a few hours of her old life, and you'll find me a liar. I adored you girls, but man, did I crave my old life sometimes! Going to the movies, being able to stay up late without having to worry about kids waking me at the crack of dawn. Going out for drinks with the girls. I wouldn't have traded you and Lila for the world, but I also missed some of my single days."

"Before Dad?" Bella asked, pleased she'd opened up to her mom instead of trying to pretend like everything was perfect.

"No, not before your father. When it was just us, doing whatever we wanted when he was home."

Bella smiled, thinking of her parents when they were younger. "Did he ever drive you crazy? I mean, actually crazy?"

Her mom sat back, smile on her face as she kicked off her shoes and tucked her feet up beneath her. Bella did the same, curling into the sofa.

"When I met your dad, we butted heads like you wouldn't believe. He infuriated me as much as he intrigued me."

"But you still knew he was the one?"

Her mom reached for her coffee and blew on it, smiling before she sipped. "Your dad challenged me, and as much as I hated to admit it at the time, I loved him for it. We still argue—heavens, you girls both know that. But we've always agreed on the important things, and I'm sure I would have been bored with a man who didn't stand up for his beliefs or one who tried to stop me from being the opinionated, outspoken person I've always been."

"My mom the feminist," Bella said with a chuckle, nudging her mom with her big toe.

"Hey, I love men, don't get me wrong, but until we have a female president, I'll continue to harp on about women's rights."

Bella loved her for it, couldn't agree with her more wholeheartedly. As kids, they'd been told they could do anything, achieve anything. As young adults, their mom had made it clear that there was no glass ceiling if they didn't believe in one.

"Mom, there's something I've been wanting to tell you."

Her mom wrapped her hands around the oversize coffee mug and sat back.

"I've been receiving letters," Bella started, feeling guilty at keeping quiet about them for so long. "This is going to sound crazy, but they're from Lila."

Her mom sighed. "I know."

"What? You know?" Bella almost sloshed her coffee all over herself.

"I've been keeping something from you, too."

She stared at her mom. "I don't understand. How can you know?"

"Because, sweetheart, I've been the one sending them."

Bella's hand shook as she moved her coffee back to the table, body trembling. "You—you . . ." she stuttered.

Her mom reached for her, stroked her hair, and left her hand to rest on her arm, warm and calming. "Lila wrote those a while

196

back, before her last tour. She put them in a box, tied string around it, and told me I was only to open it if something happened to both her and Gray. She wanted to be prepared in case the worst happened."

"And you didn't think to tell me?" Bella asked, hating how angry her tone sounded, but unable to help it. "You didn't think to just give them all to me instead of putting me through this?"

"Would it have made it any easier?" her mom asked. "She wanted you to look forward to receiving them, as something to keep you going, to pick you up when the going got rough."

"Mom!" Bella exclaimed.

"Don't give me that tone, Bella. Can you imagine how hard it's been for me, sending those letters every week without opening them, holding them to my chest and knowing that my daughter wrote them when her heart was still beating? Sitting in my home, tucking them away and swearing me to secrecy?"

Bella swallowed away any anger she had, waves of guilt washing over her. "I'm sorry," she managed.

"I wanted to read them, not because I needed to hear what she'd said, but because I wanted to see her handwriting. And I had to wait two months before Noah moved into the house, two months of wishing terribly that I could tell you what I had for you."

"How many more are there?" Bella asked, desperate to know.

She received a sad smile in response. "Lila asked me not to tell you, not to talk to you about them. I'm not going to ruin what she had planned. I can't."

Bella nodded. She understood. There was only one thing her mom could do and that was follow her youngest daughter's wishes. "Would you like to read them? The ones you've already sent?"

Her mom's eyes flooded with tears, and Bella leaned forward to hold her, to wrap her arms tight around her as she started to cry, too.

"I just want my baby girl back," her mom whispered.

"Me too," Bella murmured, holding her mom even tighter. "I don't want to mess up this being-a-mom thing, and I don't want to lose Noah, and I don't . . ." She stopped, realizing what she'd just said.

"Noah's a good man, Bella. You're the only one who's taken so long to realize it."

Bella pulled back. "Maybe I just didn't like the way he always made me feel, the way he always challenged me, put my back up against the wall." She fought a blush, thinking about the fact that he'd literally just done that to her half an hour ago on her parents' porch.

"If a man doesn't get under your skin, then there's no fire. Something about a partner has to rile you up."

"But it's more than that," Bella confessed. "I'm terrified of losing him just when I've finally started to accept him, to need him." She needed to get it off her chest, needed to share just how frustrated she was. "I can't bear the thought of letting him close and then having him ripped away, like Lila . . ."

Her mom nodded, tears glistening in her eyes. "I know, sweetheart. I've been with your father almost forty years in case you've forgotten, and more years than not, I worried myself stupid."

"But it was worth it?" Bella asked. She had never needed to hear such intimate details of her parents' relationship before but was hanging on her mom's every word now.

"Yes, darling, it was worth it. Despite all the sleepless nights, I wouldn't trade it for anything. Because it was our journey to take, and what a wonderful journey it's been."

Bella smiled. Talking about Noah with her mom hadn't been her plan. She glanced up at her mom to see her reaction. "The letters send us on a date each week. Lila's laughing at me from somewhere."

Her mom was wide-eyed before bursting into laughter. "Get out of here! That's what they're all about?"

Bella stretched out. "Yeah. Seems like she knew something I didn't. I guess she's just lucky that we're both single."

"You ladies in here?"

At her father's call, Bella pulled herself together and sat up. She had a feeling their little quiet time was almost over. "Yep, we're here."

Her dad appeared, Cooper over his shoulder, and then a moment later Noah was there. He had Will wrapped around him, legs around his waist, arms around his neck.

"The sugar high's over," Noah said. "I think it's time to go."

Bella took a quick, final swig of her coffee and rose, touching her mom's shoulder as she passed. "Let's get them in their PJs and tucked up in the car," she said. "It's been a big night for them."

She glanced at Noah, part of her igniting with heat at what they'd shared on the porch, another part wondering *What if?*, and the most sensible part of her screaming that she should run fast in the opposite direction. Because everything had changed between them, and she had a gut-deep feeling that there was no going back.

~

"Bella, there's a letter here for you!" Will called out, riding around the front yard on his bike, his little brother trailing after him. For a four-year-old Cooper was doing pretty well, but Will had two years on him and was showing off.

She was sitting inside, watching from the front window and trying to catch up on work, but the moment she heard his call, she dropped what she was doing and ran out. He was waving it in the air, ringing his bell at the same time and almost falling off as he tried to do two things at once. Bella held out her hands to stop him, and he shot straight past her, dodging her arm and giggling.

"Hey, get back here with that!" she demanded, chasing after him.

Both boys laughed, and she danced around, pretending to grab at them without actually knocking them off their bikes. After dodging around them for a while, she eventually held out her hand, and Will gave her the letter. Just like every time she was about to open one, her pulse started to race, desperate to see her sister's handwriting, to read over the words quickly, then slowly, then even more slowly the third time. Because she always read them over and over until she knew them word for word.

But this time she didn't open it, just held it to her chest, loving the fact that Lila had once held it, touched it, herself. She wanted to wait for Noah this time because this time she was almost as excited about the actual date with Noah as she was about reading the letter. She'd already organized her mom to come over and take care of the boys that night rather than wait until the following evening— now that she'd confessed the general thrust of the letters to her, she couldn't see any point in getting a sitter.

She left the boys to play and went back inside, reaching for her phone from where she'd left it beside her laptop. She sent Noah a quick text, asking when he'd be back. The boys had been so tired from their night at her folks' place, then school and pre-K the following day, that she'd taken a leaf out of Noah's book and decided to let them stay home. Although she was finding that running a business and simultaneously keeping an eye on two energetic kids wasn't all that easy.

Bella logged back in to her computer, wanting to reply to some emails, but she noticed the boys had discarded their bikes and were running back in. She sighed and closed the lid, deciding to give up for the day.

"How about we have ice cream?" Bella asked, holding her hands out for high fives as they passed.

"Yeah!" Cooper squealed.

"You're the best, B," Will said.

She spun around and walked with them into the kitchen, a hand on each of them, loving the sound of their chatter and laughter. They'd done so well, been so brave, but she felt that so often that she was scared of bringing their parents up, in case she upset them, when she needed to make sure they talked about Lila and Gray every day, no matter how hard it was on all of them.

"What was your mom's favorite flavor?" she asked as she bent to get the ice cream from the freezer. She already knew the answer—hell, they'd fought over which flavor their mom was to buy for years when they were kids, but Bella wanted them to know they could remember their mom without their thoughts having to be sad.

"Chocolate," Will replied, climbing up onto the bar stool to watch her. Bella helped Cooper up to a seat before getting the ice-cream scoop out.

"Mmm, I think we'll all have what she liked, then," Bella said. "Cones or in a bowl?"

"Cones," they both said in unison.

"Did you guys ever just sit here and eat ice cream with her?" Bella asked.

"Yeah, and with Dad, too," Will said.

"Daddy liked the one with the chocolate chip in it," Cooper said.

Bella gulped. She'd just looked at that one before, had known how much Gray liked it. "We don't just have to talk about them in our prayers before bed," she told them. "If you ever want to tell me something about your mom or dad, or just remember them out loud, it's okay."

They both stared at her, licking their ice creams the moment she passed them over.

"I miss the way Mom used to tickle me when I was falling asleep. Her fingers were really soft," Will said.

Bella nodded. "How about you show me, and I'll try."

He shook his head, ice cream already ringing his mouth. "No. I just like the way your hair smells when I snuggle you at night."

Bella nodded again. There were some things that maybe he just wanted to remember his mom doing, and she had no intention of doing anything they didn't want her to do.

"How about you, Cooper? What do you miss most right now?"

He blinked back at her, eyes wide. "I miss Daddy trying to teach me how to catch ball. He bought us mitts for Christmas."

Will's eyes lit up, excited. "Yeah, that was so cool."

"You want Noah to do that with you guys? Or was it just something for Daddy?"

They looked at one another and then back at her.

"Yeah," Will said, "that'd be awesome."

"What would be awesome?"

Somehow Noah always managed to sneak in without her realizing, his sexy-as-hell, deep voice filling her with . . . anticipation. All this time she hadn't been able to put her finger on what it was, but she'd finally figured it out.

"We're just talking about what the boys miss the most about their mom and dad."

"Okay," he said, smile never faltering until the boys turned back to the ice cream and he gave her a *what-the-hell?* look over their heads.

"It's fine," she mouthed silently, smiling back at him. "One of those things is catching ball. They thought you might like to do it with them."

He looked relieved, probably wondering what she'd been going to say. "I'd like that. You want to try your mitts out after your ice cream?"

"Yeah!" They both agreed, looking happy and content.

Bella felt like her heart was actually swelling with pride, something she'd heard moms talk about, but not really understood. They were like her little guys now—she truly felt it.

"Want one?" she asked Noah.

He nodded, patting his stomach. "I'm starting to realize that parenthood means being a little bit more slack about my diet. Kids' food is awesome."

She studied him, basked in the half grin he gave her, one side of his mouth kicking up into a delicious smile just for her. Since the other night, every moment she was around him had been charged; she was waiting for something to happen again, but it hadn't. The rules had changed, but neither of them knew quite how, and they were both holding back. And besides, there hadn't exactly been time between his going back to base for training again over the past few days since the dinner at her folks' place, her working, and everything else revolving around the kids, including each of them having a little man in bed with them from midnight or earlier. But there was tonight, and they'd both made sure to schedule it, despite the fact that they'd hardly spoken about what had happened. And now tonight was rolling around even faster.

The letter. Suddenly she needed it in her hands, wanted to rip it open and share it with Noah.

She passed him his ice cream and washed her hands, excusing herself to go get it. She left the boys talking about a cool car Noah had seen on his way home, wondering if she'd ever get used to boy-talk when all her life she'd lived in such a female-dominated household.

Bella paused in the front room, which she'd turned into her home office for the time being. It was still hard to believe that she'd sold her own place so soon after Lila passing, had given up so much but gained even more. Most of her stuff was in storage except her glass desk and the chrome and leather chair she was standing behind. She'd literally walked straight into Lila's shoes, and even though she missed her modern condo, she'd definitely found peace.

"I want to ask if I'm interrupting, but I'm scared of the answer."

Bella turned. "Can we not talk about what happened at my folks'?" she asked, forcing her to remember when she just wanted to try to act like everything was normal between them.

She watched him bite into his ice cream. "If only it were that easy," he muttered.

Bella tried to smile and pretend like everything was normal, and failed miserably. She turned around instead, reaching for the envelope and sliding her nail under the seal. She pulled it out. "I was waiting until you got home, so we could open it together." She'd thought it was something they should do as a team, to try to remind them of what they were doing, and why they were doing what they were doing, in the first place.

Noah moved to stand beside her, reading the carefully written words at the same time as she did. His body was comforting beside her, warm where her shoulder pressed into him.

November 2014

Dear Bella & Noah,

I have so many hopes and wishes for the boys, and even though I know you'll both start to think of them as your own one day, there are some things that have always been so important to me that I want you to know. Every night I tell the boys that I love them, that they can grow up to be anyone and do anything they want. As proud as I'd be of them if they studied medicine, I'd also be just as ecstatic if they were drummers in a band or talented painters. We live in a crazy world, and all I want for them is happiness.

I'm sure you're ready for another night out, but this one might take a little more planning, and if you need to change it, then so be it. I want you to go to a fair or anywhere with a Ferris wheel. Eat cotton candy, drink soda, play some stupid games, then go up into the air and forget about everything for a little while. And Bella, don't go saying they're not safe. Nothing's safe anymore, so just do it, okay? Noah, gag her and throw her over your shoulder if you have to!

I don't know what's going on with you two—whether you're both single, how you're getting on, what your feelings are. But what I can say is that no matter what, I think the way you look at each other will be changing. You're not the same people anymore because you're co-parenting two little boys who'll no doubt be driving you insane one minute, then tugging on your heartstrings the next, making you fall head over heels in love with them.

Have fun, and don't take it too seriously. It's the only way to enjoy a carnival.

Love, Lila xoxo

A Ferris wheel. Bella shook her head, cursing her sister. Lila knew how much she hated those death traps!

"Talk about pushing me out of my comfort zone," she muttered. "First shooting, now a freaking Ferris wheel? These are all things she would have loved."

Noah seemed unconcerned, his brow furrowed for a moment before he spoke. "The Santa Monica pier," he said. "If there's nothing else on at the moment, we can always go there."

"Are you sure? I mean, we could always do something else entirely." She hoped he'd fall for it.

Instead he nudged her in the side with his elbow. "Not a chance. We're getting on that wheel, even if I have to drag you there kicking and screaming. You read what she said."

Bella turned to face him, less than a meter apart as she glared up at him, hands on her hips. He was over a head taller than her and it annoyed the hell out of her that he had such an advantage.

"You wouldn't dare."

His gaze challenged her, cone lowered, no longer taking his interest. "Wouldn't I?"

Her breathing was faster, more shallow, than it had been. She almost wanted to test him, but she didn't doubt that he'd show her exactly what he'd do, how much pleasure he'd take from following her sister's words to the letter.

"So are you going to kiss me or not?" she asked, forcing herself to be more confident, to say what was on her mind rather than wait for him. She had always been the lesser one in relationships, always compromised the most and not stood up for herself, which was the complete opposite of how she was with her work. But not now, not with Noah. She wasn't going to let herself be that person again, and she doubted he'd want her to be anyway.

"Do you want me to kiss you?" he asked, staring down at her, moistening his lips with his tongue, his smile slow and relaxed, like he had all the time in the world. The anxiousness she'd seen before written all over his face was gone, his smile deliberate.

"Maybe," she murmured, transfixed by his mouth. *She should have just said yes.*

"Good," his voice was a husky whisper, his eyes telling her that he had no intention of *not* kissing her.

Noah slowly lifted his arm, hand reaching for her, cupping the back of her head. He slowly closed the distance between them, his body just far enough from hers to unsettle her, make her wish it was jammed hard to hers. And then his lips met hers, so gentle, so painstakingly soft, tender to hers like she was breakable. His mouth moved, caressed hers, over and over, softly touching his lips to hers, making her want more but desperate not to ruin the sensation of what he was doing. Because it felt knee-wobblingly good.

When he pulled back she groaned and wrapped her arms tight around him.

"I have to play ball," he muttered.

She sighed and let her fingers skim across his back then down his arms. "You do."

"How about you take some time to yourself. Go run a bath, chill, make yourself look pretty."

She laughed. "So you're basically telling me I don't look pretty now?"

He leaned in for one last kiss. "You look gorgeous right now, silly. I'm just saying to go do what girls do, without us interrupting you."

"Do you have any idea how sexy that makes you, offering to do child care while I primp and preen?"

He grinned. "I aim to please."

∾

Bella ran her fingers through her hair and checked her reflection. She felt incredible, like her old self again. She smiled as she pulled on jeans and headed downstairs, still doing up the zip and top button. Now she understood why her sister had always said the sexiest thing Gray could do was a chore like the dishes or bathing the kids for her—some time to herself and she was ready to declare her undying love for Noah. *Or maybe not quite love, but definitely gratitude.*

"Where are you guys?" she called out.

She'd had over an hour upstairs, in the bath, getting ready, painting her toenails. It had been fantastic, and now she was looking forward to spending some time with the boys before they went out.

"We're here," Noah called. "Watching TV."

She followed his voice. "I could hear you playing ball before."

"Sorry, hope we weren't too loud." He was looking up over the boys' head, one of each side of him. Or more like piled on top of him from each side.

"It was cute. I couldn't stop smiling."

"Your mom phoned. She's on her way."

Bella nodded. "Okay. I'll quickly get some dinner together for the boys."

"Don't worry. She's picking up a Happy Meal for each of them, said it was a little treat she wanted to get."

Bella grinned, pleased to get off dinner duty. It wasn't like they ate a lot of junk food. "Shove over then, boys, I'm up for watching whatever's on."

Noah's eyes met hers, warmed her like they so often did now, and she tucked up beside Will, loving the way his little hand snaked up behind her and reached for her hair, stroking gently then twirling. She'd never thought much about being a mom, mainly because she'd never found the right guy, but everything about being with the boys felt right, natural somehow.

"It's the *Planes* movie," Cooper told her, leaning forward to make eye contact. "The second one, with the rescue planes."

"Sounds good."

"Can we have popcorn?" Cooper asked.

Bella exchanged glances with Noah. She was inclined to say yes, but then she didn't want to ruin their dinner that was arriving soon, especially when her mom was doing something special for them. "How about you save the popcorn for when Grandma's here? You can finish the movie with her and eat as much as you like."

They seemed unfazed, both more interested in what they were watching than what she'd said.

"Do you have to go out?" Will asked. "Noah said it was just you and him allowed."

"It's just for a few hours. It's important Noah and I have some alone time every now and again."

"Like Mom and Dad used to have date nights?" Will asked.

She laughed. "Yeah. I didn't realize you knew about them."

"Dad used to tell me that before we came along, he had Mommy all to himself. That's why he was allowed to take her on date nights without us."

"When did you get so smart?" Bella asked, reaching over to ruffle his hair.

"Dunno." He was clearly trying hard not to grin, but the quick glance he gave her told her he liked the praise, and Bella laughed gently.

"It's good to be able to laugh again," she mused out loud.

Noah reached for her and left his hand on her thigh. "It sure is."

They'd all been through a lot, but finally there was some light at the end of the tunnel. Or at least a glimmer of hope, something to cling to and know that the pain wasn't going to be so harsh forever. But the words she'd said to him, what they'd shared on the porch, were still making her heart pound a bit too hard. They reminded her of what was at stake, why it was unfair to both of them—not to mention the boys—to be doing anything that risked ruining their friendship—and their parenting.

There was a knock at the front door, followed by a key turning, and the boys leaped off the sofa.

"Grandma's here!" Cooper shouted. Will was hot on his heels as they ran.

Noah turned to her then, one leg hooked up on the sofa. "Give me five, and I'll take a quick shower and get changed."

Bella thought he looked just fine the way he was, in worn jeans, his T-shirt faded but nice, his masculine smell so much nicer than any cologne he could put on after his shower. But she kept her thoughts to herself and merely sucked in part of her bottom lip as she watched him.

"Okay."

He went to lean forward; anticipation pulsed, a steady beat through her body, and then her mom called out and broke the moment.

"When are you two heading out?"

Bella shook her head, and Noah squeezed her knee, making her jump, knowing she wouldn't like it.

"Go have your shower," she hissed at him, trying to whack him and missing completely.

"Hi," he said to her mom as he passed. "Just trying to keep your daughter in check. She can be very . . ."—he looked at her over his shoulder, and she scowled at him—"*disobedient*."

Her mom just laughed and clucked at Noah, grinning at Bella as she came into the room.

"You look lovely, darling," she said.

Bella stood, ran her hands over the denim of her jeans. "Thanks."

"Stay out as late as you want. I've got no where to be and nothing I'd rather be doing."

She gave her mom a hug instead of walking past her. "Thanks. It'll be nice to go out."

"Serena told me more about your date with the coffee guy. And that you've called things off with him already."

"She *what*!" Bella huffed, annoyed with her friend's ability to share everything about everyone. It had been bad enough that she'd talked about it at dinner!

"Honestly, darling, when you have a man like Noah in your life, I'd just stop looking."

"Mom!" Bella exclaimed.

"I'm just saying. And your Aunt Iris feels the same way. Plus I think that after our chat the other night, maybe you think so, too."

Bella folded her arms across her chest, exasperated. "Well, I appreciate your advice *and* Aunt Iris's, but I'd also appreciate you both keeping your opinions to yourselves."

She left her mom to tend to the boys and ran upstairs to grab her shoes and her purse. It wasn't that they were wrong, but she didn't want to talk about Noah like that yet, wasn't ready to admit how she felt. Because the last thing she wanted was to finally open up to him about how she felt, only to lose him, especially after he'd made it so clear what couldn't be between them.

~

Noah shoved his hands into his pockets. Bella was on the phone, still sitting in the car, talking to a client who seemed to be having a panic attack over the colors for her new house, and he was taking the chance to get some fresh air. He was stuck between a rock and a hard place. There was something going down at work, and they wanted him back on base for a full week's training. He knew he was about to get the phone call he'd been dreading since he'd last arrived back. Hell, not wanting to leave the boys, he'd been dreading any calls since Gray had passed. But he also knew that his team needed him. He'd be training earlier in the day from now on, but he'd still be able to come home each night like he was working a regular job. When he'd done that previously, one of the guys had pulled him aside and said that word was spreading that Noah was thinking of taking early retirement—just a whisper; Noah had had to steel his jaw, look his brother in the eye, and tell him he was crazy.

"Man, you're not gonna do it, are you? You're not the only one of us with kids to think about," the guy had said.

Noah had frowned. "Where are you hearing this?" He didn't like his secrets being aired, especially when he hadn't confided in anyone. Or maybe the guys were just putting two and two together, guessing what he might be thinking.

"It's nothing, just a rumor. Besides, you know how we all get when we know something's going down. One of the guys said . . ."

When Ty had stopped talking, his voice trailing off, Noah had folded his arms across his chest. "What did one of the guys say?"

Ty blew out a breath, shrugging. "It was nothing. Just that the last time you bailed on a mission, that time you had food poisoning, it turned out cursed."

"There's no such thing as a cursed mission."

"So you say."

Noah had stopped himself from saying something stupid. "You'd be fine without me, but I'm not going anywhere. We get the call, I'll be with you."

Ty had grinned. "Good. Without you I reckon not all the guys would make it home safe. Not if some serious shit went down."

It didn't seem to matter how hard Noah tried to forget it, the conversation kept running through his head, over and over like a bad song stuck on repeat. The problem was, what Ty had said was true. They were a team—a highly focused, honed team that relied on every single member. Which meant that if he stepped back, he'd be the one responsible for ruining the dynamics. Just like when JT had died. When they'd had to bring his charred body back in pieces, in a bag, like he was trash instead of one of the most highly trained men in the world. Noah shuddered at the memory. Then there was his ongoing confusion about Bella. Since their intense moment on the porch at her parents', he'd wondered if he should break things off entirely. If he was interrupting her life—for the worse—it seemed the right thing to do. But he hadn't been able to resist when she'd asked him to kiss her. Somehow, she made all his resolutions to keep his distance a little more turn to nothing. The way he was starting to feel about her terrified him, but not as much as the thought of letting her down and being less than she deserved in a partner.

"Hey!"

He stopped, stared out at the ocean for a long moment.

"Noah!"

He filled his lungs with air and finally turned, the confused look on Bella's face quickly turning to something more relaxed. Noah was certain his mouth would be bracketed with frown lines, the stress of keeping something from her finally taking its toll. But he'd taken an oath when he'd become a SEAL, and he couldn't discuss his work with her. *But I also took an oath when I promised to take care of the boys.*

"You wouldn't believe what that client just said to me," Bella fumed, catching up to him as he started to walk toward the pier. "In one breath she's telling me that she wants to go with a more subtle duck-egg blue in her master bedroom, and moaning about the contractors she's using, and the next she's making not so subtle hints about me being a working mom!"

Noah laughed, glancing sideways at her. Maybe he wasn't the only one feeling guilty about his work right now. "If the idea didn't bug you, you probably wouldn't be offended."

She slowed, no longer keeping up with his long strides. "What do you mean?"

"I mean," he said, making a half turn so he was walking backward, keeping his eyes on her and only moving when she did, "that if the thought hadn't already crossed your mind, if you weren't already feeling guilty, then you would have just laughed it off."

Bella sighed, looking down at her feet. "I guess I'm feeling a little guilty for judging working moms in the past. I love the boys, and given what they've gone through I want to be there for them one hundred percent right now, but is it okay to be expected to give up your career just because you've got a double X chromosome?"

Noah shook his head. "No."

"Shit," she swore, glancing up, eyes swirling with guilt all over again. "I have a serious double standard. Here I am all pissed about someone who doesn't know me expecting me to be a stay-at-home mom, baking cookies and keeping house, and I'm the one who's accused you of not being dedicated to the boys because of your career choice."

He turned, looked ahead to the Ferris wheel. It should have been a lighthearted, fun evening, but instead they were back into dangerous territory all over again, talking about his job. "Accusing you of being a less than dedicated mom because you run a local interior design business is not the same as you being worried about me going off to a war zone," he told her. "I get why my job terrifies you, and to be honest, it should." *And why she feels like I'm interrupting her goddamn life.*

She was silent for a long beat, but she'd caught up to him and was walking by his side. "I still don't have the right to tell you what to do. We only live one life, and I'm all too aware of how short that life can be, after everything we've been through."

His chuckle was forced. "So you're going to happily wave me off next time I head away?"

Noah regretted his words the moment they'd left his mouth.

"No," she choked out, eyes immediately swimming with tears. "Please, God, no. Don't let this be you telling me you're about to leave."

"I'm sorry. I shouldn't have said that." He realized she was still waiting, looked like she was holding her breath to hear his words. "No. Crap, sorry, no. I'm just talking shit—don't even listen to me."

She'd stopped walking, looked shell-shocked.

"Come here," he said, forgetting his own worries when he saw how concerned she was, how terrified she'd become by his words. Noah took her hand, squeezed it tight, and didn't let go, only loosening his hold when she switched from palms pressed together to linking their fingers first. "This is supposed to be a fun night. The two of us having a good time together. Let's not ruin it by overthinking *what ifs*."

She leaned into him. "I just can't bear the thought of losing anyone else again. Of going through that feeling ever again."

He pulled her around so she was facing him, took her other hand, too. Noah watched her, looked down at the woman he'd spent so much time with lately, the woman who'd changed so much about him, probably without even knowing what she was doing. "We're not going to lose each other."

She shook her head, eyes still moist. It was killing him that he was the immediate cause of her pain. "That's not a promise you can make. Or keep," she murmured.

"True, but I can promise that I'll try damn hard. That I'll be more determined than ever to come back to you all in one piece."

Bella nodded. "Okay, then. Kind of along the lines of what my daddy used to say, so I'll take it."

Noah leaned down, kissed her before she seemed to realize what was happening. But she didn't take long to warm up, to wrap her arms around his neck, hungrily kissing him straight back.

"Come on—let's go have some fun," he muttered, kissing her one last time before dragging her along with him, tucking her under his arm. "I'm starving, so we'd better find some food."

"Ditto. It's been a long day."

Not to mention a long night. He'd found it hard to sleep, had craved being in bed with Bella, but she'd ended up in with the boys, and he was back to night terrors combined with insomnia from his guilt attacks at the position he was putting himself in. He'd always vowed never to become a dad, and look how well that had turned out. He'd always sworn never to get too close to a woman as well. And then he'd spent time with Bella. And now it wasn't just his heart on the line, it was the heart of a woman who deserved more.

They kept walking, onto the pier and toward the Ferris wheel. He felt Bella's grip tighten.

"You okay?"

"I probably should have mentioned that I'm terrified of anything that involves being high up in the air." She gulped, and he could see the movement in her throat as he watched her, trying not to be amused by the genuine terror written all over her face. "I know this sounds stupid to a freak-of-nature SEAL who can jump out of helicopters and do those crazy rolls from the top of a hill or whatever if he has to, but I can't help it."

"Were you dangled from a building as a child or something equally terrifying?" he teased.

"Ha-ha, very funny," she muttered, still not giving up his hand and making him wonder if she was trying to squeeze it off.

"And how do you know about our—how did you put it?— *crazy hill rolls*?"

"Oh, I watched a program on SEALs one night. It showed a whole lot of training stuff. Something about where you train to get tortured in ice cold water—all that."

"Uh-huh." He refused to think about the training role he'd been mulling over, the one that would involve that very ice-cold water training, among other things. The role he had to give his superior an answer about . . . *yesterday*. Or the other role that was being dangled in front of him, the one that meant a serious promotion, the one he should be finding out about within days.

"Want a hotdog?" he asked, stomach rumbling so loudly, he was sure passersby would hear it if he didn't consume something soon.

"Sure thing."

They walked hand in hand to the hotdog vendor, and Noah ordered two with ketchup and mustard, passing one to Bella. He licked the ketchup from his hand and wolfed it down, not moving from the spot.

"Geez, you were hungry," Bella said, still nibbling away on hers.

Noah shrugged. He ordered another, and they started to wander again, stopping a few yards down the pier to grab a couple of Cokes.

"You want to talk about what's, um . . . going on with us?" he asked, realizing how sudden his question sounded out loud. Just because it'd been going through his mind all day didn't mean she'd been thinking the same.

"Not really," she replied quickly. "You?"

He shrugged when what he should have said was *yes*. "I just—"

"Don't want me to get the wrong idea about us? It's okay. I get it, but at the same time I don't want to think about all the other women you've probably got scribbled down in a little black book for booty calls."

Noah swallowed the last bite of his hotdog and pulled a face. "I don't have a black book of women." He was getting the feeling that she wanted to joke around, keep things lighthearted like they'd first been when they started hanging out on Lila's dates. Who'd have thought he would be the one trying to bring up an emotional conversation?

Bella rolled her eyes, making her look childish, which in turn made him laugh. "Sorry—your iPhone contacts then."

Noah decided to play along. It was easier to have fun than to dwell on what the hell they were doing and what he was going to do about it. "I don't know who you think I am, but I'm not a manwhore," he teased. "I love women—always have, always will—but I'm not exactly in a different woman's bed every night."

She sighed. "Sorry. We're going back over old territory. I'm being silly. I was just trying to—"

"Have fun," he interrupted. "You're forgiven. Now come on. It's not impossible to enjoy ourselves if we give this a chance."

Once they neared the Ferris wheel, he could feel her balking, and he dragged her along beside him, determined to keep her smiling, at least for tonight. "How about we play a game first? I'll try to win you a teddy bear."

That made her lean in, her smile back, lips tilted up just the smallest bit at the corners, making him want them to curve more, to see her entire face light up. "That'd be sweet. I'm just not sure if you'll be able to hit the mark, though."

He squared his shoulders, rolling them back and making her laugh. He liked the sound of it; it made him feel human again. In fact, everything about being with the boys and Bella had made him feel human, which was probably why it scared him so damn much.

"I'm gonna hit this the first time. Three in a row, and that teddy will be yours."

She grinned, and he handed over a few bills, reaching for the balls and aiming the first one. He went to throw it, and she pinched him on the butt, making him falter. The ball fell foul, and he glared at her.

"Seriously?" He narrowed his gaze, tried to intimidate her.

"What? You can't deal with a little distraction?"

He frowned. "Just watch me." He was highly competitive, had been ever since he'd been given a chance to succeed outside of foster care, which meant it didn't matter what he was doing—he liked to win. Or be the best. No questions asked.

This time he aimed, and she wolf-whistled at him, but he was expecting something and hit his mark straightaway. He glanced over his shoulder. "You've lost the element of surprise. Better luck next time."

He had two balls left and prepared to throw the third, until she pressed closer to him, hand sliding around his waist, the other snaking low. Noah groaned as his throw turned to custard.

"You're wicked."

She stepped back the second he missed. He dropped the last ball and paid another few bills to get more. He wasn't giving up now, wasn't about to let her distract him. This time he focused, pushed her from his thoughts, and didn't so much as glance sideways until he'd slam-dunked the first three shots. The operator scowled and passed him a toy giraffe, which he took gleefully and thrust at Bella.

"Here."

She smiled coyly. "My cleavage didn't even impress you."

Noah stared at her, trying to focus on her face even though his eyes kept dropping. Lower. And lower. "It impresses me plenty."

They stood, staring, both immobile until Noah finally pulled away, broke the spell. He was supposed to be putting some distance between them, emotionally anyway, but it sure as hell wasn't working.

"Thanks for the toy."

"My pleasure," he replied, wishing he had the courage to pull her into his arms and not let her go—to hell with being scared of his feelings.

"Want to go brave the wheel?" she asked.

Noah nodded, hands pushed deep into his jean pockets to avoid holding hands with her. The way he was feeling right now, he didn't trust himself. Not one bit. There wasn't a line, and they stepped up. Noah pulled out his wallet and paid, neither saying a word until they were directed to their seats. They hadn't been seated long when their car began to move, a jolt making Bella gasp and shoot over closer to him, their thighs sandwiched, her hand jammed into his. He pried her fingers off his and tucked his arm around her instead, holding her against him. It was a mistake—the second her warm body was tucked to his, he wanted to keep her there forever—but he pushed away his thoughts, like he'd always been so good at doing, and looked out at the view.

"Shit," she swore, gripping even tighter and peering over the side.

"Don't look," he told her. "If you don't look, you've got nothing to be scared of."

She leaned back in, head to his shoulder. "Except for the fact that we're so high up in the air. And the fact that this machine could break at any moment."

Just as they reached the top, the wheel ground to a halt, a heaving noise followed by complete silence. Noah knew the drill—there were only a few people, and the operator had probably decided to give them a good view from the top. Only he wasn't so sure that Bella appreciated the gesture.

"Omigod," she mumbled, the words all rolled into one. "It's broken. The motor's blown up or something, and we're going to be stranded."

Noah turned and gazed down at her, taking in the tendrils of hair that had escaped, blowing around her face despite the rest of her long hair being flung over her shoulders and hanging down her back. Her lips were parted, the bottom one sucked under her top teeth as she peered over the side again.

And then she looked up at him. *Screw it.*

He reached for her, looked down at the woman whose head he now had cupped in his hands, touched his palm to her cheek on the other side. Noah closed the distance between them swiftly, not wanting time to second-guess his actions. He'd kissed her plenty of times now, had enjoyed every single one and anticipated the next, but this one he had zero control over.

His lips moved over hers like they had a mind of their own, their mouths fused, tongues colliding over and over. Bella's soft moans only spurred him more, made him more aroused, more desperate to touch every part of her. *For her to be his.*

"Damn," he muttered, pulling back.

She groaned louder and reached for him, arms wrapping tight around his neck. "No," she demanded, her whisper determined, fierce.

"We can't do this," he muttered straight back, just as his body was telling him that was *exactly* what he should be doing.

"Why not?"

He pulled her against him, the twinkling lights in the near darkness taking his attention for less than a second before his defenses were shattered all over again by the woman in his arms. Noah had prided himself on his self-control all his life, but now it was gone like it had never existed in the first place.

"Damn you," he muttered, no longer prepared to be gentle as he took her mouth against his again, relentless, not giving her the chance to say no. She'd done this to him, and he wanted her more than he'd ever wanted a woman in his life.

Bella kissed him back just as fiercely, her hunger raw, fingers gripping at his hair, one arm wrapped around his neck tight. It felt like minutes or maybe hours, Noah had no idea, and then the car they were in suddenly lurched, and they were swinging again, moving around on the big circle.

Bella eventually pulled her lips from his, but she didn't let go. He could almost smell her fear it was so real.

"You distracted me," she whispered. "From the fact that one move sideways and I could have plunged to my death."

"I wouldn't have let that happen," Noah whispered into her ear, lips grazing her skin.

She turned to face him again, arms still wrapped around his body. "Tell me how you really feel, Noah? Is this just fun to you? Am I a conquest you're going to tire of or a friend with benefits? Or is there a chance this . . ."

He pulled back, scared of where the conversation was going. He could see the hope in Bella's eyes, hope that he'd be able to give her more. Noah cleared his throat. This was exactly what he hadn't wanted to happen. "I thought I made it clear that I couldn't commit to anything serious, that I wasn't capable of being in a relationship after everything that's happened to me."

Bella's shock disappeared almost as soon as it appeared, her mouth softening as she watched him. And then he realized what it was, the look that had become familiar to him when he was younger, before he'd figured out how to make it clear to women that he was a fun-time-only kind of guy.

"You made that clear, Noah. Of course you did." Her smile faltered, and he knew she was lying. "I just thought . . ."

He braced himself, knowing the words that were coming. Trouble was, he did want more from Bella, didn't want to end what had turned into a great evening out. But he also didn't want to lead her on, pretend that what they had could turn into something that he just couldn't give.

"I can't change the way I am. The person that I am," he said softly, being careful with the words he chose. "I wish things could be different."

"So I'm not the first to think I could change you?" she asked. "Is that what you're trying to say?"

He grabbed her hand, knowing they were about to reach the bottom and be asked to exit, but not caring. They lurched to a stop before he had time to say what he needed to tell Bella, and he quickly pulled out his wallet and thrust money at the guy waiting to help them out. "Again," he demanded impatiently.

The guy shrugged. There was no one else waiting, and so he sent them back on their way again.

"I want to get out," Bella insisted, struggling to remove her hand from his.

"Tough luck," he muttered.

"Why do you even want to do this?" she asked. "Torture ourselves with whatever the hell is going on between us, then tell me that it can't turn into anything? Who does that?"

"Me," he said simply, still holding her hand. "The way I feel about you," he started, shutting his eyes, willing himself to say the words he was trying so hard to get out, "I don't know what to say."

"How about nothing," she suggested, her tone cool.

Noah knew he'd hurt her, which had been the last thing he'd wanted to do, and now he was stuck and couldn't even tell her how he felt. "I've never felt this way about a woman before. I've never wanted what I couldn't have because I've always kept things casual. Never met anyone who's made me wish it was any other way."

Her resistance disappeared, no longer fighting to pull her hand from his. He loosened his grip, ran his fingers down her wrist a little so he could stroke across her skin as he watched her.

"Noah, you don't have to let your past define you." Her voice was low, sweet and soft, but it was the expression on her face, the warmth of her gaze as she stared into his eyes, that really got him.

"Easy for you to say," he said. "I never had anyone to love me, not like you did. The two people I've"—he choked on the word, finding it near impossible to say—"*felt that way about*, have both died. Taken from me. Like I'm so broken, so cursed, I never deserved to have them in the first place."

"You can't honestly believe that?" She had tears trickling down her cheeks now.

"It's the truth," he said simply. "It's my truth." Noah opened his arms to pull her closer, wanted her against him, wasn't ready to let her go yet. "It doesn't mean I don't want you or that you're not amazing or that it doesn't crush me to think I'm hurting you. I just can't let you in."

"Can't or *won't*?" she asked, pressed to his chest, cheek to him, arms around him.

"Can't," he admitted. "If I could, I'd do it for you."

"So we stop this?" she asked. "Is that honestly what you want?"

"I want you for as long as you'll have me," Noah told her as they wheeled around. "I want to kiss you and have you in my bed. I want to parent those boys with you as best I can, but I won't hold you back if you meet someone. If you have a chance at being with someone who can give you what you deserve."

She was silent. Deathly still. Noah knew how fucked up it sounded, but it was his truth, and he could no more hide from it than he could change the way he was.

"Can we just not talk about any of this?" she asked. "I just want us to keep doing what we're doing, looking after the boys and making it work between us. With them. I don't even want to meet anyone else."

He grimaced. *But you will.* "Sweetheart, you deserve a ring, a man's heart, and a white picket fence. So much more than what a broken man like me could give you."

"I already have the white picket fence," she muttered. "We both inherited one. And look what good that did Lila and Gray."

"It did them plenty good," Noah said, moving so he could keep one arm around Bella as they neared the ground again. "They loved each other, and they had a great family. And one day you will, too."

She looked up at him. "And you'll be okay with that? Me dating, meeting someone, and getting married? You'll move out of the house?"

He braced himself, hated the visual but told her what she needed to hear anyway. "I'll do what I have to do."

"Fine," she murmured. "Thank you for being clear with me."

Noah knew, right then, that he'd ruined the easy, happy banter they'd had, the fun feeling that had been building these past few weeks. It hadn't been something he'd wanted to end, but at the same time he couldn't have lied to her before when she'd asked.

"I don't ever want to lie to you, Bella. We're in this for the long haul—with the boys, I mean."

"Yeah. We are."

They exited the Ferris wheel and walked back the way they'd come, Bella with the giraffe slung under her arm. She didn't say anything else, and he had nothing more to tell her except for the fact that he wished they'd never talked in the first place.

"You know you're going to fall in love with those boys, Noah, and they'll be the ones you risk your heart for, not me."

His body stiffened, jaw suddenly carved from stone as he stared ahead.

"You might not want to fall in love with me, Noah, but not falling in love with them is impossible," she continued in a voice brimming with emotion, moving around to walk in front of him, blocking him and walking backward so he had to look at her. "You're scared to be in love, aren't you? Even with them."

Noah hadn't liked their last conversation, but it was merry compared to this one. He gritted his teeth. "Don't go there, Bella."

"I'm just intrigued by why you can appear to love them, be so close to them, and yet be so scared of feeling the same about me. Or any woman for that matter." She shook her head. "Despite what you might be telling yourself, you're already head over heels in love with two little boys who've completely stolen your heart."

"I didn't choose to feel that way about them, okay? Damn it, Bella, I would never have put myself in this position!" He was on the verge of yelling, and he checked himself, not wanting to scare her by his sudden outburst. "Those kids didn't have anyone, and I wasn't going to let them turn into"—he exhaled—"*me*."

"You can walk away any time, Noah. I'm more than capable of making them feel loved, being there for them. And they have grandparents who adore them, so they're never going to end up . . ."

He stopped walking. "What? Messed up like me? Is that what you were going to say?"

She threw her hands up in the air. "Why are we even fighting, Noah? This was the perfect evening, and I don't even know how we ended up here."

They stared at each other, both breathing deeply. He could see the rise and fall of her chest, knew she was just as riled up as he was. And all he wanted was to tell her how stupid he'd been, that he didn't mean what he'd said, and pull her into his arms. *Only I can't.*

"I'm sorry," he said. "I care a lot about you, Bella. I really do. And if it makes a difference, I've never wanted a woman like I want you."

"Yeah, you want me, but you're not prepared to let your guard down enough to let me in. Like these past couple of months never existed in the first place."

"Bella, the reason I've been honest with you tonight is *because* I care about you. Can't you see?

"Can we just go home?" she asked, turning away from him, arms wrapped tight around herself like she was trying to shield her body from the cold. His first instinct was to embrace her, and his second was to give her space. He went with the latter, keeping some distance between them as they walked side by side. And then, seeing as things probably couldn't get much worse, he decided to break another piece of news to her.

"I meant to tell you earlier, and I know this is bad timing, but I need to head away for the entire week next week. Just to base—I'm training with my team all week, so I think I'll stay there, but I'll be back for the weekend."

She didn't say anything, just gave him a curt nod of her head— still too angry with him to answer was his guess.

When they reached the car, Bella paused when he opened the door for her, glancing up under hooded lashes. "You know, I was prepared to deal with your job," she said quietly. "To open myself up to the hurt that comes with that, because I actually care about you. For the record, this was always more to me than just some sort of fling. I was prepared to give you a chance, and you were never even prepared to give the same to me."

Noah didn't know what to say, and he never got the chance. Bella got in, shut the door, and left him standing alone on the sidewalk. He'd been humbled plenty of times, usually with regard to his career, but he'd never, ever been shot down like that before and made to feel like a complete jerk.

The way he saw it, he had two options: bail now and go back to the life he'd loved and enjoyed for so many years. Or man up and deal with the fact that he needed to change in order to survive in the real world. Either way, it wasn't an easy decision. Not by a long shot.

Noah briefly wondered if he should just give Bella the car keys and run back home to clear his head, and then he decided against it. After what he'd said to her tonight, she at least deserved for him to drive her home.

CHAPTER FOURTEEN

November 2014

Dear Bella & Noah,

I'd love to know if you're looking forward to these or dreading them. Part of me thinks they could be ending up straight in the trash, but then the other part is certain that you'll both feel you can't say no to me. This date is slightly different. I want you guys to go hiking. Just chill out, go for a big walk out in the fresh air, and talk about all the stuff you need to get off your chest. Whatever your worries, the boys will be fine. So long as you're loving them and caring for them, everything will work out there. But you two are different. To make this work, what Gray and I have asked of you, means being a team. There are things that only you two will know, about the way you've been pulled together and how you feel about that, but I want you to make a joint decision about the future. If you can't live together in our home, then make something else work. Just promise me that you'll keep the boys together and give them the kind of family that we would have. They deserve it, but you both deserve to be happy, too.

Whatever happens, know that you have our full love and support. You're my favorite people in the world, and all I want is to know that even though I'm gone, you're both still smiling.

If you've done everything, been on all the dates, then I'm so proud of you, Bella. I've made you go outside your comfort zone, and I know that couldn't have been easy for you. And whatever you think about each other right now . . . Bella, I hope you've seen the Noah that I know and adore; and Noah, I hope you've seen the Bella that I love and admire. Life's a crazy ride, and if you can be on that ride together . . . I'm going to stop writing now. Just enjoy, have fun, and cuddle my boys for me. Rock in the chair in our room, snuggle them, and whisper stories of their mommy and daddy in their ears. It's what I did to them every night I was home, just tucked them up and rocked them both to sleep. Only I was whispering stories of bunnies and other crazy characters to them, wanting to shield them from the crazy world their mom and dad lived in when we were away working.

I love you.

Lila xoxo

It had been a long week, and it was only Thursday evening. Bella poured herself a glass of wine, going past the halfway mark before finally putting the bottle down. She put the cap back on, left the bottle on the bench, and sat down at the kitchen table. Her feet were sore and she had a headache, but it had been a half-decent day. The boys were in bed early, bathed and happy, and she'd managed to work while they were at school. It was tough without Noah around, simply because she'd started to rely on him so much when it came to playing with the kids while she cooked dinner or bathing them when she was rushing around getting the laundry folded and the dishes done. But he'd been gone almost all week, and she'd started to find her rhythm. Only he'd texted a while ago and said he was on his way home a night early, so now she was braced for dealing with him all over again.

If only I had Lila to talk to. In her heart, she knew she could turn to Serena, but it just wasn't the same as having her sister. Just like she didn't want to talk to her mom right now, even though she'd usually tell her everything.

A noise alerted her to the fact that Noah was already home, and she took a few long, calm sips of the red wine before he came through the door. His heavy footfalls rang out in the hall, boots loud on the timber floor, even though he was probably doing his best to be quiet.

"In here," she called out.

No matter how she felt about him, they had to make this work. The looking after the boys and putting on a united front part, anyway.

"Hey," Noah said as he walked in, heading straight for the sofa and dropping into it.

She turned her body to watch him, the way he flopped down, body molding into the sofa and his eyes half shut. She wanted to hate him, but she couldn't.

"You look exhausted," she noted, raising her glass and taking another sip. She was drinking more wine than she ever had since Noah had come on the scene.

"It's been a rough week," he muttered. "The training was tough. A bit of down time, and it's hard to compete with the others."

She sipped her wine. *No being a bitch about the kids or what went down on our last date.*

"You get a letter today?"

Bella shrugged. "Yeah. But I can't say I'm in the mood to go along with it. Sorry."

He grunted. "I'm in the mood for sleep. But we still need to do what Lila asks."

Bella was feeling more grumpy about than endeared to her sister—she was ready to stand outside and yell up at the sky for Lila to go to hell for pairing her with Noah, even though she knew she was just overtired and being dramatic.

"The boys have missed you," she told him, not wanting to guilt-trip him, but wanting him to know that his absence hadn't gone without notice. "They're looking forward to hanging out with you this weekend."

"Bella, I've been thinking a lot about what went down between us last week," he started, sitting up, no longer looking so shattered.

"Honestly Noah, you don't need to explain yourself. It's fine. Just get a good night's sleep, and we can chat in the morning." She didn't want to talk, didn't want to do anything where he was concerned.

"You're sure?" he asked.

"Positive."

"Can I at least read the letter?"

She leaned over and reached for it, standing to drop it into his lap. Then she crossed the room with her wine and sat on the opposite sofa, turning the TV on and flicking between channels. She hadn't watched anything in ages and had more things recorded than she'd ever get the chance to watch.

"Huh." Noah made a nothing kind of noise as he read the letter. She wanted to turn and watch him, stare at his face and his body language as he read, but she didn't. Instead, she kept pretending to be interested in the screen.

"We're going hiking."

Bella laughed. *Yeah, right.* "No, we're not."

"Seriously, we could both do with the fresh air. You've had the boys all week. I have tomorrow off. Why don't you do the same, or at least just take the morning? I can collect the boys from school."

Bella shook her head. "No, I hate hiking." *And I don't want to spend any more time with you than I have to.*

232

"You know what I've always wondered? How the hell you have such a great body when you don't like outdoor stuff."

His words made her jaw drop. She was flattered, but . . . so much for not thinking about Noah like that or the things they'd done. "I run. Well, I used to run, just around the streets or on the treadmill at the gym, but I haven't had time lately."

He nodded. "Then let's run."

She laughed. "No way. You can probably run for five hours straight faster than I could run for thirty minutes."

"After the week I've had, I'd happily take it slow. Just enjoy the fresh air."

"So we go for a run instead?"

He shrugged. "Hey, nowhere does it say that we can't modify these *dates* a little."

"Fine. I'll take the morning off, and we'll run. Happy?" She could do with the exercise. It was the only reason she'd agreed.

Noah's grin made his face light up, reminded her of what she'd lost when he'd told her they couldn't have more than whatever the hell they'd had. She'd started to get used to that smile, to his knowing gaze fixed on her, his touch when she needed it. And now he was back, but he wasn't.

"I'm beat," Noah said. "I'm gonna head to bed."

She watched him go, before snuggling back and flicking through her TiVo shows. Bella reached for the throw at the end of the sofa and tucked it over herself, almost forgot about the fact she was alone instead of tucked beside Noah. What they'd had was gone, and she just needed to come to terms with the fact. Not to mention the idea of Noah having women over, because it was unrealistic to think he wouldn't at some stage. She selected *The Good Wife* and zoned out. Television was the perfect distraction. *And so is wine.*

Noah was still tired the following morning, body aching from the training he'd done all week, but it was more than just his physical strains that were troubling him. He'd just gotten off the phone with his superior, and he only had today before he had to brief his team and go. Then he was packing up and heading back to base to be fully briefed before they headed to the Middle East. It was where he'd spent a lot of time and knew some of the terrain, and it was also where he'd lost some of his best guys. In the past his deployments had been six months, give or take, but this one was going to be different. And he knew he had to tell Bella. The moment she'd been dreading had finally arrived.

He'd spent the early morning playing with the kids, pretending to be a baddie while they both got to be Spiderman, and now he was stretching beside his SUV, waiting for Bella to turn up. *Or not.* He was wondering whether she was going to show at all.

Noah walked a few steps, then dropped to do some push-ups. After having some time off, he wasn't feeling as fit as he usually did, and he didn't want to be giving anything less than his best when he was beside the brothers who trusted him with their life.

The rumble of an engine alerted him, but he dropped again, doing another twenty before jumping up to land on his feet once more. When a car door slammed, he turned.

"Show off."

He winked at Bella, then wished he hadn't. He was supposed to be making things less complicated between them, not more. Pity flirting with her came so naturally. Although the cool look she gave him put a stop to it real fast. "Just doing some training. I feel guilty about having the day off."

"Were you training all week or doing something top secret you can't tell me about?"

He collected his drink bottle from the ground where he'd abandoned it. "I was training, and I also had a few meetings to attend."

At some point he was going to have to tell her, but he knew it was going to turn everything to shit, even though he had no other option. "I wouldn't lie to you and say I was training at base if I was actually being sent somewhere."

"Want to get going?" she asked, scooping her long hair up and pulling it into a ponytail, seeming to ignore his answer completely.

Noah watched her, wished it were his lips skimming over the skin of her neck rather than her own nails as she discovered and tucked in loose strands. "Yeah," he managed gruffly.

He drank some water, offered it to her, then jogged over to put it back in his vehicle. She started off at a slow run, and he fell into pace beside her.

"Want to jog for a bit, then take a breather and chat?" he asked.

She gave him a weird sideways glance. "Sure."

Noah breathed deep, in through his nose, wanting to go faster, to run from his memories. He always felt like this before deployment—excited and amped about what they'd be heading into, but haunted by things he'd seen, things that had happened to those he cared for in the past. Those thoughts never made him hesitate, didn't change how determined he was to succeed on every mission. It just made him more mindful, more respectful of the situations they put themselves in and the lives that depended on him.

Bella was breathing more heavily beside him, but she was the one setting the pace. They ran in silence and hardly saw anyone else, which suited Noah just fine. He liked reflecting when he exercised, taking the time to get his head in the game and get rid of anything that was holding him back. And the fact that the very person he was struggling with was running beside him was somehow making it easier than when he'd been trying to focus without her at base.

After about twenty minutes Bella stopped, panting and with her hands on her hips as she slowed. "I'm going to die," she rasped.

"How long has it been since you ran?" Noah asked, stopping beside her and watching as she suffered, eventually dropping to the ground and lying like a starfish. Albeit a dead one.

"Months. I think I'm gonna be sick."

Noah dropped and held out his hands to help her up. "Sit up and drop your head down. You'll be fine in a few minutes."

She did as she was told, mumbling something he couldn't decipher as she dropped her head.

"Bella, this might not be the best time, but I don't know when else will be."

Her head stayed down, shoulders still heaving. Noah sat down beside her, knees up and arms resting on them.

"You're going, aren't you?" she asked, head slowly lifting until she was looking at him. "You're waiting to tell me the bad news."

Noah nodded. "Yeah, I am. Going, I mean."

"By choice or because you've been deployed?"

He reached for her hand, then changed his mind. "Deployment. I'd never leave the boys if I had a choice in the matter."

"So this is my life now, huh?" she asked, eyes wide as she glared at him. "I'm going to have to go home and tell the boys that Uncle Noah won't be here this weekend, then pretend like everything's okay while I wait days or weeks or months to hear from you, not knowing if you're dead or alive."

Noah sighed. "Do we have to have this conversation again? It's my job, Bella. It's what I do. I can't help that." Actually, he could help it. He'd been offered the other, more senior position that would make sure he wasn't in active combat anymore, but he just wasn't sure if he could step back yet when he'd always craved the adrenaline of his job. What he'd chosen to do for a living defined him to a large extent.

"You know what? Screw you, Noah. I know you could have taken a job here if you'd wanted to."

He raised an eyebrow. "Is that so?"

"I spoke to Dad, and he gave me this talk about how one day, when you're ready, there would be a job waiting for you on land, in America. He told me how it works, then made me feel like shit for saying you owed it to the boys to do exactly that."

"I've already been offered the position—more than one of them in fact," Noah said simply, not wanting to argue with her. Her dad had obviously been trying to make things better between them and undoubtedly wouldn't have shared the specifics, but he now felt like he was between a rock and a hard place.

"You what?" she whispered.

"I was offered a position here, but it wasn't for me. It would have kept me home, but when I started out as an officer, I had a career path mapped out, and it involved a hell of a lot more time out in the field."

"So you just said no?" she asked.

Noah shrugged. "I didn't say no lightly. But something else has come up, something I've been interviewed for a couple of times this week and only just been offered. I can't talk about it with you, but I'm not saying no, not yet. I need time to think it through." He sighed. "I want to be here for the boys, Bella, but I also don't want to resent them for killing my career."

"It's not them, it's me," Bella said, dropping her head down again. "I'm the one pushing you. I'd be the one you'd end up resenting."

"Not true," he told her honestly. "You're only pushing me because of the boys."

She laughed then, the noise strange given their low words and the silence echoing around them. "Noah, can't you see? I don't want you to go because, no matter what I said the other night, I still . . ."

"What?" he asked, dreading her reply.

"I fell for you," she said, standing up, hands on her hips. "I know I wasn't supposed to, I know you told me right from the start that you couldn't commit to more, that you didn't want more, but I did."

Fell for him? "Bella . . ."

"Don't 'Bella' me," she said, chin thrust high, shoulders back like she was suddenly infused with a strength that she'd been missing before. "I'll get over it. What other choice do I have?"

"I never meant to hurt you."

"I know that," she said quickly. "Just like I never meant to get too close to you, open myself up." Her laugh was rough, husky. "I never even liked you, Noah, and somehow everything changed. Or maybe I changed. Hell, I don't know."

She started to walk, or more like pace, and he followed, giving her some space, but not intending on letting her march off in a huff while he stayed put. He got what she was saying, because it was the same for him, and he had no idea how they were actually going to make everything work. Getting close, becoming friends and then stupidly something more, had ruined what could have been a balanced parenting act and was suddenly feeling like a bad breakup.

Bella suddenly spun around, and he almost walked smack bang into her. Noah held out his hand to steady her, but she defiantly grabbed her arm back and planted it on her hip.

"You know what I don't understand?" she said, looking angrier than he'd ever seen her. "It's that you're so damn scared of losing someone, which I get—believe me, I get it. But you're prepared to look after those boys and risk your heart there. To love them and be there for them, without hesitation."

He swallowed, carefully considered his words before saying anything. If ever there had been a right time it was now, the secret he'd held on to for seven years burning in his throat, needing to be shared. Only he'd taken an oath, promised that he'd never divulge the truth. Until he'd seen Lila's letter, wondered if she was encouraging him to tell Bella or whether she was only hinting that he should share his past with her.

"I don't know what you want me to say, Bella," he eventually said, too chickenshit to come out with it, to tell her what she deserved to know. So she could understand.

"I just want to know if you're being a jerk and pushing me away because you want to keep on playing the field or if you are genuinely so damn terrified of opening up to me, of being with any woman and opening yourself up to loss. Of letting me in so that we can be a real family."

When he didn't say anything, stood there like a statue, staring at her, she threw her arms up in the air, hissed, and marched off again.

"Bella, stop," he called out.

She didn't, walking faster, then breaking into a run again. Noah groaned, shut his eyes, and doubled over, his head starting to pound.

"I'm their father, goddamn it. I don't have a fucking choice!"

Relief hit him as the words spilled from his mouth, yelling them at Bella like an insult when all he'd really needed to do was get them off his chest—stop lying to her, keeping the truth from her.

"What did you say?" she demanded, running back, moving faster than he'd ever seen her run before.

He stood, stared her down as she ran toward him. Then she veered off the path, slipped somehow, her eyes transforming from wild to scared as she fell. Noah sprinted over to her, arms around her even though she resisted, but she'd gone over sideways and connected with what looked like a sharp branch poking out from a large shrub.

"Shit, are you okay?" he asked, helping her up and into a comfortable sitting position. Blood was flowing from her lower leg where a branch had made a solid jab into her skin.

"You're lying," she accused, voice low, not even looking at her leg. "My sister would never have cheated on Gray, not in a million years. Not even with you."

Noah pulled his T-shirt over his head and folded it, checking Bella's leg and then tying it tight. She resisted, but he was firm. "You can hate me all you like, but this is something I can deal with, so just let me."

He checked that the shirt was going to hold and sat back. Bella was grimacing as she flexed her leg, then stretched, putting it out in front of her.

"I've been wanting to tell you all this time. I should have just come out with it from the start."

She frowned, and he wasn't sure if it was from the pain or the fact that she was still angry with him. "I don't believe you. Lila would never have—"

"Gray never wanted anyone to know," Noah started.

"You're telling me that Gray *knew* about this?" she interrupted.

"Just hear me out," he said, keeping his voice even, needing to stay calm about what he was sharing with her. "They'd been trying to get pregnant for a while, and things just weren't happening. You remember how she looked into IVF?"

Bella nodded. Barely, but he saw it.

"It was so expensive, and then they found out that it was Gray's problem. That he was shooting blanks, and it killed him that he wasn't going to be able to give his wife the family they'd always talked about, always dreamed of."

"So let me get this straight," Bella said. "They turned to you, and only you? She decided to tell *you* about her infertility problems instead of *me*?"

Noah nodded. "I know it's hard to digest, impossible to process after so many years of not knowing, but Gray swore Lila to secrecy, didn't want anyone to know about his shit. He told me when we were drunk one night after both arriving home from deployment. When I offered to help out, we all agreed that it was best if no one knew, so there'd be no chance the boys would ever find out that Gray wasn't their biological dad."

Bella was in shock. She was staring at him like he'd just told her he was a superhero. Then she laughed.

"I don't believe you. It's just—"

"Why else do you think they put me down as joint guardian? We both know that you'd be perfectly capable without me hanging around, but I'm biologically their father. When we did all the legal stuff, we all decided that the boys should never know. Hell, my true dad is Gray's dad. He was the one who raised me, turned me into the man I am today. I might not have met him until I was a teenager, but he's the one who deserves to be called 'Dad,' not the guy who made me biologically. Gray's dad cared for me, taught me, put me through college. A real dad is the one who's there for you, who raises you, so in my books we weren't lying to anyone anyway."

She sucked in a breath. "You're serious, aren't you? You're actually telling me the truth."

"It's not something I'd joke about."

Bella went to stand up and he helped her, jumped up and guided her into standing.

"I'm fine."

"No, you're not." He bent and scooped her up, cradling her in his arms and heading back in the direction they'd originally come from.

She struggled for a moment, then gave in, head to his chest. After a few minutes she looped her arms around his neck.

"I want to hate you so bad."

Noah chuckled. "And now you can't because I helped your sister out when she needed it the most."

"At least I know why she always stood up for you, even when you were being a jerk."

"She treated me as family well before then. She loved me like a brother, and the feeling was reciprocated."

His chest was suddenly wet, and he realized they were Bella's tears, falling against his skin and trailing down. She never made a noise, and he never said a thing.

"Noah, I need to ask you . . ." She blew out a breath, and he could see that whatever it was, it was hard for her to say. "About changing your job. I need to know why you can't even do this for the boys? If not me, then why not them?"

He straightened his shoulders, said the words he'd told himself a thousand times over already. "It's my duty, Bella. This is what I do. It's what I have to do."

"This is just too hard for me. I can't do this, Noah—not in a million years. I can't keep," she paused, eyes locked on his. "I can't keep loving you. I will always honor Lila and Gray's wish, but nothing can happen romantically between us ever again. When you get back, we'll have to decide whether or not we can actually keep living under the same roof."

He didn't know what to say, how to respond without hurting her feelings even more than he already had. He was doing what he was trained to do, what he'd always done, what he knew best. "I know," he eventually replied.

"So this is good-bye?" she asked when they finally reached the car.

Noah dropped a kiss to her head. "Yeah. I guess it is."

"When will we see you again?"

He didn't let her go, held her tight, inhaled and smelled the sweet scent of her shampoo and perfume mixed together with her sweat, enjoyed the weight of her in his arms. If he could let go of the past, he'd give in—for Bella he would do it—but he couldn't.

There was no way he could deal with all the shit that had happened to him, let her close, like she deserved.

"I can't answer that, Bella," he said. "It could be a couple of weeks, a month, maybe longer. And if you decide you're better off without me around, then I'll find my own place when I get back. I won't ever walk away from those boys, but I'll give you all the space you need."

She nodded, pressing a soft kiss to his chest before slipping from his arms. He had no idea why the sudden burst of affection, but he wasn't about to push her away.

"I'll see you back home." Her smile was sad. "Where we can just pretend like there's nothing going on between us, like we're so damn good at doing."

Noah wanted to help her, carry her or assist her to her vehicle, but she'd already turned, was proudly struggling on her own, shoulders back and head held high. He knew what he'd done, pushed away the one woman he should have held tight and never let go of. But life was a bitch, he knew that, and nothing was going to change about the lot he'd been dealt in life.

Bella got in her car, sat there for a moment, then drove off. Noah watched her go, stayed dead still as her SUV disappeared into the distance. And only when she was gone did he curse so loud that he was certain all the birds had fled the area.

"Fuck!" he yelled. *"Fuck!"*

Silence engulfed him, left him hollow. His heart was beating fast, body reeling, hands desperate to make a fist and slam into something, *anything*. But he held it together, refused to ruin the hands that his brothers would be counting on when they were deployed. Instead, he dropped to his knees, stuffed a fist to his mouth to stop the desperate yell that was fighting to emerge, suppressing the sobs of anger. Of betrayal. *Of pure, cold, soulless desperation.*

Noah choked then, had to let it out. Tears erupted and fell in a steady stream down his cheeks, his breath ragged as he tried to catch it, sobs raking his chest. He sat there, dropped to his knees, power-less to do anything. For the first time in his life, since he'd made the decision as a boy to never let anyone hurt or humiliate him, or take power from him again, he cried until he had nothing left.

Nothing.

He was a goddamn idiot, and the only person in the world he could blame was himself.

~

Bella felt sick. Physically sick. She'd arrived home, struggled in with Noah's T-shirt wrapped around her leg, and gotten in the shower. She'd washed her hair, cleaned up her leg, and carefully bandaged it. It'd take a while to heal, but she had no intention of going to the doctor unless she needed to. And now she was standing in the living room, staring around a room that had started to feel like hers even though it wasn't, and wondering what the hell she was going to do.

She had her phone in her hand, had been about to call Serena, then changed her mind. Then she thought about calling her mom, but changed her mind about that, too. What was she going to tell her? That she was pissed with her dead sister for not telling her that her husband's best friend was actually the father of her children? It was like a bad movie, one that she'd never have believed could have happened in real life. *And yet it did.*

Instead, she sat down on the sofa and stared out the window. At the boys' bikes, left forlorn in the yard, exactly where they'd leaped off them when something else had taken their attention. It was their home, a place she could never deny them, especially not when the mortgage had been paid with the life insurance policies from their parents. It was where so many of their memories were, memories that included their mom and dad. And if she was honest with herself, it was where she'd started to imagine Noah and her raising them together, long term. Somehow she'd gone from Ms. Cynical to Ms. Fairy Tale, believing that born from all the pain she was miraculously going to end up with her own happily ever after.

Bella changed her mind and dialed her mom.

"Hi, darling," her mom answered.

"Hey," she managed, trying to sound fine, like her world wasn't completely in free fall.

"What's wrong?"

"Nothing," she lied. "I just miss Lila. I wish she were here, so I could talk to her."

"Your father mentioned that Noah might be deployed again soon. Did he mention anything to you? Your dad thought things were heating up somewhere, that Noah was trying to hint to him that he was going to have to leave soon."

"Yeah," Bella said, "he is." She was trying so hard not to cry, but her voice was cracking.

"Oh, sweetheart, it'll be okay. He'll be fine. I know how hard it is saying good-bye."

Bella nodded, tucking her knees up to her chin. She felt like a little girl again, desperate to be cuddled and reassured. There was so much she wanted to tell her mom, wished she could say.

"How much did Lila ever talk to you about him?" she asked. "Noah, I mean."

"She talked about him a lot sometimes. About how sad she thought he was, how much women loved him but that she doubted he'd ever settle down. And sometimes she'd mention what a great friend he was to Gray, that he'd do anything for him. Or her for that matter."

Bella gulped, knowing she was about to betray Noah's confidence but needing to tell her mom. It wasn't that she wanted to share something that was supposed to be private; she just couldn't deal with it on her own and needed to know if her mom knew.

"Did she ever tell you what they went through to have the boys?" Bella asked, her voice so low it was almost a whisper.

"You mean how they were going to have IVF?" her mom asked.

She sighed, deciding that it was Noah's right to decide who to tell and what he wanted others to know, no matter how badly she needed and wanted to talk about it. Her mom obviously didn't know anymore than she herself had. "Yeah. He was just saying how hard it was on Gray, thinking they weren't going to be able to have children."

"Do you want me to come over? I'm just folding washing. I was going to attempt a round of golf with your father, but—"

"I'm fine, thanks, Mom." Bella sniffled and pulled herself together, stretching out her legs. "I just needed to talk."

"I miss her every day, sweetheart. Sometimes it's so bad I don't know how I'm going to drag myself out of bed and face the day."

"Me, too," Bella answered truthfully. "And then other days I feel happy and forget about what happened, and then spend hours feeling guilty when it hits me."

"You're not alone there, Bella. Not for a second."

They didn't say anything for a few beats.

"Sweetheart, I don't want you waiting for another letter. Not for a little bit. Lila left instructions that you weren't to receive the next one for at least four weeks."

"She *what*? No way. Just send it. I need it. I can't go without them."

"She left instructions saying the . . ."—her mom's voice trailed off for a moment—"that this one had to be sent then. I don't know why, but we need to respect her wishes. The plan she had when she wrote them."

Bella didn't know what to say, but it wasn't her mom's fault, and she didn't need Bella telling her to ignore her other daughter's wishes.

"I understand. Thanks, Mom."

"Just call if you need me."

"I will."

Bella forced herself up and decided to check her emails, get a few jobs done, then go out for a coffee and have the afternoon to herself before it was time to pick up the boys. With Noah gone she was going to have to get used to it being just the three of them again, whether she liked it or not.

She grimaced as her leg throbbed, and decided to take some ibuprofen before sitting down at her desk. The last thing she needed was a reminder about Noah, so the faster she extinguished the pain, the better.

CHAPTER FIFTEEN

Dear Bella,
I wish I were there for you. You're always there for me whenever I need you. Like with the boys. Or when I'm dealing with Gray being away. Brody was an asshole—you know that, right? You're better off without him. We all knew he wasn't good enough for you, even if he did start out by impressing Dad with his Navy training.

I'll never tell anyone your secret, not even Gray. You know that when I make a promise, no one can make me break it. But know that you will meet someone better one day. You'll meet your Gray. I believe in that, and you should, too.

Go to a spa, pamper yourself, remind yourself what an amazing career you've carved for yourself because you've always known the woman you wanted to be. I'm so proud of you, and I always will be. But one day when you find The One, you need to tell him everything—your past, your fears, your hopes and dreams. Don't hold everything so tight to your chest that you never get to live and love.

Lila xoxo

Tears trickled down Bella's cheeks as she sat in a puddle of all the letters Lila had sent her over the years. They were all around her—she'd kept every single one, and after putting the boys to bed, she'd dragged them all out again. She'd brought the box over when she'd packed up her condo, but after Noah had found them that night, she'd stuffed it above the closet in Lila's old room, and now she was going through every letter all over again, reliving her past, letter by letter. They'd written about nothing and everything, two sisters keeping in touch and writing the things they would have otherwise chatted about over the phone if Lila hadn't been half a world away.

And now she was alone again, more alone than she'd ever been in her life. Except for one of her favorite letters from her sister, clasped tight in her hand.

She'd farewelled Noah ten days ago now, and she was at home by herself. Alone. She was tempted to go and curl up in one of the boys' beds just to have a warm body tucked to hers. They were sleeping better than they had been, but they were still upset about Noah being gone, confused why he hadn't been able to stay.

"Don't go, Noah!" Cooper pleaded, hanging on to his leg like he was going to be able to stop him by strength alone.

"Please, Noah. Can't you stay?"

Noah dropped to his haunches, put his arms around both boys, and hugged them tight. "I would stay if I could, guys, but I need you to be strong and look after Bella for me."

He'd looked up at her, eyes warm yet sad. And she'd smiled and pretended like everything was okay.

"It won't be for long. Noah will be back before you know it."

"How long?" Cooper had demanded.

"I don't know exactly how long, buddy, but I'll be back as soon as I can. I need to do this, I have men depending on me."

"Say good-bye to Noah, boys. We'll see him again soon."

"Bye, Noah," Cooper mumbled.

"I love you," Will had said, his brows furrowed, hands fisted like he was fighting tears, trying to be a big boy. "I love you this much." He flung his arms up as high as they would go.

Noah had looked like his heart was going to break, hugging Will tight.

"I love you, too," Cooper mumbled, stepping in for a hug.

Noah cleared his throat, glanced at Bella. "Me, too."

If only Lila had known how Bella would end up feeling about him, how her letters had drawn them together. If only she'd told her about what Noah had done for her and Gray. But then her sister had always been amazing at keeping secrets, right from when they were little girls protecting each other from getting into trouble.

And now Noah was gone. He'd walked out the door and gone God only knew where. To fight to keep their country safe. She loved that he was so proud, that he did such important work, but it didn't stop her from wishing he was safe at home. Even if he'd never be hers, she'd just found out the boys still had a father. He might not think he deserved the title yet, but she knew he did. After seeing him look after them, care for them, and take to parenting like a duck to water, even though he had no idea how good he was at it, he deserved to be their dad. Even if they never actually knew the truth of how they were conceived.

She slowly packed the letters up, put them in order back in the box. It took awhile until eventually they were all tucked away safe again. Bella tied the pink and white ribbon she'd always used to tie the box shut, and carried it up to bed with her, flicking out lights on her way up. Once she'd put the box away again, she turned, stared at the big, cold bed she should be getting into, and decided she couldn't face it. She silently crept into the boys' room, saw that

Cooper was spread-eagled across his bed, but Will was tucked up on one side of his, leaving plenty of room for her. She was already wearing her PJs, so she pulled the covers back, lay down beside him, and tucked the covers up to their chins.

Now she understood why so many moms loved to snuggle with their kids. A few months of having warm little bodies against hers, and she was heartbroken at the thought of them growing up and not wanting to cuddle her any more.

~

"So how are you getting on, really?" Serena asked, sliding her cocktail down the bar toward her.

"I'm fine," Bella said, gratefully placing the straw between her teeth and sucking a slow sip.

"You don't have to put on a brave face, Bella. If you miss him like hell, just say it." Serena's bright blue eyes never left hers. She wasn't easy to fool.

"The alternative is me bursting into tears and you having to take me home and feed me ice cream," Bella said, holding her glass up in the air. "So let's just say cheers to a night out and agree not to talk about him."

Serena clinked her glass to Bella's. "Cheers."

"I have heard from him, though. He called to speak to the boys, but the line was terrible, and we've had a few weird, crackly calls since. Other than that, it's just been emails."

Serena's smile was wicked. "I thought we weren't talking about him?"

Bella groaned. "Sorry. I think about him *all* the time. I hardly do anything else, worrying about him not coming back, what I'll tell the boys, how I'd cope if I lost someone else that I lo—"

Serena cleared her throat, and Bella coughed.

"I just don't want him coming home in a body bag or not at all," Bella muttered.

Her friend slung an arm around her and gave her a big hug.

"If anyone can cope with this, you can," Serena said, holding her tight. They stayed like that for a long while, neither caring to move.

"And if I can't?" Bella asked, biting hard on her bottom lip as it started to quiver, her telltale sign she was about to cry.

"You will. You're stronger than you realize, B."

"It's just been so hard with him away. Before he arrived, I had this careful life all mapped out, and we stuck to my plan. We were making things work. And then Noah came along and drove me crazy, tipped everything on end, and brought so much fun and laughter into the boys' lives." She paused. "That's why it's so hard, because it's not just me missing him; it's them, too."

They went back to sipping their drinks, seated together at the bar. Bella had been looking forward to a night out, just to hang with Serena and take a break for herself. Gray's mom was staying, and she'd virtually pushed her out the door and locked it so she couldn't get back in.

"This is potent," Bella said, draining another third of her cocktail and deciding she no longer wanted to talk about Noah or the boys or anything related to the past year.

"I know—they're delicious. I'm obsessed with mojitos right now."

"Hi there, beautiful ladies," came a deep, drawling voice from behind them.

Serena turned first, her smile dazzling. Bella almost giggled as she watched her friend turn on the charm.

"You look like you could use another drink," the man said.

Bella considered him, wondered if she would have been more interested if it hadn't been for Noah. The guy was handsome, with a Southern drawl, probably in town for business and looking to have some fun. Although from the look of it, it was Serena he was interested in. He was practically drooling over her gorgeous blonde friend.

"We're just having a girls' night," Serena said. "Perhaps we'll come over later and say hi."

The man looked disappointed, but Serena had left him with some hope, and so he wasn't completely dejected.

"We've got a nice little table over there," he said, gesturing to the other side of the bar where tables were paired with booth seats covered in soft fabric and littered with cushions to make it a nice place to relax. "My friend has been checking this one out all night," he said, glancing at Bella and grinning.

Bella laughed, avoiding eye contact but happy that at least one other man on the planet was interested in her. Serena managed to get rid of him, and they went back to leaning against the bar.

"You don't have to stay with me. Go have fun if you want," Bella told her.

"Seriously?" Serena said with a laugh. "I don't like being a complete bitch when a guy gets up the nerve to come over and say hi, but I'm not going near them with a ten-foot pole!"

Bella leaned into her. "I'm so pleased I've got you to keep me sane."

"Hey, that's what I'm here for. To make you laugh and forget your troubles."

"I love those boys so much," Bella said, her head on Serena's shoulder. "They're so impossible sometimes, but seeing Will all dressed up as whatever superhero he is that day and watching Cooper build some new creation after pre-K—it just makes all the hardship worth it."

"You're a great mom," Serena said. "Anyone can see that."

Bella sighed. "But I'm still not *their* mom. I'm trying so hard, but I'm never going to be able to fill that void completely."

"You don't have to," Serena said, squeezing her hand as she took a big long, last sip of her mojito. "You have to be the best aunt in the world. That's all you can be, and I promise you, that's enough."

Bella finished her drink and pushed the glass away. "Can we go somewhere with loud music so we can dance?" she asked.

Serena grabbed her purse and slid off the chair. "I thought you'd never ask."

CHAPTER SIXTEEN

Six weeks later

B ella sat outside the principal's office, waiting to be called in. She'd already picked Cooper up from pre-K, knowing that the meeting might run over time and result in her being late. She sighed, looking down at him playing with a toy Spiderman. They were both such good boys, but where Cooper had become very clingy with her and didn't want her to leave him at pre-K, Will had happily gone off every morning, only to be disruptive in class. She knew that he was acting out; she just didn't know quite what to do about it, especially given how angelic he was for her at home.

Eventually, the woman who'd originally seated her waved her over, and she touched Cooper's shoulder, nodding for him to follow. He kept his toy clutched in one hand, and she took the other, walking him into the principal's office with her. She felt like she was heading into the lion's den, straight back to being a naughty schoolgirl all over again—except that had never been her because she'd rarely gotten into trouble.

"Good afternoon."

She held out her hand. "Nice to see you again. I just wish it was under more, uh, well, happier circumstances."

The principal smiled. "These things can happen. I wanted you here today to discuss our plan moving forward, so we can improve Will's behavior."

Bella nodded, opening her mouth to speak, before being interrupted.

"Sorry I'm late."

Bella froze, turned slowly, jaw dropping. She couldn't have been more shocked if her sister had just walked into the room.

"Noah?" she asked, convinced she was imagining him.

"Hi, Bella," he said, voice deep and sexy all rolled into one. Noah dropped a kiss to her cheek, lips brushing her skin. "I picked up the message on my cell just after I arrived back in the country. I got here as quick as I could."

"Noah!" Cooper had been so busy playing in the corner that it had taken him a moment to realize who was in the room.

"Hey, buddy!" He dropped to his haunches and opened his arms, Cooper hurtling toward him at full speed. Noah gave him a big hug, Cooper's arms looped tight around his neck, then stood with the boy in his arms, to go sit beside Bella.

She was still in shock, certain she wouldn't do anything more than stutter if she tried to open her mouth.

"I'm glad you're both here," the principal said.

"Fill me in," Noah said. "Will's been acting out?"

"He has been increasingly difficult for his teacher, who is of course very understanding of the trauma he's been through, but today there was an incident where he hit another child. A boy said something to him, and he punched him rather hard in the face. His parents are quite agitated by the situation, as I'm sure you can understand."

"We are so—" began Bella.

"What did the boy say?" Noah interrupted.

Bella stared at him, annoyed that he'd cut off her apology, but not wanting to cause a scene. "You jump straight to that?" she asked, keeping her voice as calm and polite as she could.

Noah turned to her, eyes crinkling ever so at the corners as he smiled at her. She refused to be sucked in, to remember what it was like to be in his gaze, to have that smile directed at her and only her when they were alone. She'd tried so hard to put all those thoughts behind her, to move forward while he was away, but now that he was back . . . *impossible* came to mind.

"Maybe I just don't want to think the worst about a little boy who's never done anything violent in his life, or maybe I just have a gut feeling that whatever was said justified the action." He sighed. "And no, before either of you jump down my throat and tell me that violence should not be condoned under any situation, I don't agree with that. I'm just trying to understand."

Bella swiveled in her seat, digesting Noah's words. The principal looked uncomfortable.

"My understanding is that the other boy made a taunt about Will's parents being . . . er, dead."

Noah stood then, Cooper on his hip, one arm looped around the child, looking every bit the scary SEAL. If it weren't for the kid, Bella would have been recoiling into her seat herself from the ferocious look on his face.

"Let me get this straight," Noah began, lowering his voice as he glanced first at Cooper, then stared the principal down. "You call me in here, away from work, under the pretense that our *son* has problems to deal with, when in fact he was taunted about his dead parents? Sorry, but all our kid did was punch a bully who deserved it, and unless you're prepared to tell me different, that I've somehow gotten this story wrong, then I'm walking out that door right now and taking our boys with me."

Bella gulped. She might have been doing perfectly fine without him while he was away, but she was damn happy to have him here as backup right now. He looked at her, and she stood, wanting to show him her support, show the principal that they were a united front. It didn't make sense not to be firmly in his camp right now.

"Sir, we don't condone violence here."

"And the real world doesn't condone bullies," Noah shot back. "In the world I live in, no one gets away with talking smack like that other kid did."

He gave the principal one last glare and then nodded to Bella. She gathered her purse and marched out after him, too scared not to and feeling liberated for doing what she knew in her heart was right. Will was waiting for them when they emerged from the office, his entire face lighting up when he saw Noah.

"Noah!" he yelled, jumping from his chair.

Noah passed Cooper to her, and she cuddled the little boy while Noah embraced Will, holding him very tight. They stayed like that a long time, and when Noah finally pulled back, she could see that both of them had tears in their eyes.

They all walked, both of them carrying a child, and when they were out of the building, Noah slowed. "Buddy, tell me what went down today. I'm not angry with you. I just want to know what the other boy said."

"He's been teasing me for ages, telling me I'm the only kid with dead parents," Will admitted, head down, staring at Noah's chest.

Noah tucked his thumb under Will's chin, forcing him to raise it. "That's not okay. You should have told Bella."

"I know."

"And what else did he say today?"

"That my dad was probably a chickenshit soldier." Will glanced at her. "Sorry for swearing."

"It's okay," Bella said, smiling. "You're just repeating what he said." She couldn't believe other six- or seven-year-olds were even saying things like that!

"Anything else?"

"That I was gonna end up in some place for unwanted kids. Foster something."

Bella saw the way Noah's body tensed, knew how much those words would cut deep for him personally.

"That's never going to happen, you hear me?" Noah ground out, voice husky, dragged over gravel it sounded so painful. He set Will down and placed his hands on his shoulders. "When I was a little boy, that's what happened to me. And I would never, *ever* let the same happen to you, okay? Bella and I love you so much, boys, and no matter what happens or what changes, that will always remain true."

Bella had tears welling in her eyes, emotion pooling in her belly. "Noah's right," she said, "you boys will always be loved and cared for by us. And you have grandparents who would do anything for you, too."

She hugged Cooper even tighter to her and watched as Noah did the same to Will.

"I love you," she heard Will mumble.

"Me, too," Noah said back.

They started walking to the parking lot when it hit her. Noah had never said 'I love you' back to the boys. He either stiffened up, nodded, or said, "Me, too." Not once had she ever heard him tell the boys directly that he loved them.

"Want me to take them both back in my car?" Bella asked.

"I actually got a cab here. Long story short, but I really hauled ass to make this appointment."

"Then I guess we're all going in mine," she said, grinning at the boys. "How about we get ice cream on the way home?"

The boys both cheered, and she was happy, loving the fact that they were smiling and content, even if Will had had a tough day. Being around Noah again had unsettled her, but she was just going to have to learn live with it.

~

Noah had made up an excuse to get out of the house. He'd spent weeks away, had been in the pits of hell, and now he'd been thrust back into domestic life like he'd just been away working a normal job. And then he'd seen Bella, and all his goddamn intentions of staying in control and not giving in to how he felt about her disappeared like they'd never existed in the first place. Her wide mouth, honey-blonde hair, and soulful dark eyes had flicked a switch, and it was more than the way she looked. It was the way she made him feel, like he could draw her into his arms, and somehow everything would be okay.

He sucked in a breath and jumped in his SUV, gunning the engine into life and starting to drive. He'd been going to head back home, to Gray's parents' house, but there was no one he could talk to there. Not about the stuff he needed to talk about. He'd been debriefed, talked with his boys after they got home, all the usual stuff, but this time he was struggling.

Because he'd also said yes to the big new job, and it scared the crap out of him.

Twenty minutes later, he found himself parked outside Bella's family home. He stared at the front door, debating whether to knock or just turn around and head home again. Noah slumped, one hand working the steering wheel, gripping it tight, then letting go, before repeating the action again.

And then the door swung open, and Bella's father walked out, straight backed like he was still a Marine, not stopping until he was standing outside Noah's door. He put the window down.

"Afternoon, sir," Noah said.

"Son, are you just gonna sit there all day, staring at my house, or come on in?"

Noah chuckled. "Staring seemed like a good idea there for a while."

James motioned with his head and turned, heading back the way he'd come, and Noah got out and followed him, straight through the house and to a couple of big chairs facing the yard.

"Make yourself comfortable," James said. "I'll go grab us a couple of beers."

Noah sat, a million things running through his mind and not one of them ready to be spoken yet. He took the beer when it was passed to him, and Bella's dad dropped down beside him. They sat in silence for a long while, enough time for Noah to slowly sip half his beer or more, before James finally spoke up.

"I'm guessing by the fact you found your way here that you need an ear."

Noah nodded. "I was going somewhere else, and then . . ."

"You know I'll keep your secrets. You need to talk, talk. It doesn't do anyone any good holding that shit in."

Noah blew out a big breath. "We justify what we do by telling ourselves we're ridding the world of evil. That it's okay to take a life to protect our country, so long as the threat is real."

"You don't believe that anymore?" James asked.

Noah grunted. "Hell no, I still believe it."

Bella's dad took a pull of beer. "Then I'm not sure what you're asking me."

He sat a bit longer, gathering his thoughts, not wanting to break his oath and disclose anything he shouldn't. "I've been doing this job a long time, have been to places that made my training during Hell Week seem easy, but I've never, ever shot a woman." He closed his eyes, relived the moment, fingers clenching tight around his beer bottle. *"Until now."*

They were silent for a while again, neither needing to say anything.

"You want to talk about it?" James finally asked.

"Nothing to say, really," Noah told him, eyes still trained straight ahead. "I was protecting my boys, and I was staring down the lens, keeping watch as sniper, and a woman was suddenly holding a grenade. She was already dead, was about to pull it, take out innocent people and maybe one of my guys. I didn't hesitate, took the shot, but there was something about squeezing that trigger and taking a woman's life." He finished his beer in one last, long sip. "I keep replaying it over and over, but I couldn't have made any other decision. It was my only option, and I did what I had to do."

"And now you're back." James spoke softly, and Noah turned to him, knowing that he understood, that he'd been where Noah was now, knew what it was like in a way that civilians just couldn't, no matter how hard they tried.

"Yeah, now I'm back." Noah sighed. "I'm back playing dad, living in a house with your daughter, and pretending like I'm a regular guy instead of a killer. When in fact I've never wanted to be the normal guy."

"And yet here you are."

"Yep, here I am."

"Want another beer?"

"Would love one, but I'm driving and I have to get back." Noah checked that he'd drained the bottle and grinned.

"You gonna be okay, son?"

"I'm sharing a house with a woman who's the kind of girl I should be settling down with and marrying, and instead I'm trying to run as fast in the other direction as possible because I'm scared shitless of the way I feel. I'm in love with two little boys who I can't even say those words to because it scares me even more, and I've just said yes to a job that's gonna see me leave active duty and start making decisions that involve the possibility of direct meetings with the president." He balled his fists. "So no, 'okay' is probably not the right word to describe how I feel right now."

James started to laugh, his big chest heaving, and it only took Noah a few seconds to join in. It was either laugh or cry, and right now this was feeling like the better option.

"Noah, let me set you straight here. Talking about my daughter doesn't come easy, not when it involves a man, but if she's driving you crazy in a good way, then see the woods for the trees and man up. You don't meet a woman every day that makes you question the man you are, and it takes a lot for me to say that." James chuckled. "Someone said to me when I had two girls that they felt sorry for me because I had to worry about all the penises out there in the world, and they only had to worry about one, 'cause they only had one son."

Noah laughed hard then. "Sorry, sir. I don't want you having to worry about—er, mine."

James slapped him on the back. "I'd like to be only worrying about yours and no other man's, that's for sure!" Then his tone turned more somber, his face serious. "But Noah, I don't care what shit you've been through now or when you were a kid, it's time to looks those boys in the eye and tell them you love them. Just spit the words out. And if you've made the decision to stand down as an active-duty SEAL, then that's your call. If you know deep down that you've done it for the right reasons, everything will work out for the best. Trust me on that." He grinned. "And stop calling me 'sir,' goddamn it!"

Noah rose, holding out his hand. James clasped it, his grip as firm and unrelenting as his eye contact.

"And if you want my blessing to be with my daughter, you have it."

"That's not why I came here today."

"I know, but if it turns out that way . . ." James shrugged, a smile on his face.

Noah turned to leave, pleased he'd stopped by, then almost bumped smack bang into Bella's mom as he passed through the living room.

"Noah! What a nice surprise." She reached for him, standing on tiptoe to embrace him and kiss his cheek. "When did you arrive home?"

He returned the hug, amazed at how welcome Bella's parents always made him feel. They were like Gray's family—genuine people who had the kind of home life he'd once thought was bullshit.

"I arrived back a few hours ago. Spent last night on base, then rushed back to see the boys."

"Is Bella okay? We didn't see a lot of her while you were away. She was quiet, unusually quiet."

Noah nodded. "We've, ah . . ." He wasn't exactly sure what to say.

"You want to stay for a coffee? I have cookies I baked this morning."

He smiled. "Thanks, but I'd better get back."

"Let me quickly put some in a container for the boys. Something nice for them for after dinner."

"Sounds good."

She dashed around, filling the container and talking as she worked. "Noah, I sent a letter today. The last one."

His heart sank. Bella would be heartbroken.

"Do you know if she's received it yet?"

He shook his head. "No, but I think I'll head straight home."

Christine touched his shoulder. "It's been hard on me, sending these letters at the times Lila instructed. But she asked me not to interfere, to do as she asked, and I've done my best. But I think this one is going to be tough. Knowing there are no more."

"I'll head straight back. She'll be fine."

"You know, she made it clear that I had to wait a full month, but that if you were away, I had to wait until you were home. She wanted you both there."

Her hand left his shoulder, but it was like she was still holding on to him. He stayed standing, waiting. "It'll be okay. We'll be okay."

"You always managed to rough Bella up the wrong way, get her all riled up, but I think even then it was because she was scared about the way you made her feel. You're good for her, Noah, and if you let her in, I think you'd see she'd be good for you, too."

He shook his head. "You don't have to convince me about her being good for me, Christine. Trouble is that I'm not good enough for her."

She tut-tutted. "You might think you're some broken soul who can't be saved, but you're not, Noah. You're a good man who deserves a good woman, and instead of being happy, the two of you are so darn pigheaded that you'll probably both end up miserable just to spite yourselves."

Noah ducked his head, not ready to face up to her words. "Thanks for the cookies."

"No trouble. And you just drop those boys around here whenever you need to, you hear?"

He grinned to himself as he walked out the front door. The only other people in his life who'd ever been able to call him a dickhead and get away with it were his boys, his brothers in the Navy,

Lila, or Gray. Yet he'd just taken as good a whippin' from Bella's mom. Given how crappy he'd felt earlier, he was just happy to be smiling again.

CHAPTER SEVENTEEN

November 2014

Dear Bella,
Sending you these letters has either been the best thing I've ever done or the worst. Maybe it ripped the wound open even further, made you miss me more, or maybe it made you feel like I was still near. Either way, I want you to know that I love you so much, and I only did this to try to be there for you and make you happy.

Noah is a great guy, and at the very least I hope you can walk through this life with him as an ally. God only knows, the boys adore him, and I hope he's opened up to you about . . . everything.

What I've asked of you, to look after my boys and be their mom, is something no woman should ever have to ask of another. But I trust you so much and I know that in time they'll forget all about me and think of you as their real mom anyway. Don't shake your head at me either, because I'm a realist enough to know that even if you show them my picture and kiss my photo every night, I'll one day be no more than a very blurry memory.

And so this is when I tell you that this is my last letter. Don't cry or yell at me or curse, just accept that I love you. I would write a thousand of these if I could, but the truth is, I can't. It's been so hard on me writing what I have, thinking that one day they might actually be sent. Because that'll mean I'm gone and I've left everyone I love behind.

Each letter so far, every date, was actually a real date that Gray took me on when we first met. I first caught a glimpse of him at a bar, when we were both sober drivers, and the next day he found me, and we went to the beach and ate cheap and cheerful Mexican food from paper plates. Then he took me on a real date to the Italian place, the same place we went every wedding anniversary when we were both home, and then it was showing off our skills at the shooting range. The hike was next, such a short time later, but it was when he told me he loved me . . . and that he was being deployed the next morning. I sobbed my heart out that night, wishing we'd had longer, worrying about him. Realizing what my own family went through when I was deployed myself. And then he came home after months away, and we went to the fair. That was the night he proposed, and it was the best night of my life. Some people will tell you it was meeting their babies for the first time that was the most special, but for me it was seeing the look in Gray's eyes when he told me he loved me, that he wanted me to be his wife. Although watching as he cradled Will and then Cooper for the first time was a pretty close second.

This is good-bye Bella, but it's a good-bye filled with more love than you could imagine. Be kind to Noah, let him look after you, and kiss those boys every night with love in your heart and endless patience in your mind. I love you more than words can express. To the best sister in the world, the best Barbie-doll player, the fastest runner, the biggest bitch when you didn't get your own way, the most caring aunt. I'll miss you.

Lila xoxo

The sob that escaped Bella's lips sounded more animal than human. She clamped her hand over her mouth, tried so hard to stay quiet, but it was impossible. The pain filled her entire body, every inch of it, raw and stabbing. Another cry echoed out before she could stop it, her body shaking so hard it was uncontrollable.

"Hey!" Noah's deep voice rang out. *"Hey!"* Louder this time, his arms wrapping around her.

She was on the pavement, slumped outside, but Noah's big body was holding her together, keeping her from falling apart completely. His arms were firm, strong, his lips to her ear, whispering words that she knew were supposed to comfort, but she didn't hear a thing.

"Bella, it's okay," he said, not letting go for a second. "It's okay."

She fought for air, struggled to catch her breath.

"I've got you, Bella, I've got you," he murmured directly into her air.

"The letter," she managed. "Lila . . ."

Noah sighed, his chest moving against her back. "I know. It's the last one."

Bella blinked away tears that burned like acid. She'd known it was going to happen, that there was no way they could keep going. Noah had even made mention of it one night, making a joke about it, but she knew he'd been trying to warn her.

"It was her saying good-bye. Explaining"—she shut her eyes tight, the tears too hard to fight—"*everything.* I don't want it to be the last. It can't be. I need her, I need her so bad."

"She didn't mean to hurt you, to make this harder," Noah said. "There's no way she would have wanted to do anything other than show you she loved you."

Bella nodded, feeling stupid. Noah was so strong, and she was showing herself to be weak, so not in control. She'd gone weeks without him, been determined not to need him, and yet here she was in his arms again. In the arms of a man who'd so emphatically turned her down.

"This must seem pathetic to you," she muttered. "I just can't seem to hold anything together, not when it has to do with Lila."

Noah hugged her tighter, his cheek pressed to hers. "You think I don't cry just because I'm a tough Navy guy? No freaking way. When Gray died, I blubbered like a baby, and I'd be a damn mess if it wasn't for having to hold it together around the boys. And you."

She pulled away from him, turned in his arms, still holding the letter and being careful not to crumple it. "You don't have to be strong for me, Noah."

He shrugged. "Yeah, I do. And besides, I want to be."

She touched his face, palm flat to his cheek, looking up into his eyes. Eyes that had become so familiar to her but still managed to send shivers down her spine whenever they were trained on her. "You don't have to stay unless you want to be here, Noah. I wouldn't hold it against you, not after everything you've done for us. Taking all this on isn't something you voluntarily signed up for. You don't need to be here."

"And you?" he asked, his expression suddenly full of what appeared to be fury. "You think I'm the way I am with you out of some sense of duty? That I've been here every day just because a bit of paper said I should be? Because I was a sperm donor for your sister?"

She bit her lip, hard. "I just want you to know that you can walk away, that it wouldn't make me think any less of you, not after everything you've already done for us. For me." Bella pulled her hand back, self-conscious now, when before touching him had seemed so natural. "And for the record, I know you're here because you loved Gray. And Lila. That you're doing this because you loved them, not just because of what you did for them when they couldn't conceive." She sighed. "You told me how you felt before you left, Noah, and I respect that. I get it."

His grimace faded, chest visibly rising with another big breath. "We were doing okay, weren't we? Before I went and fucked everything up."

She nodded, wiping under her eyes, realizing she must be all black panda from crying. She'd been in to work earlier, eye makeup all done because she was seeing clients, and now she was a hot mess. She was at least grateful that he'd seen her at school earlier, looking half decent.

"You think the neighbors are wondering what the hell we're doing out here?" she asked with a laugh.

Noah chuckled, moving forward, his body even closer to hers all of a sudden. "Want to actually give them something to look at?"

Bella studied his face, stared into his eyes, lifted her hand to touch his cheek again. She ran her fingers down to his jaw, her other hand pressed flat to his cheek.

"What happened to not wanting anything more? To wanting out of whatever was going on between us?"

"Screw that," he muttered. "I was a jerk—still am, but now I'm a jerk who knows that he almost wrecked the one good thing he had, when it was just within his grasp."

"So what exactly are you proposing?" she asked.

Noah's expression was intense, his eyes on her mouth. He cupped the back of her head, never lifting his gaze. "I reckon my lips on yours would be a damn good start," he muttered. "Every goddamn day for the rest of our lives."

Bella could hardly breath, could only think about Noah, about what he was about to do, about how his lips would feel. His mouth was soft, then crushing, when it finally happened, when he finally closed the distance between them and made it happen. Her body was alight, full of anticipation where before it had been shuddering, drowning in pain. She should have pushed him away, still been angry with him for hurting her with his words before he left, but she couldn't be. There was no more fight left in her, not when it came to Noah, to the man she'd been pining for ever since he'd left, wishing they could have been less screwed up. That they could have given in to their feelings instead of both fighting what was so good between them.

"Noah, what're you doing to Bella?!"

Noah laughed as he pulled her in tighter, ignoring Cooper calling from the front door. Bella didn't care either, couldn't have cared less who could see them. Because in Noah's arms, everything felt right, like she was safe and cocooned and sheltered from the world. They had a lot to talk about, a hell of a lot to figure out, but she was ready to start the conversation.

"Kissing her!" Noah yelled back when he finally took his lips from hers.

Bella laughed so hard it made her cheeks ache and her belly hurt.

"But she's a *girl*!" Cooper exclaimed.

She laughed harder and Noah cracked up. "Coop, that's exactly why I'm kissing her!"

"Cooties!" he yelled, exasperated. "Now you've gone and gotten girl cooties!"

"Where the hell do they hear this stuff from?" Noah asked, head bent to hers. "And why are they *always* interrupting us?"

"No idea, but it's pretty cute," Bella replied, thankful to have the boys and Noah to pull her through and make her giggle when moments earlier she'd felt at her lowest, like she was all alone at the bottom of a dark pit.

They sat and watched the boys race down the front steps, running across the yard. She had no idea who was trying to get who, but they were both smiling and that's all she cared about.

"When I got the letter, my first thought was that you were home, and I didn't have a sitter booked. At least I don't have to worry about that."

Noah glanced down, moving her so she was still sitting between his legs, but facing away from him now, her back to his chest again. She let her head loll back, leaning into him and loving the hardness of his body and the softness of his touch as he thrummed his fingers up and down over her bare arms.

"We're going out tonight anyway," he said. "But this time we don't need a sitter. I'll organize your mom for Saturday instead."

She leaned back hard so she could tip her head and look up at him. "What's Saturday?" she asked. "And how can we be going somewhere tonight, but not need a sitter?"

He grinned. "Because tonight we're going for Italian again, only this time we're taking the boys. And on Saturday, well, we're doing a date, just you and me. We don't need Lila telling us what to do all the time."

She smiled. "So what is it?"

"What?" he asked back.

She rolled her eyes. "The date. What are we doing?"

"You'll have to wait and see." This time his smile was smug.

"Why, because you haven't figured it out yet?"

He laughed and pushed up to his feet, holding out a hand for her. She took it, palm to palm with him, letting him haul her up. Once she was standing, there was only a foot or so between them, separating them. Her heart started to race again when his eyes dropped to her lips; he was looking at her like he was ready to devour her. But this time the kiss was fast—warm, teasing, delicious, but fleeting.

"You'll just have to wait and see."

CHAPTER EIGHTEEN

November 2014

Dear Noah,
This letter is for your eyes only, and if you've received it, then it means you're getting serious about my sister. I've always imagined you guys together, been all girly and pathetic and dreamed up double dates. Of course Gray would always groan and tell me I had rocks for brains! Bella is stubborn and proud and determined, all traits I'd probably use to describe you actually, and maybe that's why you always butted heads. But you have to promise me that you'll treat her right, that you won't hurt her. She deserves a real man like you, and I want you to promise that you'll be sensitive when she needs you to be. Just promise me that you'll have her back, that if you let something happen between you, it's because you're prepared to go all the way. You need to let her in, tell her all your truths, let her see the real you. The one I've seen, and the parts of you that you've kept hidden even from Gray.

I give you my blessing, Noah, a thousand times over. If I'd met you instead of Gray, I'd have probably fallen for you myself. Your problem is that you don't believe in yourself enough. You're one of the most respected members of SEAL Team 3—I know

*that, and you know that—but your job isn't what defines you. It's
your heart and your courage and your willingness to put others
before yourself. At some point, you won't be a SEAL, though, and
you're going to have to learn to love and be loved if you want to
keep being that gorgeous, courageous man willing to put everything on the line.*

Don't be scared, Noah. Just be brave.

*I'll always love you for the brother you've been to my husband,
the friend you've been to me, and the uncle you've been to my kids.
They wouldn't even be here without you, and every night before bed
I thank God for bringing you into our lives.*

Now it's time to say my final good-bye. I love you.

Lila xoxo

Noah was nervous. A hand-clenching, needing-to-pace, pissing-
himself-off kind of nervous. Which was stupid, because they were
only going out to dinner with the kids, but he needed to tell Bella
something. Needed to man up and just get the words out. Trouble
was, he didn't recall being this nervous when he was going off on his
first deployment, or waiting to start his BUD/S training.

"Noah?"

He jumped up, having just dropped into a chair at the kitchen
table.

"The kids are just goofing around upstairs. They'll be ready
when we are." She frowned. "You okay?"

He shook his head, about to tell her that no, he wasn't okay,
then changed his mind. "You know all that bullshit I said when we
were hiking? Any chance you could just forget it all and give me a
second chance?"

Bella's eyebrows shot up, her mouth parting as she stared at
him. He could have laughed at the expression on her face, except he
was still shitting himself about all the things he needed to say.

"I've said plenty of things to you that I wish I could take back," she said, her smile returning, eyes soft as she looked back at him, caring. Maybe that's why she scared him so much, because he knew how sweet she was now that he'd gotten to know her properly, and just how easy it'd be for him to hurt her.

"I go out and do my job, keep my cool and stay calm for days or even weeks or months, and yet trying to talk to you . . ." he muttered. "I don't know what you've done to me. I think it was talking to your mom that rattled me."

This time Bella's eyebrows shot up so high it did make him chuckle.

"You talked to my mom?" she demanded. "When? Why?"

He grinned. "Now look who's all bent out of shape."

"Noah! I'm serious."

He sat back down again, indicating for her to do the same. She did, but she still looked alarmed. "It was no big deal. I just needed someone to talk to, and somehow I ended up at your folks place, talking to your dad. About war and stuff."

"Uh-huh." She looked more relaxed now. "And then my mom—"

"It was nothing. I just . . ." Now it was him ending his sentence without finishing. "Your mom just helped me put some things into perspective. About you. How I feel."

Bella looked exasperated. "You talked about your feelings with my mom!" She shook her head. "I need a glass of whiskey, something strong."

Noah laughed, fought the urge to keep the rest of what he had to say bottled up, made himself reach for her, to open up and connect with her. "You don't need a glass of anything, and I didn't tell her anything. She just saw something in me, kind of like Lila always did. That's all."

Bella seemed calmer, not so alarmed. "The whole time you were gone, I was imagining us living here for the next fifteen years, some crazy dysfunctional family, with you and I dating other people but being under the same roof. Trying to keep things normal for the boys and screwing them up in the process."

Noah swallowed, stroked her hand, looked into her chocolate-brown eyes and drew on every inch of his strength. "I don't want to screw up the boys, and I sure as hell don't want to screw up what we had."

Her smile was sad. "You make it sound like it's already gone. Past tense."

"Maybe it has." He linked his fingers with hers, shrugged. "But now maybe we can start over and check all the bullshit and fear at the door."

She bit down on her lower lip, watching him for a long beat before finally answering. "I'd like that."

"You remember that time Gray and Lila tried to set us up?"

Bella's other hand flew to her mouth, her giggling hysterical, making her sound more girl than woman. It cracked him up.

"Ugh, you were vile. So arrogant and self-centered. And you tried to tell me you were a diamond trader when I knew full well you were military."

"Hey, a million girls before you believed that story. In fact, it was my most convincing. Aside from the one about me being a chocolatier."

"A million?" She groaned.

"Okay, maybe a hundred. Oooh, and I forgot about the one when I told a very pretty drunk girl that I was a highly success-ful male stripper, touring the world. That one cracked the guys up when I told them."

They were both laughing now, but he never let go of her hand, not for a second.

"You're disgusting, but I'm not surprised she fell for it."

"Oh yeah?" Noah felt good—happy and content. It had been a long time since he'd genuinely felt like that away from work.

"So you all make up nonsense when you meet strangers, right? It's not just you?"

"We don't need anyone to know what we do. It's a SEAL thing. Maybe it's why so few of us make it through training, because the ones who go in for the glory and recognition don't have the mental toughness to finish. That's why I don't believe your douchebag ex ever made it."

Bella was still smiling when she squeezed his hand. "I've said some pretty dumb things to you and my family about military careers. I hate the idea of losing someone I love, but what you've chosen to do for a career, Noah? It's amazing. You are one of the most selfless, incredible people I've ever met."

"I don't know about all that, but I'll take it anyway," he said.

She had tears in her eyes, but they never fell. He didn't want to see her cry, to be the cause of it, but at the same time he was ready to wipe every drop away if he needed to. He wasn't running any longer. All his life he'd run, had become very good at it, but not this time. Not with Bella.

"I get it now, the guy you were pretending to be. You didn't need me to know you were a SEAL, but I took it as you being so arrogant, the way you were. I'm proud of you, and I will always be proud to tell the boys what their Uncle Noah does for a job. Just like I'm proud to have that flag flying out front, and of what my sister and dad have done for our country."

Noah blinked away his own tears, not used to being so emotional. He wasn't into feelings, never had been, but then he'd never opened up before either. "I have something to tell you."

Bella looked worried. She went to pull her hand away but he tightened his grip, didn't want to lose the connection he had with her in case he changed his mind. Even though he'd accepted the job offer, he bet they'd have him back on active duty on SEAL Team 3 in a heartbeat. He was one of the most experienced guys on the team, which was why it had been so hard for him to step down.

"I've taken early retirement from active duty," he said, almost choking on the words as they came out, not sure when he'd ever planned on saying them in his career. "A few opportunities have come up, which I always end up being pushed toward, but I've always refused, wanting to stay with my guys, be on the ground doing what I love."

"You're not going to be a SEAL anymore?" she asked, her words more of a gasp. Now it was Bella's fingers tightening around his.

"I've taken a staff position. I'll be a senior staff member, reporting directly to the Pentagon. I can't say anymore, not until I'm cleared to, but I'm not going to be deployed again. This was the last time."

Bella never said a thing, stayed so silent he wondered if she'd actually heard him.

"Bella?"

She started to shake her head. "No." she said. "No, no, *no*. Please tell me you didn't do this for me? For the boys? No matter what I've said in the past, I'd never want you to give up what you love. Never."

Noah's heart was heavy, the weight of his decision huge, but he was also at peace with the choice he'd made. It felt like a new challenge: a scary one, but a good one. "This was always my exit strategy, Bella. It's just happening a few years earlier than I expected it to. And it's my choice."

"But . . ."

He got out of his chair and dropped to his knees, holding both her hands now, staring into her eyes. "Bella, you and the boys mean so much to me. I loved my job, but those kids need a dad to be here with them, not to be worrying about losing me, too. And I want to be around. Hell, I've dodged more bullets and gotten myself out of so much shit when others haven't. It's time for me to just live a normal life. Or as normal a life as I can." He held her tight. "There's a reason that almost all SEAL marriages end in divorce, Bella, because we can't be there for the people we care about and do our jobs justice. It's just that I've never had anything in my life I've wanted more than my job before."

"I don't want you resenting us for this. Resenting me," she whispered.

"And I won't," he told her honestly, smiling when she reached for him, fingers in his hair, tugging him closer. "I was ready. If I hadn't been ready, I wouldn't have done it. Couldn't have. But going on this last deployment showed me that the timing's right. I have to do what I have to do."

He gave in, pulled up higher so he could kiss her, lips so soft at first, followed by desperation on both their parts. She gripped him tight, nails digging into his shoulders as he cupped her face, then pulled back to look at her before kissing her all over again.

"I'm scared shitless, but this feels right," he confessed.

"Me, too," she said, lips pillowy against his as she kissed him again. "Me, too."

Noah wrapped his arms around her, head to her belly as she hugged him, cradled him against herself.

"I wish Lila could see us now," he muttered against her. "See what she's done."

Bella laughed, her stomach moving against him. "You can say that again."

"Can we go get pizza now?"

Noah pulled back when he heard one of the boys speak, dropping a final kiss to Bella's lips as he rose.

"There's plenty more where that came from," he whispered into her ear.

She laughed. "Oh, there better be!"

~

It was early, so the restaurant was full of families eating pizza. Bella smiled back at a mom a few tables over when she caught her eye, and it got her to thinking how they probably looked like a regular all-American family. From the outside, no would know the pain they'd all gone through or ever imagine their struggles. But she also liked that they were a family unit, even if they were an unconventional one.

She glanced at Noah, caught his eye as he goofed around with the kids. There was no doubting how hard this must be for him, being back after doing God-only-knew-what, wherever he'd been, and giving up active duty, but she was so incredibly proud of him. How could she not be?

"What are you thinking about?" Noah asked.

The boys continued playing, toys on the table, pretending to shoot each other. She was on her own on one side of the booth, with Noah on the other in between the boys, his arms encircling them so they were tucked in close.

"You. Me. The boys." She shrugged. "Everything."

He looked relaxed, as happy as she'd ever seen him. Which helped with the shadow of doubt in her mind about his reasons for standing down. He loved what he did so much that it worried her, how he'd cope.

"You don't have to worry about me," he told her.

"Easy for you to say," Bella muttered, smiling her thanks when the waitress set down two glasses of red wine and Cokes for the boys.

"Thanks," the boys said in unison.

"They're good boys, huh?"

Bella grinned. "They had a great mom and dad, that's why."

"You're not such a bad mom yourself," he said with a wink.

"Right back at you. Those boys love you so much, they just about burst when they saw you at school."

"I feel the same about them," Noah said, still smiling, but his words were more hesitant now.

"You can't say it, can you?" she asked softly, fingers playing across the stem of her wine glass. "You can't say that you love them, even though I know you do."

Noah looked uncomfortable, removed his arms from around the boys, and folded them on the table in front of him.

"You're so sensitive and sweet in some ways, but it doesn't come naturally to you to say the 'L' word."

"I'm not sensitive," he grumbled.

"I would have said the same thing six months ago, you know, when I thought you were a complete jerk. But you are sensitive, in a nice kind of way. All tough man of steel on the outside and gooey on the inside."

He grunted. "You're right."

"About you being sensitive or the—"

"The other thing," he interrupted. "No one ever said it to me growing up, except for Gray's parents after I'd been with them for a while, and that was just plain weird. And I've just"—he exhaled, looking skyward before meeting her gaze head-on again—"never said it before. Maybe I can't."

She closed her hands over his. "Yes, you can. Just say it." Bella quickly corrected herself, squeezing his fingers. "To the boys I mean. Just tell them you love them."

"It's not that easy." He looked pissed, or maybe he was just seriously uncomfortable.

"Hey boys," she said, interrupting their game. "How much do you love Noah?"

"I love you this much!" Cooper said enthusiastically, holding his arms so wide he just about knocked his brother out when he stretched them.

"Yeah, we love you all the way to Antarctica," Will said.

Bella laughed at them, glancing at Noah, seeing him visibly suck in a breath, gulping the air down.

"How about you, Noah?" she asked softly. The boys were staring up at him, waiting.

"I . . ." he started, faltering, looking at her like he was at sea without a life raft.

Bella touched his hands again, smiled over at him.

"I love you guys so damn much it hurts," he finally said, voice gruff and deep as he slung his arms around the boys and pulled them in tight, kissing each of them in turn on the heads.

His eyes dragged over hers, made heat pool in her belly from the way he was staring at her. She'd pushed him, and it could easily have backfired, but he'd said it. Words that should have been so easy for a person to say, but for some were so damn hard.

"I hate that you grew up without being loved, Noah," she told him once the boys had gone back to playing, weren't listening to their every word. "But you're very loved now. By all of us, not just the boys. My family adores you, Gray's family adores you, and I'll bet your Navy guys do, too."

"Yeah, it's just not so easy to accept," he admitted. "When you're not used to it. When your natural instinct is to question everyone's motives when they're kind or go the extra mile."

Bella was so close to telling him the words herself, confessing that she was in love with him and probably had been for weeks, but she held back, not ready to go that far. Not yet.

"Who ordered Hawaiian?

284

"Me!" Both boys yelled enthusiastically.

Bella sat back and watched the boys, trying not to stare at the big boy in the middle. Every inch of him was gorgeous—his big broad shoulders, body hard and muscled without being bulky, face so handsome that it took her breath away sometimes staring into those blue eyes so full of warmth. Not telling him how she felt was one thing, but she was already a freight train going full steam with no brakes. The only person she was kidding was herself.

She took a slice of her pepperoni, in heaven as she swallowed the cheese. No wonder her sister had loved this place.

"Mom and Dad used to order pepperoni, too," Will said, munching his pizza and watching her.

She grinned, happy he'd brought them up. She liked talking about them, especially when they able to reminisce without it being sad. "Your mom and I grew up eating pepperoni because Granddad always got to choose, and that was his favorite. If he'd just gotten back from being away on deployment, he'd insist on eating pizza at least three times that first week home. We loved it."

She met Noah's gaze and almost melted into a puddle at the expression on his face.

"I always craved pizza when I was away, too. I'd be sitting there freezing my ass off, and I'd swear I could smell it, I wanted it that bad."

"And did you ever get it?" Cooper asked, so innocently that Bella reached over the table to touch him.

"No buddy, not until I got home. We didn't get a lot to eat, just what we needed to keep us going, and we're trained to deal with it. It's just part of what I do."

"Do you know how many people you've killed?" Will asked, still eating, asking it like it was the most normal question in the world.

"That number isn't the important one—it's how many people's lives I've saved by doing what I'm trained for."

Bella was relieved by his answer, not wanting to know. Or maybe just not wanting the boys to know, to shield them from the harsh reality of war.

"So you're not gonna tell me?" Will looked disappointed. "Daddy never would either. Said it was nobody's business but his own."

"Sounds like you had a smart daddy," Noah joked.

"Yeah, and now I've got two."

Bella almost dropped the slice of pizza she was holding. Will was happily eating still, like he hadn't just dropped an emotional bomb on the table. Cooper seemingly hadn't noticed his words, and Noah had frozen. She cleared her throat, looking between the boys, not sure what to say.

In the end, neither she nor Noah said anything. There was nothing to say. But they did both smile. Bella felt like her cheeks were going to crack she was smiling so hard, at the same time as her eyes felt like they were going to flood with tears.

"Don't kids say the darnedest things?" she murmured as she nursed her wine and took a sip.

"Hell," he said, taking a big gulp of his. "You can say that again."

CHAPTER NINETEEN

Dear Bella,

Just because Lila isn't writing you anymore doesn't mean you have to stop looking for letters. Maybe it'll be once a week or once a month, but I promise to keep our dates going and surprise you whenever I can. I'm not good at doing romantic stuff, but I will write to you. It's the one thing I actually can do because Gray's mom always made me write to her whenever I was away for longer than a few weeks, so I've had practice.

Every Thursday night will be for you and me, to go out and just be us. Not parents or anything else, just you and me getting to know each other. I'm shit scared of the future, of my new job, of being a dad to the boys and being something to you, but we'll get there. I promise. I'm stubborn and determined at the best of times, but at least what that means is that when I commit, I commit 110 percent.

Today you need to get ready for adventure. Put on your bikini under your clothes, baby, because we're heading to the beach! The kids are with your parents all weekend, your mom is swinging past this morning to get them, and we're going to learn to paddleboard,

*like you should have been doing that time you were in Mexico.
Then I'm taking you out for ice cream.*

*I feel like I'm in free fall here, but the one thing I do know is
that you've made me a better man. You and the boys.*
Noah

The boys were playing in the yard, sticks held high as they pretended to shoot each other. Bella nursed her coffee, smiling as she
watched them. No matter how she felt personally about kids and
guns, she'd had to let it go. It seemed that guns were in the boys'
DNA whether she liked it or not.

A noise made her turn, and she opened her mouth to tell Noah
what they'd been up to. Only no one was there. Bella frowned,
glancing out the window again and seeing Noah join Cooper and
Will. When she turned again, she realized there was a letter sitting
on the table. *So Noah was just in the room.*

She didn't recognize the handwriting on the envelope, her name
scrawled across it, but her heart still skipped a beat. It wasn't from
Lila, but she'd grown to anticipate what her sister's letters would
contain, and for some reason this one made her feel the same. She
set down her coffee and reached for it, sliding her nail under the
seal and opening it, eyes traveling fast over the words, greedily
digesting them. But she skipped to the end before she finished the
first sentence. *Noah.* The letter was from Noah. She dropped into
a chair and went back to the start, forcing herself to read more
slowly.

He's taking me on a date. Now her heart was really thumping. She reread the letter, tried to wipe the smile off her face and
couldn't. Bella shut her eyes and wished her sister were sitting beside
her so that they could have laughed and giggled. And so she could
have told her that she wasn't scared anymore—not scared of taking
a risk when it came to love. Noah had changed something within

her, made her want more. And she was going to jump in head first instead of holding part of herself back.

"You found it."

Bella glanced up, nervous even though she knew it was stupid to be. They shared a house together, and now suddenly he'd left her a letter, and she was a bundle of nerves.

"I guess I'd better go get the boys' bags packed?" she asked, not blinking as she stared into his eyes. He was leaning in the open doorway, arms crossed, showing off biceps she desperately wanted to drag her fingernails across.

"Already done," he said.

Bella stood, leaving the letter forlorn on the table and walking toward him, even though her bare feet felt like they were made of lead. She wanted to be close to him but yet something kept holding her back, a part of her still trying to resist, a part of her that couldn't believe all this was really true.

"Thank you," she whispered, stopping in front of him.

Noah never moved, his body language never changed. And it gave her the confidence to step in closer, to reach her hands up and place them gently on his shoulders.

"For what?" he asked.

She stood on tiptoe. "For the letter. For understanding. For everything."

Noah was still immobile, still relaxed and sexy as hell, leaning against the door, and she brushed his lips, tasted him, kissed him so gently over and over. His arms unfolded to let her closer, and she touched her body to his, grazed her chest against his and smiled when a soft moan echoed from him.

"You're trouble," he muttered, arm closing around her middle.

"You haven't even seen the half of it," she joked, linking her fingers into his short hair and forcing him forward, locking him in place so she could kiss him all over again.

A toot outside signaled someone had arrived, and she heard the boys calling out. Bella took her time, not stopping, still kissing Noah, groaning when he pulled back slightly and she dropped flat to her feet again.

"I think that's your mom," he whispered into her ear, his gruff tone only making her want to keep her fingers clenched into his arms and not let him go.

Bella laughed. "She's been telling me to start dating for the last couple of years. Believe me when I say that she won't mind seeing you taking advantage of me."

Noah tugged her closer, held her tight, mouth to her hair. She sighed against his chest, luxuriated in the smell and feel of him.

"I've been so scared of letting anyone close for so long, and now . . ." She didn't even know what to say.

"Now you're more scared than you've ever been, but there's a little voice in your head telling you that it's worth it."

Bella looked up at him, head tilted back, arms around his waist. "Yeah. Something like that."

"You ready to play today?" he asked, lightening the mood.

"I'm not exactly super sporty, but I'll give it a go," she said with a laugh, pulling back when she heard her mom's heels click on the timber floorboards.

Noah slapped her on the backside when she turned, making her squeal.

"Everything okay in here?" her mom called out.

Bella glowered at Noah over her shoulder before greeting her mom. "Everything's fine. Noah just needs to learn some manners, that's all."

Her mother laughed, eyeballing Noah over her shoulder as she stepped in to embrace Bella.

"I get the feeling like I walked in on something here. Want me to go back outside with the boys?"

"Mom!"

Noah's hearty laugh made her turn and glare at him, and then she caught her mom's smile, and she couldn't keep a straight face any longer.

"You guys are wicked. Absolutely wicked," Bella told them.

"Don't I know it," Noah growled as he came up behind her and slipped his hands to her waist.

Bella's cheeks flooded with heat, as much from the feel of Noah's hands on her as the knowing smile on her mom's face.

~

"I'm not so sure about this." Bella felt like a fish out of water. She grimaced, trying to keep her balance on the board the instructor had placed her on. *More like a girl who didn't want to end up in the water.*

"You're doing great," Noah cheered, only a few yards away but looking perfectly at ease on his board, like he'd been doing it all his life.

"You sure they didn't teach you this as part of your SEAL training?" she grumbled.

Noah laughed and she scowled, wobbling as she tried to change her balance.

A guy went past them, standing on his board and making it look beyond simple, his dog sitting up front and wearing his own buoyancy vest. The canine watched her as they passed.

"I swear that dog was giving me a smug smile."

Noah grinned. "Hey, mutt! Stop checking out my girl!"

Bella burst out laughing and promptly wobbled and fell off the board, landing with a splash in the surf. She emerged spluttering, feeling like a drowned rat. *So much for looking good for our date.*

"Couldn't you have chosen something normal, like a fancy lunch?" she demanded, water dripping off her nose as she pushed back her sodden hair.

"Your sister made you go hiking and shooting. I thought this would be a breeze," Noah said, standing now and paddling straight past her.

"Help me back up," she said, glowering at the instructor as he stood watching her. He guided her back up, and she took a big breath, steadying herself. "This damn board isn't getting the better of me, and that man isn't going to show me up."

The instructor helped her and she listened, focused on what he was telling her, blocking everything else out. And then she was standing. Bella smiled to herself as she gripped the paddle and slowly pushed it through the water.

"Take that, SEAL!" she yelled. "Whoop!"

"Not too fast," the instructor called out as she scooped the paddle through the water.

Bella was smug. So pleased with herself that she wanted to yell *"Sucker!"* at Noah. She laughed as she passed him. And then promptly fell off again.

～

The sun was lower now, not so intense, and Bella dropped her head to Noah's shoulder as they walked along the boardwalk.

"Want to go paddleboarding again next week?" Noah asked, voice low and only meant for her.

"When pigs fly, that's when I'll go again."

They both laughed, and Bella pressed her palm to his. "It wasn't so bad, was it?"

"No. I'm just being silly."

"You know what's not silly?" Noah asked, stopping and turning her around to face him, taking her other hand and pulling her against him.

"What?" Her breath started to become more rapid, eyes drawn to his mouth. Always to his full, delicious lips that tasted so good against hers.

"The way I feel about you."

His deep, gruff words lit something inside of her. "Something about us just feels right," she mused.

"I've always been too scared to let anyone close, too scared to open up, and with you, not doing that just seems stupid." He paused, stroked her cheek. "There's something about you, Bella. Something that drives me wild and soothes me all at the same time."

"So what are we going to do about this . . ."—she grinned— "*predicament.*"

"We're going to get ice cream, and then I'm taking you home."

Bella shivered, goose pimples coursing down her arms and over her body. "Is that right?"

"Why else do you think I asked your folks to have the boys for the entire weekend?"

Bella tipped her head back and laughed, body igniting with desire as he dropped his mouth to her neck, kissing all the way to her jaw. When she righted herself, he dipped his lips to her mouth, kissing her long and slow.

"Can we forget about the ice cream?" she mumbled, lips still meshed with his.

"No," he said, kissing her over and over again, clearly not giving a damn who could see. "The chocolate ice cream I'm having is the starter." His laugh was wicked. "And you're the main."

Bella slapped at him, and he caught her by the wrist, turning her arm over and nipping at the soft skin underneath.

"My mother was right, you *are* wicked." Her breathing was raspy, anticipation firing through her body, making every inch of her feel alive.

"You don't know the half of it," Noah whispered, lips warm and soft against her ear.

Bella's body molded into his, oblivious to whatever was going on around them. She was with her man, and she didn't give a damn who could see.

Noah walked close to Bella as they licked their ice creams, heading back to the car. One minute he wanted to strip her clothes off right then and there, and the next he was content just to be in her company.

"Will we have to move?" she asked out of the blue.

"When?"

"As part of your new job," she clarified. "Will we have to move to Washington?"

Noah shrugged. "I honestly don't know. I'm based here for the meantime, but I guess we'll have to cross that bridge at some stage."

When Bella didn't say anything, he nudged her with his shoulder. "I'm not breaking up this family, and I'm not leaving you, so don't go worrying about something that hasn't even happened yet."

She nodded. "I'm not. I'm just . . ." Bella sighed. "I'm a planner. Letting go and taking things as they come doesn't come naturally to me."

"Hence the uptight nicknames," he teased.

"Ha-ha, very funny."

Noah finished his ice cream as they approached the SUV, unlocking it and opening Bella's door. She smiled as she got in, and he closed her door and moved around to his side, pausing to look out at the surf one last time. He'd spent a lot of his adult life around water and near water, yet up until he'd joined the Navy, he'd scarcely been able to swim.

If you're up there, I've got your back, brother, Noah said silently to Gray as he stared at the ocean. *I've got your boys, and I've got Bella.* He blinked tears away. *And if I could have traded places with you and been behind the wheel that day, I would have.*

When he got in, Bella's hand found his almost immediately. Noah turned to face her, resisted the urge to start making out with her and instead gunned the engine into life. It wasn't far to home, but he bet it was going to feel like an eternity.

"Noah?" she asked, eyes wide as she watched him.

He kept both hands on the wheel as he pulled out. "Yeah?"

Bella's hand suddenly touched his thigh, sliding down. Lower. He hissed out a breath at the sound of her gentle laughter.

"Drive fast," she murmured.

Noah thumped his foot on the gas and had them home within fifteen minutes.

"I take no responsibility for my actions," Noah blurted as he yanked her door open and grabbed her, hauling her into his arms and over his shoulder as he marched across the front steps.

"Noah!" she squealed, thumping her fists on his back.

He kept hold, tight, unlocking the door, kicking it open and then shut behind him. He didn't stop until he reached the stairs, letting her slip down so she was in his arms instead of over his shoulder, stealing a hot, sultry kiss before taking her upstairs and walking determinedly to her bedroom, dropping her to the bed. He lowered himself before she had a chance to get away, unwavering in his desire to spend the rest of the day and night naked between the sheets with her.

Bella gasped as he pinned her arms above her head, kissing her hard and fierce. Her legs tangled around him, locked him in place, but it wasn't enough. Noah grunted as he let go of her arms so he could rid her of her denim shorts, tugging them down, sliding his hands up her slender, smooth legs as he worked his way up her body. He ran a finger over her bikini bottoms, long dry from lying in the sun before they had gone for ice cream.

"I've been waiting a long time for this," he said, keeping control when all he wanted was to lose it.

"Me, too," she managed before groaning at his fingers tracing up under her top. She obediently raised her arms as he slid it up, leaving her so close to being naked below him.

Noah had been kneeling between her legs, but he moved so he was straddling her, sitting astride her without putting his weight onto her. He took his T-shirt off, threw it across the room and lowered himself, forcing himself to be more gentle this time. But Bella fought him straightaway, wasn't content with slow kisses and soft touches.

She wriggled until he pulled back, and then she moved fast, getting away from him and pushing him back, flipping their roles. Now she was astride him, pausing to yank his shorts down and then sliding on top of him, wiggling in a way that made it almost impossible for him to let her be in control.

"You hate taking orders, don't you?" she whispered, bending and nipping at his lower lip, then his neck, before trailing kisses all the way down his chest.

"Uh-huh," he groaned. "I prefer giving them."

LETTERS TO LOVE

"I guess this will be torture for you, then," she murmured, kissing his stomach, fingers following the path her tongue had traced.

Noah grabbed her and went to flip her, but she held on tight with her thighs, refusing to make it that easy for him.

"Damn you!" he cursed.

Bella just laughed, sitting up and undoing the strings of her bikini top. Noah's breath hissed out of him again as he stared up at her breasts, groaned again when she slapped his hands away and wouldn't let him cup them.

"Nuh-uh," she ordered, holding his arms down by the wrists and lowering herself, sliding her naked chest against his.

"Who would have known you were capable of torture?" he grumbled, his frown quickly turning into a smile when her lips met his.

"Just shut up and kiss me," she demanded.

"Yes, ma'am."

~

Bella traced circles across Noah's chest, gently making circles around his nipple and tucking tighter against him. Her body felt to her like a marshmallow—soft and sated and incapable of doing anything other than lying still.

"I think this is going to rate as one of the best weekends of my life," Bella whispered against his skin, plucking at that same skin with her lips.

"You do realize we've got another, oh, twenty-odd hours before the boys get back, right?" Noah asked, mouth to her hair.

It was like they couldn't get enough of one another, both touching and kissing, still touching even after hours of being in bed.

"I plan to make the most of every minute," she declared.

297

Noah's laugh was soft, almost thoughtful.

"Bella, there's something I've been wanting to say to you. Since I got back."

She waited, listened, not wanting to interrupt him.

"You made it so easy for me to say it to the boys, but with you . . ." He hesitated, "I don't know. It's harder. More significant maybe."

Bella's pulse ignited, but she refused to react, kept her head nestled to his chest, fingers still tracing circles.

"I love you, Bella." Noah's words were so low, so soft, she almost wondered if she'd imagined them. "I love you so much that it terrifies me."

Bella pushed up on one elbow, stared into the dark eyes of a man she'd once thought was a jerk and now loved so fiercely her feelings terrified her.

"I love you, too, Noah. A thousand times over."

He leaned up, kissed her, stroked her hair. "You do realize I've never said that to a woman before. How much you mean to me?" he asked. "For the first time in years, I can sleep easy, just because you're beside me."

Bella grinned. "I bet you say that to all the women you sleep with."

His gaze was serious, unwavering. "Only you, baby. Only you."

Bella kissed him, seared his lips with hers and left them both gasping, wanting more. For years she'd never imagined she'd ever know love like her sister had, never have her own Gray. And then Noah had come along and knocked her off her feet.

"We're going to make it, Noah. I just know we are."

His kiss was sweet, his touch beyond gentle as he stroked her back. "You're the love of my life, Bella. There's nothing I wouldn't do for you. *Nothing.*"

Bella sighed and leaned into him, hands on his muscled body, mouth against his warm, full lips. She might have lost her sister and her best friend in the world, but she'd found Noah. And although she'd never stop grieving, suddenly the sun was shining on her again, and she wasn't afraid to bask in it.

EPILOGUE

The day was beautiful, the sun high, with hardly a breath of wind as Bella crossed the grass, her eyes searching out Lila's headstone. She'd barely visited her grave until now, had found it too emotional thinking of her sister in a casket beneath the ground, but today the pull had been so great that she hadn't been able to ignore it. Noah and the boys were following, but she'd wanted to have a few minutes to herself before they joined her, and so he was wandering slowly with them, pointing out trees and squirrels. Or make-believe ones, anyway.

Her heels dug into the grass, and she tried to walk on the balls of her feet. They had a low-key rehearsal dinner in a couple of hours' time and she was already dressed for it, the soft pink taffeta skirt making her feel fun and feminine. Only her nude pumps weren't exactly sensible attire for what they were doing right now. Despite her happiness, tears threatened, but she held them at bay, determined only to cry tears of happiness on the day before she was to marry the man she loved.

Bella stopped in front of the headstone, taking a deep breath and leaning forward to place her hand on it, eyes shut as she sent up a silent prayer to her sister. Then she did the same at Gray's headstone, his body buried alongside her sister's. A child's laughter on the breeze made her smile, and she glanced back, seeing her boys play. But she needed this moment alone before beckoning them over.

"Thank you for trusting me with Cooper and Will," she whispered, her lips moving but barely a sound coming out as she spoke to Lila. "Thank you for your letters. Thank you for Noah. I hope you're both watching today and tomorrow."

Bella blew a kiss to each gravestone, taking a deep breath and wishing that she could have them back for just one day. For her sister to be her maid of honor as she'd been to her, to watch as her little boys brought them their rings, dressed in gorgeous little outfits. And most of all, she wished she could see the look in Gray's eyes one last time as he smiled down at her sister and made her laugh, because that's why she'd always loved being in their company so often. Their happiness had been genuine, and it had helped her through her darkest hours.

She shut her eyes, said a silent prayer, and then called out to Noah, waving him over.

"Come on over, boys."

It didn't take them long to close the distance between them, running fast, little arms pumping. Noah didn't hurry, but his long stride meant he wasn't far behind them.

"Do you guys want to say anything to Mom and Dad?" she asked, bending low so she was at their height.

"Not really," Cooper mumbled, playing with a loose strand of her hair as it hung down.

"I don't like talking to them here. I like talking to them when I'm in bed," Will confessed.

Bella hugged them both. "That's okay. I just wanted to bring you here so we could remember them as a family. But we don't have to stay long."

Noah came to stand behind her, hands falling to her shoulders when she stood. Bella leaned back into him, craving his touch, loving the feel of his strong body against hers, the way his hands always seemed to soothe her.

"There's one other thing I'd like to do while we're here," Bella said, turning in Noah's arms and gazing up into his eyes. "Noah lost some guys from another SEAL team—he told you boys at the time—and my deepest regret is that we didn't attend those services with him."

Noah smiled down at her, rubbing a thumb tenderly across her cheek. "You were there when I needed you. That's what mattered. And I'm not even sure you could have attended even if you'd wanted to."

Bella shook her head, reaching for the boys, an arm over each of their shoulders. "What your men have done for our country is . . ." She struggled to find the right word, "immeasurable. I don't even know how to express the sacrifice. But what I would like to do is stand here for a minute in silence, so Noah can remember the men he's lost. Can we do that, boys?"

They nodded. When she glanced at Cooper, she saw he had tears in his eyes and she bent to scoop him up. "You okay, little man?" she asked.

"Did those soldiers have kids?"

Bella glanced at Noah. "Um, maybe."

"So they were daddies?"

Suddenly Bella realize why Cooper was getting so upset. "Yeah, buddy, they might have been. And that's why we have to make sure that we honor their memories."

Cooper put his arms around her neck, and Noah lifted Will into the air so he could do the same. They stood side by side, Bella's shoulder against Noah's side as they stared at the graves in front of them.

"In times of war or uncertainty there is a special breed of warrior ready to answer our Nation's call. A common man with uncommon desire to succeed. Forged by adversity, he stands alongside America's finest special operations forces to serve his country, the American people, and protect their way of life. I am that man."

Noah's voice was deep and clear, his tone commanding as he spoke the words of his Navy SEAL code. She knew the words because she'd spent so much time reading about his profession, learning while he was away about what made SEALs tick, to try to understand him better. It made the words have an even greater impact on her now.

"My Trident is a symbol of honor and heritage. Bestowed upon me by the heroes that have gone before, it embodies the trust of those I have sworn to protect."

His voice cracked then and she leaned into him, wanted to give him her strength.

"By wearing the Trident I accept the responsibility of my chosen profession and way of life. It is a privilege that I must earn every day."

He shook his head, and she put Cooper down so she could put her arms around him and hold him tight.

"I'm so proud of you," she whispered into his ear.

"They were the brave ones, the ones we lost," he muttered. "I haven't even recited the entire code, and I'm already choking up. Some goddamn SEAL I am."

She kissed his cheek and stepped back to reach for Cooper's hand. "We'll always be proud of you, Noah. Forever and always."

The sun shone down on them, warming Bella's skin and making her smile. They'd both hurt a lot and lost a lot, but she knew they were through the hardest times. Or at least she sure hoped so.

"Come on, we have a rehearsal dinner to get to!" she said, ruffling Cooper's hair and then grabbing both his hands so she could swing him around and make him giggle. Noah's laugh echoed around her, the warm timbre of his tone when he spoke making her smile.

"Come on, family. Grandma will kill us if we're not the first guests to arrive. And I'm ready for some alone time with Bella."

"I thought we were spending tonight apart?" she asked, feeling a hot blush hit her cheeks for no reason at all except for the wicked heat in Noah's eyes as he stared at her.

"Wrong. The boys are spending the night at Grandma and Granddad's, which means I get the bride-to-be all to myself."

~

Her mom poked her head out of the car and waved her down. Bella gripped Serena's hand as they descended the steps, needing her friend for support. It wasn't that she was second-guessing herself, but the nerves had started and no amount of wishing them away was working. She'd only gone five hours without seeing Noah, and for some reason the moment he'd left the house, she'd become all jittery.

"You ready?" her dad asked, holding the door for her.

Bella grinned. "Ready as I'll ever be."

The drive to the church went past in a blur, with Bella checking her makeup for the hundredth time, squeezing both her parents' hands, exchanging glances with Serena, and anxiously smoothing the skirt of her gown. She'd kept her dress simple, chosen a fitted white satin gown with a plunging neck line, and she was wearing the dangling diamond earrings her sister had worn on her own wedding day as her only jewelry. Other than her engagement ring, the solitaire diamond that Noah had placed on her finger only a month earlier. Serena was dressed in a gown, too. Hers was blue, a deep shade the same color as her eyes.

When the car slowed, Bella saw Noah, bent low with his arms around the boys. And then they saw her parents step out and squealed and pushed Noah into the church, which made Bella burst into laughter. They were taking their roles very seriously, and it only made her adore them all the more.

"Hey, boys," she said as she climbed out of the car, holding her bouquet.

Cooper ran toward her, but Will stayed still, staring. She waved him over, dropped down low so she was on his level.

"You look different," Will said, brows furrowed as he stared at her.

Bella hugged Cooper and passed her mom the flowers, other arm open for Will so she could hug him, too. "It's just because you don't usually see me all dressed up like this. You look different, too." They were wearing black trousers, white shirts, and soft blue ties, just like Noah would be.

"Can we hold your hand?" Cooper asked. "I've missed you."

"Absolutely." She shot her dad an apologetic smile. "Mind if these two walk me down the aisle?"

He came closer and kissed her cheek. "Not at all. They're your little men; they deserve the honor."

Bella blinked back a fresh wave of tears, took a deep breath, and nodded to her mom. She didn't care about discarding her bouquet; all she cared about was the little hands she was holding as she stepped toward the open door of the church. And then she saw

Noah, standing there, waiting, his face so open and happy that it took all her strength not to run to him.

The boys walked her all the way, but her eyes were trained on Noah. She didn't notice another person in the room, paused only to kiss and hug both boys as they took their places on either side of them.

"You look so beautiful," Noah said, whispering to her and leaning in to kiss her cheek, his lips so warm and soft. "Just like I knew you would."

Bella had worn her hair loose, knowing Noah liked it that way, and he gently rescued a stray strand that was touching her face.

The ceremony raced past in a blur, until it came time to exchange rings. The boys each held one, waiting for their turn to help.

"I give you this ring and promise to love you forever," Bella said, tears swimming in her eyes as she pushed the ring onto Noah's finger.

He smiled and took her ring. "And with this ring, I promise to love you for the rest of my life," Noah said in reply.

The second they were announced as man and wife, Noah wrapped his arms around her, dipping her back and kissing her like he'd waited an entire lifetime to do it.

"I love you," he whispered into her ear. "And I'll never be afraid to say it."

Bella laughed as he rained kisses down her neck. "Me, too."

~

"There's some very special people missing tonight, and it would be remiss of me not to pay tribute to them," Noah said, standing at the head of the long table and looking at the friends and family they had gathered. The table was set beneath a big tree on the grass at

Bella's parents house, fairy lights twinkling in the dark across the branches, mirrored by the candles flickering across the long table.

Bella reached for his hand, still seated, and he took it, smiling down at her before continuing.

"A little over a year ago, I lost my best friend," he started, his voice strong despite the subject matter, well practiced in the speech he'd been reciting in the shower all morning. "Gray was more my brother than friend, and I doubt I'll ever stop missing him. We fought like brothers, competed like brothers, and fiercely supported each other like brothers. Gray, not a day goes by that I don't think about you." Noah cleared his throat, knowing how emotional his words would be for everyone listening. "The truth is that we all lost a lot that day, every single person sitting around this table. My beautiful wife lost her sister, her family lost their daughter, and Gray's family lost their son. But most tragic of all is that Cooper and Will lost their mommy and daddy."

Bella stood then, fingers looped around his as she dropped her head to his shoulder, body reassuring against his. The boys had already fallen asleep, were still in their cute little shirts, lying on the outdoor sofas with blankets tucked in around them. He glanced at them before he continued.

"Bella and I would do anything for those boys, and no one loves them more than this amazing mama bear here. They may have lost their first parents, but we're sure as hell going to do everything we can to be the best damn second parents in the world."

Everyone laughed, although there were many tearful eyes present, too, and Bella leaned up to kiss him. Noah smiled down at her.

"Lila and Gray's passing was the catalyst for bringing Bella and me together, and even though odds were on us failing at even being under the same roof together for more than a week, somehow we managed to see just how right we were for each other. Bella is the love of my life, the only person in the world I've ever truly felt that way about, and been able to admit it. And now here I am, declaring my love in front of all of you, so this girl's sure changed me!"

Everyone laughed and he cleared his throat, holding tight to Bella's hand. "To Gray and Lila," Noah said, reaching for his champagne glass and raising it. "For bringing this amazing woman into my life and being the best damn friends I ever had."

"To Gray and Lila," everyone echoed, glasses clinking.

"And to us," Bella added quietly. "For the two people who never saw this coming and ended up stupidly, madly, crazily in love."

"To us," Noah whispered, just to her. "For making me a better man."

Bella tipped her head back for the kiss she must have known was coming.

"Cheers to that," she whispered back.

THE END

ACKNOWLEDGMENTS

People often ask me how to become an author, as if I'm going to offer them some magical advice, but my answer is always the same: just write. And then write some more. I'm fortunate to have some truly inspirational author friends, and when the going gets tough, it's great to know that they're there to lend a sympathetic ear and then repeat my own words to me: just get writing! On that note, I have to say a huge thank-you to Yvonne Lindsay. Thank you for being on the other end of the phone every day. I am so grateful that we have similar schedules, because knowing you're writing at the same time as I am every single day helps me to stay on track and be extremely disciplined. I honestly don't think I could be anywhere near as productive right now without you, so thank you.

I'm also fortunate to have a fabulous support crew in authors Natalie Anderson and Nicola Marsh. We might not email as many times a day as we used to before kids took over *all* our spare time, but those emails keep me going, and I wouldn't like to be without either of you. I'm so grateful to have support from both of you, and I admire you so much as authors and as busy mothers.

Thank you also to my own incredible mother, Maureen, who gives me so much of her time to help with my boys. I couldn't have written this book without her daily help, especially with my insomniac toddler. Thank you a thousand times over. My children are also very lucky to have a fantastic granddad who is extremely good at building tunnels and jumping platforms out of sofa cushions to keep them entertained.

I also have to thank my fabulous husband, Hamish. Nothing beats having a husband who will willingly play Transformers, Ninja Turtles, and Spiderman at the drop of a hat to entertain our boys. Thank you!

I'm very fortunate to work with some truly talented women, and I need to say a special thank you to them all. Laura Bradford, my very supportive literary agent, and Sophie Wilson, who was my editor on this project, thank you both for all your help and guidance. I love having you both on my team—I genuinely feel like I've hit the jackpot with both of you. Sophie pushed me so hard on this book to get it right, and I will always appreciate the work she puts into my stories. Thank you! I also need to thank my copy editor on this book, Jill Pellarin.

And last but not least, Emilie Marneur, a huge thank-you for reading the proposal for this book and believing in it right from the start. At Amazon Publishing, I have truly found a home for the stories of my heart, and this book is certainly one that I've been yearning to write.

ABOUT THE AUTHOR

Photo © 2014 Carys Monteath

Soraya Lane was born in New Zealand and was accepted to university at only sixteen years of age. She graduated with a law degree, but instead of practicing law she decided to follow her dream of becoming a writer. She successfully built a career as a freelance journalist and completed a master of fine arts degree in creative writing. Soraya is now a full-time author—and a full-time mother to her two young sons. She and her husband live on a small farm in her native New Zealand with their two dogs and four horses. Soraya is passionate about animal rights and she enjoys horse riding, spending time with her family, and reading. She hopes to be writing stories for the rest of her life.